What Am I Doing Here?

by

Jim Kesey

To Disney, Col. US Army
"All Gave Some
Some Gave All."
Jim Kesey

THREE RIVERS PUBLICATIONS
P. O. Box 283
Hebo, OR 97122-0283

This book is based on fact but is a work of fiction. Names, character, places, and incidents are either products of the author's imagination or are used fictitiously. Any resemblance to actual events or locales or persons, living or dead, is entirely coincidental.

Library of Congress Catalogue No. TX 1-050-993

Typesetting by Kenyon Haskins.

ISBN 0-9714957-0-X

Printed by Oregon Lithoprint, Inc.

# Acknowledgements

I wish to acknowledge the writer's groups in Woodland, California, 1989-92, McMinnville, Oregon, 1993-98 and a special thanks the writer's group in Pacific City, Oregon, 1998-01. They not only kept me on schedule and on task, they were a constant source of encouragement and technical assistance. I want to thank Louis Chandler, Lt. Col., Army Chaplain, retired, for stepping in as a Chaplain for the Marines, my nephews Kenyon Haskins for formatting the text, Ryan and Kory Harris for setting up my webpage, my son Guy Kesey for formatting the book cover and daughter Wendy Kesey Gale for designing and painting the cover. I wish to thank my wife and family for their encouragement and support when I returned from Vietnam. Thank you, Sharon. I love you.

Grateful acknowledgement is made to the following song writers, publishers and artists for the use of their songs:
Please Mister Custer by Darian, Delory & Van Winkle; Copyright by Patten Music, Inc.
Salt Water Cowboy by Redd Evans ©Copyright by Jefferson Music Co. 1944
Pass the Booz by Gene Northington & Ray Butts ©Copyright by Lonzo & Oscar Music Publishing Co. Inc. 1964
Detroit City by Danny Hill & Mel Tillis ©Copyright by Cedarwood Publishing Co. Inc. 1963
Amazing Grace ©Copyright by Manna Music Publishers

A special tribute to Lance Corporal Lorren Cummings, USMC who wrote the song "Marine," Chu Lai, Vietnam 1965

DEDICATION

I wish to dedicate this book to the memory of my Dad who told me there isn't a word "can't".
And to my loving Mother who taught me to care.

Veteran's Day

On veteran's day
I see the soldiers go walking.

I see my mom's dad go walking
and me and my mom very quietly wave good bye.

We seem to miss him
when he goes away.

By
Karly Kesey Gale
November 11, 2000
Age 7 and a Half (Heavy on the half)

TABLE OF CONTENTS

PART I SOUTH CHINA SEA

PLEASE MR. CUSTER

by

The Hollywood Argyles

A famous time in history
the men of the 7th Calvary went riding on.
A trembling word from the rear
a brave young man's voice so loud and clear,
WHAT AM I DOING HERE?

Please Mr. Custer, I don't wanna go.
Hey, Mr. Custer, please don't make me go.

I had a dream last night
I feel it coming back
somebody yelled look out
and there I stood with an arrow in my back.

Please Mr. Custer, I don't wanna go
Forward Ho! Oh No!

Lissen Mr. Custer. Them bushes are moven out there
I bet there's an Injun behind every one.
Mr. Custer, may I be excused the rest of the afternoon?

Look out Charlie! fffffpp Opps,
Guess you were a little late.
Oooo, I bet that smarts.

There's a red skin waiten out there
a fixen to take my hair.
A coward I've been called
but I don't want to wake up dead or bald.

Please Mr. Custer, I don't want to go.
Forward, Ho!

What's the Indian word for friend?
Kemo Sabe, yeah, that's it. Kemo Sabe, Kemo Sabe!
fffffppp No, that ain't it.
Look at them, runnin' around like a bunch of wild Indians. He he he.

1 Good Bye World

It wasn't cold now, but the feeling of despair wrapped Kohl like a shroud and made him shiver. The plane lifted off the runway in a heaving motion skyward, surrounded by silent fog, discouraging the early morning light. He appeared to be looking out the window, but didn't notice Travis Air Force Base disappearing in the fog, nor did he hear the whine of the jet engine, but he did feel. He felt it in the pit of his stomach, a constricted ache that keeps you from swallowing; the feel of sweat that runs freely down the sides of the armpits; the beads of sweat that collect on the upper lip. It was a trapped feeling, enclosing, constricting, confining, and feeling helpless and caught without a place to hide.

"You can take off your seat belt now, Sir." Since there was not a reaction, the stewardess repeated, "Sir, you can take off your seat belt." Louder! "Sir!"

"Uh?" Kohl's head jerked from the window toward the voice.

"Your seat belt, Sir."

"Oh, yeah, okay."

His hands were going to move. At least they were supposed to move. He deliberately looked at them as they clutched the black briefcase on his lap, but his gaze disappeared into the white knuckles where his fingers gripped the black Samsonite ... and the black night. He became lost within the cracks and scratches of the dark plastic. *Dusty, I love you, I do.* He heard her sweet, soft voice so clearly. He felt her pull him closer to her warm body and kiss his back. He felt the bed shake when she cried, trying to bury her sobs in her pillow ... a tear fell. It was on the black briefcase. It was there. He saw it. Moving only his hand, with his finger he wiped it away. He turned his head back toward the window. *God, I'm crying for Christ's sake.*

He wondered how many men on the plane were crying.

If I could have only ... if only. It's like looking back and when you turn around, there, right in front of your face, is a big sign that says, 'If only.' If only on such and such a day. If only it had been an inch closer or an hour later. If only I would have done that instead of letting it slide. If only I knew then what I know now. Something done. Something neglected. Something said or left unsaid. If only. Oh boy. That's all I need to start doing. To start wondering, if only? I can't change history. I know. But why me?

Kohl knew the answer. He wasn't much to dwell nor linger on the past. Not that he was a fatalist, nor believed that God had this plan for him. He accepted his plight or pleasure. And if he didn't like it he tried to change it. *I can't be looking over my shoulder at if only. I might end up sucking on my forty-five.*

Look at me. I'm flying off in some goddamn plane, to some goddamn place, where I don't want to go. Join the Marines and see the world. Bullshit! God, I feel terrible.

For the first time he looked out the window and saw the tops of the two orange spans of the Golden Gate Bridge sticking out of the fog. He also, for the first time, looked around at the other men on the plane, all military, some in civilian clothes like himself, but most in the uniforms of the Army, Navy, Air Force and Marine.

Happy New Year, you unfortunate assholes. Each within a shell, within a shell. Kohl's jaw tightened at the anger that was within him. A plane hurling through space and time, taking his dreams and places he loved. From times he didn't want to pass. Bodies, numbers and orders. It said...

From: Commanding Officer
To: Lieutenant Dusty M. Kohl, 086755, USMCR

1.In accordance with reference (b) OINC Transient Section, Mark Bks TI ltr. 10: RFE; dwr over 4650 dts 25 Nov 64.) Your orders are modified in that you will report to the Marine Corps Liaison, MATS Terminal, Building Number 3, Travis Air Force Base, Fairfield, California not later than 0800 4 January 1965, for transportation to the 3rd Marine Division (Rein) FMF (MCC 125) reporting upon your arrival at Kadena Air Force Base in

Okinawa to the Commanding General.

He read the orders again like he had the first time. It never changed. He closed his eyes and said a silent prayer. *Please, Lord, let this be just a bad dream.* As he opened his eyes, it didn't matter how hard he tried; it was still there. It wasn't going to change.

"Sir, can I get you anything?" asked the stewardess.

You'd better look at her real hard. It'll probably be the last round-eyed girl you'll see in a year. Yeah, get me the fuck off this plane.

"Why yes." As he displayed his best smile. She hadn't expected a response. "Miss? I think there has been some mistake. I think I'm on the wrong plane going to the wrong place."

The Marine Corps Corporal in the seat next to Kohl turned and gave him a questioning look and the stewardess' smile vanished from a face that was turning pale.

She asked, "Are those your orders there?" She reached out her hand and Kohl handed her his orders. She read them quickly and glanced at Kohl and then back at the orders and let out a sigh of relief.

She shook her head smiling, "Oh, no sir, you're on the right plane."

"Damn!" He took the orders back, then shrugged, and looked up at her. "Sorry. I was just kidding."

She apparently didn't find it amusing, gave him an annoyed look, wheeled and left.

"Nice ass," said Kohl smiling to the corporal sitting next to him.

The corporal looked at the retreating stewardess and nodded. But he still had a puzzled look on his face.

Kohl unbuckled his seat belt, put his briefcase under the seat, and settled back, while the plane raced ahead of the sun. *One thing in my favor, though, being a senior First Lieutenant, with only eleven months to do in the Corps on a tour where the standard duty was thirteen months. I'll probably get a nice desk job in Headquarters Battalion, like S-2, S-3, S-4 or Motor Transport Co., maybe even Special Services Officer, maybe BOQ Officer.*

Kohl smiled to himself knowing he was going to be a short timer as soon as he stepped off the plane. He continued his reasoning: *They can't threaten me like they did in Basic School. "You screw up again, Kohl, and we'll send your skinny ass to infantry." Well, they did that anyway. Then they said, "You screw up again, Kohl, and we'll send your recently married ass to Okinawa," which they did. But now, shit. What are they going to do to me now? No more shit details. I'm at the end of the line. I am on my way to the end of the world.* He grinned. *I signed up for the Marine Corps; I'll do my duty. Clean up my act for my last eleven months. Get out and start my life as a civilian. Teach, maybe, and coach too.*

Kohl looked out the window to the puffy white clouds below and asked, *What happened to December?* He smiled at the thought of Julie and how beautiful she looked floating down the aisle. He regretted that he wasn't able to enjoy it more at the time, not only did he have all of the effects of a hang-over from the bachelor party, splitting headache, eye balls webbed with reddish hue, he was also wearing some girl's bikini underwear. *I still can't remember where they came from or how come I was wearing them,* and it felt as if any moment he was going to throw-up. Bile had been working its way up his throat to the point of no return. His best man, First Lieutenant Paul M. Mays, was holding Kohl steady, or was Kohl holding him steady? *I can't lose my cookies right here in front of all these people, especially her father.* He didn't have a very good opinion of Kohl anyway. Through the eyes of the two hundred guests, the wedding was impressive with Kohl, best man, and ushers all in their dress blues and sabers. The bridesmaids were beautiful, too. The first one down the aisle licked her lips and gave Kohl a wink. She had visited Kohl two nights before in the basement guestroom of his future bride's home, in her little, short, teddy. She had caught him walking out of the shower with a towel wrapped around his waist. Everything she had was pushing to get out... tits and ass. Kohl felt the visit was no accident. *It could be a trap. The devil is tempting me. If I can't pass this test, how am I going to handle myself overseas? Handle myself. Ha, ha. Little joke there.*

"Hi Dusty."

"Hi Kathy."

"I'm sorry dear. I didn't know you were down here." Yeah, right. "I was going to take a quick shower before bed. Julie went with her mom to the store." That's a nice bit of information. "Don't mind me." Are you kidding? "Just go on with what you're doing." As she stood facing Kohl, she pulled off the straps of her teddy and let it fall loosely to the floor. She licked her lips. Her nipples must have been an inch long. What's a man to do? Maybe getting married is a bad idea.

Kohl had received lectures from not only her parents but most of his buddies too. *"Kohl, you're a screaming asshole. Nobody and I mean nobody gets married for one month and then leaves for a year in Oki. No whorin' and roarin' for you, bub. Just plain dumb if you ask me."* That seemed to be the general gist of it all. He dismissed most of their comments since they were mostly single and had few plans except to stay drunk and partake in the ladies of the night most of their liberty hours anyway.

Kohl smiled again thinking about what a wonderful time they had at Heavenly Valley, Tahoe. He could feel her soft lips touch his as they lay in front of the cabin fire. *"I love you, Dusty."*

"I love you too, Baby."

"Huh?" said the Corporal with a bewildered look.

Kohl pretended he didn't hear and looked nonchalantly at the ceiling of the plane.

When Kohl didn't answer the Corporal shrugged and returned to his book.

Hell, I'll be loonier than a fruitcake before this tour is over. Already talking and mumbling to myself. I shouldn't have let her go to the airport. It's funny, I didn't think of that until I looked at her and found I couldn't bear to leave her there. She said it was going to be harder for her than it was for me. The one leaving had the excitement of the unknown; the adventure of something new, while the one left behind is left with nothing but memories and emptiness. You should have thought more about the effects that it was going to have on her, dip shit.

As Kohl had turned and walked towards the plane, he felt like he was walking away from the most wonderful times of his life. The days and nights were gone. The sands had disappeared from the hourglass. The last touch of an ungrasping hand. *That's what happened to December, Kohl. Say goodbye.*

"Goodbye," said Kohl.

The Corporal moved his legs to the side and looked at the seated Lieutenant. "Goodbye," he answered.

"Goodbye?" Kohl questioned. "I'm not going anywhere. Well actually I am going somewhere but I'm not leaving the seat. I'm just sitting here."

"Well you said 'goodbye', Sir. Do you want by?"

"No, I don't want by. You're the one who said 'goodbye'."

"Look Lieutenant," he sounded annoyed now, "I said goodbye in answer to you when you said goodbye."

"But I'm not going anywhere. There's nowhere to go. Forget it, just forget it. This is stupid."

First stop, Hawaii. The Corporal put his book away, getting ready to disembark. He had told Kohl this was his second tour and had re-upped for Hawaii. He was single, excited and looking forward to his next three years. He wished the Lieutenant good luck. "Surfs up!" he said as he got up to leave.

Now that the plane had left Hawaii, and the corporal had left, Kohl had the whole seat to himself.

Why yes, I've been to Hawaii.

Well, what did you think of the tropical paradise?

It's hard to explain. I don't know where to start. So many things to see and do and so little time. One of the things I remember most was when we flew past Diamond Head and the big, puffy, white clouds that cast shadows over the bluest water I've ever seen. The terminal was very nice. The Hawaiian cuisine was exquisite. I dined on a grilled cheese and a chocolate shake at the airport restaurant. I went to the restroom to take a leak and heard this music and while I was looking for the speakers, I peed on my shoe. I should have kept my mind on the matter in hand. He, he, he. Little joke there. Have I seen Hawaii? Oh yes, I've seen Hawaii.

Kohl settled back and dreamed his way to Wake Island.

He woke up with a start as he heard the rumble and grind of the landing gear going down. He asked the grumpy stewardess, *She must carry a grudge forever,* where they were? She told him that they were coming into Wake Island. As the plane dipped to the port side and leveled out, he could see the island out the starboard side. *Hell, I've seen bigger islands in the Sacramento River Delta.* There was nothing on it but a tower and airstrip. Looked like the island was covered with white rocks. *Uh? Heard someone say it was bird shit. The whole island? Bird shit? Yeah, that's right.*

On the home stretch. I've come a long way since that time I talked to the Marine Corps recruiter in Denver.

*

Kohl had been receiving letters from the Draft Board for the last four months. This was his fifth year of college and it looked like it could take longer to finish. He was on a full ride athletic scholarship for basketball, which took up big chunks of time most of the school year, plus he had part-time jobs to help pay for living expenses. During this time, he had taken the Air Force Officers' test ... If a plane was traveling east at three hundred and twenty five miles an hour and had left Dallas Airport at 0630 and another plane left Washington D.C. at 0630 traveling west at two hundred and fifty miles per hour, how long would it take for the two planes to meet? ... And failed.

He talked to the Army about going to officers' school after graduation. They told him that he would have to go through Boot Camp and then apply to officers' school. However, there would not be a guarantee that he would be selected. And if he were selected, he would have to serve four years after he received his commission.

Not one to be discouraged, Kohl talked to the Navy. They told him that he would be eligible for officer's school after graduation. He asked them if they had anything on shore because he got seasick. They said they couldn't guarantee it. They trained all their officers for ship duty. So much for the Navy.

It was May now and the draft board was getting rather persistent. Kohl had received orders to take his physical. He was due to graduate in August. He didn't want to be an enlisted man. His dad had been in the Navy during the Second World War and told him..."Dusty, there's only one way to go into the service and that's as an officer. There's a lot of crap that goes on, and that crap has a tendency of rolling downhill, so the way I see it, the closer you are to the top of the hill the less crap." So...

"Yes, Mr. Kohl, we do," said the Marine with three stripes on his sleeve. "The Quantico Marines have an excellent basketball program. They play all the major colleges and universities along the Atlantic Coast and with collegiate background playing at Denver University, you shouldn't have any difficulty in making the team."

Kohl felt like he needed to explain further. "You see, I figure I can offer my country more by participating in athletics. You know, like public relations." *I can't believe what I'm saying and who I'm saying it to. Do you know to whom you're talking? A Marine recruiter. Aren't you aware of what the Marines do? Haven't you heard the stories? Seen the John Wayne movies? Can you really see yourself crawling around and hiding in bushes? Huh?*

"That's right Mr. Kohl. We feel the same way you do. Our athletic programs at all our bases are an integral part of our public image," said the Marine with the three stripes.

A clerk, with one stripe and crossed rifles on his sleeve, came in and handed Kohl's test results to the three stripes. "Well, you did very well on your test, Mr. Kohl," said the three-striper.

This surprised Kohl, because he hadn't done very well on any test in his life.

The three-striper said, "It looks like you're all ready for the Captain." The three-striper walked stiffly to the door that separated the office from the main lobby and knocked three times sharply.

"Yes?" came the reply.

"Captain, Sir? He's ready."

Oh shit! I don't know about this. Maybe I'd better go back to school and think about this.

The door opened and out marched a young man in his mid 20's, of average build, with striking red hair and freckles. He was about the same height as Kohl, just over six two and as he stood in front of Kohl, his green eyes were serious.

"Hi," said Kohl. The Captain didn't respond. He must not have heard.

"So, you want to be a Marine." His voice was low and soft but had an edge to it.

"Well, I thought maybe ... Hell, I don't know..."

The Captain frowned and glanced at the Sergeant. He looked at the application he held. "Mr. Kohl, by all indications you have excellent qualifications for a Marine Corps Officer. We need men of your caliber. I feel you have made the only choice..." he paused, "to be a Marine."

"Well, OK. I have to do something, or I'm going to end up being drafted in the Army. So I guess. I'll join up," Kohl said, letting out a big sigh.

The Captain took a sheet of paper that the three-striper handed him and he read the oath to Kohl who repeated the lines after him. Kohl ended with, "I do." *Jesus, sounds like I'm getting married.* Little did he know?

The Captain looked at the three-striper. His expression showed nothing. The Captain returned his gaze to Kohl. His jaw muscles were working. "It takes a special man to be a Marine. He must be strong physically, mentally, and emotionally. It's the same as in team sports, where there is little room for the individual. It takes a team effort, each depending upon one another to do his best. The team is only as strong as its weakest link. The Marines eliminate the weak links. At Officers' Candidate School these weak links either quit or get kicked out. The Marine Corps prides itself on being the best. This feeling of pride we share was founded on our glorious past, a living tradition that inspires every Marine to be the best. It isn't going to be easy, Mr. Kohl. You will never experience anything in your life that will be as difficult as making it through Marine Corps Officers Candidate School, that is except for one thing..." the Captain paused for affect, "... combat."

As Kohl left, he felt confused. He felt a sudden feeling of pride in going back to the frat and telling everybody that he had joined the Marines. And yet he was uneasy, like he might be making a big mistake. He reassured himself that the Captain has to say all that rah, rah stuff to keep the queers out. He thought he could take anything the Marines could dish out.

Kohl would make a good Marine officer. There were reasons that Kohl wasn't fully aware of. He was a leader. Through his activities in athletics at Huntington Beach High School, California, he not only was a premier basketball player but also lettered varsity in football as a split end, ran quarter mile for the track team and was on the C.I.F. championship mile relay team. He was a team player. His coaches and teammates liked and respected him.

He always gave a maximum effort, followed directions, and yet took the initiative. Since getting the scholarship to Denver University, he had been called upon to play an even greater role in the leadership of the team by earning the starting point guard position his sophomore year. His final year he led the league in assists and averaged fifteen points per game. That won him honors in the Skyline Conference. During the summers he worked for the Huntington Beach Recreation Department as a Recreation Leader, where he coached and supervised youth activities. He was authoritative without being bossy. He was conscientious without being pious.

Kohl remembered vaguely his first encounter with the famous Marine Corps Drill Sergeant. The vague memory was because on that day in October when he reported to the Marine Corps Officers Candidate School, at Quantico, Virginia, he was high. He had smoked a fair-thee-well-civilian-life joint at the Quantico bus depot. It was a mistake and an unfortunate beginning, as he came "bippy-boppen" into the cement squad bay that faced the beautifully gold tree-lined Potomac River. He began by giggling at the Drill Instructors, with their Smoky Bear hats. He thought they looked funny. They did not find his humor amusing. It went down hill from there. The Captain recruiter was right. To Kohl, it wasn't the physical, or the class work, it was the constant 'in-your-face' harassment. Kohl remembered the time he was carrying a swab and bucket down a hall. He didn't see the DI until it was too late. He was supposed to yell, as loud as he could, "gang way" and press himself up against the wall. The DI grabbed Kohl and threw him against the wall. He took hold of the bill of his cover and pushed the bill and his fist into Kohl's face. This was quite a reach for the shorter DI. Fear was Kohl's' initial response and as the DI continued the pushing and yelling at what a fuck-up he was, Kohl's' fear turned to anger. *Come on you little fucker. Call me anything you want because it don't matter. Do anything to me, push-ups on coke bottles, crawling for miles on my belly in the mud, because it don't matter. It's like water off a duck's back. Just rolls off. Come on, you ignorant little fuck head, give me your best shot.* When the DI took his hand down, Kohl looked straight into the opposite wall, showing no fear, nor anger. Nothing. His expression was without emotion. The DI smiled and continued walking down the hall. It was the turning point for Kohl without him knowing it. When a candidate at OCS got to the point of realizing that they could take anything the DI's could dish out, you were on your way to becoming a Marine.

*

Kohl shuddered and woke up. He saw the lights of Naha, as the plane made a right-bank for a landing approach into Kadena Air Force Base. He wondered who would be there to meet him and what his new billet would be. *I'll probably spend a couple of days to get squared away and all.* He was already thinking about the return to the mainland. He considered transit time (five days), accumulated leave (thirty days), and rehabilitation time (fourteen days). He could be back stateside sometime in September. That's only nine months.

2 Swift, Silent and Deadly

I'm a short timer, so don't give me any shit. Kohl stepped from the plane's ladder to the tarmac and walked to the terminal.

"Lieutenant Kohl?"

"Yes?"

"I'm Lieutenant Spade." He grasped Kohl's outstretched hand with a firm grip. Spade smiled briefly. "Lance Corporal Rutkowski will pick up your gear." Second Lieutenant Spade had a wide, friendly smile that showed a mouth full of big white teeth. He was clean-shaven for this time of early evening, with neat short-cropped hair. He was shorter than Kohl and heavily muscled.

As Lance Corporal Rutkowski picked up Kohl's luggage and swung the sea bag over his shoulder with ease, Kohl noticed the thick-muscled body with shoulders starting just below his ears. He also was neatly groomed, with razor-sharp creased fatigues. All three walked toward the front entrance.

Lieutenant Spade was talking, but Kohl wasn't paying too much attention. His mind kept wandering, and it was hard to stay focused after the long flight. The running dialogue was distracting him. The Second Lieutenant was talking about the island and something else that Kohl's tired and cluttered mind was having a hard time grasping. In a corner, back within the recesses, through long corridors of blackness, something was not right. Kohl looked at Spade's big mouth, with all those big white teeth, talking.

Kohl interrupted him. "Who did you say you were with?" as they entered the clear, cool air outside.

"Third Recon. Battalion," he answered with great exuberant pride.

Well good for you, you gung-ho prick. He probably has duty tonight and Headquarters Battalion has sent him down here to pick me up.

"... Father in the big two ... Ohio ... down south near ... around October ... outstanding outfit ...As far as I'm concerned..." Lieutenant Spade droned on. "... the best ... swimming ... Corps ... about six miles ... having a ball ... bars, girls and booze ... trained ... officers ... the c.o.'s a real stickler ... enjoy ... Yep, you'll really enjoy yourself."

Enjoy? Enjoy? Did he say, enjoy? He's talkin' 'bout fuckin' Recon for christ's sake. They were approaching the jeep and Kohl noticed the insignia on the side. 'Third Recon' with a skull and crossed swords inside a banner with the words underneath, 'celer, silens et mortalis.'

"What's 'celer, silens et mortalis' mean?" Kohl asked.

"It means, swift, silent and deadly."

Kohl was getting that feeling again. His heartbeat was quickening and the knot he felt in his stomach was working its way up his chest. *Don't get all excited now Kohl. This can probably be explained.*

"Who did you say you were with again?"

"Third Recon, man," he said, as they climbed into the jeep and started driving north.

"Which way is Headquarters Battalion?"

Lieutenant Spade pointed south. *We are going the wrong fucking way. This can't be for real.* "Oh, shit."

"What's that, Lieutenant?"

"I said, 'Oh shit'. Where's my orders?"

"I'm sorry Lieutenant. Here. Sorry. Forgot to give them to you. I'll turn on the dash light so you can see."

"Yeah, Okay." Kohl read his orders.

7b/pers/rog
1320.1
ser: 5-65
5 Jan. 1965
Memorandum endorsement
From: Commanding General, 3rd Marine Division (Rein), FMF

Permanent change of station: orders to-
1. You reported this date.

Now there's an intelligent statement.

2. You will further report to the Commanding Officer of the organization indicated after your name.

Kohl frantically looked over the list of about thirty names until he found his.

First Lieutenant Dusty M. Kohl 086755/0302 USMCR (Third Recon. Battalion)
1. You are to report to this organization at 0800 this date.
2. You will report to Company "A" for duty as a Platoon Commander.

Oh brother. There it is.

Kohl knew about Marine Corps Reconnaissance and the function within the Corps. Recon was an elite unit, the best of the best. They usually worked in four-man teams. They scouted out areas for the advancing troops or dropped behind enemy lines to observe and record enemy movements. These guys were supposed to be tough. They like to hurt people just for the fun of it. They don't get excited at the sight of blood, even if it's their own. They like to get dirty and crawl around in mud and hide in bushes. Kohl's worst nightmare raised its ugly head. A laughing, drooling skeleton was dancing and running beside the speeding jeep. The eyes glowed in the dark and the medallion that hung from its' neck said, "swift, silent, deadly." The skull screamed in a shrill cry, like fingernails on a chalkboard. It brought chills to Kohl's skin. He made out what the skull was saying. "Oh boy. Oh boy. Fresh meat." The skull said it over and over, again and again.

Lieutenant Spade gave Kohl a momentary puzzled look, as he continued on with his enthusiastic rampage about Third Recon "It's an outstanding outfit..." His voice searched for a reassuring nod or an affirmative response.

There was a ringing in Kohl's ears. The cramp in his stomach had moved into his throat. "I think I'm getting sick," said Kohl softly.

"What?"

"I said, I think I'm going to throw up. Goddamn it anyway."

"Pull over, Ski," Spade said.

The Lance Corporal swerved the jeep to the side of the road and skidded to a stop. Kohl got up out of the back seat, climbed over the front, walked hurriedly to the rear of the vehicle, stooped over, gagged and threw up. It wasn't much and didn't take long. The air was cool and felt refreshing. He raised up, and looked at the stars. He smelled the air, as he took in large gulps of it. It smelled wet, like rain.

Kohl turned and walked back to the jeep and climbed in, stepped over Spade, into the back seat. "Must have been the long plane ride, excitement and all ... you know."

"Sure. You okay now?"

"Yeah. Fine. Just fine. Couldn't be better." The sarcastic tone did not escape Lieutenant Spade.

Kohl's immediate feeling of disappointment turned to disgust. Tears were starting to form in his eyes as he thought of what he left behind and what could lie ahead of him. *The Corps really did it to me this time, didn't they? Life has its little surprises and that gung ho prick had better shut the fuck up or I'm going to smash all those big white teeth down his muscle-bound throat.*

Lieutenant Spade lifted his foot, pulled up his pant leg, and removed a pack of Camels out of his sock. He shook one out, tapped it down, lit it with a Marine Corps Zippo, inhaled deeply, turned to Kohl, and shook one up for him.

Kohl shook his head no.

Kohl couldn't get it out of his mind what was happening. *They really did it. They really did it this time. My God, recon for-cryin'-out-loud. Why does this have to happen to about the most ungung-ho guy in the Corps? It's bad enough being in Oki, let alone recon. Fuck me, recon.*

Kohl had anticipated that as a senior First Lieutenant, he would probably be somewhere in headquarters or maybe a Company Executive Officer. Never in his wildest dreams did he ever expect to be a Platoon Commander in Reconnaissance. He suddenly felt very tired. His anger disappeared in a feeling of surrounding helplessness.

*

No, it's not a bad dream. You're awake. For a few seconds he couldn't remember where he was. It wasn't only raining out it was pouring. He lay there looking at the pale, yellow, concrete block walls, trying to remove the remaining cobwebs from his mind. *Better get moving, cowboy, because you have to check in at 0800.* The hot shower didn't help the deep gut-wrenching, depressive state that was slowly consuming him. Still dripping wet, he sat on the top bunk. The rain literally poured from the gray-black sky. The buffeting wind was sending sheets of rain, wrapping his heavy shoulders, and pulling him under the heavy blanket that covered his world, this morning of the sixth of January 1965. *Got to get my act together here. I've got a long way to go, so I'd better get with the program.*

Kohl looked at his reflection in the mirror. His eyes were a little red. He scowled at a wrinkle in the collar of his neatly pressed khaki uniform. He took his shoes from the plastic bags and gently rubbed a smudge from his heel with a piece of cotton. Kohl spoke to the mirror. "This is stupid. I'm polishing my shoes and it's raining so Goddamn hard out there. It's like a cow pissin' on a flat rock."

"My name is Lieutenant Kohl," he said as he walked into the Battalion Headquarters office.

"Welcome aboard, Lieutenant," said the duty NCO. "You are to report to Captain Heart of "A" Company."

Kohl handed him his orders. The NCO signed two copies, kept one, and gave the other thirty or so back to Kohl. "Nice weather," Kohl said.

"Yes Sir. Kind of does this here."

As he left Battalion Headquarters to the quonset hut of "A" Company, he ran and tried to jump to high spots, but it wasn't working. There seemed to be about an inch of water over everything. He finally realized that trying to keep his shoes dry was a lost cause. He burst through the door of "A" Company, with the wind and rain close behind. Water dripped from his raincoat leaving puddles on the cement floor. His garrison cover was soaked and no longer had its starched crease. He took off his raincoat and hung it on the coat rack by the door.

"Jesus! Hi, Top. Christ, it's pouring," said Kohl in good humor.

"Hello thar, Sir. It flat puts 'er out this time a year, come to think of it, when it rains, this is how it does it. Yep, flat puts 'er out. Ya, must be Lieutenant Kohl," drawled the tall, thin hollow faced First Sergeant behind the desk. "The Captain's expectin' ya. Go on in."

Kohl handed the First Sergeant his thirty copies of orders and walked into the Captain's office. Behind the desk sat a thin dark complexioned man with a soft face, thin mouth, and long straight nose set under dark brown eyes.

Kohl stepped sharply to the front of the desk and came to attention. "Lieutenant Kohl reporting as ordered, Sir."

The Captain looked up from the 'whatever' on his desk and with a very busy look, coupled with a, 'Don't bother me,' look and said unenthusiastically. "Welcome to Third Recon, Lieutenant."

"Thank you, Sir. I'm glad to be here." *Aahhhh, I can't believe I said that.*

"It's good to have you aboard." He pulled out Kohl's folder and opened it up. "We can use an officer like you, Lieutenant. Your record shows that you work very well in the field. I see that you have gone to Jungle Survival School, Escape and Evasion School, POW Interrogation School and you have your Scuba Certificate. But ..." *Oh no. Here it comes.* The Captain leaned back in his chair while Kohl remained at rigid attention and looked at him. Kohl knew what was in the fitness reports. Not good. It told about the three times that he had Office Hours with the Battalion Commander at Pendleton. The Captain continued..."But you seem to have a problem in garrison?" *Was that a question or a comment? Should I respond?*

A long pause. *I guess it was a question.* "Yes Sir, that seems to be a problem."

"Well Lieutenant, I hope all that foolishness is left behind. We like good field officers. You have received numerous accommodations for your combat abilities in many of the training exercises at Camp Pendleton. That's a rarity and is probably why you have been sent to us. But, a warning Lieutenant, you fuck up in my outfit and your ass is grass, and I'm the lawn mower." *Oooooooo, what ya going to do? Huh?* "We are a proud outfit. Only the best Marines come to Third Recon and then we make 'em better." *Then how in the hell did I get here?* The Captain leaned forward to make a point. "We're where the action is. As you know, the Marines are the first to fight. Well, Third Recon is there before the rest."

What the hell is this jerk-off doing? He's talkin' to me like I'm some brown bar. Here I am standing at attention, not a "at ease" or "have a seat," or "how's your flight over," or "kiss my ass," or "how-de-do."

"Your platoon is out in the field today. They'll be out there for a couple more days. Tomorrow we'll go out so you can get acquainted with your men."

Kohl continued to look straight ahead at the wall behind the Captain. *Oh joy. How can I contain my excretment, I mean... excitement?*

"You can go unpack and get squared away, and I'll see you tomorrow at 0600."

"Aye, aye Sir. Will that be all, Sir?"

"Yes, that'll be all." Kohl started to do an about face and leave when the Captain continued. "Oh, by-the-way, you have duty Friday night. *And the shit keeps rolling along.* "See you in the morning." He motioned with his head that he was finished and Kohl wheeled and left his office.

What a bunch of horse shit. He smiled and nodded to the First Sergeant, retrieved his raincoat and soaked garrison cover and braced himself.

The First Sergeant said, "See ya tammarra, Lieutenant"

He opened the door and ran outside into the whirling wind and rain. *Yeah and your ass sucks buttermilk.* And sprinted toward his BOQ.

*

He changed out of his wet uniform and put on his sweats. He sat on the side of the bunk with his chin in his hands. *Pete's on this island somewhere. I need to talk to somebody about my predicament.* He glanced at the phone. Lieutenant Richard (Pete) Peterson had come over about two weeks before Kohl and according to his wife, was in Supply Battalion. Pete and Kohl had been in the same outfits since OCS.

Kohl had taken an instant liking to Pete at OCS. He was friendly and easy to talk to. Kohl could tell he was an athlete by the way he walked and moved. He was always in trouble for laughing at the Drill Instructors when they would do something funny to one of the other candidates. Pete suffered the consequence by doing push-ups time and time again. But he would crank out push-ups like a yo-yo. He had played football at Utah State as a defensive back. He was strong, fast, and agile and was the best in the company in the physical fitness test. He was close to six foot and weighed about one hundred and ninety pounds, had black curly hair and blue eyes and a broken nose that made him look attractively rugged.

In the beginning, there had been over eighty officer candidates in Kohl's platoon, but they were eliminated for bad knees, bad feet, bad attitudes, and poor physical condition. For those who did not have 'that Marine Corps Officer look,' the DIs found ways of weeding them out. Both Kohl and Pete had done well in the physical aspects and the academics. One of the major difficulties for them were inspections. The 'junk-on-the-bunk' inspections had them cleaning, scrubbing and shining on most weekends, while the rest of the platoon went on liberty.

On the night before graduation, they knew they were going to make it. So they went down to the Club and proceeded to get drunk. At about two in the morning, they staggered back to the squad bay carrying two six-packs of Black Label beer. Most of the platoon had returned from liberty and were asleep. Kohl and Pete took off their clothes, collected the beer, and went to the showers. They turned on both banks of eight showers, plugged up the drains with towels, sat down, drank beer and sang as many Elvis songs as they could remember plus, 'Duke of Earl' and 'Under the Boardwalk'. They were in the middle of 'Earth Angel' when they noticed, through blurry eyes, their Drill Instructor standing at the entrance to the showers. He was standing in about an inch of water that was cascading over the thresh-hold, down the hall, down the stairs, snaking its way out the front entrance toward the Potomac River.

Empty beer cans were bobbing in the shower water. Kohl and Pete tried to stand, slipping and falling, crawling on hands and knees, trying to brace themselves against the tile walls. Finally by hanging on to the showerheads, they managed to pull themselves upright. Kohl was overcome with fear. *This is the end.*

The DI said in a surprisingly calm voice, "What's going on here?"

Kohl and Pete looked at each other to see who was going to handle the question. Kohl saw in Pete's eyes that he was about to explode in laughter. So Kohl swallowed, cleared his throat and in a shaky voice said, "Shur, we, ah ... the Candi ... aaah, Candatesles, Shur, we're ah, cellbrating ...ss. Burp! Scuse me, Shur."

"You queers," the DI continued in a calm voice, "shouldn't be celebrating until after you graduate. Now, turn off the showers, pick up the beer cans, clean up the water in the halls, and hit the sack. You two have a big day tomorrow."

Kohl and Pete looked at each other. They couldn't believe what they had heard. They both stood as stiffly as possible and answered strongly, "Sir, yes sir!"

The DI turned and sloshed down the hall. Kohl and Pete looked at each other and Kohl could see the smile start in the corner of Pete's mouth. They laughed so hard they slipped and fell. They were going to be Marine Corps Officers.

*

After about five calls Kohl found Pete at Embarkation School.

"Lieutenant Peterson."

"No shit. I hear you're learnin' how to crate pussy."

"Kohl? That you? When did you get in? Where're you at?"

"I got in last night. How ya doin'?"

"Oh hell! I can't believe I'm over here. I thought I was going to get out of it. How was your wedding? Sorry Sue and I missed it but you know.... had to go and see the folks before I left. I'll meet you after I get through here. Where did you say you were?"

"First of all the wedding was great. I'll have to tell you what happened to me and Mays. You won't believe where I'm stationed."

"Well, tell me?"

"I'm a Platoon Commander at Third Recon. Battalion."

"You're what?"

"Recon."

"Did you say," Kohl heard at the other end the beginning of a chuckle, "Recon?"

"Yes, I..." Pete was laughing hard now. Kohl was yelling into the phone for him to shut up. He dejectedly sat on his bunk and waited for the laughing to stop. "Pete? Goddamn it. Come on, this isn't funny." Pete was still laughing. "Fuck you, Pete. I'm going to hang up. This is not remotely funny. This is serious."

"Oh my." Pete was still laughing.

"I'm glad I made your day."

Pete stopped long enough to emit a feeble, gulping, "You sure did," then resumed laughing.

"You sadistic son-of-a-bitch." Kohl paused again to wait for Pete to compose himself. "Come on Pete. God damn it to hell anyway." The frustration was evident in his voice.

"Sorry, ol' buddy." But Pete kept giggling. "I have to admit, it's pretty bad news."

"Bad news, hell. It's horrible."

Pete took a couple of deep breaths. "I'm sorry. Just couldn't help it. I've been feeling sorry for myself, thinking of all my problems, ya know. Now I may not be in too bad a shape after all. Man, did you get the shaft. Oh man. Oops. Hey, I've got to get back to class, where it's warm and out of the rain. Where I can sit on a chair, instead of my helmet."

"Fuck you."

"See ya tonight, around six thirty. Oh sorry, I mean eighteen thirty. I'll have to remember you're in recon now. Everything by the book. Gung-ho! I'll see ya at the Camp Schawb "O" Club. Semper fi, mutha fucker."

"Yeah. Whatever."

3 Slow, Noisy and Harmless

The alarm went off at 0500. Kohl and Pete had spent the previous evening feeling sorry for themselves, trying to drown their sorrows. *Yuk. My tongue feels like a potato chip. God, do I have a hangover.* He showered and climbed into his utilities in a slow, fumbling manner, followed by his field jacket and finally his poncho. He left the warmth of the BOQ and slogged over to the chow hall, got himself a cup of coffee and a donut, then shuffled over to "A" Company, climbed into the back of the Mighty Might-Jeep (no top), and drove in a steady drizzle to the area where "A" Company was training. Captain Heart introduced him to his platoon. They were standing in the rain, in their ponchos, waiting to get the word to move out on a compass exercise.

Kohl felt the rain trickle down the back of his neck, as he clogged and sloshed along in a mucky-red quagmire. A steady bone-soaking drizzle was falling. The red mud stuck to his boots and every step seemed to add an inch in mud and a pound of weight. With a pocketful of cookies that Julie had sent, Kohl ate, and smiled as he recalled the notes he had found tucked into various places in his suitcase. *What a sweetheart she is.* He put another cookie in his mouth. In front of Kohl was a five-man team, making observations on terrain, vegetation, weather conditions and structures.

The team stopped. Kohl leaned up against a tree, not paying too much attention. They were having some kind of a discussion about what to do. They were looking at a map that was wrapped in plastic to keep it from getting wet. Kohl could hear them talking. Every once in a while, one by one, they would look around at the Lieutenant.

"Let's ask him. Come on Ford," said one of the team members.

Corporal Ford, the team leader, was a small, stocky, black man. The other team members were Hernandez, who probably didn't weigh more than one hundred and thirty pounds;Thompson, who looked big and heavy, and carried the PRC-10 radio. Beach and Sales looked alike. Both were about the same size with fair hair. Kohl could not tell their rank because they all wore ponchos.

Corporal Ford folded the map, put it back into the mapcase and said, "Nope. Let's go this way."

"I don't think we should, Ford," said Beach. "I think we've gone too far already."

"Ask 'im," said Hernandez.

"He doesn't know what the fuck's goin' on," said Beach.

"Shssssss! He'll hear you, Beach," cautioned Ford.

"He ain't said nothin' all day," continued Beach.

"I heard him say something, but I couldn't understand it. I don't think he was talking to me anyway, cause he was looking off somewhere," said Sales.

"He was singing, not talking," said Hernandez.

"Dang it," Corporal Ford said. He wanted to impress the new Lieutenant, with how well the team worked. "Let's move out. And stay spread out," added Ford, as they headed out.

Hernandez was point. He did a little dance and headed up the hill.

Kohl moved along at the rear of the column, and as he topped the hill, he stopped and looked. Kohl ducked his head smiling.

Have you ever heard how the Fuqawi Indian tribe got its' name?

No, how?

The Indian Chief and his tribe, after wandering around the plains for days, climbed a hill and looked out across the valley and the Chief said, "Where the fuck are we?"

It was still raining, but the clouds were high enough that he could see the valley below. Everything was so green. *No wonder, the way it rains here.* He was surprised that even though he was soaked, he wasn't cold. Corporal Ford had kept the small group moving steadily. The water continued down the back of his neck and the red mud made his legs feel like they weighed a ton. Still it had been a rather pleasant walk. *This Goddamn mud would stick to a baboon's ass. Sure is a pretty valley. Uh oh. Kohl? You're thinking weird. This could be dangerous.*

"Games? Why yes, I love to play games."

"All right you guys. I want you to go out there and walk around in the rain and mud, hide in bushes. Oh, and don't take food either.

"Why in the rain? Can't we wait till the weather is nicer? And, why no food? Can't I eat my cookies?

Oh, don't you know? You have to practice.

Practice?

Yeah, practice. You know, at being miserable. It's a little game Marines play- practicing being miserable. Once you get used to being miserable, you won't know when you're miserable. Even when you're miserable, you won't be miserable because you're used to it. Understand? When you start enjoying these little walks in the rain and mud and hungry, you're cured of being miserable. Have another cookie."

"Why, thank you. I think I will."

Kohl smiled, as he saw Hernandez slip and fall on his butt.

"What time we gettin' back, Ford?" asked Thompson.

"Keep quiet, Thompson!" answered Ford.

"This fuckin' radio is gettin' heavier," Thompson grumbled. "And how in the hell am I going to get across that?" He said pointing to the rain-swollen stream about six feet across.

"Come on, lard ass," said Beach, who had easily jumped to the other side.

"I'll get wet."

"What's a matter bubble buns, you're all wet anyway. Why not just wade across?" taunted Hernandez.

Thompson shook his head no. He looked up and down the creek trying to find a more suitable crossing. By now everybody had crossed except Thompson and Kohl.

The men, under Ford's urging, continued up the trail.

"Will you guys wait! Shit," Thompson complained, as he paced back and forth along the bank. He gave a questioning look back at Kohl, who stood under a tree, watching. He looked across the creek to the retreating figures, as they slogged up the hill. Thompson shot a quick glance back at Kohl, took his M-14 rifle off his shoulder, grabbed it like a javelin, and threw it, muzzle first, into the muddy bank on the other side. It stuck.

Kohl had to turn his head, so Thompson wouldn't see him laughing.

Ford and the others had stopped about fifty yards up the hill and stood watching, waiting to see what Thompson was going to do.

Reluctantly, Thompson backed up about twenty yards and took a loping, sliding run at the creek. With arms pumping and a determined grimness, he slowly began to pick up speed. As the creek bank approached, he realized too late, that he didn't have the speed to jump across. He tried to stop but slipped on his last step. The heavy PRC-10 radio pulled his shoulders back while his feet were trying to find traction in the red mud. As his arms searched upward, his hands clawing the empty air, he let out a small cry of "Oh shit!" He was now air-born, hanging, suspended horizontally, above the water. He dropped, sending seismic waves up and down the stream. He now became a human dam. The radio was stuck in the creek bottom mud. His legs and arms were thrashing wildly in the air like a turtle on its back. The water began cascading over his stomach. "Help me, for Christ's' sake. I'm drowning."

Kohl was laughing so hard, he had to hold himself up by grabbing a tree limb, and the team had fallen onto the muddy trail, rolling in hysterical laughter.

With the force of the water,Thompson was able to roll over onto his hands and knees and crawl to the other side. He lay gasping for air, half out of the water, on the muddy ground. He looked like a beached whale.

The team came sliding back down the hill. They were laughing and making fun, while Ford checked the radio. Even though it was covered in plastic, it had gotten wet and wouldn't work until it dried out, which wasn't going to happen on this trip. They had seen Kohl laughing as hard as the rest. It cleared the air a little. Instead of an uptight officer, he might be all right after all.

Kohl jumped easily over the creek and they all resumed walking up the trail.

Kohl had been walking along most of the day with his mind adrift in waves of thought. He took it for granted that the team knew where they were going and were hitting all their checkpoints. Now it was starting to get dark. And it got darker. No moon, no stars. The steady, silent light rain blanketed the groping, slow moving team from one compass checkpoint to another.

Kohl was bringing up the rear, with his hand on Beach's shoulder. In turn, Beach had his hand on Sale's shoulder, then Thompson, Ford and at point was Hernandez.

Ford stopped each in turn also stopped. Nobody said anything.

Kohl heard the rustling of a poncho and saw a slight flicker of light. He thought Ford was making a map check. It was now so dark that the team had to mark their last known position on the map and measure the distance and compass reading to the next position. Ford had to count the number of paces, any deviation from the compass line on the map had to be measured and compensated for.

Much to Kohl's surprise, he heard a barely audible, "Lieutenant?" It was Ford.

"Yes?" asked Kohl.

"I think we're about two miles south of base camp. We only have two more check points, Sir."

"Thompson?" Ford whispered. "Where's Hernandez?"

"He was in front of you," answered Thompson.

"Hernandez?" hissed Ford.

"Horseshit, Ford, " said Beach in a normal voice. "Who's goin' to hear us out here?"

"We're on a mission, pretending to be in a combat situation here. Now keep quiet," Ford whispered forcibly.

"Are we lost?" Thompson whined. "This radio's killing me, and the inside of my legs hurt."

"No, we're not lost," Ford answered without whispering. "Hernandez?" he said, louder this time.

"Hernandez?" hollered Beach.

"Beach. Shut up! We're still on a mission. You can't go around hollering like that," commanded Ford.

They heard a scream and indistinguishable noises.

"What was that?" Everybody was quiet, listening.

"I think we've found Hernandez," Beach giggled.

"Hernandez?" Ford now yelled as loud as he could.

"Come on. It sounded like it came from over this way," said Beach, as he cautiously moved to the front. They slowly crept forward, each holding on to the shoulder of the person in front.

Inching their way along, stopping every once in a while to call, they heard a faint, but recognizable stream of Mexican swear words. "Penche covron. Mutha fuckin', pendeho."

"Hernandez? Holy shit! Stop!" Beach yelled.

Kohl bumped Sales, who bumped Thompson, who bumped Ford, who bumped Beach.

"Don't fuckin' touch me! There's no ground here. There isn't a fuckin' thing in front and below me but air," said Beach who was now on his hands and knees. "Hernandez?"

They all looked into total blackness.

"Hold on, hold on! We are talking total blackness, here. Not just dark. I'm talkin' black. No light from the moon or stars. Have you ever been in a cave? You walk with a light and then you turn it off. You can hear breathing. You can hear water dripping. You can smell the dampness. You can feel the cold. But ... you can't see shit. Nothing. Zero. Zip. You can close your eyes and open them and it's no different. Do you understand?

Hello? We're talking dark, real dark ... Understand?"

"Down here, you fucking queers." It was Hernandez.

"Careful," cautioned Beach as Ford inched forward.

"Hey, yeah, no shit. I don't want any of you muthas fallin' on top of me, especially lard ass Thompson."

"Fuck you. You fuckin' grease ball," muttered Thompson. The rest laughed.

Ford asked, "Where're you at?" He tried to put his pen light on where the sound was coming from.

"Here. Further to the left. Wait. No. I mean right."

"Which way? Cripes!"

"Right. Yeah, right. It's hard to tell. I'm upside down."

"Up-side-down? What are you doing upside down?"

"What the fuck do you queers think I mean? Excuse me, Lieutenant. I'm hanging upside down in a ... tree. I think. My ankle is wedged, caught or something, anyway ... Do I have to draw you a fucking picture? Get me the fuck down ... up."

Ford said, "I'm goin' down to get him."

Ford started crawling forward. "There's nothing here."

"Hey, Ford you got shit for brains?" said Hernandez. "You think I just walked down here? Hey, no shit, I'd kinda like to get down from here. All my blood's runnin' to my cabeza."

They sat in the wet grass quietly, each waiting for the other to make a decision.

Kohl cleared his throat. He imagined them all looking at him. "Let's take off our belts, use the straps off the radio, lower someone over the side and see if he can reach the tree Hernandez is in." He could hear them taking off their belts. He handed his forward. They already knew who was going over the edge, Beach. Thompson wrapped the end of the belt around his arm, since he was the biggest; the rest scooted behind each other, holding onto each other's waistband. Then they lowered Beach over the edge.

"I've got a hold of a limb," said Beach. "Slippery though."

They heard him grunting and groaning until he finally said, "I've let go now, Thompson."

They were leaning over the edge and peering into the coal-black night.

"Hello there, you fuckin' little greaser."

"Your ass."

"I found the little fucker."

"Can you get him down?" asked Ford.

"Hell, Ford. I just got here."

"My foot's up there."

"Where?"

"There."

"Oh." More grunting. "I can't get it out. Can you lift up to take the pressure off it?"

"I tried. I don't have anything to hold on to."

"Hey, you guys? I can't get his foot out of the tree."

"Well, do something, Beach," Ford commanded.

"Just leave him there and we can come back and get him in the morning," Thompson said in a droll voice. Everybody giggled.

Hernandez asked Beach, "What are you doing?" There was a moment of silence, "Don't do that, Beach. I don't think that's a good idea."

Ford shouted, "Beach, what's going on?"

They heard Hernandez yell and the sound of crashing limbs breaking followed by a thud, a grunt, and a moan.

Ford called to Beach in a frightened voice, "Oh, my God, Beach? What happened? You okay Hernandez? Hernandez?"

Hernandez moaned, "Fuck me, I'm dead." There was a sigh of relief from up above. "I'm going to cut your fuckin' throat, Beach. You're a dead man."

The sound of more limbs moving and breaking. It was Beach climbing down the tree. "You okay, little buddy?" Beach's voice showed genuine concern.

"Bend over. I'll show you nine inches, you dumb, mutha fuckin' gringo."

Ford asked, "Is he okay, Beach?"

"Yeah, I think so. You okay?"

"Just don't touch me. Leave me the fuck alone."

Ford asked, "What did you do, Beach?"

"I untied his boot."

Kohl muffled a giggle.

Ford asked Hernandez, "How come you kept walking when the rest of us stopped?"

"I didn't know you guys had stopped."

"Well you know when you don't feel a hand on your shoulder, you're supposed to stop. Right?" asked Ford.

"Yeah, I know," said a chastised Hernandez. But in a lower voice he added, "But Ford was playing with my ear."

Beach laughed.

"I heard that," Ford said, but there wasn't any threat to his remark. Ford took the pen light and shined it on the map. The mission had been compromised. He found where they were on the map and told Beach where they could rendezvous. Beach tried to find Hernandez's boot but gave up.

Supporting a limping Hernandez, they walked slowly toward the rendezvous.

The five of them labored along the muddy trail back to camp. Hernandez was limping along without a boot and holding on to Beach. Thompson was walking straddle-legged, because his wet pants were rubbing the insides of his thighs raw, and Kohl brought up the rear.

What a lovely way to spend an evening. 0330. Here, have another cookie.

Well thank you. I think I will. Go recon. Waahoo!

Hey. I'm impressed. Swift, silent, and deadly?

I think it's more like slow, noisy, and harmless.

*

Kohl jumped out of the six-by and ran across the parade deck towards his BOQ room. It was 0600 and he had been thinking of nothing else but to get some sleep since about 0400. He was wet, cold, muddy, tired, and hungry.

"Hey, Kohl!"

He turned toward the familiar voice. Jogging towards him, looking like a pulling guard, jumping puddles and holding on to his cover to keep the wind from blowing it off, was First Lieutenant Paul Mays. He rushed up to Kohl, grabbed him, and lifted him up, pinning both arms to his side in a bear hug. The rain was pouring down his flat face and dripped off his smashed nose into a grinning mouth.

"Havin' fun?" Mays dropped Kohl back to his feet. Kohl was able to breathe again.

"Your ass, you miserable little shit," Kohl answered with a tired smile.

"It's good to see ya here. I heard you were coming. You sure didn't waste any time playing recon man." Mays was hopping back and forth and looking at the sky. "What do you say we get out of the fuckin' rain."

They ran to Kohl's room at the BOQ.

Kohl took off his rain soaked, mud splattered clothes and climbed into the shower. Mays followed and sat on the toilet seat, as Kohl asked, "What are you doing here?"

"I'm Battalion S-2. Some shit, uh?"

"You, S-2? Doesn't S-2 stand for intelligence?" Kohl was laughing as he climbed out of the shower. He cleared his throat, lowered his voice, and in a serious tone said, "Lieutenant Mays, what do you think of the enemy situation?"

Answering in an equally serious vein, Mays responded, "I think we ought to castrate the CO's and fuck all their wives."

"We might as well. They sure been screwin' us."

"I got news for you Kohl. They ain't through yet."

"Whatsha mean?"

"We're going afloat."

"Afloat? You're shittin' me. I'm still suffering from jet lag. I haven't unpacked yet."

"Well don't, ol' buddy boy." Then in a John Wayne drawl, he said, "We're makin' a break for it, Pilgrim." Then, in a sing song voice, "We is goin' afloat. Oh, yes we is. Goin' afloat, afloat, afloat. In a big ol' boat."

"I've only been here two days. Besides, I've got the dirty duty Friday night. I don't even know the guys in my platoon yet. I'm not even supposed to be here. Are you shittin' me?"

Mays shook his head no. "I wouldn't shit you. You're my favorite turd." Big smile.

"Come on Mays. Why would they do that?"

Mays shrugged his shoulders. "I guess they like ya." Another big smile.

"I get sea sick. Pete told me last night that 1/9 is going. What's that got to do with me?"

"You're recon patoon is attached to 1/9 and I'm the S-2 liaison Officer. We start loading tomorrow. I know all this shit man. I'm the intelligence man." He used his superhero voice.

"How many platoons in this Battalion? Uh?"

"I don't know. Twenty?"

"They chose my platoon? Give me a fuckin' break. Tomorrow?"

"What? Is there a fucking echo in here or something? Tomorrow. Got that?"

Kohl said, "I don't like it here anyway."

4 Liars Dice

Kohl was finally on board ship. It had been a long day. He had been up since about 0330 and it was close to 1800 now. He would have been here sooner except the six-by he was riding in was in an accident.

"Well, I see you finally made it." Mays met Kohl coming up the gangplank of the AKA USS Union. Kohl stood at attention, saluted the bridge and the flag, and then requested permission to come aboard. "What took you so long?" continued Mays. "I've been here for about two hours waitin' for your skinny ass."

"Where's the cabin?" Kohl grinned at the word as he thought of a cabin by a lake. Mays pointed down the passageway. They started walking towards where he had pointed.

"What took you so long?" Mays asked again.

"We were up at White Beach, and comin' around a corner was this guy in this little tiny car, on our side of the road. I've never seen a car that small before. Anyway, he was heading right for us. There was no way in hell that six-by was going to stop or swerve to miss him. He went right under the front bumper. We hit that little sucker and rolled that car between the right front wheel and fender."

"Anybody hurt?" Asked Mays.

"No. He was kind of beat up a bit. And talk about scared. We had to pull the little boogger out through the window. He was shaking so bad he couldn't stand up."

Mays took Kohl to his cabin and Kohl immediately started to unpack his suitcase, when the curtain swung open.

"Hi!" said a Navy Ensign as he entered and put something away. Kohl and Mays answered back as he left.

Kohl asked, "Who's that?"

"Must be your roomie," Mays answered with a wink.

"Why is it that Navy ensigns all look like queers?"

Mays added with a short laugh, "Because they are. And you'd better sleep with your back to the bulkhead and keep one eye open. I'll see ya later. I'm goin' to finish unpacking." He drew back the curtain and left.

Kohl unpacked and put Julie's picture on the wall, then he sat down and wrote her a letter.

> Hi Sweetheart,
>
> I'm on board ship, the USS Union. Got here about seven tonight and I'm pooped. Been up since three thirty this morning. I just got to Okinawa, and I'm off again to bob around the ocean for a while.
>
> I've been trying to learn my job and get everything squared away plus get to know my troops.
>
> Thursday morning, I went out to the field as an observer in reconnaissance. The wind was blowing and it was raining like hell. They were on patrol and I went along as an observer. It wasn't bad walking. I got to see what the island was like. The pine trees are short with lots of branches. Apparently it was logged heavily during the war. The brush is thick and green, just like most places where it rains a lot. The ocean is a deep blue-green with a lot of coral rock. I'll probably do some scuba diving while I'm here. I bet it will be prettier than diving in Laguna.
>
> Pete came over the other night. He was feeling pretty down. Did you know Sue is pregnant? Due in July sometime.
>
> After I got back from the field, I ran into Mays. Remember he's the guy at Pete's New Years party who threw the red smoke grenade in the house. Anyway he's in recon too, in fact we're on board ship together. He feels lousy. His wife went back east, Boston I think, to stay with her folks while he's over here.
>
> We're going to Hong Kong first. That should be bitchin'. Then on to the Philippines. Then we float around in the South China Sea for awhile, and in March we come back to Oki.
>
> The sun's shining today. Not a cloud in the sky. I hope it's a good omen.

I'm anxious to hear from you. It will take a while before the mail catches up with me, especially if I keep moving.
Hope the ol' car doesn't give you too much trouble. Love you, Kitten. Keep your chin up and those big blue eyes shinin'. I'll be home before you know it. Here's my new mailing address.

1st Lieutenant Dusty M. Kohl
1st Battalion, 9th Marines (A Co., 3rd Recon. Bn.)
Marine No. 11
c/o Fleet Post Office
San Francisco, Calif.

Kohl was putting the letter in the envelope when the cloth curtain gave way to Mays' hairy arm. In poked the smashed face, "Let's go you skinny shit."

"Where?"

"Let's go see Pete."

"I'm beat, Mays. I'm hittin' the sack."

"Come on. You'll have plenty of time for that. We could take off tomorrow. We might not see land for days, months, who knows? Come on. We won't stay long." Kohl shook his head no. "Come on. I already told Pete we'd come see him before we left. Come on. Let's go."

Kohl shrugged, grabbed his cover and said, "Oh well, what the fuck."

*

"Isn't that Captain Tuttle over there?" Pete pointed.

Captain Tuttle was wrapped around a beer bottle. The stack of empty bottles on the table was a sign that he had probably been there for a while.

"Howdy, Skipper," Mays waved as they approached the table.

Captain Tuttle lifted his big square head. Through squinted eyes, he gave the three Marines a puzzled look. His head swiveled from side to side as they sat down. Then a small light of recognition began to form across his white freckled face, first with a half grin, as though one side was still frozen from a novocaine shot.

"Looks like you're ahead of us, Skipper," continued Mays.

Captain Tuttle finally managed a uniform smile that showed a broad mouth full of white teeth. He waved his arm for them to sit down which they had already done. His arm hit the only beer bottle that had any beer left in it and it spilled, foaming over the table into his lap. The waitress came over quickly with a damp cloth to wipe up what remained on the table. The Captain didn't even notice that he had knocked the bottle over. He looked over his shoulder toward the bar, waved his arm again, and hit the waitress in the chest. He hadn't noticed her until the impact of his arm. "Around fer, burp! Scuz mmm, erybody." He focused his red eyes on the young lady, "Okay?"

"Jesus, Skipper, you're ripped," commented Pete.

"Fuckin'-A-John-dingle-derry ... berry." He looked for his beer. He started peering into the empty beer bottles to find one with beer in it.

Kohl, Mays, and Pete had all been in the same platoon at basic school where Captain Tuttle was their Platoon Commander. He was a graduate of Georgetown School of Law. Most of the platoon commanders were captains or senior first lieutenants, and most were regular Marines. They were eagerly aware of the impression they hoped to project to these young and newly commissioned second lieutenants. Being a Marine was serious business. Being a Marine officer was not a privilege to be abused. It was a badge to be worn with honor and dignity. They were there to learn how to be an officer and a gentleman, not 'goof around'. This was not a college dorm.

However, Second Platoon Lima Company was different. The platoon had more than its share of 'hell raisers.' One cold night the Platoon was standing in formation, being disciplined because one of the officers had returned to quarters, from the firing range, with live ammo. Word got around, even before they were called out to formation, that the ammo had been planted by one of the other platoons because Second Platoon had the company's highest scores. They were to stay in formation until the guilty Officer came forward. Captain Tuttle went to bat for the Platoon without results. The Platoon eventually broke ranks and started a bonfire using their rifle stocks. The whole Platoon was confined to quarters for one week and had to pay restitution for the burned stocks. They never discovered who had brought back the live ammo.

Through coaxing and sign language, they found out that Captain Tuttle had been in Okinawa for about two months and was the Legal Aid Officer to the Ninth Marines. He said he was celebrating his wedding anniversary.

"I've got three deuces," Kohl said in a controlled deadpanned voice that matched his blank face. He slowly slid the leather dice cup to Mays.

Mays tipped up one end, looked at Kohl, and stuck up his big fat middle finger. He picked up the cup and dice, then shook and slammed the cup down on the table. The beer bottles rattled. He tipped the corner of the cup up and looked, grinned, licked his lips, took a long pull on his beer, burped and slid the dice cup to Pete. Mays, with a frozen smile said, "Three fours."

Pete grabbed the cup, peeked under, pulled out three fours, then shook the remaining two dice. He peeked under and nonchalantly moved the dice cup to the Skipper and said "Four fours and a three."

"Skipper? Your turn," said Kohl.

Captain Tuttle looked at Kohl. "Uh?"

"Your turn. Four fours and a three, to you, Skipper."

Kohl thought they were going to have to quit. It was getting late anyway. On the table in front of Kohl, he had three full beers, and the others had at least one full one. The Captain was very drunk now and had trouble following the game. He had, in fact, lost almost every hand since they began playing two hours earlier.

"Another round!" yelled the Captain.

"No! Wait Captain. You haven't lost yet. It's your turn." Kohl turned to address the others. "We had better go."

The Captain was fumbling with the cup, trying to put the dice in it.

"Captain? We'd better go. Mays and I have to get back to the ship."

The Captain had just successfully put the two remaining dice back in the cup then turned to Pete, and asked, "What did you have?"

"Four fours and a three."

"Your ass, and you're a lyin' sack of shit."

"You've already picked up the dice, Captain"

"Oh, yeah! Lost again?"

"Yeah."

"Another round over here!"

"No, Captain." Kohl turned and waved off the waitress "Let's finish our beers and go. Captain? Mays and I have to go back to the ship."

"Bottoms up," said Mays as he drained his beer in a series of noisy gulps. "Wanna see my wedding pictures?"

Kohl and Pete answered in unison that they didn't.

"You really should see them. I look ravishing."

Kohl answered that he had seen them four times. "Yeah, but Pete hasn't seen them. Have ya, Pete? Wanna see how pretty I looked in my dress blues?"

"Yeah, well, may ... oww! Shit!" Kohl had kicked Pete in the shin under the table.

Kohl asked Pete, "Do you think you could take the Captain back."

"Yeah, I can do that," Pete said while rubbing his shin.

The Captain had barely spoken all evening. His far away look focused on the bottle in his hand. "I got pitchures." He slurred in a soft voice. He moved the beer bottles with a sudden swipe of his arm in a noisy rattle, some tipping, and rolling off the table. He took out his wallet and started removing its contents out in search of his pictures. "There they are." He picked them up one by one, out of the spilled beer on the table and handed them to Kohl. The three Lieutenants had met his wife, Judy, and their two kids at a party at his house while they were in Basic School. They passed the pictures around. One was of his wife and ten-year-old daughter and the other showed his four-year-old boy, standing next to him holding on to his leg. They commented how pretty his wife was and how cute his kids were.

"You saw his pictures," whined Mays. "Why don't you want to see mine?

"No, Mays. Let's go," said Kohl as he got up.

"Ass holes ... and fuck everybody!" Mays blared.

The fifteen or so people in the Club looked around. Kohl gave an apologetic shrug and turned to grab Mays to leave. Mays knocked Kohl's hand away. Kohl didn't like it when Mays had too much to drink. He got mean. As they were walking out of the club an Air Force Officer didn't move far enough out of Mays' path, so Mays shoved him. Kohl and Pete let out an "Uh oh."

"Fuckin' fly boy," Mays said. And as the Air Force Officer turned around, Mays quickly grabbed his tie with his left hand and started to jerk him into a smashing right. It was happening so quickly that neither Kohl nor Pete could stop what would happen next. But to the surprise of everyone, as Mays yanked the Officer's tie, it pulled loose. It was a clip-on tie and was lying limply in Mays' left hand. Mays looked at it surprised that the head was not attached to it. The Captain started laughing and was soon followed by everyone in the club: except for the Air Force Officer, who was as white as a sheet. Mays handed the tie back to him.

They staggered out of the club. It was dark and raining again. Mays ran and tackled a ten-foot palm tree. He lay on the rain soaked ground with his arms wrapped around palm fronds of the uprooted palm tree.

"Nailed that son-bitch," he said, as he staggered into a standing position. He walked over and leaned into the cab window that was parked at the curb. "White Bitch, please."

"That's White Beach, Mr. Cab Driver. White Beach," Kohl corrected.

Pete helped the Captain into another cab.

Kohl went over and shook Pete's hand and said, "See ya in about three months, Pete."

"Take care ol' buddy." Pete smiled weakly and climbed into the cab. The Captain had already passed out.

5 Cat on a Raft

Kohl awoke from the thudding of his head. *Bad headache.* He stuck his foot out of the bed and put it on the floor. *They say it'll stop the bed from spinning.* Didn't work. Kohl thought he really must be hung over to be feeling like this. Not only was his head spinning, but also the whole room seemed to be moving. He soon realized the thudding of his head was not completely the result of a hangover, but because his head was hitting the headboard. The room was moving because the ship was moving. He felt his stomach tighten and saliva was starting to collect in his mouth. He swallowed. Quicker than he had expected, the bile began to collect to the point of no return. Sooner than he wanted to, he staggered from the bed to the bathroom, which fortunately was only about eight feet away. "Uuuughaaa." *Up comes what I think of the Corps.* He gagged again. *Oh shit this is terrible. I'll never do this again. Promise.* "Uuuuughhaaaa." *Oh bad. Wheeooo. God, I hate this.* He laid his head on the toilet seat waiting for his stomach to calm down.

Mays stuck his head through the curtain. "Hey, Kohl? Where're you at?" Pause. He heard Kohl moan from the bathroom. "Oh. How you feelin'?"

"I feel terrible."

"Let's go eat. It'll make you feel better to have something in your stomach." Mays heard Kohl heave again. "Ah, never mind. Bad idea. I guess I'd better go. See ya later."

While lying in his bunk, looking at the ceiling, Kohl recalled the reason he didn't join the Navy. *You get seasick. Remember?*

Then what the hell are you doing out here in the middle of the fucking ocean?

He couldn't sleep. He had been in bed for three days. He was beginning to wonder if it was going to be like this for the whole duration. As long as he was lying down he felt fair, a little groggy, but probably because he was chewing Dramamine like M&M's.

He thought of Julie. He couldn't do much of anything else. But he had to take her picture down from the bulkhead because it would swing out and bang back against the wall, which was annoying. He thought of how beautiful she was and how much he loved her. He felt remorse because he hadn't written her since they shipped out. Even to sit up in bed made him sick. He could read by rolling over on his side, as long as he didn't get his head too far up. *How am I ever going to get back on a sleeping schedule?* He looked at the clock. It was 0200. *Now I'll probably sleep till 1000 and miss breakfast again. Can't stand those fish smelling eggs anyway. Be careful talking about food, Kohl.* He gagged. Too late. He bolted up and charged for the bathroom. He leaned over the bowl, felt his stomach turning inside out. Nothing came up but Dramamine, saliva, and the stomach bile that strung down his lower lip. He had thrown up so much that his stomach muscles were sore. He returned to his bunk, weaving from the rolling motion of the ship. He gave a disgusting look at his roommate. *Look at that fat son-of-bitch just lying there dead to the world.* Kohl resented him. *How can you resent him? You don't even know him. What does he think of you? Always in bed. Is the big bad Marine sicky, sicky? Maybe it's that grin he gives me when he passes me in the morning. I don't belong on a ship. I'm a land man. I love the ground, dirt, rocks, trees, and stuff like that. It's not natural for man to be floatin' around on the water.* He closed his eyelids.

The light from the passageway made its way through the curtain that swayed first into the room then back out into the passageway. The light blinked off and on throughout the night. The ship creaked and groaned as the metal hulk rolled from side to side, breaking the constant and persistent roar of the big diesel engines that propelled the pointed steel hull, cutting, then peeling the black sea into rolls of white foam. He tried to put more padding between his head and the headboard. He scrunched further down into the bunk.

The light glittered through Kohl's closed eyelids. He saw visions of golden aspen leaves. The sun briefly warmed his face. He listened intently for the sound of the small stream nearby, knowing its sound but not recognizing the noise he was hearing. Oh, yes. It was a logging truck followed closely by billowy clouds of fine powdered dust, hanging in still air, choking leaves, collecting on moist lips. But there were more trucks one after another. The roar of the trucks never seemed to stop. The dream was not right. He uncovered his eyes by lifting his eyelids, revealing the confines of the small cabin. He recognized the constant roar of the ship's diesel engines. He felt the hesitation, the strain and groan as the ship tried to cut through a swell, then a sigh of the engines, a slight pause and then a shudder at the impact of another wave, over and over again. The ship tore the sea apart with its bow, like a rusty wedge. The torn edges were whipped by the wind into a towering spray that rained upon the ship. The metal monster lifted, twisted, rolled, bucked, and heaved. It provoked, disturbed, and disrupted the ocean's flow. The constant force of the persistent waves put a strain on the twenty-year-old rivets. The sea was winning. A never tiring force eventually to swallow, without so much as a small bubble, a sea burp, between horizons and after several eternities, a bent and barnacled piece of tubing will be belched upon some quiet sandy shore without notice to anyone that matters.

He closed his eyes again to shade them from the light in the passageway. The intercom whistled. A droning voice announced to expect heavy rolls through the Taiwan Straight. *Expect, hell. What do you call what we've been having for the last two days?*

What Kohl didn't know was that the convoy had hit the perimeter of a typhoon and it was going to get rougher.

I don't belong here. I feel like a cat on a raft. I love the ground. There is a feeling of security when you can stand on something solid that isn't moving. I feel safe on the ground. I'm familiar with it. It feels comfortable. I'm a land man. I like flowers, trees, birds, and animals. I like to roam the beaches, climb rocks, play in fields of clover. I like the kind of water you can drink, jump across, or see across or swim across. Where land meets sea in waves, I like that. Where sea meets sky and meaningless clouds in all directions, I don't like that. Makes me feel uneasy. Kohl grinned at himself. God must be a Marine. That son-of-a-bitch. Excuse me God. Are you trying to tip us over?

It was an uneasy sleep.

"Look at him. There." Pointing. " See? That's the Lord. Just sitting there on the edge of that storm front." The Lord's legs were dangling down so

His toes could play in the ripples in the ocean. He was throwing rocks into 'His pond'. He was tanned by the sun and stars and his white hair whipped around his face and forehead by the wind that brought the front closer. He displayed the concentration of His amusement. Tight lipped, He heaved a big rock in a shot put motion close to the thing in the pond. Just to make waves and splash it. "Oh, darn," said the Lord. "Got too close with that one." He sank it. It was gone. Kohl felt the shock of cold water. "The Lord sank the boat. Goddamn Him. Hmmm. That won't work. Can't damn God."

The Lord stood up and bent over searching for a good skipping rock. One that would beat yesterdays record. All the way to the California coast. Sixteen skips.

It was hard for Kohl to see over the waves. But the Lord was high in the clouds. He had His arm cocked. His arm swung forward in a slow graceful arc, horizontal and close to the water. It was going to be a good throw. The wrist snapped, putting the necessary spin on the smooth flat rock. Kohl saw the spray of the first skip from the stone that God threw. Excitement climbed into Kohl's throat. It was a good throw. It could go all the way to California. He followed the flight of the rock as it continued to glide above the reach of the lapping water. Kohl tried to gauge and anticipate where the next skip was going to be. His excitement swelled when he realized it was going to enter the water within swimming distance. Kohl had to make it or he would drown. He had to make it. No telling when God would throw another rock this way again. Kohl started swimming as fast as he could until he got tired. He realized he had a long ways to go and should be pacing himself. The waves rose and fell pushing him forward one minute and pulling him back the next. His clothes dragged him down. His arms hurt and shoulders ached. His boots became lead weights on his feet. He should have taken them off, but he didn't have time now. He watched the stone as it spun toward him. "It'll hit about twenty yards ahead." Kohl was gasping for breath now. His swimming strokes were labored. It was like slow motion. Barely moving. He could hardly move his arms out of the water. "I've got to make it. I've got to. Can't give up. Push. Push. Never give up. Just a few more feet." The stone entered the water in a powerful shower of spray. Kohl was startled by the size of the rock. It must have been two hundred feet in diameter. The stone surged to the surface almost directly under him, flipping him into the air and in a torrent of rushing water he tumbled back onto the rock. He landed on his back and immediately rolled over. The joy he felt was short lived, because now he was groping and clawing for a hold on the smooth slick rock. The spinning rock was propelling him out to the side, away from its center. His knees hurt, as they slowly scraped towards the edge. His fingers were so numb from the cold water that he felt nothing. They scratched and searched for a hold. He watched as his fingernails tore away from the flesh and his raw fingers were leaving ribbons of blood on the sun-bleached face of the stone. He cried from the pain. As he slipped closer to the edge the pull became stronger. His fingers were cramped into claws and the tips of his boots were now open sores of exposed toes. His sobs were heavy. "Oh, God. Don't leave me here in the middle of the ocean. I want to go home." All his strength was gone. He was swirling in sobs of despair. He lay face down on the stone, tearing his left side raw. Suddenly he was flung, hurling into space, falling, slowly, pinwheeling, with arms and legs outstretched, dizzy...

Thump! The water was hard. Kohl's eyes popped open. Black. Confused and breathing hard, he swung his arms and lifted the sheet that covered his head. Light poured in. His face lay on the cold floor. He saw bare feet. He rolled over and looked into the laughing faces of the Navy officers. Kohl saw the hairy arm of a laughing Mays reach through the air and helped him to his feet. He limped from his wounds. He wiped salt water from his face.

"Holy shit, Kohl," laughed Mays.

"Hey, man. Quite the show," said a laughing face.

His roommate said, "Yeah, you were yellin', cryin' and thrashin' around before you fell out of bed. Man you were really great. Better than Collins here, last week." They all laughed again.

Kohl, sitting on his rack, asked, "What did he do?"

His roommate continued as Collins turned and walked back to his cabin, "Collins was running down the passageway yellin' that a giant pussy was going to eat him." They all laughed and returned back to their cabins.

The fat roommate said, " Yeah you really put on a show. Good night."

"Good night." Kohl looked to see what time it was. 0430. *Maybe I'll have breakfast this morning. I'm awake.*

*

USS Union (AKA -106)
Fleet Post Office
San Francisco, Calif.

Do not remove from ship.

To the north ocean, to the south ocean, every where you look there is water. You can put the ship's orders in a bottle, cork it, and throw it over board.

Plan of the day for Tuesday, 12 January 1965
OOD watch list
08-12 & 20-24 Lt. J.G. Billings
12-16 & 00-04 Ensign Collins
16-18 & 04-08 Ensign Silverman
18-20 Lt. J.G. Hanover

Uniform of the day: Officers and CPO's wash khaki short sleeved shirts blue steaming caps optional.
Other enlisted men dungarees, blue working caps.

Carry out the daily under way routine as prescribed in Chapter II, USS Union Organization, and Regulations Manual except as modified below:
0800 Pay day
1030 The Medical Officer will conduct sanitation inspection.

That is a pecker check.

1245 Holiday routine for X Division

Notes from the desk of the Commanding Officer:
1. During our trip to Hong Kong, we will be passing through the Taiwan Straits and will be steaming close to the Communist Chinese mainland. It is obvious that in these areas we should be well prepared for attacks. That is why the General Quarters Drills was repeated yesterday. However, in view of the performance during the drill and during the AA Shoot, it is doubtful that we would survive even a minor attack. Sound Powered Phones had been removed from the G. Q. Stations and not returned and some had been left out in the open and rusted. Plus the covers on Sound Powered Outlets had been left off so that salt water had shorted out some of the lines. Helmets had been removed from the Gun Tubs. During black out there were portholes with out covers. Many hands were obviously not doing their best to man their stations as fast as possible

and some were not manned at all. This points to a lack of awareness of the dangers that exist in these waters. Attacks occur suddenly, as in the Tonken Gulf Incident. The Commies will not warn us in advance, so with all the gasoline and ammo we are carrying, we have to be ready now. We not only have to do it right the first time, but better than the last. We have to be prepared. Do your part. It's your neck. Mistakes out here can be fatal.

2. Division photographs will be taken today commencing immediately after payday. These will be the last pictures to be taken for the cruise book.

3. Information concerning the procedure for obtaining tax-free liquor is published and available at the supply office. Only one gallon per enlisted man, three gallons per CPO/NCO and five gallons per officer.

4. While in Hong Kong it is strongly urged that the buddy system of traveling in pairs be stressed. Hong Kong has an abundance of entertainment, sight seeing and shopping. On the other hand it is also famous for pick pockets, clip joints, unsavory merchants and venereal disease.
Drunkenness of U.S. military personnel will not be tolerated. Marine Corps personnel observed to be unduly under the influence of intoxicating beverages will be returned to their ships by the Shore Patrol without delay.

Tattoos. The occurrence of personnel receiving tattoos will be called for Office Hours and disciplinary action will be taken. In Hong Kong contracting infectious and venereal diseases is very high. Persons engaging in sexual intercourse have approximately 10 to 15% chance of contracting venereal diseases so protect yourself. Go to the ship's doctor for the necessary supplies. Better safe than sorry.

5. The winner of the ship's raffle is LCpl. Beach, USMC. Congratulations.

6. Commanding Officers non-judicial punishment was held on 13 Jan. and the following punishment awarded Seaman R. B. Stanley for

insubordination towards a Petty Officer. Awarded: three days confinement of bread and water, extra duty for 30 days and reduction in rank.

7. To prevent the flow of US dollars into Communist China through Hong Kong, only authorized agencies will be used for exchange of US to Hong Kong dollars. The Chinese take US currency out of circulation. We are fighting the Commies not feeding them.

8. The following liberty hours of Marine Corps personnel are as follows:
1200-2400 E4 and below
1200-0100 E5 to E6
1200— E7 and above and all officers. Return time will be at the discretion of the company commanders.

9. By agreement with British authorities, liberty can now be granted to Kowloon. Privileges may be withdrawn if trouble arises between US personnel and British servicemen.

10. Out of bounds areas: the roof tops in the Wanchai District, bounded by Arsenal St. on the west, Percival St. on the east, Gloucester Rd. on the north and Hennessy Rd. on the south. Again it must be stressed that there is a prevalence of venereal disease.

6 Hong Kong

Kohl and Mays got off the ship's liberty boat at Fenwick Pier.

With arms and face to the sky Kohl shouted, "Land! Land! Oh my God, solid ground. Ain't it beautiful?"

"You make it sound as though you've been afloat for months instead of six days," Mays said.

"Months, days, hours. What's the difference? Anytime is too long for me." Kohl ran up the cement steps to the sidewalk above. A grinning Mays followed closely behind.

"While you're thinking of land, I'm thinking of slant-eyed pussy." He looked to the left to check for traffic. "Come on." He stepped off the curb to cross.

"Mays!" Kohl yelled, as he grabbed Mays' shirt collar and yanked. With the horn blaring, a taxi zipped by, missing Mays by inches. With the force of the pull and Mays jumping back, they both landed sprawled on the sidewalk.

"You crazy sonbitch!" yelled Mays. "Get on your own fuckin' side of the road!"

"Jesus, almost got hit. Didn't even slow down. Little fucker would have drug you clear to China. Close. Fuck me," Kohl said excitedly.

Mays glared at Kohl and said, "We're in China, you dumb fuck." Mays got to his feet and brushed the seat of his pants off.

Kohl was still sitting on the sidewalk. He looked up at five grinning sailors. The one in front reached a long arm down and helped Kohl up. Kohl checked for soiled spots on his civilian clothes.

"A lot of guys get hit here." The sailor said. "Everybody in Hong Kong drives on the wrong side of the road. Just like England, ya know. And the cross walks? Don't mean shit. They don't stop for nothin'. See ya guys."

"Thanks," answered Mays and Kohl, as the sailors turned and left.

"Shit, that was close," Mays said as they jogged across the street. "Just goes to show you what can happen. One second you're here, thinkin', seein', feelin', then pppuuffft. Gone, done, adios, kaput and some dude you don't know, readin' over you while someone else is throwing dirt in your open eyes."

Kohl gave Mays a disgusted side-glance, "That's a morbid way of looking at death."

"True though. Nothing pretty about being dead."

"Yeah, but you don't have to talk about it."

"Let's get laid," Mays said.

"I'm going to the bank of Hong Kong then to the China Fleet Club," Kohl said.

"And then screw? Oh. There's one." Mays points. "There's one." Mays points at another young girl. "There's one. Ooo!"

"Come on Mays. Knock it off." People were starting to look.

Mays continued to point and yell. "There's one. Oooeee!" Mays stopped, grabbed Kohl's arm, and wheeled through the swinging doors into a dark bar. "Ooooeee! Here I is, honey."

The bar was dark and cool in contrast to the sunny warm outside. Kohl ran into a chair. So much for that close one-eye bull shit. "Damn. I can't see a fuckin' thing."

Kohl recalled a lesson learned the hard way at basic school. They were on night maneuvers and had become blinded by a flare. An old Gunny, who was one of 'the enemy,' caught the blinded officers, took off all their clothes, except for their skivvies and boots, and marched them through the cold January night to the POW holding pens. After he had his sadistic fun of push-ups and sit-ups in the mud and snow, he gave the shivering lieutenants their clothes. Around a warming fire, he told them why they needed to keep one eye closed when a flare pops. Then when it's dark again at least you've got one good eye. He said it saved his life at the "Frozen Chosen" in Korea and maybe it would save their lives one day. All through OCS and basic school, they had heard that before. But, they accepted the Gunny's comment to be worthy of remembering to be tucked away and recalled some day. He also told them it was good to close one eye before you went into a bar during the day. The Lieutenants asked, why? He said walking into an unfamiliar bar blind, you could get sucker punched and not even see it coming. At least he had given them something they felt they could use in civilian life. It's not like they were going to go through life closing one eye because of white phosphorus flares popping in the night.

They groped their way toward the faint light at the bar. An English looking gentleman, with a thin mustache and thin gray hair smiled and greeted them with a friendly, "Hi." They took the two empty stools to the man's right and ordered two pints of whatever they had on draft from a six foot, heavily muscled, tan bartender who wore a black silk tank top that showed a black hairy chest and a gold medallion. He looked Mediterranean.

Kohl's eyesight was beginning to adjust to the dark and was beginning to make out forms.

An elderly overweight man approached the English looking gentleman. "Say, Harry. Introduce me to your young friends here," as he nodded and smiled. "I'll take care of that, William," he said as the bartender brought the Marines their beer.

Kohl leaned over and said, "Thank you." Mays nodded. Kohl whispered to Mays, "Sure are friendly."

Mays began looking around for girls, as they took long gulps of the cold beer. Kohl could feel it all the way from his mouth to his stomach.

"My name's Harry and this is my friend Chester. Where you boys from?"

The four of them stared at each other, smiling.

Kohl started to answer, "We're from...." When Mays turned around with his back to the bar, grabbed Kohl's arm, leaned over and whispered, "Somethin' ain't right."

"What?"

"Look around. There ain't no women."

Kohl looked again. "Maybe it's too early."

"Hell, it's one-o-clock. And besides there's always hookers."

The man named Harry put his hand on Mays' thigh and said, "You boys just get in?"

Kohl thought he saw the smiling man wink.

Mays looked at the hand on his leg and then at Harry. Mays grabbed the man's wrist in his vise like grip and jerked his leg up. Harry screamed as the wrist snapped.

"You fuckin' faggot!" Mays snarled as he smashed his left fist into Harry's nose. Blood splattered.

Kohl stood up in shock, but out of the corner of his eye he saw the bartender swing a bat at Mays who had his back turned. Kohl shoved Chester into the bar. The bat deflected off Chester's head and hit Mays with a glancing blow to the shoulder. Mays whirled and blocked the next blow with his forearm. He grabbed the bat with one hand and with the other he grabbed the bartender by the hair and smashed his face on top of the bar. Now Mays had the bat. Kohl and Mays were standing back to back, surrounded by about fifteen or so patrons. Kohl saw a few with knives others were holding beer bottles. Mays swung the bat in an arc to keep them at a distance.

"Get out of the fuckin' way, you fuckin' queers!" Mays yelled.

With Kohl in front, they moved towards the swinging doors. The bartender, blood running from his smashed nose, was on the phone to the police.

A small man darted at Kohl, slashing with a knife in a sweeping arc. Kohl blocked the man's arm with his left forearm, spun to his right and caught him with a right elbow to the side of his head. The man went down. Mays continued to swing the bat. When they were about five yards from the door Kohl yelled, "Go!" Mays turned and they bolted for the door. Blinded by the sun as they ran from the dark bar, they ran into and over the people on the sidewalk. Mays in his pulling-guard-crouch didn't even slow down or try to swerve to miss pedestrians. Kohl peeked a quick glance and saw five or six men chasing them. They ran through traffic crossing the street. They heard the sirens. Ducking into a narrow alley, they ran through an open door into a restaurant kitchen, much to the surprise of the cooks who began waving their arms, throwing pots and yelling at them. They slowed to a walk and entered into the dinning area and sat down at a table. The room was crowded. A few people looked up as they walked in.

They looked at each other. Both were breathing hard. Mays picked up the menu and said, "Lunch?"

Kohl gave Mays an annoyed glance as he watched the five men who were chasing them pass the restaurant window. Kohl's heart was still racing. Adrenaline had his every nerve on edge. He leaned over the table, glared at Mays and snarled. "You dumb mutha fuckin' ass hole. Fifteen minutes in port and already we've had a fight and now we've got the fuckin' cops after us. Out-fuckin'-standing. Just out-fuckin'-standing. You know we could have left that place without any trouble, but noooo. Not Mister 'bust-your-face' Mays. Fuckin' ass hole. Could have got us both killed." Kohl was shaking with anger and frustration at Mays' nonchalant attitude.

"So we had a fag fight. Big deal. Forget about it."

The waitress came up. Mays handed her the bat. She instinctively took the bat and held it. Kohl could tell her mind was racing, trying to understand all of its ramifications. Finally she took the bat to the kitchen and returned. Since the menu was in Chinese and she did not speak English, they pointed to what other people were eating and ordered. Mays tried to make small talk but Kohl was still angry and ate his meal in silence.

*

The Bank of Hong Kong took up most of the block and rose skyward with black and white marble pillars. As Kohl and Mays walked in, their eyes locked on the guard who was standing next to one of the pillars. He wore a black denim suit that fit tightly on his six-foot-four frame of about two hundred and twenty pounds. Wiry cord muscles stuck out from his neck that kept a dark, gaunt head straight. His eyes were steel gray and moved across the patrons in a slow distinct motion. He had a black handlebar mustache that matched his long black hair. His cheeks were high under deep-set eyes. His mouth was nothing but a firm, thin line. He had a long nose with a pronounced bump on top, as if it had been broken several times and never fixed. Next to his left hand was a shotgun with a magazine clip in it. His eyes stopped and fixed on Kohl and Mays. They both quickly looked away.

"Good God," Kohl whispered to Mays, as though the guard would hear them forty feet away. "You see that guy?"

"I noticed."

"Did you ever see anything as scary as that?

"No. If you held up this place, that son-of-bitch would blow a hole in your belly the size of a dinner plate. He'd make a good DI, wouldn't he?"

"Yeah. Scary. I remember that at the bank back in Huntington Beach, we had this little old man about 65, kind of heavy and short. He had rosy checks and would smile and greet everybody, open doors for little old ladies and point you to the right counters. I don't even think he had a gun," reminisced Kohl.

After exchanging their currency, Kohl and Mays went their separate ways. Neither of them had the money the Navy guys had. The Navy guys had been saving for months just for Hong Kong. Mays and Kohl had been on leave before leaving the States and had received only one pay period since. Kohl walked around Hong Kong. He went to the China Fleet Club, bought a camera and a string of cultured pearls for Julie.

He entered the Hilton Hotel and looked at suits, tape recorders, and radios for sale on the first floor. Later he took the elevator to the top of the Hilton where there was a cocktail lounge. He ordered a beer and enjoyed the panoramic view of the Hong Kong Harbor, with a background of brilliant blue sky, scattered with white fluffy clouds. Pearl colored skyscrapers surrounded the blue harbor. The harbor itself was active with military ships, freighters, and sampans. Looking towards mainland China he saw high green mountains dotted with isolated high-rise apartments and houses. He looked at the view and drank beer until sundown, wishing Julie could be next to him to share this moment.

His thoughts were interrupted when he heard Mays' familiar voice, "Hey, Kohl." He was with three other Marine Lieutenants from the convoy, Joss, Wheeler and Mesherwitz.

"Ya hungry ol' buddy?" he added.

"Yeah sure." He shook hands with the three Lieutenants. They had all been together at Basic School and Camp Pendleton.

The five of them took the ferry to Kowloon and ended up at the Grand Hotel for dinner. They had a table that overlooked the airstrip and the harbor.

*

Heads turned at the combination of Mays' loud voice and the laughing Marines. Joss's face was red with embarrassment, as he was the current brunt of the joking Marines. The red luster was further enhanced by the third Whiskey Sour on an empty stomach.

Bill Joss was born and raised in the little town of Fallon, Montana. His graduating class was only twenty-five. The closest neighbor to his parent's farm was a mile and a half away. He went to Boise State where he got his Engineering Degree in four years with a three-point-seven. He wasn't much of a ladies' man, which lead to a lot of kidding at Basic School. He was called the oldest Marine virgin.

"I'm not either a virgin. I ... have had ... experience," said Joss in a forced whisper.

"Joss," Mays shakes his head no. "Sheep don't count." That brought on uproarious laughter.

"You know, every time he hears the 'baaa' of a sheep, he gets a hard on," kidded Wheeler.

"I even heard that back on his farm in Montana, the sheep were so afraid of him that they walked backwards when he was around," said Mays.

"You shouldn't talk, Mays, you won't see me walking into a queer bar," said Joss then he flipped them the finger and left for the restroom.

"Escuz me gennalmen." The waiter tapped Wheeler's heaving shoulder. Wheeler's head was on the table. He looked up with tears in his eyes. "The gues are compraining. You are too roud. Prease be sirent or we have to ass you to reave." He turned and left.

Wheeler squinted his eyes and said in a sing song voice, "We're too roud and have to ass you to reave." They all started laughing again.

Out of the corner of his eye, Kohl saw an elderly gentleman with white hair coming toward their table. The gentleman cleared his throat. They looked up and quit laughing.

"I'm sorry gentlemen," he said in an English accent. "On behalf of the management, I'm going to ask you to leave."

"Okay, Sir. Sorry," Wheeler said as he shrugged self-consciously.

Mays brought out a piece of paper, unfolded it and said, "Fuckin' Limeys."

"Sshhh! Mays. Shit," said Kohl nervously.

"Okay, where to now? We have to chart our course," continued Mays.

"I'm going to get Joss out of the bathroom," said Wheeler.

"Isn't that the Ship's Bulletin, Mays?" asked Kohl.

"Yeah, now listen. Out of bounds area. Kawloon."

"Oh shit," says Kohl. "No way."

Mesherwitz was looking over Mays' shoulder. He never seemed to say much, just grinned, and drank.

Mays continued, "The area from Jordan Road, north to Boundary Street and from Nathan Road to the Waterfront is out of bounds after sunset. Well, that pretty well says it."

"Says what?" Wheeler asked as he returned with Joss. Mays told him.

"Isn't that out of bounds?" asked Wheeler.

"Yes. And I wonder why," said Mays with a grin. "Let's go. Time's a wastin'."

The five walked from the Grand Hotel. "Nice place, wasn't it?" said Wheeler.

"Wonder how the food was," asked Kohl.

"We sure as hell won't know now, thanks to loud mouth over there," grumbled Joss.

"Come on Joss, don't be pissed," Wheeler said. "We'll get you something to eat." He flicked out his tongue.

They stopped at a cocktail lounge. Mays checked to see if it was on the list. It was.

"Is this a brothel?" asked Joss.

"I think so. It's on the list," answered Mays.

"Glad to know we are in the right place. Can we eat here?" asked Wheeler.

"Yeah, but it'll probably taste like fish," said Mays laughing.

"I hope we don't get picked up by the MP's," cautioned Kohl.

For a bar it was too light. In fact it looked like a '50's cafe with slick, red, plastic booths. There was a bar and a center area for dancing to a juke box that was playing songs from the '50's. Kohl felt his neck redden. He felt uneasy being in a place like this, at least that was what it was supposed to be. It must be the bright lights. Can't hide. Three girls from the bar walked over to the booth where the Marines had just settled.

"Out-fuckin'-standing. Now that's what I call service," Mays said as he stood up and the first girl slid in between him and Wheeler.

Mesherwitz got out of the booth and picked up two chairs while one girl sat with him and the other slid in between Joss and Kohl.

"Here ya go."

"How's that."

The girls nodded.

"Well now," said Mays grinning and rubbing his hands together.

"Buy me drinkey?" said the girl leader.

"Yeah sure. What do you want?"

"House drink fine," answered the leader.

Mays hailed the waitress. "Two Scotch and waters, one Whiskey Sour for pussy Joss, two San Miguels and three house drinks."

She said thank you and turned to leave.

Mays added. "Oh, hey, lady. Bring that jar of beer sausages. Okay?"

She nodded and shuffled off.

"Money for juke box?" asked the girl leader with an outstretched hand to Mays, who was doing all the talking.

"Oh, for christ's sake!" He pulled out a handful of change, offered it to her, as she picked out the coins she wanted.

The drinks came along with the beer sausages. Mays paid. The bartender gave a slip of paper to the head girl. She shoved it in between her flat breasts.

Mesherwitz asked. "Aren't we going to get anything to eat? I'm hungry."

"Yeah, queer boy," added Joss. "If you and your damn big loud mouth hadn't run amuck we would have had chow by now." Joss was still upset over Mays making fun of him.

Kohl saw Mays bristle. "Well order something, asshole. I ain't your fucking mother. And I got the sausages for you, Krout. So shut the fuck up and let's do some serious drinking."

Wheeler took out a sausage and put it between his legs and said, "Hey Mays. I got something you can eat."

The tension broke as everybody laughed.

Mays grabbed the house drink from the girl next to him, looked at it, sniffed it, and tasted it. "It's coke. How much did I pay for a tea cup of coke?" The Marines shrugged.

"Gook money."

"No, it's not. It's British. Dumb college jocks," Joss grumbled, which was mostly true. Mays and Krout played football, Kohl played basketball, and

Wheeler was a swimmer.

The girl leader said they couldn't drink on the job.

Wheeler bought the second round and started a conversation with the head girl. Mays and the girl he was dancing with were grinding their hips together in rhythm to the music of Ray Charles singing "Georgia."

Kohl and Joss took turns smiling at the girl that sat between them.

"What you name?" she asked.

"Who me?" said Joss.

"My name is Linda," she said. Kohl couldn't quite bring himself to believe that.

"My name's Bill," said Joss.

"You Sailo man?"

"No, we're Marines," answered Joss.

"Oh, that nice. I like Maeen."

She probably likes anything with money and a dick, mumbles Kohl. She turns to Kohl. He smiled.

"My name is Lu Quong," said Kohl.

Joss gave Kohl a troubled look and took a big gulp of his Whiskey sour.

"No, no. You tease me. You name Kohl. They say it."

"That's my nick name. My real name is Lu Quong."

"That's right," said Mays as he slides into the booth with his girl. "He's tellin' the truth." Joss took another drink and tried to understand what was going on.

"You see," continued Kohl, "Not many people know, just my closest friends. But when I looked at you, I don't know ... something inside me said 'I've got to tell her'." She nodded. "You see during the Second World War my father was in China fighting Japs, where he met and fell in love with a woman who was half Black-Russian and Chinese. She became his wife and my mother. So, when I look into your eyes I see Mom."

"Aw, gee whiz, Kohl. That's real sweet," sighed Mays.

"What's a Black Russian? I thought it was something you drank," inquired Joss.

He leaned around the girl in the middle and looked at Kohl. "You don't look Chinese."

"Would you care to dance, Linda?" asked Kohl.

She nodded.

Joss ordered the third round. Wheeler and Krout left with two of the girls.

"You know, Linda? Joss has the hots for you."

"What's hots?"

"You make his dick stick out. He told me when you were dancing with

Mays."

"Don't you like me? I like you."

"Oh, yeah sure, but I have a girl."

"Here?"

"No. Back home."

"That okay. Make no different. I make it with many who have girl."

"Yeah, well. Joss needs you. He's shy and he's afraid to ask to spend the night with you."

The record ended and they returned to the table. "Come on, Mays. Let's go."

Linda slid in next to Joss and gave him a big smile. She touched his leg and slowly moved her hand to his crotch. Joss gave a slight jump.

It was three in the morning when Mays and Kohl returned to the Hilton. Mays told Kohl he would see him later and went over and talked to a cab driver as Kohl went up to the room.

*

The next day Kohl went sightseeing. He rode a trolley up to the top of the mountain overlooking the harbor. The warm sun consumed his body as his eyes absorbed the colors of Hong Kong Harbor. He strolled along garden paths of flowers. He lost himself in the sounds of birds. He felt lucky. *Yes, lucky.* He felt lucky to be able to see this city. He stopped at a park and watched a group of men play Cricket.

When he got back on board ship he couldn't find his wallet. Frantically, he searched everywhere. It probably had been stolen on the crowded trolley. This meant that he would have to report it to the XO, Lieutenant Commander Hangerber. His military I.D. and driver's license would have to be replaced. His American Express would have to be canceled. The XO would not be happy about this. ***Why me?***

He spent the last day on board ship. He was in his cabin reading, when he recognized Mays' footsteps coming down the passageway. Mays poked his smashed face in.

"Where in the hell have you been?" Kohl asked.

Mays looked tired. He staggered into the room, then flopped onto the bed, rolled over and gave Kohl a pained look. "Gawd, my peter's broke. This beautiful girl and me were together for two days. I lost track after twenty times."

Kohl gave him a doubtful look.

"Man, she was great. I'd be all done in and ol' peter would just lay there, all pooped out. Then she'd find ways to bring the magic wand to life you wouldn't believe."

"I don't want to hear all the gory details."

"My aren't we stuffy today. But just one more thing. I made her climax five times in one screw."

"She probably was pretending."

"No. I could tell. Her pussy quivered."

"Really?"

"I'm not shittin' ya."

"They'll tell you anything for money."

"That wasn't true with this chick. In fact the second day she didn't charge me."

"She probably made a bundle the first day." Kohl saw Mays' neck swell and his jaw tighten.

"You're starting to piss me off, you skinny-assed fucker. Just because you don't approve of my actions, don't give me any of your high-and-mighty bull-shit. You live your life, I'll live mine."

"Don't get your ass in an uproar. I'm just rattlin' your cage. Sorry," Kohl added quickly. "I finished the letter to the Commandant and my Congressman, asking for an early out. Here, read it and tell me what you think."

Mays took the letter, gave Kohl a chilling look and said, "Well, she did."

"Okay, okay. Read it."

Mays got comfortable and read the letters. They would wind their way through the chain of command, first to the Commanding Officer of First Marine Battalion, Commanding Officer of Third Reconnaissance Battalion, Commanding General of the Third Marine Division and finally to the Commandant of the Marine Corps. The request was for an early out in September, instead of December, so Kohl could teach school. If he got out in December he wouldn't be able to teach until the following September. This, he said, would prove an "undue personal hardship." Mays finished the Commandant's letter, then started the letter to the Honorable James B. Utt, Jr.

"Oh. I like this. 'I want to continue making America a better and stronger place to live by working with the youth of America. I am asking for your help, your advice, and your influence.' What a bunch of bullshit."

"I thought it sounded pretty good."

"Man, this is going to get you nothin' but trouble. The COs don't like letters to the Commandant, and you'll end up with every shit detail they can think of."

"What the hell did I do to deserve this?" Kohl said as he swung his arm around.

"Well, getting the Battalion Commanders' wife drunk at our Battalion party wasn't bad for starters. And then when she ran out of the house, naked as a jay bird with those big tits a floppin' all over and jumped into the pool, well, I'd say that was the straw that broke the Colonel's back."

Mays didn't know the half of it. Kohl first met Carol, the Battalion Commanders' wife, at the Sandpiper in Laguna Beach two years earlier. That was about a year before he met Julie. She had approached him and asked him to dance. She hadn't volunteered her last name, and he hadn't asked. She only said that her husband was a Marine Officer and was gone most of the time. Kohl liked her immediately. She was attractive and had a snide sense of humor. She was noticeably older, mid-thirties maybe. She was tall, but what Kohl noticed first and foremost were her large breasts. He could not keep from staring. When Kohl and Carol danced, her breasts jiggled, rolled, bounced, swayed beneath the low cut dress. They went to a motel later that night where Kohl had one of the most erotic nights he'd ever had. When they parted ways the next morning, there was no mention from either one of them about seeing each other again. But she called Kohl a couple of months later and they met at a motel in San Juan Capistrano.

The next time he saw her it was at the Battalion party. That was when he found out she was the wife of his Battalion Commander. They began dancing and then one thing led to another. They were both drinking heavily and found their way to one of the upstairs bedrooms. She had her clothes off and had her head between Kohl's legs, when her husband, Colonel Hastings walked in. Kohl was not in a position to run, with his pants down around his ankles. But nothing stopped Carol from running screaming out of the room, down the stairs, through the patio and jumping into the pool. Colonel Hastings was an intimidating big man that could break Kohl into little pieces. Kohl's drunken mind was racing, *(well maybe more like a slow trot)* as he pulled his pants up. He was scared and embarrassed. The Colonel just stood there and finally told Kohl to leave. Kohl slowly inched his way around the big man and left.

Mays continued talking. "He was so pissed at his wife. They had a terrible fight after he finally got her to come out of the pool. Weren't you with her? You left right after she jumped in the pool. What happened? You never did tell me. It was funny though." They both laughed. Kohl's laugh was a little uneasy. "Runnin' naked as a jay bird, with her big tits a floppin'. Man that was bitchin'. Not a bad lookin' ass for a women in her thirties," Mays added. "Were you with her?" Kohl nodded his head, yes. "Thought so. Yep, he sent your skinny ass here all right. You think this is an accident?" Mays made a "fffpt" sound. "Then you're dumber than you look." Mays groaned as he got up, grabbed his crotch and said, "Come on ol' boy, let's get some rest."

Kohl wrote Julie a letter and told her he had finished writing the letter to the Commandant and his Congressman in hopes of getting an early out for September. He told her he'd probably be back in Okinawa around March with a good possibility of being transferred to a nice desk job in Headquarters Battalion.

7 *The Mickey Mouse Man*

The convoy left Hong Kong Harbor in the night. The next morning the Officer's Mess was full of smiling faces with reddened, swollen eyes and laughing stories from their Hong Kong shore leave.

Kohl greeted everyone with a cheerful good morning even though he wasn't feeling well. He received a few muffled greetings in return. This was similar to most of the other greetings he had received since he had been on board.

"Kohl, isn't it?" said the Ensign with the Mickey Mouse watch.

"Yes," Kohl answered.

"Who's that colored Corporal you got?" he asked.

"Must mean Corporal Ford."

"Yeah, anyway, this colored Corporal," he started as though he had been interrupted, "knocks on the bulkhead outside my cabin, which is next to his," as he points towards Kohl. "Boom, boom, boom! I jumped. Almost cut myself shaving. I wondered, what the hell's going on? I'm standin' there in my skivvies, see. 'Who is it?' I ask. 'Suh, Corporal' ... uuuh. What's his name?" he asked as he turned to Kohl.

"Ford, Corporal Ford."

"Yeah," he continued in southern drawl and trying to sound like a black man. 'Corporal Ford, Suh.' I ask him, 'What do you want?' And he ducks through the hatch and stands like he's got the runs with his butt puckered." The ship's officers snickered. "Then he asked, 'where's Lieutenant Kohl?' I told him, that I didn't know, but I would guess that if he wasn't in his rack, he was probably down at sick bay getting more Dramamine." That brought a few more chuckles. "And then he blares out, 'All troops are present and accounted for, Suh'." Everybody laughed. "And I said, 'Why in the hell are you telling me?' And he says, 'I'm supposed to report that everyone is present and accounted for sir, but I can't find nobody to report it to, but you.'" Everybody laughed except Kohl, who just smiled uncomfortably.

Kohl's smile was a mask and his anger was building. He was embarrassed and uncomfortable.

Another man added, "You know how those grunts are, they train them to follow orders so they won't have to use what few brains they've got to make decisions on their own."

"What brains?" added another. They laugh.

Lieutenant Commander Hangerber, who was sitting at the head of the table, cleared his throat. "Pass the milk, please."

Kohl finished the rest of his meal in silence, as the Navy officers continued with the stories of what they had bought in Hong Kong, from whores to stereos. Kohl realized he was going to be with these guys for the next three months and was going to have to get used to the harassment. It would help his reputation if he could get over being seasick. The Ensign, with the Mickey Mouse watch, seemed to be the one who was putting either Kohl or the Marines down every chance he could. His name was Silverman. He was about six foot one and two hundred pounds, but the weight was not proportioned properly. He was shaped like a pear, with narrow shoulders and wide hips. He had black wavy hair and a light complexion. His accent was East Coast, probably New York, or New Jersey.

The word was the convoy was heading back to Okinawa. Once the ship got out of the harbor and into open sea, Kohl got sick again and didn't make it for the evening dinner.

"You have to eat something," said Mays that night.

"I can't even stand up and walk to the galley without getting sick. Say, could you do something for me? Go down to sick bay and get me some more Dramamine."

The intercom came on. "Tonight's movie will be 'To Hell and Back' starring Audy Murphy."

Kohl made it up to shave the next morning with the intention of going to breakfast, but after he finished shaving he lay back down. At 0800, after Kohl had dozed off.... "Boom! Boom! Boom!" Kohl bolted upright then realized it was only Corporal Ford and lay back down with a moan. "Come in, Ford. And for Christ's sake, knock that shit off, hittin' the wall like that. Hell's bells."

Ford steps in. "Sorry, Sir. How's the Lieutenant this morning?"

"I feel like hell."

"Sorry to hear that, Sir. Sir, I came to report that all the troops are present and accounted for."

"Of course they are, Ford. Damn it anyway. Where are they going to go out here in the middle of the friggin' ocean? Jump overboard? Goddamn it anyway." Kohl was still upset from the ribbing he received at breakfast a couple of days ago. Then he realized that Ford was just doing what he was supposed to do.

"Sorry, Sir. I thought you wanted a report every morning, Sir."

"No, it's not necessary, Ford. Just when we are in port or when someone is actually missing, or if you actually have something to report. How are the troops doing?"

"There are a few who are sick. I think the Lieutenant would feel better if he would go topside for a while. It's nice out and the fresh air would probably help, Sir."

"Thanks, Ford. Sounds like a good idea. What are you guys doing to keep busy?"

"Keeping our gear squared away, Sir. Checking radios and rifles, writing letters, and playing cards. Plus we have PT every morning at 0500 on the fantail. We try to keep busy, sir."

"That's good. I should be feeling better tomorrow. I want to start having training classes. Anything else?"

"No, Sir."

"That'll be all."

"Aye, aye, Sir." Ford did an about face and left.

Kohl took out the platoon personnel folders and made a master sheet with each Marine's pertinent information.

Name	Rank	Job	Age	Ht.	Wt.	Nationality	Hair/eyes	Home	Married	Education
Kohl, Dusty	1st Lt.	Plt. Com.	26	6'2"	180	Cauc.	Br/Blu	Huntington Beach, Ca.	yes	B.S. Degree
Ford, James	Cpl.	Plt. Sgt.	22	5'8"	165	Nigro	Bl/Br	Oakland, Ca.	no	H.S.
Marcellius, Lewis	Hn.	Corpsman	21	5'10"	175	Greek	Bl/Br	Ft. Brag, Ca.	no	H.S.
Spallenski, Benjamin	PFC	Radioman	19	5'9"	150	Polish	Br/Gr	New York, New York	no	H.S.
Grant, Edward	Lcpl	1st Sq. Ldr	21	5'10"	175	Nigro	Bl/Br	Portland, Or.	yes	GED
Woods, Billy Joe	PFC	Rifleman	18	5'7"	145	Cauc.	Bld/Blu	Sayer, Ok.	no	no
Flowers, Anthony	PFC	Rifleman	20	6'1"	195	Nigro	Bl/Br	Birmingham, Al.	yes	H.S.

Harris, Stewart	Pvt.	Rifleman	20	6'4"	210	Nigro	Bl/Br	Denver, Co.	no	H.S.
Sale, Danial	Lcpl	2nd Sq. Ldr	20	5'8"	145	Am. Indian	Bl/Br	Cedar Pass, S.D.	yes	no
Hernadez, Julian	PFC	Rifleman	19	5'6"	135	Mexican	Bl/Br	Salinas, Ca.	no	no
Thompson, Mathew	PFC	Rifleman/Alt. Radio	19	6'1"	210	Cauc.	Br/Br	Chisholm, Mn.	no	H.S.
Charlet, Timothy	PFC	Rifleman	18	5'9"	165	Cauc.	Br/Br	Yreka, Ca.	no	H.S.
Beach, Thomas	Lcpl	3rd. Sq. Ldr	19	5'9"	145	Cauc.	Bld/Blu	Dimmitt, Tx.	no	H.S.
Schultz, Willaim	PFC	Rifleman/Driver	19	5'9"	155	Cauc.	Rd/Gr	Athol, Id.	no	H.S.
Thorogood, Maynard	PFC	Rifleman	20	5'7"	140	Am. Indian	Bl/Br	Darien, Go.	no	H.S.
Handle, Buford	Pvt.	Rifleman	21	6'0"	160	Nigro	Bl/Br	Compton, Ca.	no	no

*

Kohl worked on a training program. He even made it to lunch, ate a little, made it back to the cabin, and threw up. The same thing happened at dinner. That evening the ship's doctor, Lieutenant Ben Dorfman, came in to look at him. He told him to eat in small quantities. Mays brought him some crackers and poggy-bait from the PX. Kohl noticed some improvement.

Kohl felt better the next morning and went to breakfast.

"Well, well, well. Look who's here, up and about this morning," said the Mickey Mouse man.

I really don't like this guy.

Lieutenant Commander Hangerber said, "Lieutenant Kohl? We had a little rough weather through the straight; but-by-and-large this has been pretty smooth sailing. It usually takes about three days to get your sea legs. You'll get used to it and start feeling better, I'm sure."

"I'm feeling pretty good this morning, Sir. I guess I'm a ground man," answered Kohl smiling.

"I'd say you're more like a bed man," said the Mickey Mouse man. They all laughed, except the Lieutenant Commander.

"I'd say you're a dead man if you don't shut your fuckin' mouth," snarled Kohl.

The Mickey Mouse man made an "Ooooooo," sound, but his smile was nervous.

Lieutenant Commander Hangerber cleared his throat. "Excuse me, Lieutenant Kohl. We do not tolerate foul language at Officers Mess."

"I apologize, Sir."

"And, Ensign Silverman?"

"Yes, sir."

"The Marines are guests on our ship. I expect them to be treated with dignity and respect. Do you," he turned and looked at all the officers," and all of you, understand?"

"Yes, Sir," they said.

*

It was a beautiful day. The blue sky was sprinkled with popcorn clouds. Being topside sitting in the sun and fresh air helped Kohl feel better. Mays found him leaning against the stack, aft of the bridge.

"Heard I missed a little excitement this morning at breakfast," Mays said as he pulled his tee shirt off and sat down next to Kohl.

Kohl couldn't understand how Mays got and kept his heavily muscled chest so defined. Kohl never saw him work out with weights.

"I don't know how exciting it was but that Silverman is starting to get my goat."

"That fuckin' fat-Navy-fag-Jew needs to be knocked down a few notches but there's not a hell of a lot you can do about it out here. Wait till we get to port, then clean his clock."

"How come nobody ever gives you shit?"

"Well, for one thing, I'm not a California 'perty boy' like you. And another thing, I don't put up with any bullshit, which you do. And another thing, people by and large look at my face and can tell those are battle scars. And another thing, I really don't mind hurting people. I mean, I'm not standin' around with my thumb up my ass waiting for someone to take the first punch."

*

Kohl had always perceived Mays as a grenade about ready to explode. He needed a release valve to let out his hostility and anger. It was football in college and now it was the Marines.

At OCS, during pugil stick exercises, nobody wanted to fight Mays. Candidates did not have a choice, however. The DI's picked who fought whom. Pugil sticks were used to train Marines in hand-to-hand combat. They were broom handles with pads on each end and were used to resemble rifle thrusts and butt swings. A person fought with pugil sticks in the same way a boxer would fight using left jabs and right crosses. The fighter wore football helmets with a single bar for face protection.

Candidate Klugman was tall and skinny and had a difficult time in all of the physical training, from forced marches to the PT tests. He had a high, squeaky voice and when he called cadence the DI's were always harassing him to lower his voice. "From the diaphragm. You sound like a goddamn faggot," they would say. The DIs were constantly finding something he did wrong and having him do pushups, except he could only do about ten before he lay trembling on the deck, struggling to do more. This day, he was picked to fight Mays.

Mays went to work on him immediately. Klugman was cowering from the blows, hardly fighting back. He was backing up, mostly trying to ward off the constant barrage of blows. The ring of candidates kept pushing him back into the center of the ring. The DIs were yelling for him to fight back, calling him a yellow-bellied-coward and a sissy.

A chant started. "Kill 'im, kill 'im, kill 'im." It grew louder and louder.

Mays' blows to Klugman's face and head made him stagger. Mays hit him with two jabs and a ferocious right-butt swing. Klugman fell to his knees, dropped his pugil stick, and covered his head with his arms and hands.

The DI's now joined the candidates chanting, "Kill 'im, kill 'im."

Mays was in frenzy and had the pugil stick by one end and was whaling on his opponent's head and arms. Klugman's helmet had spun around and Mays continued to hit the candidate as he slowly sagged to the deck. With one violent swing, Mays knocked his helmet completely off. Blood flowed from the nose and mouth of the defenseless Klugman, as he lay helplessly unconscious. Mays continued the onslaught of blows to the limp body.

The DIs immediately jumped in and stopped Mays. The chanting stopped. The DIs looked worried. Klugman just lay there. The medics were called and they came running, but efforts to revive him from his unconscious state were to no avail. He was later carried off in an ambulance and was never seen again. Nobody asked about him.

*

"I thought we were going back to Oki," said Kohl.

"We were, but now we're going to Subic Bay. Supposed to be there about thirty days. Great huh?"

"I'm for anything that will get me on land. I'm feelin' better today. I'm going to have class this afternoon, even. How 'bout that shit?"

Kohl looked at an atlas in the stateroom to see where Subic Bay was. He knew it was a Navy base and somewhere in the Philippines but that was all. In the atlas he found Subic Bay on the Island of Luzon north of Manila, surrounded by jungle and tropical seas. *Could be fun.*

*

The Reconnaissance Platoon was sitting topside with their legs crossed and hands folded in their lap, ready for their Lieutenant's first training class.

"Good morning, men," said Kohl.

"Good morning, Sir," they answered in unison.

"I finally made it out of bed." That comment brought a few chuckles. "How many of you have been sick?" Approximately half raised their hands.

"We should have requested a different cruise line," commented Kohl, that comment brought on a few more chuckles.

Kohl cleared his throat. The speech he had worked on for the last few days was taken mostly from a lecture that he had attended while he was at Interrogation School at White Beach, San Diego. He wanted to pump the men up for the possibility that they might land.

"The last briefing I was at we were told that South Vietnam is, at this moment, marked by civil unrest. General Nguyen Khanh has ousted Tran Van Huong, who took over as Premier last November, in a bloodless coup. The battle of ideas is being fought and the communists are winning.

"There are approximately 7,000 people an hour that are converted to the Communist way of thinking. The world today is truly under a new type of war, a war of ideas, a battle of minds.

"The majority of the people in Vietnam are poor and uneducated. They have no real freedoms. They spend most of their time and efforts in trying to survive. Over the centuries they have been ruled first by warlords, then by the French, but now, they are in the midst of a battle to choose between democracy and Communism. They do not know what democracy is, what it stands for, or what form of life it can bring. This nation knows little or nothing about the truth of what the end result will be if the Communists control the government."

Kohl noticed that the men were still sitting at attention and said, "Make yourselves comfortable, men," and then he proceeded.

"If we land in Vietnam, it is our duty to protect the people from Communism so they may be free to live in freedom as we do in America. But these people don't know the great gifts we have to offer. They do not know freedom as we know it. Those who are weak from starvation and those who have their lives at stake do not know what it is we can offer so they can live life free without fear. Yet our efforts fall upon ears that have heard lies from the Communists.

"Communism is like a red blood as it stains its way into the lands of poverty and the weak, to clog minds by force and propaganda. It's like a weed when it multiplies into many. A fence will not keep the weed from spreading. Victory comes by destroying the weed and then planting anew. Democracy needs nurturing and cultivation so it can grow strong and fight off any infestation that seeks to destroy. There has to be a change from ignorance to enlightenment that can only come through education. Through education, we can teach what freedom is. Only through strength and power can we protect these freedoms in order to educate."

The troops were starting to fidget. Kohl looked around and some had closed their eyes as they relaxed in the warm sun.

As Kohl droned on, "The Communists have pulled no punches in their expressed desire for worldwide domination. Their Asian Empire is expanding, especially with China fueling the Communist fire.

"The Communist's claim to have a no-class society, where everyone is equal. But that's a lie. They have a working class, peasants (proletariat), a middle class, made up of military officers, government officials, educators and scientists and the party elite. Just to make the Soviet society more equal, Joseph Stalin killed millions of his own people to insure that he wouldn't have anyone to threaten his power. The Communists also have class distinction between the Indians in Siberia, the Orientals in Mongolia, and the dark skinned people along the Caspian Sea, all ruled by white Russians.

"They believe the way to change is not through democratic means but through revolution. Even though the Russian Communists have a beautifully written democratic constitution, they have dictators who interpret and change the constitution as they see fit.

"What we should do as a nation is to educate the illiterate to our way of thinking. I think we should back the masses instead of supporting dictatorships. We have to set the example of what it is that makes America so great. As individuals, we have to live up to our American heritage and what we stand for. We take pride in our homes, families, and country. We practice and live up to the morals and norms of our society. We worship our God of choice; we do not discriminate against any American, no matter his race, color, religion, or creed. We are Americans and these ideals are worth fighting for. As a Marine, be grateful. We are the saviors of the downtrodden and the poor. We offer liberty and freedom.

"The Communists mean business when they say they are planning to take over the world. Vietnam is just one more step toward their goal of worldwide domination. They fight for what they believe in and we must fight harder for what we believe. Good will prevail.

'Many people say, 'Why should we be the ones that fight against Communism?' The reason is that we can't afford to have the Communists too close to our shores, which could and does endanger the lives of our people. Who would ever believe that we would have a Communist country just twenty-five miles from the shores of the United States? The communists are a threat. Look, what happened with the Cuban Missile Crisis? As Marines, we have been trained and schooled to fight for freedom and to keep the world at peace and discourage the Communist threat. We will prevail.

Are there any questions?" Kohl saw a hand raise. "Yes? And what's your name?"

"PFC Schultz, Sir."

"And what did you want to ask?"

"Lieutenant? When's the next mail call?"

Disappointed that the question had nothing to do about the speech he had worked on the previous day, Kohl answered, "The Convoy has to get close enough to land for a chopper to reach us. We're heading towards Subic Bay now, so we should be getting mail within a couple of days. Are there any more questions?" Another hand was raised. "Yes? And your name?"

"PFC Handle, Sir. Can we have a smoke break?"

Kohl was dejected. He thought it was either over their heads or they didn't care. "The smoking lamp is lit," ordered Kohl. They all got up, stretched, many lit up and started talking. Kohl said, "Thanks for your attention and I'll see ya tomorrow." But they didn't hear as he turned and walked back to his cabin.

8 Subic Bay

The next afternoon the USS Union drifted into Subic Bay. The harbor was ringed with lush tropical vegetation and palm trees; the shore covered with large, round, smooth, brown, volcanic rocks but no sandy beaches. He could see the towering green mountains to the east.

Liberty went at 1700, but Kohl had dinner on board ship first. He caught a Jeepney at the pier that took him to the Officer's Club.

After a couple of drinks at the club, he noticed several high-ranking Marine officers going upstairs. He recognized Lieutenant Connie Fitzsimmons, who was his Battalion's Adjutant at Pendleton. "A fucking kiss-ass-queer," according to Mays. Fitzsimmons had always seemed uptight, very precise, and particular. He wasn't a field Marine. It was as if he did not want to get dirty. But, he was one squared-away Marine in garrison. He had short-cropped blond hair that made him look bald and a square jaw that didn't match his baby face. His thin nose was sunburned and peeling.

Kohl got up from the bar. His legs were unsteady, but he blamed it on being aboard *(the fucking boat)* the ship. He walked up the stairs. He really didn't care that much for Fitzsimmons, but Kohl thought it was better than sitting alone at the bar, besides the drinks were probably free. He spotted Fitzsimmons about the same time Fitzsimmons saw him. Fitzsimmons was listening to something a barrel-chested Colonel was saying, and gave a recognizing glance and nod toward Kohl. Fitzsimmons didn't especially care for Kohl either. It was no secret. They had both expressed their views at the

San Mateo Officer's Club at Camp Pendleton that ended up in a fight. It was a good fight, neither one had a distinct edge over the other. The result was that they respected each other and got along better afterwards. Fitzsimmons didn't care for Kohl's laid-back attitude, as he mistook it as a sign for not caring. He didn't like the way he was always fraternizing with the NCOs either. It was not something an officer was supposed to do. He didn't like it when Kohl drank too much, because he got a little out of control sometimes. Fitzsimmons was always in control. Kohl walked towards Fitzsimmons.

*

When Kohl moved from one place to another, he didn't walk, he strolled. His step was springy and close to a swagger. He never paid attention to the way he walked before OCS ... "Walk like a Marine, candidate, not like a goddamn sissy." Followed by, "Some of you maggots are bouncin'," then, "goddamn it, cuttin' edge a da boot, cuttin' edge a da boot. Unt, tup, thirp, forp." The DI would run up to the side of Kohl and yell in his ear. "You friggin' turd! You got ears, maggot? Can't you understand the Queen's fucking language? What did they teach you queers in college?" He continued to yell, as Kohl tried to march the way the DI wanted. He did not dare turn his head nor glance at the DI. Finally out of frustration, the DI threw up his arms and yelled. "Stop! Woa! You son-bitches." The platoon shuffled into one another and stopped. "Turn around." They shuffled around to face the DI. "You people march like you're strolling along a friggin' beach. Wiggling your butts and swinging your shoulders and bouncing up and down like friggin' yo-yos. You!" He pointed to Kohl. "Come 'er."

Oh my God. He's pointing at me. Oh, I'm dog meat. "Sir, yes Sir," shouted Kohl. He did an about face and walked stiffly around the platoon turning square corners and halting in front of the DI, did a left face, took two steps forward, saluted and said, "Candidate Kohl reporting as ordered, Sir." *Ooops.*

"What did you say, maggot?" the DI yelled.

"I'm sorry, Sir..." Ooops, wrong answer.

"Sorry?" The DI was in Kohl's face now, yelling and swearing so that his spit was flying everywhere. "Sorry? Did you say sorry?"

Don't nod your head. Don't move a muscle. Just stare straight ahead.

"Marines don't say, 'sorry'. Marines ain't sorry for nothin'! We might be gravely concerned but never sorry." There were a few snickers. The DI glared at the platoon over Kohl's shoulder.

"Sir, I mean, Sir. Sir, what the candidate meant to say, Sir, was ... Sir, Candidate Kohl reporting as ordered, Sir."

Satisfied with his answer, but not the manner in which it was presented, he sneered at Kohl. "Candidate, you are a disgusting low-life maggot."

"Sir, yes Sir," Kohl answered.

"I'm going to stop you from bouncin'. In fact," as he stepped back to address the platoon, "I'm going to stop everybody from bouncin'. You maggots ain't civilians anymore. Your ass is mine, and your soul belongs to the Marine Corps. You're not walkin' some twitchin' cunt through the park. You're supposed to be marchin' all as one. No bouncin', no bobbing heads no swinging shoulders. Got that? Now girls, I want you to follow Candidate Kohl, here. He's going to be your leader. In fact, we're through marching for today. We're going for a walk ... a long walk."

Kohl heard the "huh oh's" from the platoon.

"You can bounce all you want because you are going to walk on your toes. And if I see one heel hit the deck, I'll keep your goddamn skinny asses out here all night. Did you hear me?"

"Sir, yes, Sir," they said in unison.

A puzzled, but game, Kohl called cadence, while everyone walked on their toes. There was laughing and horse play at first, but after the first twenty minutes it had vanished. Most of the other platoons on the parade deck were watching and making catcalls. It had been over an hour, and all the other platoons had gone to chow. Bewildered passerby's watched this group of men walking and turning on their toes. By now the calves of the their legs were tight knots, cramped so bad it felt like the calf muscle was behind the knee. From the middle of the parade deck, the DI calmly walked over and told Candidate Kohl to halt the platoon. They stopped but couldn't put their feet flat because of the cramped muscles. He told them they were finished for the day and hoped that tomorrow there would not be any more bouncing. They gingerly walked back to the barracks.

The next day at drill, their calves were still cramped and sore ... but no bouncing.

*

Fritz straightened his medium six-foot frame and said to the approaching Kohl, with his hand out in greeting, "I'm the General's Aide," and pointed his thumb to the rear.

Well la-dee-da.

Kohl shook the outstretched hand and took a quick glance. It was General Victor "Brute" Krulack himself. Physically an unimpressive man of only five feet six and slight-of-build, he got the nickname of "Brute" from his Annapolis days to make fun of his physical stature. But those who knew him were in awe of his military knowledge and strategies. Next to him was another General that Kohl only knew through pictures. It was General Lewis Walt, Commander of the Third Marines. General Walt towered over General Krulak. He was a big man, built like a football lineman.

Fritz asked, "What are you doing here, Kohl?"

"Came in this afternoon. I'm afloat with 1/9. I'm a recon platoon Commander."

Fritz raised his eyebrow in respect, as they joined a small group of officers. He introduced Kohl.

Kohl made small talk then excused himself to get another free Scotch-on-the-Rocks and returned.

General Krulack turned slightly and caught Fitzsimmons's eye, which wasn't hard to do because he hardly took his eye off the General. He gave a slight nod and Fitzsimmons walked briskly to his side. He whispered something in Fitzsimmons' ear then Fitzsimmons walked to another group of officers.

Kohl returned his attention to the group of officers he was with before Fitzsimmons left.

"Lieutenant Kohl, wasn't it?" the short Major asked.

"Yes, Sir."

"Who are you with?" he asked.

"Came in this afternoon with 1/9," answered Kohl. He watched Fitzsimmons jumping from one group to another, within beckon and call of the General and his guests.

Kohl asked, "Who are you with, Major?"

"I'm part of General Walt's staff. Here for a series of meetings with General Krulak. By the way, my name's Simms. I try to make sure all you guys have bullets and beans."

"Lot of brass here. What's all this about?" asked Kohl.

"Ever since the Gulf of Tonkin incident in August of last year, we have been run amuck with rumor."

"I can't understand what the big deal is. North Vietnam attacking the USS Maddox with three patrol boats firing torpedoes. Come on. What a joke."

"It's no joke Lieutenant. We have never allowed a country to attack property or personnel of the US-of-A and get away with it. Not if we expect to be able to hold our head up with pride. It doesn't matter how ridiculous it appears to be."

"Well, what were we doing there in the first place?"

"We have to protect our interests in the Southeast Asia. It's not as simple as it sounds. We now have the authority 'to take all necessary measures to repel any armed attack against the forces of the US and to prevent further aggression and so on.'"

Kohl and the Major made another trip to the bar.

The Major asked Kohl. "I bet you're excited about the prospect of going into Vietnam?"

Kohl's mental reflexes had deteriorated by this time, and it took him a few moments to catch what the Major actually said. *Did he say what I thought he said?* The idea of going to Vietnam had not been something he thought would happen. And, if it was a possibility, the thought of being excited about it was the furthermost thing from his mind.

Kohl asked, "You really think they will send 1/9 to Vietnam?"

"Sure looks like it." The major looked around to see if anybody was listening. "That's why the Generals are here in Subic Bay."

"Are you shittin' me, Major?"

"Nope."

"I mean, this floating around in the South China Sea is just for show, isn't it?"

"No." The major looked puzzled. And added, "You're in recon, right?"

"Yes."

"I detect some hesitation in your voice. Is there a problem?"

"Hell, yes, there's a problem. A big problem."

"Don't you want to go?"

"Do I look like a friggin' moron? Hell, no, I don't want to go," said Kohl as his voice got louder.

"There are hundreds of Marine officers who would give their left nut to be in your shoes. Hundreds, including me."

"Well, Major," said Kohl sneering," If your ass is in so much of an uproar, you go. As far as I'm concerned, I'm not real excited about the prospect of ending up in a body bag."

"If you don't want to go, first of all, why are you in the Marines and two, why are you in recon, one of the most prestigious outfits in the Marine Corps?"

"Yeah, I'm a Marine and proud of it. I was all prepared to go to Cuba during the Missile crisis. But I don't know about this Vietnam thing. The South Vietnam government is all fucked up. And being in Recon was a mistake. To tell the truth, I'm really not too thrilled about it. I didn't ask for the billet. Besides, I'm a short timer."

"I don't see what you're so concerned about. Once the Marines get in there and kick some ass, run those commie bastards back into North

Vietnam, it'll be over in a couple of months. No sweat, no strain," said the confident Major.

"I don't think it's going to be that easy."

"I think you had better get your head on straight, there, Lieutenant. You've got a bad attitude. I wouldn't want you in charge of my men."

"I think you've got me all wrong, Major. Its not like I have second thoughts about serving my country or doing my job as an officer, I just don't know if this Vietnam thing is..."

The Major interrupted Kohl, "Your purpose is not to ask why, but to do or die."

"What kind of bull-shit answer is that?" Kohl's voice was raising, and it caught the attention of Fitzsimmons. Some of the other officers had turned their attention to the raised voice. Fitzsimmons moved closer to Kohl.

"With all due respect, Sir," Kohl continued. That comment was a prelude to comments to follow that bordered on insubordination. "As far as I'm concerned, you can take my place and crawl around in the fucking bushes if you want, and I'll take your job and hand out fucking blankets," Kohl snarled.

"Well, I think you're getting way out of line here, Lieutenant," the Major said, putting the emphasis on the 'Lieutenant'.

Fitzsimmons quickly moved to intercede before there was trouble. But before he could reach Kohl, he heard him say, "I think you're full of shit." Kohl had a cocky, drunk sneer on his face. "You fucking office poge."

The major was noticeably flushed and his eyes glanced around the room to see if anyone else had heard.

Fitzsimmons approached and said to Kohl, "Hey, Kohl. There's somebody I want you to meet. Excuse me, Major." He grabbed Kohl's arm and led him away from the Major to the top of the stairs. "Kohl, darn it. You're not even supposed to be here. And if you stick around you're going to get into trouble. You've already pissed the Major off. So why don't you go back down to the bar, or better yet, back to the ship."

Why, you little prick. Kohl felt like he was being patronized and was going to tell the faggot Fitzsimmons, to fuck off, when the General gave Fitzsimmons a signal. So he quickly said goodbye and left. Kohl was left with his mouth open but he slowly turned and walked down the stairs and up to the bar and asked for a drink-to-go. The bartender refused. On his way back to the ship, he muttered to himself. "*Fuckin' career officers. All think that we should be grateful for a war. All the glory medals and stuff. Which would be fine if nobody got killed. I wouldn't mind that, glory and hero stuff. If we could all throw rocks at each other, what a bitchin' war that would be. Or if we all wore boxing gloves ... and the winner is ... The prob-*

lem is we have countries that say, "my gun's bigger than yours." Must be a male thing. It's like going deer hunting except the deer shoot back. And I've got a wife now. I don't want my gun to get broke. I only have a few months left, and I'm outa here. And here I am in Recon. Now ain't that a bitch. Should trade places with the fucking gung-ho Major and let him poop-n-snoop and hide in bushes and get shot at, and I'll sit in his nice office and hand out blankets and stuff. Kohl walked, mumbling, and fuming all the way back to the ship.

*

The pain behind Kohl's right eyeball woke him up. He started to rise up and the room began swirling, then he remembered why. *This is stupid. Why do I do this? I feel terrible. End up acting like an asshole and get in trouble telling a superior officer that he's full of shit. Not too bright there, Lieutenant.* He got up to go to the bathroom and went back to bed. He could sleep a couple more hours before battalion briefings at 1000.

Following the briefings on board the USS Vancouver, where 1/9 headquarters was located, Kohl and Mays headed for the gym to get some of the 'sea kinks' out. They quickly changed into their issue gym gear, checked out a basketball, and walked out on the court. Mays grabbed the ball out of Kohl's' hands and dribbled in bursts around the gym, all bent over, making his short body look shorter than his five foot eight. He dribbled under the basket, whirled and shot. Hit the bottom of the rim. Grabbed the bouncing ball, dribbled to the top of the key and shot the ball like a shot put. It was short.

"Not enough umph, I'd say," said Kohl.

Mays glared at the bouncing ball as though it was its fault. He zipped over and retrieved the ball and dribbled around all bent over then quickly threw the ball at the unsuspecting Kohl, who was jogging around the court. Kohl swatted the ball from his face, retrieved it, dribbled twice, and shot a graceful jump shot from the side. It fell short.

"Not enough umph, I'd say," said Mays.

Kohl and Mays spent most of the afternoon playing basketball. Kohl felt good and looked forward to getting in shape again after a two-month lay off. His spring was gone because he could not dunk the basketball. His outside jumper was going everywhere except in the basket. But it felt good to be playing again.

Mays was not a good basketball player, but in a game of horse Mays beat Kohl two out of three. Mays would shoot with one hand from mid-court, bounce the ball from the floor into the basket, shoot over his head with his back turned to the basket and from his knees at the free-throw line. He was good at it because he played with guys like Kohl all the time.

They played one-on-one to twenty, win by four. Kohl spotted Mays ten points.

Kohl was shooting mostly set shots and jumpers until he got warmed up. He made a quick fake to his left and tried to drive past a slower moving Mays.

"You can't do that, for Christ's sake," Kohl protested.

"Do what?"

"You can't stick your arms out like this." Kohl held his arms straight out from his body.

"Why not?"

"You're supposed to block me with your body, not with your arms."

"Same thing."

"Is not." Kohl showed Mays how to shuffle his feet and move his body into a blocking position.

When they resumed play, Kohl dribbled to his right, faked, and moved around Mays to his left. And then Mays blocked him with his shoulder and sent Kohl sliding across the floor.

"You can't do that either," said Kohl from a sitting position on the floor.

"I blocked you with my body."

"That you did. I must admit. But you're supposed to have your feet set."

There was a puzzled look on Mays' face. Kohl realized he was wasting his time. They continued playing and Kohl was ahead by two and needed one basket to win. Kohl drove around a flat footed Mays and took off for an easy lay-up. Mays hit Kohl with his shoulder at about the hip. Kohl grabbed the air for balance, emitted an, "Oh shit," just before he hit the floor on his back and shoulder and slid into the wall.

Mays ran over and crouched over him. "You all right?" Kohl shook his head no. "You did some pretty weird shit while you were in the air. No shit. You all right?"

"No, I'm not all right. You friggin' moron. You could have killed me. That isn't what I had in mind when I said 'get your body in front of me'. My shoulder hurts." Kohl hadn't moved anything yet. He was afraid to move because he might find something wrong.

"You all right?" Mays repeated.

"Yeah, I think so?"

"Move something then."

Kohl moved each appendage carefully. When he was satisfied that nothing was broken, he took a helping hand from Mays and got up slowly. He rubbed his bruised shoulder. They steamed and showered, then proceeded back to the ship.

Kohl was looking forward to spending the next two weeks in the Philippines. He looked at the special service's bulletin on sights to see, swimming pools, yachting, movies, gyms, handball, and the nice Officer's club and good food. *This is going to be out-fucking-standing.*

The 1/9 C.O. was having an inspection tomorrow morning, but after that Kohl and his troops were free to go on liberty. *I'll go to the gym, maybe work out the soreness from the beating I took from Mays. Then dinner and a few drinks at the Officer's Club.* Kohl slept well.

9 Who's In Charge Here?

Then ... there was a shudder. Kohl bolted upright. "What the hell's going on," he said to his nameless roommate who was dressed and proceeding out the hatch.

He gave Kohl an annoyed look. It was like he did not want to be bothered. He answered matter-of-factly "We've moved out. Been underway for about four hours now."

"Moved out? We just got here ... there."

The Lieutenant Junior Grade left without answering.

Kohl yelled after him. "What for?"

What is his name anyway? Been here a couple of weeks and still don't know his name. Kohl got up, shaved, dressed, and made it to breakfast.

Mays came in and sat down beside him. "Mornin'," he said cheerfully. "South China Sea."

Major Sims was right after all. Like my Grandpa used to say, "If you run around the barnyard long enough, you're bound to step in it sooner or later."

"What?" asks Mays.

"Never mind. Just thinking."

Kohl went back to his cabin and lay down. He was getting that old feeling again. He started reading the FMF 2.2 Amphibious Reconnaissance book. *I'd better start learning some of this stuff.*

> "The term 'reconnaissance' means a mission undertaken to obtain, by visual observation or other detection methods, information about the activities and resources of an enemy or potential enemy, or to secure data concerning geographic characteristics of a particular area ...
> ... The primary mission of the reconnaissance platoon is to conduct ground reconnaissance and observation in support of the Marine Battalion...
> ... The reconnaissance platoon is not equipped, nor is it their purpose, to execute decisive or sustained combat. They must accomplish their mission through stealth, maneuver, and rapid reporting.

Kohl knew what the qualifications were to be in reconnaissance. He had his doubts about Thompson and Handle but the rest looked qualified. They had to be in excellent physical condition and possess qualities such as speed, endurance, and strength. They must have a knowledge of basic infantry skills such as map and aerial photography, use of the compass, land navigation, how to conduct a patrol, the art of camouflage and silent movement. They had to be excellent swimmers, preferably with scuba certification, be expert riflemen, knowledgeable in artillery, tank and vehicle operation, have radio communication skills, escape, evasion and survival techniques, and intelligence gathering techniques.

Kohl could understand now why they had chosen him to be a Reconnaissance Platoon Commander. He met most, if not all the criteria. *There was the answer to 'why me?' Maybe you weren't put here because you're a fuck up after all. Thirty to sixty days off the coast of Vietnam. I can't believe this shit.*

There was a knock on the bulkhead. "Come in," Kohl said.

It was the Captain's Orderly. "The Captain requests your presence in his cabin, Sir."

Huh oh. I wonder what I did this time. Shit. Was it the night at the 'O' Club or when I told the Mickey Mouse Man that I was going to kill him? He followed the Orderly up to the Captain's quarters. The Orderly knocked, opened the hatch and Kohl saw that the table was set for two.

"Join me for lunch, Lieutenant Kohl?"

"Thank you very much, Sir. I would be honored." *Play the role Kohl. I wonder what he's got on his mind.*

The Captain of the ship. Sounds like something you would holler down a deserted hallway. You would slam yourself against the bulkhead to let this hulk of a man stomp by. But not Captain Harold Henderson. He was a man of medium height and slight frame. He had gray curly hair with stretched tan skin that gave him a distinguished look. He had a crooked smile that was warm and friendly. He talked all through lunch with Kohl nodding his head and trying to make sure the Captain did not notice that he was starting to get sick. They walked out on the deck after lunch. It was a smooth day, with sunny skies and a warm breeze.

"I guess you've heard Lieutenant, that we are going back to Oki."

"We are? No, Sir, I didn't know." Kohl tried to keep the excitement from his voice.

"Well, we are. We should be there in a week," he added.

They talked about home, wives, and kids. He showed Kohl around the bridge.

"I always like to have the Marine officers up for a visit. The Marines have a special place in my heart. My dad was a Marine Major at Guatacannal. He didn't make it home. I was around 10 or 11 at the time."

Kohl sat in silence for a time as the Captain looked out the side hatch. "Sorry, Captain."

"It was a long time ago. Thanks for coming up." Kohl shook his hand and then left.

He went back to his cabin and wrote a quick letter to Julie to tell her the good news. He had just written her yesterday to tell her he would be in the Philippines for two weeks. Now they had just left the Philippines for the South China Sea and in less than twenty-four hours it had changed. Now they were going back to Okinawa. *Maybe a nice Headquarters billet. Lie in the sun. Do some scuba diving in those blue waters. No mud. Eight to five. No weekends. No boat.*

Dinner was noticeably livelier. Everybody was smiling. The movie was "Music Man."

After the movie, Kohl returned to his cabin. He didn't feel too bad at all. The ocean was like glass. Mays poked his face through the curtain.

"Da word is Subic."

"This afternoon the Captain himself told me we were going to Oki."

"Nope. Subic."

"How do you know?" Kohl was growing irritated.

"I'm S-2, remember? I was just up to the com shack and saw the teletype. Subic."

"So we're going back. Flip a big uee in the South China Sea. This is horse-shit. What kind of a cluster fuck are we involved with here? Doesn't any-body know what the hell's going on? Well, I don't care. I don't give a big rat's ass. I just don't want to float around off the coast of Vietnam. It's okay with me if we go back to Subic or Oki, just to get my feet on land. I don't care where we go." *Hold on here, ol' buddy. Let's exclude Vietnam from that last comment. Oh yeah.*

*

Now that Kohl was back in Subic Bay, he felt relief. His recon platoon was attached to 1/9 and he was only responsible for his own troops. No senior officer to report to, which he liked. He had visions of running training programs for his platoon the way it should be. To learn things that if, *heaven forbid,* they were to land in Vietnam, they would be prepared. Training programs back in Pendleton were prolific in standing, waiting, and doing repetitive, unproductive busy work; just to keep the troops occupied.

Nobody talked about Vietnam, even though it was on everybody's mind. And most of the young boots were afraid. Kohl could see it in their eyes. Still there was an air of excitement at the thought of action. The fear came as a result of not knowing what may lie ahead. They were confident in themselves and their abilities. With the brass, there was a tension in the air, an energy, electrically charged atmosphere, like the sound of a scratch on chalkboard. They looked at war as a way to prove them selves, make rank and get medals. As career Marines, this was their job. This was what they were trained to do. Kohl didn't want them getting too anxious and throwing Marine bodies on the beach without good reason. There were eager lieutenants who wanted to go; they had visions of John Wayne at Io-Jima. *Didn't he get killed in the end?* And "Battle Cry" with Van Hefflen. Kohl's vision of war was more like 'Custer's Last Stand.' Kohl had heard the older NCOs talk about Korea. But they didn't talk about the glories. They talked about the pain, hardship, death and dying. They talked about the freezing cold or the jungle heat. They talked about how it was to fight an enemy who was not afraid to die. The NCOs will follow their gung-ho officers, not because they want to go to war, but because it is their job to keep the troops alive. It is up to them. They know what war is and what death looks like. The pictures they painted were not of glory and were not pretty. When the bullets start flying, staying alive takes on a whole new meaning.

The Marine Corps motto, "The first to fight" could also mean "the first to die."

*

"I'm a changed man. I'm up. I'm making a comeback. You see I've had a hard time getting motivated, but now ... the motivated Marine, runs on land and likes this. I went over to the USS Vancouver this morning and found out the hot scoop. Twenty days in Subic. Why, that's fine. Training sessions, basketball games, island tours. This young ambitious Marine has ideas of fun and frolic.

The First Battalion of the Ninth Marine Division was standing in formation for afternoon muster. Afterwards, Kohl called his troops over to the side and told them to stand at ease. "Men, the latest word is, we'll be in Subic Bay for at least twenty days, and this is what I'd like to do..."

"Don't plan on it, Lieutenant," Kohl turned around as the 1/9 XO walked by.

"What's that, Sir?"

"Don't count on staying. We're moving out at 0800 tomorrow."

He wanted to ask, *"To where? What for?"* but he thought, *"Oh, what the hell."* He turned to his troops, shrugged, and called liberty.

Kohl went down to the gym and shot around, played a pick up game of three on three, took a steam and hot shower.

He walked to Alongipo, a small town outside the base and bought a French harp. He had always wanted to learn how to play the blues like Sonny Terry. It was something that he could do topside onboard ship, plus it would be easy to carry around. He found one, then walked over to the Caleinte "O" Club for drinks and dinner with his buddies.

Kohl joined Mays, Wheeler, Mesherwitz, and Joss at the bar. He pulled out a stool and sat down.

"What'll it be, Sir?" asked the bartender.

"I don't know. What would you recommend?"

"How about our Subic Special?

"Sounds great."

The club was noisy. The new Ray Charles record 'What'd I Say' was playing on the jukebox. What few American girls that were there were dancing with their husbands.

Hey, mama don't you treat me wrong
Come and love me all night long
Oh, oh, hey, hey, all right, now
See the girl with the diamond ring
She knows how to shake that thing
Oh, oh, hey, hey, all right, now

Kohl watched the bartender make his drink. Two shots of light rum, one shot of brandy, orange juice, Seven -Up, a pineapple slice, and a cherry topped with red wine. Tasted like a Maitai. Kohl drank leisurely listening to the music and the ship stories of the lieutenants. He asked for another as they waited for a table in the dining room.

"Phillips!" Joss yelled. "Over here!"

They all turned to see Lieutenant Andy "Tarzan" Philips walking into the club. He had been at OCS and at Camp Pendleton with them, until he transferred to Force Reconnaissance. He got his nickname for his Tarzan yell. He was one of the most "gung ho" Marines Kohl had ever met. He was one of those Marines who loved the Corps. He was tall and stocky, with a pockmarked face, sleepy eyes, big nose, and ears that stuck out from the side of his head. Kohl was somewhat surprised, because Phillips looked like he had lost a lot of weight, his eyes had dark circles, and his cheeks had a hollow look. Phillips smiled and with a noticeable limp joined his buddies at the bar.

Mays said, "Jesus, Tarz, I hate to say it, but you look like shit."

Leave it to Mays to say what everyone else was thinking.

Phillips ordered a Seven-Up.

"Hello, my fellow comrades."

The others all said hello.

"Heard you got married, Kohl." said Phillips.

"Missed ya, Phillips," Kohl paused, looking at Phillips, "Couldn't wait for the rest of us. You were in a big assed hurry to get over here early, huh?" said Kohl.

"I got married too. Wanna see my pictures?" asked Mays.

"Nooo!" they all answered in unison.

"Besides, your wife is tooo ugly...," said Joss.

"How ugly is she?" asked Wheeler.

"She's sooo ugly, that..."

"Don't even go there, you little sheep fucker. You still pissed at me because of Hong Kong?" asked Mays. Without waiting for an answer, he turned to Phillips and said, "What's the deal, Tarz? What's wrong? You look like you've been sick. Malaria? And what's this Seven-Up shit? You used to drink Southern Comfort by the gallon."

Phillips put his arm around Mesherwitz's shoulder. "I may not look too hot right now, but I look a lot better than I did two months ago. I just got out of the base hospital yesterday. You guys are looking at a Marine who has much to be thankful for."

"Jesus, no shit," said Joss.

"I knew it," said Mays.

"What's to be thankful for? I wouldn't call being in the hospital as something to be thankful about. What happened?" inquired Kohl.

"Let's go to that table in the corner," suggested Phillips. They picked up their drinks and went to the table.

"I hope you guys will bear with me on this. It's still pretty hard for me to talk about, what happened, and all. It's hard for me to find the right words. Sometimes I don't know what's real and what's not."

"Say, Tarz. We're here, man," encouraged Kohl. "We don't want to pry, except for Mays over there." They laughed uneasily and nodded, as Kohl continued, "But maybe it would help if you talked about what's wrong. You're not going to die are you?"

"No, but it was close. Real close. And for all I know..." Phillips trailed off into his own thoughts. He leaned forward with his elbows on the table, swirling his glass, his mind searching for words. He quietly began to talk. "What I'm about to tell you guys cannot leave this table. I am under orders not to discuss what happened. Please honor my wishes."

"What ever you say, Tarz. Our word is our bond," said Wheeler.

"Semper fi," said Joss.

"Hear, hear," they said in unison, with glasses raised in a toast.

"Our recon outfit had been running LPs and OPs in North Vietnam during November and December."

"North Vietnam?"

"Not so loud. But that's right."

"We're not supposed to be up there, are we?"

"Officially we're not," answered Tarz.

"Shut up you guys, let 'im finish," said Mays. "What where you doing up there?"

"Like I said, we were running patrols up there. They would chopper us in and drop us. Then we would set up and see what the North Vietnamese Regulars were up to. I had been on six patrols and the last three had been in about the same place. They wanted us to go on another mission to the same area again. I told our people that by now NVR probably knew we were around there someplace and that it was risky to keep going back. They told me how important it was that we get the information about NVR troop and supply movements and so on. Well, they dropped us in there under the cover of darkness. Even though NVR couldn't see us, they could sure hear the Hueys and knew that we were there some place. That was about two months ago now. There were six of us. We were only two hours out, on our way to the designated OP, when we got hit."

The lieutenants let out a moan, and as Phillips continued softly and slowly, they leaned closer.

"I knew with the first burst of fire that it had dropped the front three men and I was hit in the leg. But I managed to get off the trail out of the line of fire. As I crashed into the brush, I hit a trip wire on a Pangi trap. It was a bamboo pad with bamboo stakes tied and mounted on a bamboo pole that had been pulled back. When I hit the trip wire this pole swung around and caught me in the small of the back. It lifted me clean off the ground. As I was hanging there, I looked down, and swear to God, saw the stakes sticking out my stomach." He paused and took a gulp of his Seven-up.

"You mean, you were..." stammered Joss.

"Shut up, Joss. Go on, Tarz," said Mays.

"I can't remember too much about what happened after that. I was drifting in and out of consciousness. I could hear shooting and talking but my vision was blurry. I remember them poking me with their guns. There was no pain. I didn't feel anything. I don't even remember being afraid." He stopped and took a deep breath. He wiped his eye with a finger.

While he had been talking he didn't look up from the table. Not once did he look at his friends.

"Lewis, Bernards, Juliet, Phillips and Roberts, gone. Just like that. They were just kids. I was their officer. I was responsible. I should have been more ... our luck was running out. I just knew it. Maybe, I could have..." He shook his head.

His buddies gave him time to continue.

"The next thing I remembered was bright lights. As my eyes began to focus and I looked around, I realized that I was on an operating table, with people dressed in green standing over me. It was a hospital."

"What? How in the hell? Whose?"

"I know. I know. It was a hospital, all right, and it was ours, a hospital boat. It's all guesswork from here but this I know. A chopper on patrol in the South China Sea found me by accident floating in a dugout canoe twenty-five miles off the coast of North Vietnam. The bamboo stakes were still sticking out of my stomach but mud and grass had been packed on top of my stomach and back. The doctors think the NVR left me there to die and that some villagers found, doctored and put me in a canoe to drift out to sea. The doctors said another reason I didn't die was because I was tall and instead of the stakes puncturing my lungs, it hit in the small of my back."

"Man, you are one lucky son-of-a-gun," said Joss.

"I don't think luck had anything to do with it." For the first time he looked at them. "Too many things had to go right. I was left there to die and should have. I think I was chosen to live. I was selected to survive for a reason. I don't know why I was chosen, but I was. God came down and lifted me to safety. Every little insignificant detail came together so I could live. I owe my life to Jesus Christ my Lord and Savior. I am not the same man I was. I have been reborn. I have been resurrected. I have been given a second chance at life."

Tears were freely flowing from his eyes. He made no effort to hide it. Joss put his arm around Phillips. He could feel his bones and the softness where once was a hulk of a man.

"A toast," said Mays. "To the Second Coming, and he's a Marine."

They held their glasses high, each silently expressing their own private fears, their own hidden horrors, their own doubts as to their mortality. Who controlled their destiny? Does God really care who lived and who died? Does he choose? Does he pick and select people like a farmer picking apples? This one I will keep and the other I will throw away.

"What are you going to do now?" asked Kohl.

"They are sending me back to the 'World' in a couple of weeks. I lost part of my stomach and some other things are pretty screwed up. So, I'm through. Discharged. I'm going to go to seminary school. My life is in the hands of the Lord now. It's pay back time."

Kohl had just finished the third drink and was starting his fourth when the group was told their table for dinner was ready. He stood up and turned to follow. Either the floor wasn't where he thought his foot was or his foot wasn't where the floor was. When he got up and took a step he fell flat on his stomach with an "ooooff" and his fourth drink went flying. Kohl looked around, puzzled and embarrassed. Even with the loud talking and music everybody looked and laughed. Mays reached down and helped him up.

"What the hell happened?" asked Kohl.

"It's those drinks. Kind of sneak up on you," said Mays.

"And how," answered Kohl. He didn't feel drunk or high. But he was having a difficult time navigating his way to the table. They ate their dinner in subdued conversation. Noticeably absent was the horseplay. They consoled, encouraged, and wished Tarz the best.

*

The first day out, Kohl stayed in bed again. Sick. That evening, when he was in the head throwing up, he heard someone call his name. Kohl stuck his head out.

"Darken ship," the sailor said.

Kohl closed the porthole and put the cover over it. It was hot and sultry in the cabin. With the porthole closed, it was stifling. They were now twenty-five miles off the coast of Vietnam.

The next day Kohl felt better and went to dinner. The weather had cooled some and the ocean was calm. As he stood on deck, the sun's late afternoon glow silhouetted the mountains of Vietnam. Even though Kohl hated being on board ship and the dreaded nausea that it caused him, the thought of landing in Vietnam was worse. He wasn't afraid. Fear for his life hadn't crossed his mind. He was young and immortal. Death happenened to other people.

It could happen, you know.

Yeah, but don't say it.

What? Death?

I told you, don't say it. I don't want to think about it. Bad luck.

What do you think it's like? You know to die.

Man, what's with you. I don't think it would be a fun thing. I don't want to hear about it anymore.

Kohl started singing.

"When Irish Eyes Are Shining and the world was bright and gay."

*

The next morning there was a rap on the bulkhead outside the cabin.

"Message for you, Lieutenant," said the Communications Chief.

The message was marked SECRET. Kohl's heart felt like it was going to leap out of his chest. It was a frag order. It read: "Be prepared to land on Red Beach." *Oh, shit.* He continued, "and protect the air strip in Danang." Kohl's mind raced. *Don't they give these frag orders to all battalions that are afloat ... don't they? Kohl recalled, Sure they do. That's just to let me know what to do if they give orders to land. Besides, the U.S. Government doesn't want to get involved in Vietnam, at least not any more than we already are with military advisors and providing military supplies to fight the Viet Cong. At least that's what Johnson's been saying. But I haven't been up on the news too much since I've been out here. They only give us the information that they think we need and then reduce it by half. Here I am a Marine that voted for Johnson because I thought he would keep us out of war. If Goldwater had been elected, we would be doing mop up operations by now and heading home. None of this floating around shit.*

"Would you sign this, Lieutenant?"

"Yeah, sure." Kohl forgot he was still standing there. He scribbled his name on the security sheet attached to the clipboard.

"Thank you, Sir." He turned and left Kohl with his thoughts.

After dinner, Kohl went to his cabin to get his French harp so he could go topside and play. He had been doing this almost every night since they had left Subic Bay. He didn't see it on his desk where he thought he had put it. He looked around his rack, suitcase, closet, pockets, nothing. While he was down on his hands and knees looking under his bed, his roommate, Lieutenant J.G. Billings, stumbled over Kohl as he came through the curtain and stepped on Kohl's hand.

"What the...." he said.

"Oooooouuah. Son-of-a-bitch!" Kohl said, shaking his hand in the air.

"What are you doing down there?" There was no concern in the fact that he had stepped on his hand, and when he smiled it wasn't a friendly smile, more like a smirk.

"I'm looking for my French harp. Seen it?"

"Nope. Sure haven't." He picked up something and left.

Kohl looked in a few more places. This had happened a couple of times before. Once he found it in his sock, another time under his pillow. This time he found it inside the Marine Corps Amphibious Training Manual. Kohl's hand still hurt from where Billings stepped on it. *Fat son-of-bitch mashed every bone in my hand.*

At breakfast the next morning when Kohl walked in, Lieutenant Commander Hangerber was talking about going back to Subic Bay. Kohl didn't ask any questions. He just sat and listened. Maybe they were playing games at his expense. Mays was there and caught Kohl's eye and nodded yes. Kohl smiled to himself. *Go back, circle around, turn to your left, turn to your right, stand up, sit down, fight! fight! fight! Walk on land, walk on water. We will do what ever you say, because it don't matter!*

"I'll have two eggs and toast, please," Kohl said to the Philippine steward.

*

Kohl had felt a quiet slow heat burning in the pit of his stomach from the resentment towards him by the ship's officers. He knew there was some merit to it. He had brought a lot of it upon himself. He openly showed signs of not wanting nor liking being on board ship. However, the last couple of weeks, he had tried to improve his attitude, especially now that he wasn't sick anymore. A few things in the beginning he thought were funny, especially the time they wrote on the sole of his right boot "left" and on his left boot "right." It upset him when they hid his French harp a couple of times. It was a combination of feelings from being sick most of the time; being confined on a small area for a long period of time; not knowing what was happening about Vietnam; plus he was home sick and he had only completed his first month.

Kohl had received a letter from Julie on the first of February. It was post marked the fifteenth of January. Fifteen days to get a letter. *Well, no wonder.*

*

"I've got a letter here for Lieutenant Kohl. Where is he?"

"He's at Subic."

"No. Not there."

"He must be in Oki, then."

"No. Not there either."

"There he is."

"Where."

"Over there."

"That's not him."

"Then where is he?"

"I thought you knew."

"I thought I knew too, but he keeps moving. Why don't you ask someone who's in charge."

"Who's in charge?"

"No. Who's on first."

*

It's a game. Somewhere in a Georgetown bar some Pentagon Military Officers are sitting around a table. "The table here is the South China Sea. Here. I'll move the beer bottles over here. Now, they will be the Philippines. This bar rag will be Vietnam, and this napkin will be Okinawa. Okay?"

"Yeah," said the Admirals and Generals sitting around the table.

"The salt shaker will be the USS Union and the ash tray will be the USS Vancouver and the pepper shaker will be the USS Hanricko. Here, we'll put this little cocktail umbrella in the pepper shaker to make it the flag ship."

"Good idea. Good idea," said the men nodding their heads.

"Hold it. Shouldn't the salt and pepper shaker be closer to the San Migel

beer bottle?"

"Yeah." (Move, move.)

"No. Wait. I think it'll look more balanced if they were closer to the napkin."

"Really? Okay." (Move, move.)

"Oh dear."

"What?"

"We left the ash tray out there all by itself. We don't want to break up the set."

"You're right. We had better move the salt and pepper shakers back." (Move, move.)

"Now, that's better."

"Lets put the French fries on the bar rag."

"I can empty the ash try on the bar rag too."

"Good idea. Yeah, do it."

"How 'bout catsup too. Like this."

"Looks like blood. Ooooo!"

"Well, I think the salt and the pepper should be spread all over the French fries."

"What shall we do with the mixed nuts?"

"We can put those on Hawaii."

"Naw. Let's put them on the bar rag."

"With all due respect, Sir, the bar rag is all gooey and mushy. It looks awful.

Oh, General you're drunk aren't you?"

"No, I'm not. And you don't know what you're talkin' about. I out rank everybody here and I say that's what to do. Now do it."

They pour the mixed nuts on the bar rag and shake the salt and pepper on the French fry's stir it with swizzle sticks and say, "It's just making an awful mess, General. General?"

He didn't hear because he had passed out.

*

"Who in the hell's in charge here, for Christ's sake?" Kohl yelled at Mays, as they stood topside in the warm night.

Mays shrugged, looked off disinterestedly. It was unanswerable anyway. Minutes passed as they looked out into the dark expanse of the ocean. Suddenly Mays turned his head toward Kohl, with his eyes aglow and a tight grin.

"Let's go see the Doc."

"Hell of an idea," answered Kohl. Kohl had become friendly with the ship's doctor, Lieutenant Ben Dorfman, since Kohl had been seasick so much of the time. At one of Kohl's visits, he had confided in Kohl, a secret that he could never divulge to any of the ship's officers. "I can't tolerate any of those pricks, and I sure can't trust them," said the Doc to Kohl, during one of his visits to pick up another ration of Dramamine.

"Think he's up?" asked Kohl.

"Up or out," snickered Mays, as they made their way to Doc's cabin, which was down by the sick bay.

Kohl knocked lightly on the door so as not to wake him if he were asleep. He had a door.

"Who is it?" was the answer.

"Kohl and Mays," said Kohl.

"Oh. Yeah, okay. Come on in."

The Doc was sprawled on his rack reading an old copy of Playboy with an orange drink in his hand. He was dressed in a government issue v-neck tee shirt and boxer shorts. He lowered the magazine as they entered. "Not sick are you, Lieutenant?" he said smiling and winked at Mays. "Have a seat, gentlemen. Care for an orange juice?"

"That's what we came for, Doc.Thought you'd never ask," answered Kohl.

The Doc got up, walked to the foot of his bed, took a screwdriver off the dresser top, and pried up the top cap that covered the bedpost, reached over and from under his mattress. He pulled out a three foot length of surgical tubing, stuck it into the bedpost, knelt down with a cup and siphoned a clear liquid into two cups. Vodka. He poured in just enough orange juice to give it color and flavor. "Here's the juice, Bruce."

"Thank you, Doc," they said.

Any liquor on board ship had to be locked up in supply and registered with the supply officer. The good Doctor smuggled it into his room while he was in port, which wasn't any big problem for an officer, except if he got caught. The Doc had it concealed in two three-foot long beakers that were in the hollow portion of his bedposts. The caps of the posts were easily pried off and the beakers were filled with Vodka. He kept a fresh supply of orange juice and ice from the enlisted galley, in exchange for non-reported Penicillin shots. The Doc had it covered. He kept to himself, and stayed close to drunk all the time. They just thought he was laid back, walked, and talked funny.

"What do you think of my set up, Mays?"

"Not bad, Doc. Not bad at all."

"Any ice?"

"Hell yes, I've got ice. What kind of an establishment do you think I run here? It's over there in the fridge where I keep the urine samples. Don't get it mixed up. The ice is the clear hard stuff," he laughed at his joke. "I know how you Marines are. Score a little low in the I.Q. tests." He laughed again. Gave them a salute.

"Speaking of brilliance, Doc, it wouldn't take a rocket scientist to think if you had a choice of being stateside or on this fucking boat, the smart person would pick stateside, lying next to some sweet young thing, pulling in about sixty grand a year," teased Kohl. "You don't sound too bright to me," he continued.

"Wrong, banana breath." Doc gave Kohl a long look. His smile was sure. He appeared to have the situation in hand. He had justified his existence to this way of life many times before.

"Yeah," echoed Mays, "What's a nice doctor doing in a place like this?"

Doc laid down his girly magazine and took a long swig of his orange drink. He said, "You grunts can't see the forest for the trees. What you see is a small bare room. A ship in the middle of the ocean going in circles. But you don't see the whole picture," gesturing with his hands he took another drink and began. "After I graduated from med. school at USC, I did my intern at Presbyterian Hospital in Phoenix. After three years I stayed on as staff." He laid his head back against the headboard and took another drink. "I worked hard, in fact I busted my ass. Long hours. Shit everything was so ... How can I put it? So ... intense. I mean uptight. You know. Like there wasn't any room. There wasn't room for a personal life. I was working day and night. There was no room for mistakes. I know that sounds funny. I'm a doctor. I'm not supposed to make mistakes. But anyway, everything was compressed. Too many patients and not enough time to think. I thought it had to be better in private practice, so I joined a small clinic in the 'burbs'. Things settled down for a while. I even got married. My practice was growing and before I knew it, there I was again, no time. I'd be home, getting a little from my wife or whoever, and I'd get beeped, or the phone would ring. Or I'd be going to the bathroom at the hospital and on the intercom I'd hear 'Doctor Dorfman, line 3, Please.' Nine times out of ten it would be some cunt that had an emergency that just couldn't wait. They needed someone to talk to ... give them a placebo and pat them on the ass and send them home. I still worked long hours and sure, I was making plenty of money and gettin' all kinds a women. The clinic really packed them in. Looking at sweaty cunts and smelling wheezing breath of dying old men was getting to be a drag. I was never home. Finally, I just quit going home. Then I quit going to the office. There I was in the prime of life at 35 and realized I wasn't having any fun. So I sold my interest in the clinic and traveled around for a while. Ended up in San Diego, walked into a Navy recruiter's office and said 'take me away'. So ... look real hard. You'll see what I've got. I've got it made. I'm pretty much my own boss. I get to go to Japan, Hong Kong, Taiwan, Philippines, Guam, Australia, New Zealand, the Mediterranean, France, Spain, New York, San Francisco, San Diego, all at government's expense. I get paid a good salary with good benefits. I can retire when I'm 55 on some seashore in Central America. I've got it made. No sweat, no strain. I treat pimples and venereal disease. Anything serious comes up; they pick them up with a chopper and take them to the nearest port hospital or to another ship with better facilities. No complaints from my patients, plenty of liberty. Plenty of slant eyed pussy. No liability suits. Now tell me, gentlemen, do I have it made or what? Want another orange drink?"

*

Kohl's head hurt ... again. He had spent the night in Doc's cabin.

Later that morning, the Captain's orderly found him lying on the sun deck and told him the Captain wished to see him. Kohl entered the Captain's cabin. The Captain told him to be seated. As always, Kohl was concerned about what the Captain wanted. He wondered if he found out about last night. But the Captain quickly interrupted Kohl's thoughts of concern when he spoke in his soft quiet voice.

"Lieutenant, we have a serious problem." *Oh, shit. Here it comes. He knows. Oh man, I'm dead meat.* "One of your troops ... " the Captain paused as the color came back into Kohl's face," got into a little trouble. I have a report here, concerning the conduct of a..." he looked at the report, "PFC Harris. One of your men, isn't he?" Kohl nodded his head yes. "This incident happened while we were in Subic Bay. This is a complaint filed by Marine Major Tom Blue." Kohl made an unintelligible sound. "Do you know the Major, Lieutenant?" Kohl nodded yes. The Captain handed the report for Kohl to read.

*

Kohl had heard about the incident involving PFC Harris from Corporal Ford. He had also talked to Harris personally about the incident. In fact Major Blue made certain that Kohl heard about it. Major Blue blamed Kohl for his divorce, and would do anything to get back at Kohl. Major Blue had been Kohl's Company Commander back in Pendleton. He had been a Captain at the time. Kohl had met Captain Blue's wife, Nancy, on many occasions. She was a lot different from Captain Blue. She was friendly, suffered from few inhibitions, a real Southern belle from South Carolina. He was a straight arrow, a born again Christian and a graduate of the Citadel. At the Marine Corps birthday party two years ago, Nancy was sitting alone while the Captain was talking in another room with a clustered group of officers. Kohl liked Nancy as a friend. Even though she was attractive, there was no impropriety in their relationship. She was always fun. The life of a party. Kohl walked over and asked if he could join her. She gladly accepted. They danced most of the evening, laughing and drinking. When Captain Blue finally came back, he took Kohl to the side and told him he could see how they were laughing and carrying on. That they were purposely trying to embarrass him. He told him to stay away from his wife. He said that he wasn't blind, that he could see what was going on. Kohl had told him that his intentions were strictly honorable and that they were just having fun. Nancy soon saw what was happening and joined to tell her husband that he was way off base and owed them both an apology. He said to hell with them both and left the party in a huff. Kohl took Nancy home soon after. She called him the next day and wanted to meet later that day. Kohl told her that the Captain had said not to speak to her again. She started crying. She said she didn't have any friends to talk to; she wanted his opinion on something. She said he would not find out, that they could be careful. "Very careful," she said. Kohl rationalized that it didn't matter what he did, the Captain would be mad anyway, but he did not want this meeting to get out of hand, so he agreed to meet her for lunch in San Clemente. He thought lunch would be safe. She came in wearing dark glasses, which was unusual for a foggy day. When she sat down he could see one side of her face was swollen and red. Her lower lip was puffed. They talked over lunch about what she should do. Kohl said, "Well, to tell you the truth, Nancy, I think he's an asshole and always will be." He could tell things could have gone further with her but it would not have been fair to her. Not at this time in her life. She left for South Carolina two weeks later.

*

Testimony of Major Thomas C. Blue, USMC, 066068.

I stopped in the Subic PX accompanied by Major James L. Ripple. We were both in uniform. Three Marines, also in uniform, were

> standing at the magazine rack. One of these men, later identified as PFC Stewart W. Harris, was talking in a loud voice and using language such as "fucking" and "shit" and "fuck you" and so on. The PX was crowded and there were women present. I ordered PFC Harris to leave. Then he pushed his cover to the back of his head, placed a hand on his hip, and smiled. He made no move to leave. I ordered him to wait for me outside the PX. When I approached him, he had his hands in his pockets and did not salute nor come to attention.

Kohl handed the report back to the Captain. In the Marine Corps a Marine was not to have his hat (cover) on indoors, nor was he to ever have his hands in his pockets. Some Marines, in order to break the habit, sewed their pockets shut.

The Captain said, "Bring PFC Harris in, Corporal."

"Aye, aye, Sir." The Corporal-of-the-Guard moved quickly through the hatch and brought a six-foot-four black man who weighed about two hundred and ten pounds. The Corporal dropped his hand from the man's strong arm. The prisoner walked smartly to the front of the Captain's desk, stopped, and in a slow deliberate low voice said, "PFC Harris reporting as ordered, Sir." His jaw was set. He quickly glanced at his Platoon Commander.

The Captain read him his rights under U.C.M.J. Article eighty-one. "Do you understand those rights, PFC Harris?"

"Yes, Sir, I do."

The Captain continued, "PFC Harris, this Officer's Mast has been called because you have been accused of violating Article One-Thirty-Four, and eighty-nine of the UCMJ.

Kohl watched Harris as the Captain read the statement of Major Blue. Kohl had read Harris' folder: North High School, Denver, Colorado, fullback and quarter miler, poor grades, boot camp fights, but after three months in Third Recon Battalion, A Company, First Platoon, he had been promoted from Private to PFC. Fitness reports indicated he was a good field Marine but got in trouble in garrison and that was mostly when he was in the company of a friend of his by the name of Private Bufford Handle. Kohl didn't care for Private Handle. He appeared to be lazy and resented taking orders. Harris had recognized Kohl from the games he had seen at Denver University and on TV. They had briefly talked about Denver and Colorado.

"What do you have to say for yourself, PFC Harris?"

"Sir, I know I did wrong, Sir. And I'm sorry, Sir." he looked at Kohl. "Sir, it won't happen again, Sir. I promise."

Good. Just the way I coached him. Accept the charges and keep your mouth shut.

"Did you say those words like the Major said?" asked the Captain.

"Sir, there was three of us and we was talkin', but not loud like the Major says, and I don't know why he picked me cause we was all talkin', Sir."

I do.

When Kohl had talked to Harris about the incident earlier, Harris had said the Major asked what outfit they were with. And when he found out Kohl was his Platoon Commander, he pulled him out from the rest and wrote him up.

But Harris continued, "Captain, Sir. If I may, Sir. The Major was...."

The Captain cut Harris off. "I'll ask you again, did you say those words the Major said you did?"

"Sir, we were all talkin'. I could have, Sir."

"Do you have any questions for PFC Harris, Lieutenant Kohl?"

"No, Sir."

Harris looked disappointed.

"Any final words, PFC Harris, before I pronounce sentence?

"Sir, it just seems like I was singled out, Sir."

Kohl was trying to catch his eye, to signal him to keep quiet. He could tell by the Captain's look and tone of voice that he did not want to hear any more. He could tell that Harris had gone too far.

Harris continued, "Seems like everywhere I go, I'm somebody's lackey."

Kohl cringed.

"Ain't no difference whether here or in some honky town in Colorado."

The Captain abruptly stood. His face and neck were red. Kohl couldn't understand the bitterness in Harris. It hadn't been prevalent in their discussion before. He knew how Major Blue felt about what he called "uppity niggers." He had seen it happen in his Company back in Pendleton. Captain Blue on several occasions when he had held Office Hours with some of the colored Marines who had been in trouble, had commented that he didn't like the way they walked. "It is unbecoming of a Marine to walk like that," he had said.

He could see that Harris was way out of line at Subic Bay PX, and did not want to lose face in front of his friends. This was a case of a colored enlisted man and a white southern officer who happened to have a grudge to settle with Harris' Platoon Commander.

"Very well. PFC Harris, I have no other recourse but to charge you with bringing discredit upon the naval services and showing disrespect under Article eighty-nine of the Uniform Justice Code towards an officer of the USMC. I hereby award you fifteen days in the ship's brig, followed by thirty days of restriction to the ship when we are in port, reduction of rank from PFC to Private and to forfeit

Forty-two..."

Kohl saw a pained expression on Harris's face.

"... dollars for two months this second day of February of nineteen sixty-five. You are dismissed."

"Aye, Aye, Sir," Harris replied. He wheeled sharply and left with the Corporal- of-the-Guard on his shoulder.

The Captain was still standing and said, "Lieutenant, as senior Marine Officer on board ship, see that these orders are carried out."

"Aye, Aye, Sir."

The Captain shook his head. "Don't the colored folk realize that by serving in the Armed Services they can improve their social and economic stature?" The question was not asked in a way that Kohl needed to answer.

Kohl shrugged his shoulders. "Will that be all, Sir?"

"Probably was high on something, do you think?"

"I don't think so, Sir. PFC Harris seems to be all right."

The Captain continued, "Better keep an eye on him. Yes, that will be all."

10 Survival

The convoy was back in Subic Bay and Kohl was at the Caliente Officers Club stuffing himself. He had salad, steak, potatoes with sour cream and butter, mixed vegetables, rolls with jelly, chocolate milk, apple pie topped with ice cream and coffee. The next morning at breakfast, he had pancakes, two eggs, bacon, milk, juice, and a cinnamon roll. Why was he gorging himself? The Battalion was going on a four day Survival Jungle Training Course.

At 0730, the Battalion moved out under blue skies in six-byes, to an area in the mountains where the troops were to disembark. Each company had a Filipino guide to show the Americans what they could and could not eat in the wilds of the Philippines. Each Marine had one pound of rice. The company commanders and Kohl checked their troops to see that absolutely no food was smuggled into the jungle.

Kohl's fifteen-man platoon was the last to leave the main road into the jungle. Joss' platoon had turned off about a half mile earlier. The Filipino guide followed a trail along a small stream. It was cool under the jungle canopy. Kohl was in his element. He enjoyed the field at times like this, exploring and experiencing the new surroundings. He was fascinated with the different shrubs, flowers, vines, trees, and especially the bamboo. He saw some as big as eight to ten inches in diameter and forty to fifty feet tall. But just as Kohl was getting warmed up for a long stroll through the jungle, the Filipino guide stopped.

"We camp here," he said.

"We just got off the road. Let's go further," suggested Kohl.

The guide reluctantly moved on but soon stopped again and said, "We camp here."

Kohl said, "no" and moved on up the stream. The guide continued to protest about going further. Kohl eventually took the lead while the guide fell further and further behind. After about five miles Kohl came to a fork in the stream. There was a sandy shore, big rocks, majestic waterfall, and a deep clear pool. Kohl stopped and took off his pack. A perfect place to camp.

"This will be our home for the next four days, gang. Not bad, huh? Where's the guide?"

They all dropped their packs and looked around for the guide. He was gone. *So much for showing us how to live off the land.*

The troops quickly disrobed and went swimming. Afterwards they lay in the sun in the small clearing. They also relished the walk in the jungle and the feeling of being on land again. Kohl took his camera that he had bought in Hong Kong, and hiked up the stream. His eyes took in everything, as he walked and jumped from one rock to another along the clear blue stream. This was more than he had imagined. He recognized some of the plants as indoor plants back home. He saw the Split Leaf Philodendrons clinging to large Mahogany trees that climbed as high as he could see into the canopy above. There were Bromeliads growing in rotting logs along with Staghorn Ferns. He saw orchids in a large variety of colors and clusters of brilliantly colored flowers and ferns that grew ten to twelve feet tall reaching out over the stream bed. He felt as if he were in paradise. The bamboo amazed him at how big, straight and tall it was. He found a deep pool at the base of a small waterfall. He removed his clothes, swam in the cool water, and basked in the sun, as he lay stretched out on a rock. He watched beautifully feathered birds fluttering from one enormous tree to another. He was curious if there were any tigers or snakes around. Off in the distance he had seen a couple of monkeys. He did not return to camp until late in the afternoon.

The troops were lounging around and had a small campfire going. Thorogood and Charlotte had caught some pink shrimp that resembled the American crawfish without the pincers. They had broken off and shelled the tails, then mixed them with the rice that was boiling.

The men horsed around and showed pictures of their girlfriends, wives, and children. They told stories until way past midnight. The next morning they finished off the rice and boiled more shrimp for lunch.

That afternoon Kohl conducted a three-hour class on escape and evasion. The setting and conditions were ideal. In the background was the sound of the waterfall; calls of tropical birds filled the air. The men were lounging in the grassy clearing between the streams; their bodies warm from the afternoon sun.

"If you're behind enemy lines or your position has been over-run, what is the first rule?" asked Kohl.

"Hide," said Beach.

"Don't get caught," said Grant.

"You're both right. You need to do everything you can to keep from being captured. You have to have the proper camouflage, stay quiet and still. How many of you have been deer hunting?"

Marseilles, Woods, Harris, Sale, Charlotte, and Thorogood all raised their hands.

"Where's Shultz?" asked Charlotte.

"Taking a dump," said Ford.

"I've hunted possum and coon, does that count?" asked Flowers.

"I've hunted girls, does that count?" asked Hernandez.

"In your case it probably would," said Beach, "because anything you'd catch would be a dog."

Hernandez threw a small stone at Beach, while Kohl continued, "The point I want to make is, when are you able to see the deer, Charlotte?"

"Usually when they move, Lieutenant."

"Right and what else, aah, Harris?"

"When they make noise."

"Right and what else? Anybody?" Kohl didn't receive any responses so he added, "When they do not blend in with their surroundings or they are out in the open. You can hide by lying on your back and scooting feet first into the grass or brush and pull the cover over your body, then role over on your stomach and lay quietly and wait for nightfall before you move. So what enables us to detect someone or something is movement, sound and what about smell?"

"Yes, Lieutenant. That too," said Harris.

"Why is that?"

"Like aftershave," answered Harris.

"Or if Bubba farts," said a laughing Woods.

"Shultz did not go to the bathroom. He's right here, within ten feet of us. Look around and see if you can see him," said Kohl.

"He's probably in the bushes back there," points Spallenski.

"Do you see him, Ski?"

"No, but that's the only place where there's cover."

"Don't get up. Just look. He's here. Close."

"Okay, Shultz. Stand up."

To the surprise of the men, he wasn't in the brush to the rear of Kohl, but to the rear of the troops near the point where the two streams met. Schultz had dug a shallow pit and covered himself with sand and clumps of grass with the help of Corporal Ford. He stood up and brushed himself off.

"Good work, Shultz. Now, the next thing is, what would be the first thing you do if you're caught?" asked Kohl.

Ford poked Thompson who was dozing off.

"What?" asked Thompson as he jolted upright.

"What would you do Thompson?" asked Kohl.

"Aaaa ... Sorry Lieutenant. What was the question?"

"Tell him Charlotte," said Kohl.

"The first thing I'd do if I was caught..."

"Besides shit your pants?" said Hernandez.

"I'd ... Fuck you, Hernandez."

"I don't think that would work," laughed Thorogood. "Might confuse them though."

"Go on, Charlotte," said Kohl.

“I'd..." Charlotte turned and glared at Hernandez. "I'd escape."

"The best time to escape is when you are first captured and why is that? Handle?" asked Kohl.

"I don't know. Nobody's going to capture my ass, Lieutenant."

"But, what would you do if it happened."

Handle shrugged.

"Anybody?"

Corporal Ford said, "Because they are unorganized and often times are confused."

"Right. Let's say that you have successfully escaped and have made it back near your lines or friendly forces. What should you avoid?"

"Getting your ass shot. That's what," said Grant.

"And what should you do to keep that from happening?"

"Don't go in at night," said Thorogood.

"Don't attach to a patrol," said Grant.

They continued to talk into the night about how they would react to being captured and how they would try to escape.

"Let's just hope that we won't have to use any of the things we've talked about. We are all trained to overcome pain, cold, hunger, thirst, fatigue, and loneliness. We were told to never give up and to try to keep a positive attitude."

*

Escape and Evasion School for Marine Corps Officers was held in Bridgeport, California, high in the Sierras. It was mid-March and there was still snow on the ground in places. It was cool during the day and below freezing at night. Kohl was the only infantry officer among the wild and crazy pilots from El Toro Marine Base. After class, Kohl would hang out at the bar and play a dice game called twenty-one. The second week was the practical application of what they learned the first week. They were divided into five-man teams. Each team was given a camouflage parachute, and each man had a poncho, a pound of rice, matches, toilet paper, "K" Bar, safety pin, some crackers, and salt. They had been instructed to use a safety pin for a fishhook and nylon thread from the parachute for fishing line. But they didn't find Kohl's salmon egg hooks and length of two pound test leader hidden on the inside of his cold weather hat band. The teams were taken to a forested valley that had a stream running through it. The instructions were to live off the land for four days without getting caught by the "enemy," which were the instructors. If they caught you, for punishment, they would throw you into the icy cold stream. The teams' camps were considered "safe areas."

Kohl's team set up camp about a quarter of a mile half way up the north side of the mountain from the valley stream. With fallen pine poles and rocks they made an enclosure next to a large tree stump with the parachute over the top. By the time the camp was set up the sun had gone down it had turned cold. They made a fire, boiled some water, and ate some of the rice. Afterwards they rolled up in their ponchos and went to sleep. Even with the cold, the parachute held their heat well. Next morning Kohl got up at dawn and left to go fishing while his team members were still sleeping.

It was a cool, clear morning when Kohl left camp. He walked south up the side of the mountain away from the stream. After about a half mile he started angling to the east up the valley. When he felt he was safely out of the area where the "enemy" was, he started down the mountain towards the stream. Since Bridgeport was also the site for cold weather training, Kohl was able to find discarded "C" ration cans of cheese in the snow. He picked up a couple of cans for fish bait. At the stream's edge, he cut a willow pole about eight feet long and tied on his line and hook. He made sure the end of the pole was limber because he didn't want the line to break and lose the valuable leader. He baited the hook with cheese and crept towards the edge of a deep pool. He caught three eight inch brook trout out of that pool and moved down to another pool and caught eight more. By this time it was only about 10:30. He packed up his catch, concealed his line and hooks back in his hatband, and walked up the south side of the valley. He found a discarded ammo can and he put the fish in it and filled it with snow. He spent the rest of the day resting, dozing, and dreaming in the sun.

It was about dusk when he got back to camp. He found his team members shivering around a roaring fire with their steaming, wet clothes hanging from sticks. They had been caught fishing and had been thrown into the creek. They boiled some more rice and broiled the fish in empty old pop cans they had picked up. They asked Kohl if they could go with him the next day. He did not want them to go. It was easier to travel alone. Rather than argue with them, he told them they could. But the next morning he left without waking them.

He went west over the ridge into another valley and found a beaver pond where he fished most of the morning. He had found a wooden crate and made a quail trap in a Manzanita thicket, using crackers as bait. He had learned how to make a quail trap from his grandfather who lived in Camp Nelson on the western slope of the Sierras. It took almost four hours before a covey of quail came into the area. He had been dozing when he heard their bobwhite call. He returned to camp with a nice mess of fish and two quail. Again he found them huddled around the fire cold and wet. They were upset because he had not taken them. They had given up on fishing and were trying to pick greens and dig for roots.

"I thought you guys were going to stay away from the creek?" asked Kohl.

"We did," said the sandy-haired pilot. "We were looking for those wild onion bulbs and Donkey Ears over there when they snuck up on us."

"This is horse shit," said the tall one.

"Listen, it's up to you guys, but about a half mile up the mountain there's a small meadow where I think we can dig bulbs and pick greens. And I need somebody to look for cheese "C" ration cans for bait. I don't think the instructors will look for us there."

The next day, Kohl trapped a gray squirrel and caught more fish. On the morning of the fifth day, the teams mustered for the walk out of the valley.

One of the instructors walked up next to Kohl and asked, "Where have you been?"

"Around," said Kohl.

"You were supposed to be out looking for food. Not just stay in camp," said the instructor.

"He didn't stay in camp, Sarge," said one of Kohl's team members.

"If it hadn't been for Kohl, we would have starved to death," one of them said.

"In fact we ate pretty good. Fish, quail..."

"Quail?"

"Yeah. And Squirrel."

The sergeant gave Kohl a questioning side-glance.

"It's true Sarge. Saved our ass."

*

By evening their stomachs were growling. Thompson kept talking about food and everyone was getting sick of it. They complained about the Filipino guide leaving and some said it was the Lieutenant's fault for walking too far into the jungle.

Kohl had taken Corporal Ford aside earlier and explained a plan he had for that evening. Corporal Ford had expressed some concerns about the Lieutenant's plan but Kohl was able to convince Ford of its worthiness, plus he said it would be fun.

That evening, just before dark, he gathered the men around the campfire. "Well, I would say that by now we know how it feels to be hungry. Wouldn't you say?"

There was a chorus of, "Yes, Sir." and nodding heads.

"I think we should be practicing something we need to practice. Don't you think?"

There was an answering chorus of, "Yes, Sir."

"Tonight we're going to run two patrols," Kohl said. He saw their eyes light up. "The first patrol will be a four man team, that will sneak back to the base to buy food."

There was a mixed chorus of "What? Aw right! Outstanding. How can we do that?"

"Hold it! Hold it! Now listen. I'm not saying we shouldn't be learning to live off the land. But our guide took off. Didn't they tell us in Survival School to be creative and imaginative? Well, we are. Now I'm not talking about just walking into the base PX and buying some food. You will be on a mission. It has to be done right. You can't be seen leaving the base camp area and you can't be seen reentering. You can't get caught or we'll all end up in deep doo-doo. This will require the best of your stealth skills."

"The second patrol is a test. I want to see how good you guys really are. This four-man team will find where Lieutenant Joss' camp is and do a complete reconnaissance on his platoon. You will assume you are in enemy territory. Corporal Ford will fill you in on the details. What do you think? Is it worth the risk?"

"Yes, Sir," they all said.

"I will ask for volunteers."

They all shouted and raised their hands.

"Corporal Ford will choose the teams and brief them."

Lance Corporal Seal's team was chosen for the base patrol. They were instructed to stay off the main roads and to stay in the shadows once on base. They collected money for the food and made a list of what to get.

Kohl reminded them, when Thompson persistently requested steaks, "You can't go into the PX at 2200 and ask for sixteen steaks. We have to keep it simple so as not to bring undue attention to the mission. We can't let any of this get out."

Lance Corporal Grant's team was chosen to recon Joss' platoon. He briefed his team and made sure PFC Billy Joe Woods put camouflage on his face and the backs of his hands.

"Hey. How come Bubba doesn't put any on his big, pink, fat lips? Uh? How come?" sneered the cocky Woods.

"How would you like a fat lip, you hillbilly white trash," retorted Bubba.

"Woods. You's one dumb sumbitch. Remember what happen lass time?" said a cautioning Grant.

"It was an accident," explained Bubba. "I didn't mean to drop 'em. I was jus playin'. Didn't do it on purpose."

"Let's get movin' children," said Grant.

"Bring something back from Joss' platoon," said Kohl.

"Like what, Sir?"

"I don't know. Think of something."

They did a time check. It was 2000 hours. The teams were to be back by no later than 0200.

Kohl and Ford watched the two patrols disappear out of the campfire light and into the darkness of the jungle.

"Ford? What was Grant talking about?"

"You mean what Flowers did to Woods, Sir?"

"Yeah."

"Sir, as I understand it, some of the platoon had gone to Naha for liberty. They had rented a hotel room, were drinking and partying, when Woods got Flowers upset about something. Which is hard to do, you know, Sir. Flowers doesn't get too excited about anything. Anyway Sir, he hung Woods by the ankles off the three story balcony ... and ... dropped him ... not on purpose, Sir. It was by accident. His hand slipped, he said because of the thrashing around Woods was doing. Luckily, Woods fell on a palm tree and into some bushes. That broke his fall, plus being drunk probably helped him too."

Grant's team returned first and gave Kohl a complete briefing. Kohl was impressed with the information and their professionalism. Kohl asked what they brought back and Grant handed him a boot.

"A boot?" asked Kohl.

"Not just any boot, Lieutenant," Grant answered.

"What's so special about this boot?" asked Kohl.

"It belongs to Lieutenant Joss, Sir," said a grinning Grant proudly.

"I did it, Lieutenant. Me," said an excited Woods. "Crawled into their camp while they were sleeping. Piece of cake, Lieutenant."

"Man, is Joss going to be pissed," laughed Kohl. "You guys did an outstanding job. Well done."

The team that went to the base returned near the deadline of 0200. Kohl was beginning to worry that they may have been caught, but they came bounding in with big grins on their faces.

They roasted marshmallows and ate candy while they expounded on their exploits. Woods told anybody who would listen, in minute detail, of his "taking of the boot."

The next morning they had eggs, bacon and cinnamon rolls, then after lunch Corporal Ford gave a class on "How to Develop a Patrol Plan." He used Grant's Patrol as an example. Their last evening they roasted hot dogs with pork and beans. The next morning the camp was policed and secured. Nothing was left as an indication that anybody had been there. They moved out along the trail back to the main road to get picked up.

They got to the road and were waiting for the rest of the Battalion when Lieutenant Joss' platoon came out of the jungle onto the road. Kohl noticed that Joss only had one boot on. Kohl's platoon started to laugh until he turned and cautioned them. When the rest of the Battalion arrived to pick them up in six-byes, Joss was red with embarrassment as they pointed, jeered and laughed at the Lieutenant.

"Hey, Lieutenant. What happened to your boot?"

"Man, he must have got real hungry. Did you eat your boot, Lieutenant?"

"Hey, Lieutenant. I saw a monkey wearing your boot."

"That was no monkey. That was Corporal Jones."

"Hey, Lieutenant One Boot."

The name stuck. Joss became known as Lieutenant One Boot.

11 Manila

Joss had asked Kohl, before they went on the survival course, if he wanted to go to Manila for the weekend to visit his aunt and uncle. Kohl had told him that he would like to go. Joss' aunt was his mother's sister and worked for the U. S. Embassy. His uncle had a job in agriculture under the U.S. State Department. When they got back to the ship they got cleaned up, packed, then headed for Olongapo to catch a bus to Manila.

They bought a case of San Migel beer and boarded a 1939 International bus. It had been a school bus at one time. The yellow paint was peeking through the peeling, pale-blue cover coat. The right front bumper was held in place by wire and the windows were in various degrees of open, closed and out. They picked out a seat that had most of its padding and covering but it was impossible to get comfortable because of the over-crowding and the undersized seats that were built for the smaller Filipinos.

The motor started with a cough and a roar due to a non-existing muffler. They sat and watched the onslaught of men, women, and children. To Kohl's surprise chickens and goats also crowded onto the bus. There was a little girl about five pulling an old woman with white eyes and as she passed Kohl she held out a dirty, skinny hand and Kohl put an American dime in it.

Kohl asked, "Joss, how come you only had one boot this morning?"

"When I got up, I couldn't find it. Looked everywhere. I guess some animal came in during the night and carried it off. A monkey maybe. Do you think?"

"Probably. I've heard of coyotes taking shoes and boots. They like the salt, I understand. Sounds logical."

"Sure made me look stupid."

"You sure did. Here," said Kohl as he handed Joss a beer.

The country was an assortment of lush, green mountains and terraced rice fields. Kohl noticed that there were large areas that were burned like a forest fire. Joss told him that a nomadic tribe called Greetos burned the areas to scare game into snares. Some nights in Subic Bay he could see the fires burning in the distant hills.

After about two hours of winding roads, up and down mountains, with drop offs into space, with dust swirling from speeds only Parnelli Jones would feel comfortable with, the bus halted out in the middle of nowhere on top of a ridge. There were no houses or buildings, just a wide spot in the road. Kohl noticed everybody was getting out of their seats to get off the bus. Joss tried to ask some of the Filipinos why they had stopped, but they didn't understand English. The Marines exchanged glances. They were the only ones left on the bus and looked out the window as they saw the passengers relieving themselves. The women hiked up their dresses or dropped their pants and squatted. There was no effort to conceal them selves. After two hours of drinking beer, the bumps and curves encouraged Kohl and Joss to join the passengers to the bushes.

The bus continued toward Manila. It flew down the mountain roads with the horn blaring. At first Kohl thought it was to signal the village that the bus would be there to pick up passengers but he soon found out the bus was warning the village to get the kids, water buffalo, chickens and cars out of the street. The bus never slowed down. Non-stop to Manila.

Beer cans were now littered all over the floor and rolling from one side to the other. There was goat urine and chicken manure, crying babies and nursing mothers with sagging breasts. The beer had dulled their sense of fear and their sense of smell from the sweat, animal crap, and urine. The bus careened around corners, often on the wrong side of the road, with two hundred-foot drop-offs, no guardrails, over bumps that sent them flying into the air. They could feel the back end fish tail as it hit soft spots on the gravel road. The bus would honk and pass cars, trucks, carts, even around blind corners, even with cars coming the other direction, forcing many off the road. Apparently the right-of-way went to the biggest vehicle. Even with all the beer, their knees were weak when they finally got off the bus in Manila.

They staggered out of the bus terminal drunk, smelly, and sweaty then picked out one of the six yelling taxi drivers. Joss gave him his aunt and uncle's address. They didn't have a clue where it was.

The cab left the curb in a jerk, swinging across three lanes of traffic into the oncoming traffic, which was stopped momentarily at a traffic light, then careened back into his side of the road, weaving in and out of the slower moving cars. As the traffic slowed to a crawl, he weaved back into the oncoming traffic. With horns blaring, he crossed three lanes, went onto the curb. The pedestrians scattered like chickens with a fox in a hen house. Then back into traffic, around cars stopped at an intersection, back into his own side again. Neither Kohl nor Joss saw any thing after they first drove into the oncoming traffic. They were both lying on the seat with their hands over their heads. He finally stopped briefly at a traffic light. Actually, he just slowed down before he ran it. Joss reached up and grabbed the driver by the throat.

"Pull over! Pull over! Goddamn you! Stop!" Joss screamed at him.

"No hold up! No hold up! No money!" screamed the driver frantically, as he began to pull over to the side. "No money. Please. No money."

"We aren't going to take your fuckin' money," Joss yelled at him, but the driver didn't seem convinced.

"What you want then," the driver asked in a less frantic voice.

"We want you to slow down. Drive slower. Understand?" continued Joss.

"I lose money. Too much time. Have to hurry," said the driver. He said he was paid by the mile and the sooner he could get his fare delivered the sooner he could get another.

"How much will it be to take us where we are going?" asked Joss.

"Ten American dollars."

They gave him a twenty-dollar bill and told him to drive more carefully.

It was dark by the time they arrived. It was a two-story stucco, Spanish-style house trimmed with brick. Joss' uncle met them at the courtyard gate. They walked along a brick path; through vine-covered arbors and tropical plants of hibiscus, ferns, and Weeping Benjamina, and into a large open entry-way of glazed brown tile. All the while Joss' uncle chattered excitedly. His aunt greeted them in a brick archway off the foyer that led to the kitchen. She was small, about five feet tall and eighty-five pounds. She had black hair pulled back into a bun that accentuated her thin narrow nose. The uncle was as big as his aunt was small. He had thick red hair, freckles, and a ruddy rugged face. He was over six feet tall and built like a bull. They both looked fit for being in there mid-forties.

"Kohl, I'd like you to meet my Uncle Earl and Aunt Opal Witherspoon," said a smiling Joss.

"Pleased to meet you and I appreciate Joss's invitation. I just hope it's not an imposition," said Kohl. He had to make a special effort to pronounce his words because his tongue felt thick from all the beer they had been drinking.

"Not in the least, Lieutenant," said Opal. "We're glad you could come."

Kohl felt a little embarrassed. He and Joss were both drunk, plus they both looked and smelled terrible.

"I apologize, Sir, for our appearance. Our bus ride was quite an experience," said Kohl.

"If we would have known sooner, we would have driven over to pick you fellas up," said Earl apologetically.

"I know you would have Uncle Earl, but we didn't know for sure if we had the time to come down or not," said Joss. "Uncle Earl, if it's all right with you, could we get cleaned up a bit?"

"Sure. We have everything all set up for you. Carlos here will take your things and show you to your rooms," said Earl smiling. "After you've had a chance to get refreshed from the trip, you can join us out on the veranda."

They took showers, shaved and dressed for dinner. They each had nice clean comfortable rooms with windows that overlooked the back yard. The evening was warm and sultry. They came down the stairs together and Joss lead Kohl to the veranda where his aunt and uncle were sitting. They each had a tall drink.

"Can I get you boys something to drink?" Uncle Earl asked.

"What's that you have, Uncle Earl?" asked Joss.

"Maitai. Carlos makes a fabulous Maitai."

"That sounds good to me. How about you Kohl?"

"That would be fine if it's no trouble, Sir."

"No trouble and cut the 'Sir' crap," he grinned

"Sorry, Sir, I mean...."

"Earl. Just call me Earl. Well, well. Hi, sweetie," said Uncle Earl as he saw his daughter step out to the veranda.

Kohl and Joss stood up.

Kohl felt his heart thump and his knees got weak. She glided towards them. She barely touched the tile floor with her bare feet. Her long red hair cascaded over her shoulders and framed a freckled face and green eyes. Her fine delicate features were in contrast with her full red lips. She was wearing a long white cotton dress with thin straps over the shoulders.

Joss whispered, "Close your mouth, Kohl," and in the next breath, "Well, if it isn't my kissin' cousin."

"Don't you wish, Billy boy," as she took his hand and stood on her tiptoes and kissed his cheek. She turned to Kohl.

"May I introduce you to my Marine buddy, Dusty Kohl. Kohl, this is Wendy.

"My pleasure," Kohl said as he bowed slightly.

She made a small laugh. "Dusty Kohl?"

"My father thought it would be funny," said Kohl.

"I think it's cute," she purred.

"And so are you," Kohl added. *What, may I ask, are you doing? You are married. Knock it off.*

"Wendy, you sure have changed since I saw you three years ago. What year are you now?" asked Joss.

"I just graduated from high school and I'll be going to UCLA this September."

Carlos came out with the Maitai's.

"Daddy, can I have one too?" asked Wendy. Her words dripped with honey.

Uncle Earl gave her a glare and resumed talking with Joss. Wendy's neck splotched with embarrassment. She pursed her lips and went to the kitchen. When she returned she had a Maitai drink in her hand. She ignored her fathers glance and smiled at Kohl.

Carlos returned and told them dinner was ready. As they proceeded to the dining area, Wendy came up beside Kohl, slipped her hand onto his arm, and gave him a warm smile.

I'm married. I'm married.

The dinner was good American food, steak, mashed potatoes, gravy, and fresh green salad, with a fine red wine. After dinner they returned to the veranda and spent most of the time asking Joss how everything was back on the farm in Fallon, Montana. Out of politeness they asked questions of Kohl.

Wendy asked, "Daddy, can we take them out on the boat tomorrow?"

"I've been thinking that we would all go out tomorrow. What do you think, Opal?"

"Sounds fine with me. It's up to the boys though."

Joss said, "Sounds great. How 'bout it Kohl?"

"Fine with me."

"Oh, thank you, Daddy. I can hardly wait to show them our special beach," said Wendy excitedly.

Kohl left them to talk about family and walked into the garden below the veranda. The night was clear and warm. He lay down on the cool grass and fell asleep looking at the stars.

He heard something and woke with a start. Wendy stood looking down on him with her back to the house. The light showed through the thin white cotton fabric and silhouetted her legs.

"I'm sorry, Dusty. I didn't mean to startle you. We are retiring for the evening and I didn't think you intended to spend the evening asleep on the grass when you have a nice warm bed upstairs, even though you are a tough Marine." She laughed lightly.

"Just laid down to look at the stars and the next thing I knew, I'm dead to the world." Kohl got to his feet and stood facing her. *God, is she beautiful. I'm married. Can't forget that. Damn, I could crawl into those eyes.* "Sorry. I was staring."

"I know. I don't mind. I was staring at you too."

She took a step forward and stood with her head tilted up. Her lips were slightly parted. *It would be so easy to take her in my arms and kiss her. That's what she wants. Stop thinking with your dick.*

He scratched his nose with his left hand. "Shall we go back in?"

"If you wish." She sounded disappointed.

They walked back to the house and she slipped her warm tiny hand in his.

The next morning they had breakfast on the veranda and made plans for the day. The servants prepared the lunch baskets. They loaded up the Land Rover and drove the five miles to the harbor. Kohl was pleasantly surprised at the size of the boat. It was a thirty-foot Chris Craft Cabin Cruiser, with two Cummings diesel engines. Kohl couldn't keep his eyes off Wendy. She had on a long silk summer dress with a blue and yellow floral print. She was also making small talk and giggling at everything Kohl said, even if it wasn't funny. Both Earl and Opal showed mild concern over her attentions to Kohl.

They finished unloading the supplies from the Land Rover into the boat, had started the engines, and were beginning to heave to when they heard the Filipino servant yelling. He ran down the ramp to the dock and waving, trying to get their attention. He came to a stop next to the boat.

In panting breaths, he said, "Sir, Earl. The Marine Lieutenants have been called back to the base. They are to go back immediately." He looked at Joss and Kohl.

Joss said, "What did they say exactly, Carlos?"

"They asked for you, Lieutenant Joss. And when I said you were not here, they asked if I knew where you were and I said I did and they said that I was to tell you and Lieutenant Kohl to return to the base immediately because they were ... leaving."

"Leaving?" asked Kohl. *What is this shit? We were supposed to be in the Philippines for at least two weeks. In another five minutes, we would have been gone.* Kohl looked at Wendy, who was biting her lip in disappointment. *Boy, I wish I could have seen her in her swimsuit. Mmmm, mmm, mmm. Better yet. I wish I could have seen her without her swimsuit. My, my my. Ass and tits pokin' out all over.*

"Yes, Sir. That's what they said. That they were leaving."

"When were they leaving, Carlos?" asked Joss.

"They said 1400."

"Shit. That only leaves us with a little over three hours. Shit. We'll never make it," said Joss, obviously worried.

"I'll take you boys back to the bus station," said Uncle Earl.

"No, you don't need to, Sir. We can take a cab. You folks go on and continue your outing as planned," said Kohl.

"But it was for you," whined Wendy.

"Why thank you, Wendy. I really appreciate everybody's hospitality, even though it was short lived," said Kohl sadly.

"It was good to see you again, Uncle Earl and Aunt Opal," said Joss. "And always a pleasure to see my kissin' cousin." He gave her a wink.

Wendy followed them off the boat and walked about ten feet up the ramp.

Earl hollered at the retreating Lieutenants, "Say boys, let Carlos take you back to the bus station. Okay with you, Carlos?"

"Yes Sir."

Kohl purposely didn't look back until he reached the top of the pier, then he turned and waved. *I'm so fuckin' horny. I've been walkin' around all morning with a hard on. The muscles in her ass-cheeks could have cracked walnuts.* "Damn." He let out a big sigh. *God, was she beautiful.*

Joss was looking at Kohl and said, "Come on. Man, I could see where that was heading," as they continued walking towards the car. "You're married, or did you forget?"

"She made me forget everything. A stiff dick has no conscience."

"Well, in a way I'm glad we're leaving ... for both your sakes. I don't want to see Wendy getting hurt."

They caught the first bus out and it stopped at every village between Manila and Olongapo.

"Man, we're going to be late. There's no fuckin' way we're going to make it back by two," said Joss.

"Nothin' we can do about it, Joss. Not our fault."

"Yeah? Try explaining that to the CO."

They finally arrived back at Olongapo and caught a Jeepney to the harbor. The ships were gone.

They looked at each other not knowing what to do.

"I knew it. I Just knew it. This is out-fucking-standing," said Joss, exasperated as he looked out into an empty harbor. "We're fucked."

They knew that missing the ship was going to be very embarrassing. They walked over to the office of the harbormaster and he said that the USS Vancouver was still anchored out in the mouth of the bay and was sending the Captain's launch back for stragglers. Joss and Kohl were relieved that they were not the only ones. When they finally arrived at the USS Vancouver, they received catcalls and ribbing from the other Marine Officers.

Kohl followed Joss to his cabin where Joss changed out of his civilian clothes into the uniform of the day. In walked Wheeler and Krout.

"You guys picked a hell of a time to go sightseeing," said Wheeler smiling.

Kohl asked, "What the fuck is going on anyway?"

"Don't know. Somethin' must have happened in Nam," shrugged Wheeler.

Kohl asked, "How am I going to get back to my ship?"

"Transferred at sea," said Wheeler. "Saw 'em do it once."

Kohl did not ask how that was going to be accomplished but his imagination ran wild.

The Battalion Commander held a briefing that evening and Kohl found out the reason why they left in such a hurry,

"Ten-hut!" said the Battalion XO, Lieutenant Colonel Snell.

In walked the Battalion Commander, Colonel McGraw, a big man with a hawk nose and balding head.

"Be seated, Gentlemen. I have called you here this morning in an effort to keep everyone informed about the current situation in South Vietnam. Two days ago the Viet Cong attacked the U.S. helicopter base at Camp Halloway near the town of Pleiku. Nine helicopters and one transport plane were destroyed and fifteen planes were damaged.

"But that's not the bad news. They also blew-up the U.S. military barracks. Eight Americans were killed and one hundred and twenty-six were wounded. Our President has initiated retaliatory raids against North Vietnam. Because of the raids both China and Russia are threatening to intervene on the side of North Vietnam. Men, we've been pussy-footin' around the Commies too long. The sooner we land in Vietnam, the sooner we can start kicking some commie ass. I'm as frustrated as you are about floating around out here in South China Sea. I will do my best to keep you gentlemen apprised of the South East Asia situation. Keep your troops informed and continue your inspections and training programs. That'll be all."

"Ten-hut," said the XO. Then he added, "Carry on."

The officers shuffled out of the conference room.

"This is probably it, Huh?" commented Joss.

"Do you really think so?" asked Kohl.

"What do you think, Skipper?" Joss asked to the passing CO, Captain Vallenti of Lima Company.

"This is serious. Whenever US personnel are threatened, wounded or killed, we take it as an attack on the US government. We take swift and decisive action. Always have and always will. Nobody pushes us around. They'll pay."

"Do you think we'll land Skipper?" asked Kohl.

"I don't know. It depends on how effective the air strikes are. If they can cause North Vietnam and the Vietcong to rethink their military effort in South Vietnam, we probably won't go in. But I don't know. We just have to be ready, though, in case we do land."

Three days later, the tenth of February, they had another briefing and were informed that two Viet Cong, each carrying two fifty pound explosive charges, blew up another U.S. Barracks. This one in Quinhon. Twenty-three US personnel were killed.

It was also the day Kohl was going to be transferred back to the USS Union. *The Son-of-a-bitches would pick a day when the wind's blowing and the oceans like a churning caldron.* They shot a harpoon like gun with a rope over to the USS Union. The ships were about one hundred yards apart. The rope was attached to pulleys that hooked onto a metal chair. Kohl, still in his civilian clothes, was scared, plus he was starting to get seasick. He put on a life jacket and they strapped him in the chair. They slowly began pulling him towards the USS Union. With the ship's rising and falling in the swells, Kohl would zoom up one second and plunge down the next, almost touching the ocean waves. He felt at any moment he would crash into the sea. The chair swung back and forth worse than any roller coaster ride he had ever been on. The sudden drops and jerking motion took Kohl's breath away. The ship's rails were lined with sailors and Marines jeering, laughing, and yelling. Kohl's knuckles were white and his hands were cramped from hanging on to the heaving and rolling chair. His face was in a constant and very concerned grimace. After what seemed like and eternity, a sailor finally grabbed him. They had to pry his hands from the chair railings.

12 ... And In This Corner ...

As Kohl walked to his cabin he tried to control his shaking legs. He pulled back the curtain and saw Mays lying on his rack.

"Well, no shit. Did you finally decide to come back? Nice little roller coaster ride you had there, ol' buddy."

"I'll tell ya. That would have scared the shit out of me if my anal sphincter hadn't been clamped shut."

"How come they didn't send the Captain's launch over?"

"They said it was too rough. Besides, they said they needed the practice pulling that chair across. Lucky me, uh?"

"You sure know how to stretch a two day liberty into six."

Kohl changed into his khaki uniform. "Yeah, it was hard over there on the Vancouver, with it's air conditioned cabins and state room, where I could fraternize with my own kind."

"What happened anyway?"

Kohl told him about the trip to Manila but didn't mention Wendy. Nothing happened anyway. He told Mays about the Battalion Commander's briefing and what the latest scuttlebutt was. Mays walked with Kohl to get his mail and then went on to his cabin.

Much to Kohl's disappointment there wasn't any mail from Julie, only an inter-military correspondence from his Company Commander, Captain Heart.

1:DHB:njg
1900
6 Feb. 1965

First Endorsement on 1st Lieutenant Dusty M. Kohl's ltr. Dated 20 Jan. 65

From: Commanding Officer, A Company, 3rd Reconnaissance Battalion
To: 1st Lieutenant Dusty M. Kohl 086755/0302 USMCR
Via: Commanding Officer, 1st Battalion, 9th Marines

Subj: Early release for reasons of personal hardship; request for

1. Redressed and returned for resubmission with a request for additional information.
2. Please find your letter to the Commandant of the Marine Corps so enclosed.
3. The Battalion Commander has asked that I address the Battalion's concerns, that even though you may have a legitimate reason for seeking an early release, it is highly unlikely that such a request would be made at this time. We are asking that the Commanding Officer of 1st Battalion, 9th Marines review your request and make such recommendations to us since you are attached to his Battalion and your records are available to him.
4. However since your main concern is financial security and since your release dates are not compatible with the school semester, it is our recommendation that you request for an extension until June or July of 1966.

Captain F.A. Heart

Fucked again, Kohl. You're out here in the South China Sea about to land in South-fuckin'-Vietnam. You're not going to get out early. What makes you think that they are going to give you any breaks? You think you're going to get out of this whole thing unscathed? What planet are you living on? You are in for the long haul, ol' buddy. Get used to it.

That evening at dinner everybody had a good laugh at Kohl's expense. Kohl knew it was coming and had prepared himself for the razzing that was to take place. After all, it was all in fun, wasn't it?

"What time is it?" said Ensign Collins in a froggy voice of Buster Brown.

"It's How-Dee-Doo-Dee time," said JG Billings.

The Mickey Mouse man added, "You know it's hard. Marines are products of their intensive training. They get up when the sergeant rattles the trash can and go to sleep when it's lights out. Causes some very confusing moments when there isn't a trash can around."

"Why don't they use a watch?" asked JG Billings.

"They would just get confused with all those numbers," said Silverman.

"Here Lieutenant. We all chipped in and got you a gift," said Ensign Collins. It was wrapped in bright green wrapping paper.

Kohl said thank you, smiling, knowing it was another effort at fun. He unwrapped the small box and opened it. It was a watch that they had changed the face to look like a sundial.

"Why thank you," Kohl said.

"We thought it might be easier for you to read," said the Mickey Mouse Man.

I really don't like that guy.

"There's an instruction sheet, Lieutenant."

Kohl unfolded a small piece of paper. He read it out loud for their enjoyment.

"Only good when sun is out."

"That's the bright round thing in the sky," continued Billings.

Lieutenant Commander Hangerber cleared his throat and the ribbing stopped. Kohl finished his meal in good humor.

After dinner Kohl went back to his room to write a Valentine poem to Julie.

With a lonely heart I did roam,
looking for a loving home.
One to treat it kind and gentle,
to give that something kind of special.

'Twas in December, 'long 'bout evening,
when your eyes sent my heart reeling.
Next to your heart it snuggled there,
to live forever in your loving care.

But to keep a love that's been so true,
Just to make sure you still do,
Can I ask, if you don't mind?
Will you be my Valentine?

He folded and tucked it into an airmail envelope. Licked the flap, but he was thinking of December as he walked to the galley for the mail drop.

*

The next day, under clear, blue skies and a calm sea, the ship stopped. The Captain launched his boat and threw out some rafts and buoys so the sailors and troops could go swimming. The sailors and Marines tried to out-do one another diving off the side of the ship. Before long there were sailors and Marines holding up scorecards for each of the dives. The ship had a Boatswain's Mate who could do beautiful flips, with twists. The Marines only had a couple of crazy guys that didn't know anything about diving but would try anything. PFC Woods was one of the crazies. He would jump off and start spinning, ten or twelve times before he would hit the water. When he landed on his back, on the third dive, they pulled him unconscious into a boat. The Marines cheered and gave him tens. The afternoon was followed with a bar-b-que on the fantail. Everybody seemed to have a good time.

After the bar-b-que, Kohl was walking back to his cabin when he saw Silverman, the Mickey Mouse Man, walk out. He smiled and nodded to Kohl as they passed in the passageway. Kohl had assumed he was in his cabin to see JG Billings, his roommate, but he was not there when Kohl entered. Something caught his eye. He turned, stopped, looked at his desk. The picture of Julie. There was something wrong. *Those fuckin' sea-maggot bastards.* Kohl muttered through clenched teeth. His eyes filled with tears as he picked up the picture of Julie. Somebody had drawn, in black grease pencil, a penis in her mouth. He quickly grabbed a moistened towel and rubbed it so hard, he broke the glass. Shaking with rage, he burst outside to get some fresh air. He took in great gulps of air until he slowly regained his composure. Even though he couldn't prove it, he had a feeling "the Mickey Mouse Man" probably did it.

On February sixteenth, with the USS Union floating three miles off the Coast of Danang, South Vietnam, Kohl heard rumors that they were going to land. No date was given. President Johnson had started the bombing of

North Vietnam the raid was called "Rolling Thunder." Adding to the uncertainty of the situation was the South Vietnam's President General Khanh's government had been overthrown. Now there was conflict between the ARVN troops. The government was in turmoil.

Since returning to the USS Union, he had been with his troops every morning at 0500 on the fantail doing PT before breakfast. He spent the rest of the day reading military manuals, conducting classes, sunbathing and writing letters. He spent a lot of time thinking of Julie and waiting for the mail, which was having a hard time catching up with the fleet. It had been fourteen days since they had mail call. They watched the latest movies like 'The Music Man,' and "Two For The See-Saw." He and Mays were sent in the Captain's launch to the USS Hanricko for a 1/9 briefing. They were told that there were ten Chinese Divisions on the North Vietnam border. From reading and listening to stories about how the Chinese entered the Korean War, Kohl did not relish the thought of having to fight the 'yellow horde.'

Kohl found out on the eighteenth of February that they were going back to Okinawa on the twenty-eighth and would arrive on or about the fifth of March. It was apparent that they were not going to land after all. He had mixed emotions. He had convinced himself that he could be in a position to make a difference. He was proud to be a Marine and an American.

The next morning at breakfast, Kohl walked in while Lieutenant Commander Hangerber was expressing his concerns about the crew's slow and lackadaisical attitude during General Quarter's drills. Sitting at the table with the XO was Ensign Murray Silverman, Lieutenant Junior Grade Steve Hanover, Lieutenant Junior Grade Tom Billings, Ensign Bill Collins and Mays.

"I would like to know what happened to the ear protectors that are supposed to be at the gun turrets, Murray?" Hangerber asked as though exasperated.

"Sir, I found two of them down in the engine room. Tom's people must have been using them for ear muffs."

"They were not using them as ear muffs," protested Billings. "I don't know how they got down there. You're just trying to cover your butt, Silverman, because your guys lost them."

"We didn't lose them. Your men stole them," Silverman shouted.

"Sir, that's not true. And Sir, that isn't all we're having trouble with. Since it's been so hot at night, the men have been hiding the porthole covers so during General Quarters the port holes won't be covered," complained Billings, trying to deflect the blame from himself onto someone else.

"But it gets hotter than hell down there in the hole. The sailors and Marine troops don't get any air down there. Besides I have been assured that they have kept all the lights out," said Collins glaring at Billings.

"You can't use that as an excuse, Bill, for Christ sake! Just one lighted cigarette or a match can be seen for miles. You know that," Hanover argued.

"How do you know, Steve? I haven't seen your ass below topside in a month. I think you forgot how fuckin' hot it is down there," yelled Collins.

"You had better watch your language. You're way out of line, Ensign Collins. You had better think of the consequences before you spout off something you'll regret," threatened Hanover.

Lieutenant Commander Hangerber kept clearing his throat, but nobody was paying attention while the Navy officers were yelling at each other.

"I'm not afraid of you, Steve."

"Well you'd better be, you skinny little prick."

"Gentlemen, please?" said the Ex O.

Mays scooted his chair back, dabbed his mouth with his napkin, yawned and stretched as he rose and said, "Well, Collins. You sure scared the hell out of me. See how I'm shaking? I must say, it's been a charming and glorious morning with you idiots." They stopped yelling for a brief moment with a shocked look on their faces, as Mays wheeled and left.

"He can't say that and get away with it, Sir," protested Silverman.

"Well, he has a point," answered the Lieutenant Commander.

"I don't see the Marines busting their ass around here," chimed in Billings.

"The Marines don't have anything to do with what we're talking about," said the Lieutenant Commander. "They have other things to worry about."

They were all glaring at Kohl as he got up to leave. "Excuse me, gentlemen. I had better go work on my tan."

*

"You won, Kohl. You won."

"Who are you?"

"I'm 'The Big General In The sky'."

"What did I win?"

"Come on, guess?"

"Naw, tell me."

"Just guess, come on."

"Skates?"

"Skates? Why would you think you had won skates?"

"I don't know. Always wanted a pair of skates. The good ones. You know with the plastic wheels and that stopper thing on the front."

"Well, it's not skates."

"Tell me then, I give up."

"Come on. Think of something else."

"A trip home would be nice."

"Nope. Sorry. That wasn't included in the cruise package."

"Quit playing games with me. I'm tired of playing your stupid games."

"Well, they're your games too, you know."

"Well, I don't want to play any more. So tell me. What did I win?"

"Why Lieutenant, you have won another forty-three days on board the luxury cruise ship, USS Union."

"That doesn't sound like fun to me."

"It's not that bad. Your vacation cruise could be worse, ya know."

"Well pardon me if I'm not jumping with joy. And what, may I ask, am I going to do for forty-three days?"

"Look at it this way. In your spare time..."

"That's all I have is spare time."

"You can practice doing nothing. You can watch the ship rust. You love doing that. You could count waves and see if the seventh one is always the biggest. Nothing is the best thing to do when there's nothing to do."

*

Kohl and Mays were lying on the sun deck when Kohl broke the silence and said, "Mays, something's happening. Either I'm becoming paranoid or..." Kohl shook his head and continued. "I've been noticing things, small things mostly. Those guys and how they act, things they say... that I don't quite hear or understand. Things coming up missing or moved. It's weird, hard to explain. Do you see it, or am I imagining things?"

Mays was picking his nose and trying to flick a big brown piece of crud from his finger that he had excavated.

"For Christ's sake, Mays," Kohl pleaded.

"I'm listening."

"No, that's not it. Here. You're fuckin' disgusting." Kohl threw him a towel. "Well?"

"Well what."

"What I just said."

Mays shrugs.

"Come on. Am I imagining this or what?"

"Personally I think they're a bunch of pricks, trying to get your goat. You're too easy going. Shit, I don't know. Grin and bear it." Mays gave Kohl a false grin with clenched teeth.

"You're a big help, asshole."

"Besides the French harp and the picture deal, what have they done?"

"I don't know. Like I say it's hard to explain. I walk into the galley and it seems like they stop what they're talking about and change the subject. Or make remarks. I haven't had one long conversation with any one of them and I swear I've tried. I'm telling ya, I'm not this way. I usually could care less. I get along with everybody."

"Listen Kohl, we're short timers. We only have to put up with this military bull shit a few more months. Just keep focused. It doesn't matter. You've got more to look forward to than most of those Navy queers. That fat Jew, Silverman knows he's getting to you. Don't let it show, man. Remember Quantico. Like water on a duck's back. Besides if we do land, things could get a hell of a lot worse than being on board with these yo-yo's."

"You're right. I'm over-reacting. I'm just getting fed up with now we land and now we don't. This is horse shit."

"Don't sweat it, man."

"Oh what the hell. Like you say, who gives a big rat's-ass anyway."

Mays got up to leave and turned, "Like my sweet departed Mother told me once. She said, 'Son, shit's always brown.'"

There was a long pause. Kohl thought there was more words of wisdom coming. "What's that supposed to mean?"

"I think what it means is that no matter how hard you look and wish it was a different color, it's always brown, except baby shit which is sometimes green but that doesn't count."

*

Hi Sweetheart,

I say to myself that it's a good thing being out here because of all the money I'm saving. It's for sure I can't blow much out in the South China Sea. We just received word today that we will remain here for forty-three more days. So that means three more pay days. No lie, we are going around in fifteen-mile circles. It makes me laugh. I can't believe it myself. Of course you never know what will happen. Our extension out here didn't appear to be because of any emergency or anything that I'm aware of. However, you are probably getting a lot more information than I am, that's for sure.

By the time I get back stateside, I'll be a big, strong, tanned, good lookin' stud. I might even be pretty good at the French harp.

The only thing I don't like about staying on this rust bucket is that the tempers are getting shorter and there's not a whole hell of a lot to do. You can imagine how I feel because you know how I like to walk and roam around. Well even with all this space around me, I feel trapped.

It's 1:30 am. We had our weekly Sunday steak barbecue on the fantail today.

I bet you're relieved that I'm out here because you know, at least, I can't get into trouble.

I love you, baby. Miss you more than I can bear sometimes. Time seems to just crawl by.

Love always,
Dusty

*

Kohl was working out with his platoon every morning. He was sunning himself in the afternoon doing push-ups and chin-ups and was starting to gain back the weight he had lost when he was seasick. He got a letter from his folks and his Dad even wrote some, which was unusual. His little brother wanted to know what it looked like out here. He wrote back that it looked blue.

He gave the platoon an assignment to write their autobiography, all in an effort to get to know them better, plus give them something to do. Some of the troops turned in the assignment but Corporal Ford told Kohl that some of the men could not write very well. So Kohl said those who wanted to write could and those who didn't feel comfortable writing could talk to him personally.

Kohl read the personal history reports from Ford, Marseilles, Spallenski, Thompson, and Schultz.

Corporal Ford was from a tough neighborhood in Oakland, California. His father was a Baptist minister and ruled the Ford household of seven children with an iron hand. Ford liked the Marine Corps and wanted to make it a career. Navy Corpsman Marseilles was from Fort Brag, California, where his family ran a small fishing fleet. After his tour he wanted to finish college. PFC Spallenski was from New York where his father owned a pub in the Bronx. Kohl had heard he was street tough and complained about everything, getting his name of 'Bitchin' Benny.' PFC Thompson was from Chisholm, Minnesota. He was an all conference tackle. He didn't write much. He said he had lived a 'pretty boring life.' Kohl had talked to Ford about his concern of his weight. Ford said he worked out, was strong, and ate like a horse. PFC Schultz was from Athol, Idaho and the driver of the communication's jeep. When Kohl asked him where he was from he told him he was from Sandpoint. He wanted to go to college after his tour was up.

Lance Corporal Grant was the first platoon member Kohl interviewed. He was from Portland, Oregon, 21 and married. He got his GED in the military. He took his job of squad leader very seriously.

"I might stay in the Corps, Lieutenant. They say if I reup, I'll get a bonus plus my choice of three duty stations. My tour will be up in May and then I'll be stationed stateside for the next three years."

The next Marine Ford sent up to Kohl's cabin was PFC Woods from Sayer, Oklahoma.

"Shit, Lieutenant. I was on my way to juvy when the Juvenile Court Judge gave me a choice to either join the Marines or go to jail. I chose the Marine Corps."

"May I ask what you did to get in trouble?"

"Beat the shit out of my Step-Dad, Sir. The cocksucker. Excuse me, Sir. He was a drunk and beat my Mom. So, I worked him over with a baseball bat. Hit him as he walked in the door from work. Bamm! Right in the fuckin' face. Home run."

Kohl had read Woods file and found that he had been kicked out of school so often that he quit going after the eighth grade.

PFC Flowers, from Birmington, Alabama, was the next one up. He was happy go lucky, always smiling and helpful. He was married and had two children and was only 20. He had gone to a segregated school and had little association with white people. Kohl felt he intimidated Flowers. He talked in a slow, careful manner, always respectful, but with down cast eyes.

"What was it like going to a segregated school?" asked Kohl.

"I don know, Su. Dat's juss da way et was."

Next to talk with Kohl was Private Harris. Of all the men in the platoon, he was the most physically prominent. At six feet four inches and over two hundred and twenty pounds, he held a commanding presence. Nobody in the platoon bothered him except PFC Woods, who wasn't afraid of anything or anybody. Harris played fullback for North High in Denver. He had hoped to get a college football scholarship but his SAT scores were not good enough.

When Lance Corporal Sale came to talk to Kohl he just sat in the chair answering, no Sir and yes Sir. He was one eighth Arapaho from Cedar Pass, South Dakota. He lived most of his life on the Pine Ridge Indian Reservation.

He attended the Chemawa Indian School in Salem, Oregon. He was very quiet. He said he was married and had a child but did not live with them. He said his wife's father ran him off and that was when he joined the Marine Corps.

Kohl couldn't help but smile every time he saw PFC Hernandez. He was the platoon clown. He was from Salinas, California. He had eight brothers and sisters who all worked in the fields with his parents. He joined the Marine Corps on his 18th birthday because he wanted something more than working as a migrant in the fields.

PFC Charlotte was from the logging-mill-town of Yreka, California. He had run away from home when he was 16 and ended up in juvenile hall in Sacramento for grand theft auto. He also was given a choice of Marines or jail. Like Woods he chose the Marines.

Lance Corporal Beach was from Dimmit, Texas. He said it was so boring there, he just had to get out. He also would like to make the Marine Corps a career. He boxed amateur at a Boxing Club in Amarillo.

Kohl had a difficult time talking with Private Handle. He slouched in the chair and his remarks were contemptuous, as if to say, "Don't waste my time." He was from Compton, California, had never made PFC in the two years he had been in the Corps. He had been in the brig twice once for insubordination and the other for drug possession.

"It appears that you don't like the Corps, then why did you join?"

Handle rolled his eyes under the heavy eyelids and said, "I joined on a dare. Five more months and I'm out-a-here."

PFC Thorogood always had a wide grin across an equally wide brown face. He was from Darien, Georgia. His great-grandfather was full blood Cherokee. He was married and couldn't wait to get back home to fish and hunt along the Altamaha River and crab in the estuary.

"My uncle Zeek, see, has this swamp buggy. Well we can take that thing anywhere we want, almost. In the summer me and my cousins spend days out there on the river and never go home hardly. Man, we have so much fun swimmin' and fishin'. Lieutenant, you'd love that place. I can't wait to get back.

"I've got four Uncles that live up by Pine Harbor and."

"Excuse me, Reb. But I've got a meeting with the Captain in about ten minutes, so..." *Liar, Liar. Pants on Fire.*

"I understand, Sir. It seems I get talkin' about home and can't stop."

*

After Thorogood left Kohl let his mind drift playfully into a vision of four years ago at his Grandfather's farm in the Sierra foothills.... *He smiled as he stood underneath a big maple. The white billowy clouds let through enough warm sun to evaporate the sweat that had collected on his forehead and upper lip.*

Sometimes his brother didn't want to come, Kohl walked too fast, and it was difficult for him to keep up. Kohl usually left him lagging behind in his haste to get to where he was going. He always liked this old maple. Even as he got older, he still enjoyed climbing the moss-covered limbs.

Walking through the barley fields gave his little brother hay fever. Kohl could barely distinguish his blond hair from the golden barley swaying in the afternoon breeze. His brother stopped to pick bachelor buttons that usually wilted or got smashed before he could get them to Grandma. He would get to playing and would stuff the flowers in his pocket. He always seemed surprised when he would pull out the matted leaves, stems, petals, and dirt. Kohl smiled as his brother walked up the trail, pulling up his pants to keep the legs from dragging in the dust. He squatted down in front of him and admired his already wilting flowers. The dust had collected on the sweat around his white mouth and red cheeks. He was breathing with difficulty but tried not to show it by taking slower and deeper breaths. And when he breathed Kohl could hear the rattling wheeze. His brother didn't say anything about Kohl leaving for the Marines the next day nor about the pain in his heaving chest.

*

The latest letter Kohl received from Julie was pervaded with concern for his safety. She was taking a Current History class at Fullerton State and was beginning to see the danger lurking in Vietnam. She wrote, "I don't know what I'd do if I never saw you again." That statement was a real shock to him. The thought of not returning home had never occurred to him. Kohl was currently fifteen miles off the coast of Vietnam and she probably knew more about what was going on than he did. He wrote and told her that they were probably exaggerating about a war. That it would be too much for the United States to risk. "I'll never have to set foot in Vietnam. Mark my word," he wrote.

*

USS UNION (AKA-106)
FLEET POST OFFICE
SAN FRANCISCO, CALIF.

PLAN OF THE DAY FOR MONDAY, MARCH 1, 1965

OOD WATCH LIST
08-12Lt. J.G. Hanover20-24 Ensign Silverman
12-16Ensign Silverman00-04 Lt. J.G. Billings
16-18Lt. J.G. Billings04-08 Ensign Collins
18-20Ensign Collins

MCD: 2ND DIVISION

Carry out the daily underway routine except as modified below:

0700Rendezvous with Task Force Group 76.6 CONPHIBRON ONE and staff transfer from Henrico to Lenawee. Commanding Officer, USS Union designated as OTC.
1230Rendezvous with USS Platte.
1300Station lifeguard detail.
1330Station the refueling detail.
1400Refuel
1500Refuel completed.
1800Task Group 76.6 detached.
SunsetDarken ship.

NOTES

1. LTJG Billings will distribute cigars today. LTJG Hanover will distribute cigars tomorrow.

P. J. Hangerber
Executive Officer

*

Kohl had just returned from a briefing on the Vancouver with the 1/9 Staff and the word was that the Battalion was going to land at Danang in two days, March 4th. They said the landing would probably be unopposed, but there could be demonstrations, such as rock throwing, spitting and maybe some sniper fire. They were told that the Viet Cong were slowly encircling the city and the Battalion would be used to protect the airfield at Danang. They gave Kohl and his platoon wills to fill out. The filling out of the wills had a detrimental effect on the cocky attitude of Kohl and his troops. The "I don't think we'll land" theory, along with the other theory of "nothing is going to happen to me," were beginning to look rather precarious. The letters he received from Julie were getting more frantic. He wrote that the news probably exaggerated the situation. He said he had the real scoop and that he was not in any real danger.

Kohl had always had a private concern about not having a Staff Sergeant for his platoon. The platoon TO called for a Staff Sergeant but he had felt that as long as they were floating around out in the South China Sea, Corporal Ford could handle the job. Now with his platoon landing and conducting patrols for the Battalion, he wanted the experience and guidance of a veteran Sergeant. So he requested that Recon Battalion send him a man as soon as possible.

The next two days were busy. Kohl briefed his platoon and held inspections of their 782 Gear, rifles, radios, and other supplies. Kohl wrote letters to everybody. He couldn't tell them they were landing. He was told that the planes from Danang Air Base had bombed Hie Pong Harbor. The rumors were spreading like wildfire and the latest was that the Viet Cong would retaliate by attacking the airfield at Danang. He also heard that the ARVN forces were in disarray and airport security a joke.

*

The landing on the fourth of March was called off. It was now a day later. The USS Mount McKinley joined the Task Force that night. It had come in from Subic Bay and had the Fleet Admiral and Marine Corps Chief of Staff. Kohl and officers from the other ships were taken to the McKinley for another briefing.

As Kohl and Mays were being transported to the McKinley on the Captain's launch for the briefing, Mays said, "It looks like this is the real McCoy this time, ol' buddy."

"All the big mucky-mucks are chompin' at the bit, I bet."

"How 'bout you?"

"Not, me. And you?"

"I don't care one way or another. Of course, I'm not going to be snooping and pooping around in the bushes like you. So it's different I guess."

As the officers shuffled into the briefing room and took their seats Task Force Commander Colonel McGraw said that it looked like they were going to land for sure a couple of days ago, but it was unlikely now. Kohl let out a sigh of relief. *I knew they wouldn't do it.*

Kohl felt emotionally drained upon his return. He briefed the troops of the latest on again, off again saga. When Kohl came topside he began shaking uncontrollably. He looked at his trembling hands. *What the fuck's wrong with me?* He sat down on the deck with his back against the bulkhead, with his head in his hands. He closed his eyes and listened to the rumble of the ship and the crashing waves. Control. He had to be in control. *Deep breathes. Calm down. Come on. Get control.* But he was not in control. His emotions were being jerked and pulled from an emotional high one moment to a depressing low the next. It was like getting ready for a football game, putting on your uniform, warming up, waiting for the opening kick and then having the game called off. Not just once, but time and time again.

*

"I've got my gun and I'm ready to rumble. Where is everybody?"

"Uh, Sir? Nobody's here."

"We were supposed to have a war. You know, bombs, tanks, planes and stuff."

"I know, but you're the only one here, Lieutenant."

"Am I the only one who got the word? What happens if nobody shows up?"

"I guess we can go home, Lieutenant. Can't have a war if nobody shows up."

*

Kohl left the deck and was on his way to the galley for a glass of milk when he saw Silverman and Collins leaving the evening officer's mess. They were laughing as they walked toward Kohl.

Kohl's throat choked dry and his heart felt like it was trying to break out of his heaving chest. As Silverman approached, Kohl bounced to his right, dropped his left shoulder, and dug his left fist into the soft-relaxed stomach of Silverman. He watched Silverman's eyes bulge in shock of the attack as the air whooshed from his lips. *In the dream his stomach felt softer.* By now, Kohl's right fist cracked against the Ensign's left cheek. He felt pain run up his forearm. *In his dream he's supposed to fall. He isn't falling.* Kohl hit him on the side of the head with a left hook and watched his head bounce off the wall. Silverman's eyes were still wide and he couldn't catch his breath. Then Kohl hit him with a straight right to the bridge of the nose. Blood splattered. Silverman's knees buckled and Kohl hit him two more times as he slid down the bulkhead to the deck. It was all over in less than five seconds. Kohl stepped back from the crumpled Silverman. Collins had turned around and took a few apprehensive steps toward Kohl. Mays was there first and grabbed Kohl but it wasn't necessary, he was finished.

"...and the winner is Lieutenant 'Don't Tread On Me' Kohl," Mays said as he raised Kohl's arm. "You don't look so good Silverman," he added casually.

Silverman was gasping for breath and was being tended to by Collins. Collins stood up and faced the Marines. His lips were pursed and his hands were clenched at his side.

Mays laughed at the tall, skinny Collins. The laughing changed suddenly into a frozen grin, "You so much as fart and I'll break your skinny little fuckin' neck."

"Just let it be, Collins," said an approaching Hanover. "Go get the Doc."

Silverman moaned and threw up. His face was beginning to swell. Blood was running from his nose, mouth, eye, and ear and from the back of his head.

Lieutenant Commander Hanberger had heard the commotion and was walking swiftly down the passageway, followed by Billings. He looked at Silverman then at Kohl. His mouth was set in a thin line and he cleared his throat. Between clenched teeth he told Kohl to go to his quarters, that he was under ship's arrest. Kohl nodded and walked to his room. His hand hurt. *I wonder if I broke it.* A guard was placed outside his cabin. *Where in the hell am I going? I'm a prisoner anyway.* Kohl remembered William Bendix saying in 'The Life of Riley'; "Well this is a fine predicament I've got myself into." His roommate came in, glared at him, got some of his things, then left.

About an hour later, Kohl answered the knock on the bulkhead and the Captain's Orderly came in smartly and told him he was to escort him to the Captain's Cabin. Kohl was led by the Orderly and followed by the Guard to the Captain's quarters. The Orderly knocked and opened the hatch and let Kohl in. The Captain came in off the bridge, removed his hat, and lit a cigarette. "Sit down Lieutenant," he said in his usual calm soft voice. He pointed to a chair. The Captain remained standing, leaning against his desk. He looked out the window into the darkness for a long time before he spoke.

"You may think I'm up here confined in my cabin and the bridge, that I'm isolated as to the goings on of the ship. Well I'm not. Not only does my X O, Lieutenant Commander Hangerber, keep me informed, but also I am constantly aware of the pulse of the ship. After all I am the Captain. It's my job. I know most of the enlisted men on my ship by name and especially the Officers. I know you too, better than you think. I think I know what happened and I know why." He turned from the window, looked at Kohl, and sat down in an easy chair across from him. "You may not understand my actions, but I have my reasons and it's not what you probably think. Your behavior was reproachable. You inflicted extensive damage to Ensign Silverman. However, I will not proceed any further than our discussion tonight." *What? Did I hear him right?* The Captain got up, walked to the open hatch, lit another cigarette, and looked out the window. "You're a good man, Lieutenant. You made a mistake. It appears that this was an isolated incident. There is a tremendous strain on everyone right now.

"You will remain confined to your quarters. Your meals will be brought to you. You can continue to hold training sessions for your troops. You will not be allowed visitors. This will be an oral reprimand. Nothing will be made in writing. No entry will be made in your personnel file. This incident never happened as far as I'm concerned. The ship's crew has been told that the Marine Task Force Commander will handle the incident. You must never reveal what we have discussed this evening." He turned and looked at Kohl and said, "I am confident that you will not make me regret this. That will be all, Lieutenant."

"Aye, aye, Sir."

Kohl was totally confused. He had expected at least Office Hours, and a letter of reprimand. He expected to be brought up on charges of aggravated assault. He could have lost his commission with a dishonorable discharge.

Well that was one way to get home early.

Knock it off you dumb fuck. That's the last thing you need, to go home in disgrace.

Why did the Captain do that? Does he know something that I don't?

You don't need to know, Kohl. You're off the hook.

The weather had changed. It was raining and the wind was blowing. Kohl asked the Guard to go get the Doc, he was starting to get seasick again.

"Well how's Joe Palooka doing?" said Doc as he entered.

"I just need some Dramamine, Doc. How's Silverman?"

"I had him sent over to the Hanricko. You broke his nose and I think he had a concussion."

"Will he be all right? I swear to God, I don't know what happened to me."

"Yeah, he'll be fine. Here. Let me look at that hand."

Kohl held up his swollen hand. He winced as the Doc pushed at the bruise on the top.

"Might have a broken hand here, slugger." He let out a small chuckle. He wrapped it with an Ace bandage and said, "Happy landings, Kohl."

Happy landings. What did he mean by that?

Kohl spent all the next day in bed and wished privately that they would land so he would not be sick any more.

*

It was 1200 hours on the seventh of March when Lieutenant Commander Hangerber pulled back the curtain to Kohl's cabin and said, "We got word. Land the Landing Force."

"Oh shit! For real, Sir?"

"For real," he answered. The XO stood in the doorway for a few seconds and looked at Kohl.

"When do we go?"

"We start off-loading at 0400. Your troops will be in the second wave and will start off-loading at 0600."

"Well, this is finally it. No turning back now, is there, Sir?"

"No turning back."

"I'm sorry, Sir. I apologize for what I did to Silverman. I don't understand what happened. I..."

The XO sat down in the only chair in the cramped cabin and held up his hand to quiet the stammering Kohl. "Lieutenant." He cleared his throat, and said, "Two things come to mind. I could see it in your eyes, that you were very uncomfortable on board ship. Am I right?"

"Yes, Sir."

"It's not an uncommon feeling. Being on board ship takes some getting used to. The confined quarters and confinement to the ship for long periods of time gives some people claustrophobia. Even with a large expanse of ocean around us, some people get the feeling of being trapped."

"All I know, Sir, is that I feel uncomfortable."

"That's a claustrophobic symptom, as well as shortness of breath, a pounding heart beat, sweating and so on. The other thing is that you have been under constant turmoil. Worried about what's going to happen. The uncertainty of it all. Whether we were going to land or not, can't help but take an emotional toll on you. The Navy officers feel the same, except we are not faced with the danger that you may be facing." The XO stood up. "Be careful, Lieutenant. I pray to the good Lord that our political leaders know what they are doing." He let out a big sigh and added almost to himself, "But.... I have a funny feeling about this whole Vietnam thing." He walked to the hatch and held out his hand and Kohl grabbed it in a firm handshake. "God be with you," he said and added with a grin, "Silverman was an asshole anyway."

PART II
DANANG

Salt Water Cowboy
By
Redd Evans

Who is that great big wonderful man,
wearing that fine coat of tan?
He's a Salt Water Cowboy
with the whole world for his range.
Just a Salt Water Cowboy
and the herd he rides is strange.

He's a roundin' up his country's foes
where ever they may be.
He's a Salt water Cowboy.
A United States Marine.

Git along little nippy,
I can hear my singing pal.
I'm takin' you to pasture in a barbed wire corral.
He's the salt of the earth boys
And he's long and lank and lean.
He's a Salt Water Cowboy
A United States Marine.

Git along suki yaki,
Sang the man from the golden west.
I'm gonna brand your carcass with a star striped U.S.
Oh! You don't have to worry.
He will keep your pastures green.
He's a Salt Water Cowboy
A United States Marine.

13 Land the Landing Force

Kohl went below to give the troops the word, then went back up to his cabin and packed. At about 1500 hours he and Corporal Ford passed out body armor, gas masks, ammunition, hand grenades, radios, and three days C rations. The convoy moved closer to the proposed landing site. They were about eight miles out now. It was raining, with wind blowing and heavy swells. Kohl was nauseated. Land was starting to look better even if it was Vietnam. After inspecting the troops, he reviewed the landing procedures.

"Okay men. Let's go over a few things. Just a quick check," said Kohl.

There was a moan from the troops.

"When we get the word, we will assemble on the port side of the ship and form in a column of threes. We will be in the second wave and will probably be asked to set up LP's and OP's somewhere around the perimeters of the landing area. Now the first three over the side will be Ford, Thompson and Harris."

Kohl wanted the biggest and strongest men down in the landing craft first so they could hold the cargo net out and away from the side of the ship.

"When we disembark over the side, what are some of the things we should remember?" Kohl asked.

PFC Spallenski responded, "Keep your helmets unbuckled."

"And why is that Ski?" asked Kohl.

"Because, Sir, if you fall into the ocean you could brake your fricken neck," he added.

"What else?"

"When you're climbing down, don't look down," said Harris.

"Good. And,"

"And, when you're down, don't look up," said Harris.

"Keep your hands on the vertical ropes," said Hernandez.

"And why is that," asked Kohl.

"To keep lard ass Thompson from stepping on your fricken fingers, Lieutenant."

The men chuckled.

"Keep abreast," said Schultz.

"Good. That's good. Now listen up. We've done this many times before; it's no big deal. You men can go get some rest now. We probably won't get much for the next couple of days, at least. I anticipate that we will disembark sometime around 0600. I'll make sure you get plenty of time to prepare. Good night."

Mays was the Embarkation Officer. Besides Kohl's recon platoon, there was a squad of motor transport personnel that would be on the same LCU (Landing Craft Unit). Mays had to see that all the Marines and their gear were ready to off-load and in the proper order.

"What did I do to deserve this shit. I probably won't get any sleep tonight," he complained.

"You've been fuckin' around here now for two months with nothing to do and now that you have to start earning your big GI bucks, you start whining," said Kohl sarcastically.

"Fuck you. I hope you're the first Marine casualty."

*

Kohl awoke with a jerk as he bolted upright in his rack. He heard another bang against the side of the ship. It was 0400. It was beginning. He got up and dressed. Topside, he could hear men yelling and swearing. He was the only one in the officer's mess, until Lieutenant Commander Hangerber rushed in and told Kohl they were to disembark at 0630. It was now 0500. He finished his breakfast and notified the troops.

Topside was a frenzy of activity. Running, yelling, noise of winches, banging, blinding lights. It was chaos. They were off-loading an LCU as the ship was rocking port to starboard. With the LCU suspended from a boom, the craft swung out then back, banged into the side of the ship. "Keep the guide ropes tight! God damn it!"

The LCU crashed into the side of the ship again, this time knocking the rudder off.

Kohl noticed that one of the two LCU's in the water was taking on water and the bilge pump could not empty it fast enough. It soon sunk out of sight.

"We lost that one. Son-of-a-bitch," yelled the Boatswain's Mate.

They finally got the LCU into the water but it was useless without a rudder. They were now lowering a Mighty-Mite jeep into the one good LCU, when one of the sailors lost his hold of one the guide ropes, the jeep started to spin, and wrapped the other rope around the cables. As the jeep twirled, it hit the side of the ship and scraped paint from the side and broke off the front fender. When it stopped spinning, it started unwinding the other way. Seeing that they couldn't get it into the LCU, they brought it back up on deck to try again. There was a lot of cussing and screaming going on. Kohl was fascinated at how unorganized everything was. Here it was, the real thing. This was not a practice. This was what everybody trained for.

This looks like the fuck up from hell. What a grand and glorious day this is going to be.

Mays looked at Kohl and shook his head in disbelief. They called for Kohl's Platoon to disembark. Out of the eight LCU's in the water, four were afloat and capable of movement. Kohl's men formed a column of threes with Ford, Thompson and Harris in the lead. These three strong men would hold the net out from the side of the ship and keep it taunt, as the LCU would rise and fall in the eight-foot swells. Kohl would be last. He would follow the squad from Motor Transport.

By the time the recon platoon was down, Ford, Thompson, and Harris were exhausted fighting the eight-foot swells. They had been struggling with the rising and falling LCU, trying to keep the net tight and doing the job well. Kohl yelled down for three more Marines to relieve them. Grant, Flowers and Woods took immediate control as the Motor Transport personnel began to climb down the nets. Though all Marines practice climbing down cargo nets, most of the practices were on dry land. For the Motor Transport men this was a major ordeal. They were having difficulty timing the jump from the net to the pitching LCU. There were three at the bottom, three in the middle and three just climbing over the side. After two of the three at the bottom jumped into a rising LCU, the third Marine misjudged. By the time he started to step off, the LCU rapidly descended. He hesitated and turned to his left. He lost his grip with his left hand and the weight of the pack, rifle, and flack jacket caused his upper body to fall backwards. Luckily his right foot caught in the net keeping him from falling into the ocean or onto the side of the LCU. The flat-bottomed boat rose and hit the side of his head. Blood spread across his face. He tried to reach and pull himself into a pike position when the LCU rose again and hit him in the back. He cried out in pain, lost his grip again and fell back against the cargo net.

"Help me," he moaned.

"Keep the net tight!" Kohl yelled.

Grant and his men were doing their best to keep the net taunt.

"You men! Get off the net! Climb back up! Now!" commanded Kohl.

The jerking and tossing LCU rose and hit the Marine on the shoulder and the side of his head. He hung limply from the net. Blood was dripping from the top of his head. More men where holding the net but as the LCU rose again, there was a surge of water that swung the LCU away from the ship and as it swung back and up, it trapped the fallen Marine between the side of the LCU and the ship. Kohl was already over the side and heard the crunch of bones. Ford and Harris where now on their way up. Harris reached the Marine first and with his powerful right arm he lifted the limp Marine out of harms way just as the LCU was rising again. Kohl had a rope and tied it under the Marine's arms. Ford untangled his foot and they began to pull him up. The ship's doctor had arrived and gave instructions to those sailors who were handling the unconscious Marine. They placed him on a stretcher and took him to sick bay.

The rest of the men were loaded without incident. The accident played silently in Kohl's mind. The horseplay and comic chatter of the men was noticeably absent. They gazed into their hands, each with their own thoughts of the unknown, of fears both real and fantasy.

The LCU joined those from the Hancock and Vancouver and rendezvoused in a circle to make up the second wave. One of them was taking on water, so the LCU that Kohl was on pulled up alongside and took aboard an anxious rifle platoon standing in a foot and a half of water.

It was 0830 as the LCU's pealed off to form a straight assault line toward the beach. Kohl was crouched at the front of the LCU with his back against the side. The Second Lieutenant, of the platoon they had just picked up, stood and looked through the peephole in the landing ramp. His eyes were wild. He licked his lips and looked at Kohl. Kohl smiled and nodded.

"Lock and load!" shouted the Second Lieutenant.

The recon platoon looked at Kohl questionably. He nodded. Ford answered with instructions to lock and load. The men stood up, slammed the magazines in and sent a round home. They buckled their helmets, adjusted their packs and flack jackets.

The Second Lieutenant returned from the front viewing hole to the front of his platoon. His breathing was quick and shallow. Kohl wondered if he might hyperventilate and pass out. The Second Lieutenant's Sergeant was squatting comfortably in the back and giving reassuring pats to the troops to his front.

The amphibious tractors, that Marines called "Iron Coffins," rolled out of the water onto the beach. Kohl could see the men run off the ramps in the back onto the beach. The second wave was about two hundred yards out. He didn't hear any firing, which he thought was a good sign. The LCU's were at full throttle. At about one hundred yards out the LCU jolted to a stop and the ramp dropped. The young and eager Second Lieutenant bolted upright and headed to the front of the ramp and stepped off into the ocean and disappeared. His sergeant yelled for him to stop but he didn't hear over the engine noise. As his platoon walked cautiously forward they turned to look as the yelling sergeant told them to stop.

Kohl gave a sign to his platoon to wait. The troops moved forward into a position to disembark. With the weight of the troops in the craft moving from the back to the front and with the help of another wave the LCU was lifted off the sand bar and continued toward shore.

Kohl stood up and said, "I don't know what to expect but let's give 'em hell and good luck."

The LCU roared toward the beach and came to an abrupt halt within ten feet of the shore. Kohl, his troops and the other platoon stepped off the ramp into six inches of water and ran yelling war cries, up the beach to the tree line and fell into the sand.

They lay in the sand. Something was not right. Kohl heard music. To his left he noticed the Marines who came in the Am tracks were walking around with civilians. He stood up to get a better look.

"What's going on, Lieutenant?" asked Ford.

"Damned if I know. Do you hear music?" asked Kohl.

"I think so," answered Ford.

"I'm going down there," he pointed," and find out what's happening."

As Kohl walked down the beach he began to see Vietnamese waving along the tree line. He was soon met by a lovely young girl who put a lei around his neck and said, "Welcome American Marine." He was speechless. As he continued toward the sound of music, he saw a platform with dignitaries, and South Vietnam Army Officers welcoming the landing Marines with hand shakes and hugs. A large banner read, "Welcome Gallant Marines." The band was playing the 'Marine Corps Hymn.'

This sure isn't Guadalcanal. What kind of war is this?

Kohl walked up to a Major who was climbing out of a jeep with a Shore

Party insignia on it.

"Good morning, Major," said Kohl.

"Morning, Lieutenant. Can you believe this shit?" asked the Major.

"What's going on?"

"Just got here. Flew us in this morning to take care of all this shit," he said as he waved his arm.

The LCU's continued to land and off-load troops, who milled around at the surprising welcome. LCU's with equipment and supplies were starting to pile up and needed to be off-loaded.

"We could use some help. Got an outfit?" the Major asked.

"Yes, Sir. Doesn't look like there's anybody to fight at the moment."

"I'll get it cleared through your commanding officers. Try to line up some more men for me, okay?"

"Sure."

Kohl walked back to his troops through a swarm of activity. He wasn't prepared for what was happening around him. He was glad that there wasn't any resistance, but he still felt a let down. Dressed to kill and prepared to fight. *Are you complaining, Kohl? Disappointed are you? Let's get your priorities straight here, ol' buddy. Number one, you're off the fuckin' boat. Two, you're not dead.*

Kohl told Ford to find a place to stockpile their gear, leave a two-man guard, and then take the rest of the platoon and report to Shore Party. He then found the Platoon Sergeant that had landed with them.

"My name's Kohl, Sergeant."

"Chambers, Lieutenant," he said as he stuck out his hand.

"What happened to your Lieutenant?"

"I don't know. We should have seen him swimmin' around out there by now. Don't you think, Lieutenant? It was just out there, wasn't it?" he said as he pointed.

"Yeah. I think so."

"Think he drowned? The LCU went right over the top of him." Then the Sergeant added under his breath, "The dumb little fuck." He looked at Kohl. "Sorry. I told him." The Sergeant shrugged. "I'd better go find the Company Commander and tell him what happened. Maybe they can send out divers or something."

"Hey, Sarge! Look!" yelled one of his men pointed towards the surf.

Something was floating in the rough sea about seventy-five yards out. It was hard to tell what it was. Kohl and Sergeant Chambers ran over to the nearest LCU and pointed out the floating object to the Coxswain. The LCU left with the sergeant and one of his men to investigate. Kohl called Ski to bring his PRC-10, so he could call battalion and tell them what was going on. Ford had his binoculars on the object in the ocean.

"Can you tell, Ford?" asked Kohl who was now in radio contact with Battalion Headquarters who were still on board ship.

"Can't tell, Lieutenant."

The LCU was alongside the object now and Ford was giving Kohl a description of what was happening.

"They're pulling something up, Sir. It looks like a body, Sir."

Kohl saw a Mighty Mite jeep heading towards them, dodging Marines, gear, and equipment. It looked like medics. Kohl waved them down. The LCU ran up onto the beach much further than normal. He'd never get off now. As the ramp fell, Kohl saw Sergeant Chambers holding his Lieutenant in his arms. Kohl, Medics and the small band of Marines ran up the ramp into the LCU.

"He's dead," said Chambers.

The medics checked him, put him on a stretcher, and tied it to the back of the jeep. The small group of Marines stood watching the jeep drive off.

Kohl and his platoon spent the next two days and nights unloading equipment and supplies from the LCU's into trucks. The beach was littered with LCU's and vehicles that were stuck in the sand. Aluminum matting was brought in to help keep the trucks from getting stuck. A forklift was trying to get an LCU off the beach when the prongs broke through the front and now were both stuck with water pouring into the LCU.

On Kohl's first night in Vietnam he ate a can of cold chicken noodle soup from his "C" ration pack and tried to find someplace to get a little rest, but with a cold steady drizzle and sand fleas he didn't have much luck.

*

The day after the landing, Kohl found Mays scurrying around trying to get trucks unstuck. Mays told him that they had the first Marine fatality yesterday. The Marine on the cargo net had died from internal bleeding. He said the Doc couldn't handle it and because of the rough seas they couldn't land a Chopper to take him to the hospital in Danang.

"The Doc fuckin' panicked," said Mays disgustedly. "You know, I think he may have been drunk. He was going fuckin' nuts. Hands shaken'. Cryin'. Shit, Man. The kid just laid there and bled to death and Doc didn't do shit!"

"I think the, 'I've-got-it-made-theory', just went out his port hole. Don't you think?"

"Fuckin' A."

"We had a brown bar jump off the front of our LCU yesterday. He's dead too," said Kohl.

They stood in silence for a while looking at their boots.

Mays broke the spell, "Hell, the VC don't have to worry. We'll just stay here on this fuckin' beach and kill each other."

With most of the equipment and supplies off-loaded, Kohl and his troops were taken by truck to the Danang Air Base. On the way, they passed under banners that said, "The Vietnam People Welcome Marines." Along most of the route people stood and waved and yelled, "Ello".

Kohl was surprised at how many South Vietnamese troops there were. It seemed every young male was in uniform. They were small and thin. The women, for the most part, were attractive. They wore silk pants with wide pant legs and long silk jackets with high necks. Most of the houses looked neat and well cared for but had fences made of barbed wire. Home sweet home.

Kohl's outfit camped in an open area and immediately erected pup tents. Soon after they arrived, choppers started bringing in more troops. There was a fenced in field next to their camp and Sale, Charlotte, and Woods were standing, talking, and looking at the cows in the field. They were like miniature light brown Brahma's with a slight hump on their front shoulder with small horns. They only stood about four-foot high. Woods hollered for Spallenski from the Bronx to come look. Ski climbed out of his pup tent.

"What?"

"Come 'ere and look at these things," Woods yelled.

Ski walked over and with eyes wide in surprise said, "I've never seen one of those son's-a-bitches up close before."

They gave him a questioning look.

"What are you talkin' about".

"A damn deer. Never seen one up this close before," said an excited Ski.

"Deer? They ain't no damn deer. Hey, everybody! Ski saw a deer," said Charlotte who was from Yreka, California where he had gone deer hunting every fall since he was ten.

Ski realized he had said the wrong thing and his face started to get red. "Well how in the hell am I supposed to know what a friggin' deer looks like, you assholes." But it was too late now.

Thorogood walked up and in his southern drawl said, "I'll be damned. A New York deer right here in Vietnam."

14 Hill 327

The First Battalion Ninth Marine's Operations Officer, Major Krinshaw, found Kohl and asked if anyone in his platoon had sketch capability. He wanted to have them go to the top of Hill 327 and sketch the terrain. Kohl said he had troops who had the ability. He gave Kohl a French map and showed him where Hill 327 was. Kohl could sketch some and asked if there were any artists in the group. Flowers said he could draw.

"I don't mean stick figures here, Flowers. We have to sketch the hill up there."

"He can draw, Lieutenant," said Grant confidently.

"Okay. Grant, get your team saddled up. Schultz, you'll drive us up to the base of the hill and drop us off. Take rifles, noon chow, soft covers and, Ski, you come too with the Prick 10."

Kohl still did not know what to expect. There had been some VC sniper fire but nobody seemed too concerned. *They must not be good shots. The Marine Corps sniper squad, with their single shot bolt action Springfield rifles hit what they aimed at. Damn sure.*

Schultz dropped them off at the bottom of the hill and was told to return in four hours.

They took a trail up the side of the hill. It was steep and took them an hour to get to the top. He and Flowers sat down and started to sketch. From the top, looking east they could see Danang, the airport and sticking out on a peninsula was a mountain called Monkey Island. To the north, they could see the beach where they landed and a river surrounded by salt flats. To the south was another large river called Riviere de Tourane, a large expanse of coastline and a mountain called Marble Mountain. There were no trees on hill 327, just brush. It was a beautiful view, ribbons of streams and rivers white puffy clouds, white beaches, and a blue ocean. But most astounding to Kohl were the rice paddies. He had seen pictures in National Geographic and he had seen the large rice paddies in the Sacramento Valley, but it was nothing like what he saw in the valleys below. The whole valley floor was divided into small contoured mosaics of green. To the west where highlands.

What a lovely place to have a war.

*

It was March 12th; the sun shined hot when First Battalion Ninth Marines started up the hill. They marched through a community called Dog Patch. The children along the way chattered and clamored for cigarettes and candy. They would grab the hands of the Marines as they waved and patted the heads of the kids. But soon many found their rings and watches gone. The children would feel and pull the hair on their arms because the Vietnamese didn't have hair on their arms. Bulldozers were already cutting a road up the side of the mountain. The objective was to secure hill 327. Kohl's platoon was to secure hill 181, which was where the battalion headquarters was going to be. They were to set a perimeter to the north of the ridge. From the battalion's vantagepoint they would be able to protect the airfield in Danang. When Kohl's platoon got to the top of hill 181, they began to clear a helo pad. Then they set up their area of perimeter security and assigned teams their areas of responsibility. They also started to dig foxholes.

At the Battalion briefing Master Sergeant Blacksox walked up to the front of a hastily erected CP tent and addressed the officers gathered. "Gentlemen, you may remove your bars, or, if you want, put them under your utility lapel. It will not be necessary to salute. For you officers who haven't been in combat, I'll explain a few things. This is guerrilla warfare. The enemy will pick the time and the place to attack. And it will be mostly hit and run. Snipers are already shooting at us, but it appears to be mostly harassing fire. Charlie will try to shoot the officers, the radio operators and your corpsmen. You can't do much to hide a PRC-10, but you can help protect yourself by removing your bars and having the corpsmen remove their Red Cross arm bands."

Battalion Commander Colonel McGraw added, "However, military protocol and gentlemanly standards will be maintained." *Does that mean I'm going to have to continue to kiss your ass, Colonel?* "Everybody has been given their areas of responsibility. Keep your men alert. None of those little commie bastards are going to hit the airport during my watch. Understood?"

"Yes, Sir," they said in unison.

There was one hundred percent security the first night on the hill. That meant every Marine along the perimeter was awake. It wasn't any secret, everybody was spooked. It was just a matter of degree.

The next day they worked on their two man bunkers, filling sandbags and digging into the side of the hill. The platoon was able to sleep a couple of hours before the second night of one hundred percent watch.

Kohl's platoon sector was to the north about fifty yards from the battalion helo pad. Every time a chopper would come in they would run for cover. The dust would fly and cling to the sweat on their skin and clothes. On the third day on the hill, the chopper brought in another platoon from Third Recon. Battalion. Kohl, along with some of his men, went up to meet them and he recognized Second Lieutenant Spade. The men from his platoon saw some of their friends from Camp Schwab. They were in support of 3/9 that had joined 1/9 on the hill. Along with Spade and his platoon was Kohl's new platoon sergeant he had requested.

Kohl was sweaty, smelly and dirty as he walked up and shook Spade's hand. Spade's eyes were darting around.

"Welcome to Hill 181, Spade. Your area is over there," pointed Kohl.

"Hello, Kohl, this is Staff Sergeant Fontain, your new platoon Sergeant," said Spade.

"Glad to meet you, Sergeant," said Kohl. "Good to see you again, Spade." *You fuckin' gung ho brown bar.*

"Well, I'd better go report in. I'll talk with you later, Kohl," he said as he hurried off in the wrong direction.

"Spade, it's this way," pointed Kohl.

Kohl turned to the Sergeant and said, "A little excited, isn't he?"

"With all due respect, Sir, but you'll have to excuse me. He liked to have drove me bug shit. He wouldn't shut his mouth, the whole flight over here. I almost threw him out the back end of the GV."

"I know what you're talkin' about, Sarge. He met me at Kadena Air Base when I first got to Oki. He droned on for a solid hour on our drive to Camp Schwab. And, you'll have to excuse me ... we haven't had much of a chance to get cleaned up. Sarge, this is Corporal Ford. He has been the platoon sergeant and has done one hell of a job just getting us to this point. Ford? Gather the men. Hernandez? Take the Sarge's gear and stow it, please."

"Yes, Sir. Lieutenant."

Kohl introduced Sergeant Fontain to the platoon. As with anybody new, they observed him with a skeptic eye.

"I'll accompany you to the CP," said Kohl.

Sergeant Fontain barely came to Kohl's shoulder. He had a slight build. But the feature that stood out was his handlebar mustache. It stuck straight out to the sides of his face to a fine point. He had clear blue eyes and a long, sharp nose. After Kohl got him checked in they went back to Kohl's unfinished bunker and sat on the sandbags and looked over the valley to the north.

"I'm glad you're here, Sarge. Corporal Ford is a good Marine and has done a great job, but I need experience, Sarge. I can't take chances with these kids. I think I've got the makings of a good outfit. You, of course, will know better. I just want you to know that I'm not one of those know-it-all officers. I know my limits and my abilities. I only have about eight months to do in the Corps and I'd like to go back alive. Cover my ass, will you?"

The Sergeant had listened quietly, nodding his head and looking out across the valley. "Was just a kid, like these boys, scared half to death, when I found myself in Korea, Lieutenant. I know how they feel. I won't let you down, Sir. If you'll excuse me, Sir, I'd like to go and get acquainted with First Platoon St. Joe Alpha Company."

"Oh, by the way Sergeant, we have our first patrol tomorrow morning at 0400," said Kohl.

*

Reveille went at 0200. It was still hot and the mosquitoes were waiting for the Marines to crawl from their mosquito nets. Just putting on his clothes made Kohl break out in a sweat. He thought he might be sweating because of his nervousness. He groped around in the dark trying to find everything he needed. He had spent a lot of time thinking about how this patrol should be run. He didn't want anything to go wrong. He wondered if there were really VC out there or was it just jumpy troops firing at animals and strange noises and shadows the last two nights.

He had to inspect the platoon in about a half an hour to double check that everyone was ready to go. Now that Sergeant Fontain was here, he felt some of the pressure relieved. He heard the platoon up above getting ready, checking out the PRC-10's, filling canteens, receiving their ammo and grenades.

The night before Kohl had told them what was expected of them. They were to recon the hills and gullies to the front.

Front? You mean, to the west or to the north?

I guess so.

So, you mean that to the east and to the south is secure?

Well, to the east is Danang. It looks safe. I don't know about to the south.

So, what you're saying is the front is to the west, north, south, and you're not sure about the east.

Have you noticed that up here on this hill, we are in a three hundred and sixty-degree perimeter? That should give you some kind of a clue.

Kohl's Platoon was going out with Wheeler's platoon. Wheeler's outfit was to provide protection and to clear a helo pad while recon conducted patrols. The word was that VC were in the area and recon would try to confirm that information. Kohl's platoon had moved out and was now on top of Hill 327 where they were joined by Wheeler's platoon. They heard an occasional round go off and the pop of an illumination 81mm mortar round that sent out a brilliant light. Kohl realized that, yes;Americans really do have a fear of the dark.

Flares, the American nightlight. Who sees who anyway? I bet the VC see more than we do.

Wheeler said, "How you doin' buddy boy? Havin' fun yet?"

"My butt is so puckered, I haven't been able to take a crap for two days", said Kohl. "Sure is dark," he continued.

"Wonder what's out there?" Wheeler asked.

The only camouflage Kohl's platoon had was carbon paper and Tough Skin. Woods was giving Harris a bad time because he put carbon paper on his lips.

"Ready?"

"Ready."

"Lock and load."

The sound of the rounds entering the chamber of their M-14's filled the silent night. They passed through "Jake's Outpost." It was now 0400. Wheeler's platoon was in front. As they walked along a trail on top of the mountain ridge, the column would stop periodically and send out a fire team point. In the dim light of distant flare, he could see the bushes move. *Monkeys? Goats? VC?* Kohl tried to keep his men spread out without losing eye contact with the person in front. This was hard because it was very dark. Every time the column would stop Kohl's men would face out in opposite directions. They had been walking for about forty-five minutes when they stopped briefly and moved out again. For some reason Kohl felt his back was exposed. He looked to his rear and couldn't see nor hear

Corpsman Marseilles. Nobody was there.

I can see it now. Recon on it's first mission, lost half of its platoon in the dark.

Kohl heard them over a little rise.

Oh, we're recon all right.

"Where did they go?" asked the frantic Corpsman.

"Shit Doc. I should have known a fuckin' squid would get us lost out in this fuckin' country..."

"Sshhh listen. I think I hear them over there."

Doc came panting up to Kohl. "Sorry, Lieutenant."

Kohl hit him as hard as he could just below his left eye. Doc staggered back against Lance Corporal Sale.

Damn that hurt. Kohl shook his right hand. The same one he broke when he hit the Mickey Mouse Man.

"What was that for, Sir?"

"That was for not paying attention," said Kohl as he seethed in anger. Then he hit him again. This time Doc crumpled to the ground. Sale helped him up. Kohl's hand was throbbing now.

"Jesus, Lieutenant. What did I do now?"

"That was ... for ... just because, that's all. Just because. You, God damn, stick to me like you're trying to butt-fuck me. Got it?" There were a few giggles.

"Yes, Sir. Got it. Ain't going to happen again."

I really can't blame him much. 'Keep interval.' we always say. 'Don't bunch up.' But with it so friggin' dark, you have to be within reach of the guy in front because you can't see.

At 0700, Kohl dropped off his first three-man patrol of Ford, Beach and Thompson. They were to patrol the finger to the south and explore a patch of woods that overlooked the battalion lines. S-2 thought if there were VC, that's where they would probably be. About a mile further along the main ridge, Kohl sent out the second patrol consisting of Grant, Woods and Ski. They would recon a ravine to the south. The third patrol, of Sale, Hernandez, and Schultz, were to follow a trail to the north.

Kohl saw a prominent rock about fifteen feet high off to his left. He walked over, climbed the rock and look around. He couldn't resist. The rock drew him like a magnet.

Oh, there's a rock. Climb it.

"Lieutenant? I wouldn't do that if I were you," said Sergeant Fontain.

"Why?"

"You stick out like a sore thumb."

He's right you know you dumb fuck. Get your ass down. You aren't back home deer hunting. Here the deer shoot back.

Kohl climbed down and said, "You're right, Sarge."

Sergeant Fontain got a call from patrol number two and told Kohl that first patrol was surrounded by VC and were being chased back up to the top of the ridge. Kohl called in the patrol that he had sent north and contacted Wheeler for backup. Sergeant Fontain tried to contact patrol one, but nothing.

"Probably down in some canyon," said Sergeant Fontain.

As soon as the third patrol was in, they retraced their trail back to the place where they had dispatched the first patrol. Kohl thought they could go to the west of the drop-off-point and out-flank the VC, but the brush was so thick they had to turn back and continue along the ridge.

"This is where we left them," said Kohl.

As they stood silently, bushes started moving to their front and right side. They all saw it and immediately hit the deck in a three sixty pattern, with weapons all pointing out.

"Hold it. It could be the patrol," cautioned Sergeant Fontain.

Or it could be a whole company of VC. Shit.

Just then they saw Beach cautiously enter the clearing at the top of the ridge. He saw the Lieutenant's signal and headed for the perimeter. He was followed by Thompson, then Ford.

Ford ran crouched over and scooted next to Kohl.

"How many?" asked Kohl.

"Bout ten, maybe."

"Where are they besides up there?" pointed Kohl.

"I think they're all around us," said Ford.

They heard talking and saw more moving bushes. Wheeler's platoon had by now formed a scrimmage line along the ridge. Sergeant Fontain threw a grenade at some moving bushes to the front as Wheeler's platoon moved forward for the sweep through the area. There was some sporadic automatic rifle fire into some of the bushes.

Always liked playing hide and seek. Oli, oli, oxen free! Come out; come out, wherever you are. Everybody home free. I give up.

"Keep contact with your flank," yelled Wheeler's sergeant.

Kohl and his platoon watched Wheeler's platoon walk through the area. Nothing. Gone. Disappeared.

"Where in the hell did they go?" asked Kohl.

"You sure it wasn't just monkeys, pigs, or whatever goddamn animals they have over here," asked Wheeler excitedly. He was still pumped from the activity.

"No. I heard gook talk."

Kohl and his platoon went back to the CP area by the rock and Wheeler's platoon went back to their task of clearing a helo pad.

Kohl asked Ford what happened.

"Sir, after you left us, we went down the ridge and as we got near the bottom we stopped at the edge of the trees and watched a group of five men in black PJs talking. In order to get a better look Beach climbed a tree. Then Mat just happened to glance to the side and saw a man in khakis run from some brush, across a small clearing into some more bushes." ***Khakis could mean North Vietnamese Regular Army.*** "I don't know if they knew we were there or not until we started seeing movement all around us. I tried to reach you on the 'prick-ten', but nothing. Then we got hold of Grant's patrol. I wanted to get the heck out of there but by the time Beach was down out of the tree, he started taking off his clothes."

"Fuckin' ants all over me," complained Beach who had his pants down around his ankles. He was exploring his crotch for ants. "These fuckin' little buggers bite like hell. Gotcha, you lil-son-bitch. Man you ought to have seen lardass climb back up that hill, radio, and all. Shag ass is what he did. Shag ass."

"I noticed you weren't too far behind there, Beach," said Thompson.

"Anyway," continued Ford cutting off the bickering, "we would move, they would move. We'd stop and they would stop."

"I saw one run across in front of us with a carbine, Lieutenant," said Beach.

"We finally got on top of the ridge here and we expected them to start rushing us. Then we saw you guys."

"Fuckin' ants are in my butt crack. Little bitty sneaky devils."

"Ants?"

"No. The VC."

15 *Shadows in the Dark*

The shooting started about 2300. Kohl sat in his bunker and stared into the black night, watching a few flickering lights down in the valley. He had constantly warned his men about shooting at noises, shadows and moving bushes. He told them, "Don't shoot. It will give away your position. If one crawls into your blanket then you can shoot. But even then I'd prefer that you use your "K" bar. Silent. Remember?" The sporadic shooting went on most of the night with an occasional flare. He heard some M-50's open up. That wasn't supposed to happen either. He thought that maybe they were shooting at a real enemy this time. In the night, alone, the imagination has a way of creating its own nightmare.

About 0400, Kohl saw the Battalion medical vehicle leave the CP area and head up towards hill 327. He was heating his "C" rations over a can of sterno when the med. truck came back down the hill. About an hour later Sergeant Fontain called down to tell him there would be a staff meeting at 0930 in the Colonel's tent.

It was about 0800 when Kohl saw Mays walking up the dusty road. Every time his foot hit the fine powder, it would send out a cloud that floated in the still morning air. "Heard about the meeting?" asked the approaching Mays.

"Yep," answered Kohl.

"Did you hear what happened up on the hill last night?"

"No." Pause. "Are you going to tell me or am I going to have to wait for the meeting? I'm assuming that's what it's all about. Am I right? Was all that shooting coming from "K" Company? Did they get hit last night?"

"In answer to your questions, yes, yes and no. I don't know all the details. But, last night one of Joss's fire teams that was manning OP number four, had been firing at noises and shadows all night. This one hundred percent security shit is starting to get to the troops. Well anyway, about 0330 the men at OP number four heard something not far from the front of their foxhole. Three of them crawled out of the fox hole to investigate."

"Oh, shit! You gotta be fuckin' kidding."

"I'm not kidding, pud pounder. You would think they would know better. But anyway, after about fifteen minutes the guy that stayed in the foxhole heard something to his rear. Scared shitless by this time, he whirled around and emptied his 22 round clip into his three Marine buddies."

"Oh, my God! No!"

"One had three rounds through the stomach. Dead. The other was shot in the head. He's dead. And the third was shot through the arm and leg. He'll live but will probably lose his arm at the elbow."

"The troops are going to have to get some sleep, Mays, or this shit's going to happen again. There's no need for it. How many days has it been now? Seven isn't it? These troops have to get some rest. We just got here, for Christ's sake. And no tellin' how much longer. Is anybody telling the Colonel this? He was in Korea, wasn't he?"

"Yeah, but you know how that goes. He figures if he's up all night, everybody else has to be up too. Do you have your men all set up for tonight's patrol?"

"And that's another thing. We go out on patrol. Come back and work on our bunkers then go on watch. Is there something missing from this picture? Huh?"

"Hey, don't go jumpin' my bones."

*

The patrol consisted of Grant's and Beach's squads plus Sergeant Fontain. It was the first joint patrol with ARVN troops. The patrol was to follow a road along the base of hill 327 to the outskirts of a hamlet called Phuoe Li. There was a curfew after dark. Anyone seen outside their home was considered VC. Kohl was in the S-2 tent with Mays when they got a call from the joint patrol.

"Cobra two, Cobra two. This is Zebra, over." Kohl recognized the voice of Schultz.

"Zebra. This is Cobra Two, over," answered Mays.

"Cobra Two. This is Zebra. Our partners will not proceed. Over."

Kohl looked questionably at Mays and asked, "What the hell's he talkin' about? Is he saying the ARVN's have stopped?"

"Zebra. This is Cobra Two. Say again, over?"

"Cobra Two. This is Zebra. Wait one."

The radio hissed in static.

Schultz came back up on the radio, "Cobra Two. This is Zebra. To proceed with the mission may not be possible. Over."

"Zebra. This is Cobra Two. What is your nearest checkpoint? Over."

"Cobra Two. This is Zebra. We are five hundred meters north of Check point Bravo. Over."

Major Krinshaw walked in and said, "What's wrong?"

"I think the ARVN's have quit or stopped. I don't know for sure," answered Mays.

"Why?" asked the Major.

"Don't know, Sir."

"Well, find out."

"Yes, Sir."

"Zebra. This is Cobra Two. Over."

"Cobra Two. This is Zebra. Over."

"Zebra. This is Cobra two. Why won't partners proceed? Over."

There was a long pause. More static. Then came the voice of Sergeant Fontain. "Cobra two. This is Zebra two. Not able to respond to your last request. Over."

"Sure. That's right. He can't tell us over the radio that the ARVN's are afraid of the VC. Show me on the map where they are?" asked the Major. Kohl pointed out there position.

"They've gone far enough. I don't want to cause a major incident here. Call 'em back."

"Aye, aye, Sir," said Mays.

At about 0200 the patrol walked into camp. Kohl asked Sergeant Fontain to join them in the S-2 tent.

"What the hell's going on, Sergeant?" asked the Major angrily.

"Sir. I really don't know exactly. Everything was going fine until we hit checkpoint Bravo. I noticed that the ARVN squad was starting to lag farther and farther behind. I stopped the patrol and asked the interpreter what was happening. So he went back to where they were sitting. I heard them talkin'. They had squatted down alongside the road and lit up their cigarettes. I couldn't believe it. In about ten minutes the interpreter returned and told me they wouldn't go any further."

"Why?" asked the bewildered Major.

"Because ... Well, the interpreter said that they didn't want to go any further because there might be VC up ahead."

"Well, shit. That's the point isn't it? No wonder we're here. For Christ's sake. I can't believe this shit. Come on Sergeant. You've got to tell the Colonel about this. I can't believe it," the Major said muttered to himself as he and Sergeant Fontain walked out of the S-2 tent.

Kohl was proud of the way Sergeant Fontain handled himself in front of the Major. He was confident and self-assured. Kohl liked him. He was soft spoken, which was hard to believe since he was a DI at Perris Island. His light-blue eyes were almost gray. But he had sternness to his gaze, and Kohl had seen that icy stare on a couple of occasions.

*

20 March, 1965

Dear Julie,

I lose track of the days so easily. One day is just like the rest. I have a chance to write now that is if nothing happens.

It's 10 o'clock at night and I have my bunker fixed good enough so no light can get out. My troopers made me a desk and I have a real chair. They brought me some candles too. I have a place that is about five-foot high, four foot wide and five foot long. I'm sorry I haven't written lately. I just couldn't.

So here I am in Danang, Vietnam. Settled into a sandbagged bunker with bushes all around me and a beautiful breathtaking view of the valley below of green rice fields and a blue harbor. I bought a small transistor radio and I can listen to the Grand Ol' Opry on the Armed Forces Radio out of Saigon.

I got three of your letters today. They smelled so sweet. I've got them under my folded up field jacket that I use as a pillow.

Huh oh. I hear Captain Fellows talking to one of my recon men. He's standing post. Probably giving him shit about something. Every chance he gets, he's always coming around ragging on me about something. I think he's bored. He's a little weird. The other day he said it would tickle him to death to be able to hear a VC scream if he threw a white phosphorous grenade at him. I tell you he's crazy. People like that can fight these friggin' wars.

I hear mortars going off now. Shooting illumination because somebody thinks they hear or see something. These poor kids end up half the time shooting at shadows. My men though are pretty good about keeping their cool.

They just got back from running a combat patrol about six miles from here. They said they wounded a couple of VC, found the blood but said they were either carried or crawled off into the brush. When they got back I had beer waiting for them that I got down at the airstrip. They were tired. Two days without sleep.

The other night I heard on my little radio Harry Belefonte sing "Green Grow the Lilacs" and I went into a hundred dreams of you.

Last night one of my men, PFC Thorogood from Georgia, got a Dear John letter. His wife wrote that she had filed for divorce. All he could say was "I can't believe it." It really shook him up. He's a great kid, smart and good looking. I asked Captain O'Riely, our Battalion Chaplain to talk with him. You don't want some kid going off shooting himself or others over something like this.

This thing we're in over here is not all that it's played up to in the States. They probably think we are fighting tooth and nail. The only reason we're here is because of some political thing that I'm not fully aware of. We should be leaving in a couple of weeks though, at least by the end of March. The VC doesn't want anything to do with the Marines. So far they have been staying clear.

I miss you so much. These first three months have been long. What's depressing is I've got six months to go. So I'll sign off for tonight. Tomorrow is Sunday but it could be Tuesday for all I know. All I want is you. I love you so much. It will be another honeymoon when I get home and then I won't ever leave you again. Promise.

I love you sweetheart,

Dusty

*

"Howdy, Sergeant Higgens," Kohl said to the approaching Marine. They shook hands. The Sergeant had been a Mortar Platoon Sergeant in his old Battalion at Camp Pendleton. He had the same billet now.

"Howdy, yourself, Lieutenant," he drawled.

"Say what was happening up on the hill last night? Had a hell of a time trying to catch some shut eye," said Kohl smiling.

"Aw, gee, Lieutenant. Really sorry 'bout that. Hate to see the Lieutenant lose his beauty sleep," said Sergeant Higgens, returning Kohl's smile.

"By the sound of all that fire power, the gooks know where all your automatic weapons are now. You must have been attacked by at least a battalion of Regulars."

"Ya, sure."

"What was the body count this time?" teased Kohl.

"Four goats and a cow. No C rations tonight. No sirree. We have fresh meat for supper? Care to join us?"

"Why, thank you, Sarge. Thought you'd never ask. After all that shootin' and no sleep, I figured that least you could do was offer me a meal. You know though, it makes it a little rough on Lieutenant Lance." (Lieutenant Lance was the Battalion liaison officer between the Marines and the villagers.) "He'll have to pay some gook who drove those midget, hump backed cows and scrawny goats into our trip wires for his VC friends." Kohl laughed at what he was going to say next. "I heard the night before last, you had 81's landing on the other side of the mountain. Killed three goats. You guys must really be hard up for fresh meat. You're going to break the Marine Corps bank paying for dead animals. You don't have anything against animals, do you? Or are they VC animals?" laughed Kohl.

"Heard about it did you?"

"Oh yeah. But it wasn't you?"

"Oh, heavens no, Lieutenant. You know I wouldn't make a mistake like that. It was one of your cohorts, Lieutenant Childers. Double clicked."

"Sounds like Childers. It's your job to keep an eye on him. When I'm out there, I don't want him droppin' rounds on me."

"I'll do my best Lieutenant. But you know as well as I do that he's dumber than a damn post."

"Trueness comes from your lips, Sarge. See ya tonight."

"See ya, Lieutenant. We have a new motto. 'You shoot it, we cook it.' "

*

It was 0330. Kohl had been monitoring the field phones since 0200 when he took over from Mays. He was reading a book, drinking coffee and trying to stay awake until 0600 when the night watch would conclude. He wished something would happen.

"Brigs, Brigs, You out there?" said a whispering voice.

"Yeah. Stoges, that you on?"

"Yep. What's happenin' out there?

Brigs chuckled and said, "Joe thought he saw something move or something, anyway he shot Corporal Higgins in the foot. Dumb ass."

"Joe?"

"No. Higgins. He was crawling out to Joe's post to try and catch him sleeping." Brigs chuckled again, "I don't think Higgins will do that again."

"In the foot, huh? Ticket home?"

"S'pose so."

Heard from Eddie, Brigs?"

"Got a letter from him Friday. He's in Hawaii. Some shit uh? Fuckin' Hawaii, while we're over here in this fuckin' place."

"You goddamn jackasses, do your socializing' at the titty bar. Now get your asses off the tactical phone."

"Fuck you, Gunny," said a voice disguised as Bugs Bunny.

"I know who said that."

"Wasn't me, Gunny," said another disguised voice.

"Wasn't me, Gunny," said another in falsetto.

"Sure as hell wasn't me, Gunny," drawled another.

"Not me, Gunny," said another in a singsong voice.

"What the fuck's going on here?"

"Sorry, Captain," said the Gunnery Sergeant.

"Don't Sir me. You know this is a tactical line. Gunny, I want the names of all those who had watch from 0300 to 0500 on my desk first thing in the morning."

"It's already morning, Sir."

"I know that."

"Well what time then, Sir?"

There was a pause in the phone conversation.

"Zero eight hundred. Yeah, zero eight hundred," said the Captain.

"Post number one all secure, Sir."

"Post number..."

The Gunnery Sergeant cut him off. "Shut up! I'm supposed to call you. Now get off the fuckin' line."

"All right, Gunny."

"Sorry, Gunny."

*

Mays called on the tactical phone to tell Kohl that Major Krinshaw wanted to see him. It was about 2100 hours and very dark. As Kohl walked down the road to Headquarters, the sentry stopped him.

"Halt! Who goes there?" the sentry asked in a shaking voice.

"Lieutenant Kohl."

"Advance to be recognized," he said.

Kohl walked cautiously forward. He thought he was about ten feet from him but didn't know for sure. *God. I hope this kid doesn't shoot my ass.*

"Halt!" There was another pause. "Not recognized," said the sentry.

Well, no shit Dick Tracy. It's darker than shit. I'd have to be standing on your fuckin' chest before you'd see me.

"Take it easy, Marine. Don't shoot me," soothed Kohl.

There was another pause before the sentry asked, "Thrust!"

Shit. The pass word. What's the password? Damn. Can't remember.

"Thrust!" said the sentry more forceful than before.

"Uh, listen Marine," Kohl gave a self-conscious, nervous laugh. "I'm afraid I forgot the password. Sorry."

There was another long pause.

"What's the capital of New Mexico?"

Shit. What is this, a quiz show? He must have seen this in a movie somewhere. I'd better answer him.

"Albuquerque," said Kohl confidently.

"Wrong," said the sentry.

"Shit. I didn't do very well in geography. What is it?"

"I can't tell you."

"Give me another one."

"Who won the World Series last year?"

Damned. Buggered again.

"I don't follow baseball. Look, if I were a VC, I would have shot you by now. And besides I'd be talkin' with a Vietnamese accent. Right?"

"Yes, Sir.

"Will you please let me pass. I have to go see Major Krinshaw."

"OK, Lieutenant. You may proceed."

"Thanks. What is the capital of New Mexico anyway?"

"Santa Fe."

"Oh, what's the password?"

"The password is foreword. You know, thrust - forward."

"Thanks. Sure is dark, isn't it?"

"Sure is. Good night, Lieutenant."

"Good night. You're doing an outstanding job, Marine."

"Thank you, Sir.

*

Kohl's bunker was cut into the north side of Hill 181. It was enclosed on two sides by sandbags, the back wall consisted of the hillside and one wall was made from a shelter half. The top was covered with corrugated steel panels. The inside was about four feet wide, eight feet long and five feet high. It had a small desk and a fold up cot with a mosquito net and frame. In the front was a gun port about twelve by eighteen inches.

Major Krinshaw introduced a sound technician from Division Headquarters and two technical advisors, to Kohl. They wanted Kohl's platoon to try a new listening device. Sensors were placed in front of each of their positions and each position was given earphones. The purpose was to be able to hear movement of a crawling enemy. However if there was a breeze or slight wind, it was hard to tell the sound of the wind from the sound of an enemy crawling. If small animals, such as monkeys or goats were moving in the area, it sounded like crawling enemy.

Kohl had spent hours on the earphones. Every noise was that of the VC enemy and every night it seemed, they got closer and closer. He had started putting his cocked forty-five under his field jacket each night.

He felt himself drifting. "Wake up!" he heard himself say. He could see his own body lying on the cot with the earphones on. He thought he was having an out-of-body experience he thought was reserved for dead people. The spirit could see in the dark and could see the bushes moving. By looking hard into the blackness, he could see a crawling VC. "Wake up!" He caught a glimpse of something shiny. The VC was crawling through the firing hole and was now kneeling next to Kohl. That's me. Wake up!" The VC slowly lifted the mosquito net and drew his knife. No, it was more like a machete. "Open your eyes. Wake up." The VC clasped his soiled hand over Kohl's mouth and quickly drew the razor sharp knife across his throat. The spirit couldn't believe what he was seeing. Blood was spurting out of the gaping wound.

Kohl gasped for air but couldn't breathe. He tried to cry out but couldn't speak. He tried to wake up but his eyes wouldn't open. He blinked, but it was hard to tell the if his eyes were open or closed. He was losing blood. He could hear the whizzing, as he tried to breathe from the jagged hole in his windpipe. He was dying. He struggled and tried to sit up. Then his cot collapsed and he found himself on the dirt floor of his bunker. He moved his hand to his throat expecting to find a gaping hole. Instead he found his dog tag chain wrapped tightly around his neck and to one of the legs of the cot. He got it untangled and lurched out of the bunker in the night air. He took in great gulps of air. Then vomited.

16 Gilloppo's Raid

Most of the platoon was sitting and talking by the helo pad cleaning their rifles or sharpening their 'K' bars. Sergeant Spalding was there. He had just arrived in Vietnam and had looked up Kohl who had been his platoon commander at Camp Pendleton. Everybody was swapping stories when Sergeant Spaulding asked Kohl to tell his troops about the time that they were "the Guerrillas" in a war game at Camp Pendleton.

Kohl leaned back against a sandbag and began. "My name was Colonel Pablo Gilloppo. It rained for the first three days while our platoon hid in a ravine. I was getting calls on the Prick 10 from the umpires complaining that I wasn't doing anything. I told them, 'Well come find us then.' My idea was that after a few days the troops on patrol would start losing their enthusiasm and start getting lackadaisical. After the third day I started sending out patrols to observe the Regimental Headquarters perimeters. That was going to be my main objective, to infiltrate the Regimental Headquarters and neutralize all the staff," Kohl laughed. "We painstakingly identified where every OP, LP and fox hole was located, plus gullies, vegetation, trip wires and flares. We observed the roads leading in and out of the compound, the kinds of vehicles and times of travel. We noticed that the MP vehicles were not checked.

"On the night of the attack, I took two fire teams and went down to Camp San Onofre. I found two MP's sitting in their pickup. I told them what we wanted to do and asked for their cooperation. So they wouldn't get into trouble, I told them I would back them up when they said they were hijacked and forced to comply. I rode up front to keep the MP's under guard while the rest climbed under a tarp in the back. At the same time, Sergeant Spaulding took his two squads to sneak as close as possible to the perimeter lines. The attack was to take place at 0200. The MP vehicle was waved through the checkpoint at 0150 and they drove around behind one of the buildings. We put blank rounds in the dumpster next the Regimental Headquarters. Then we set it on fire. When the rounds went off in the dumpster, it was the signal for the two squads to move closer while the men on watch were distracted by the activity in the rear. Ninety percent of the occupants in the headquarters tent went out to see what was going on, while at the opposite side of the tent we came in blazing with our M-14's on full automatic. We wiped out the entire Regimental Headquarters without them firing a single shot. The shooting was the signal for the two squads to breach the perimeter lines and run for the com. tent. A lot of our men were well within the lines by the time the signal came. It was pandemonium. There was ultimate confusion. The com. tent was over run and destroyed. The Regimental Commander and most of his staff were declared dead by the umpire. Three of our men were captured but the rest of us ran off into the dark. The Regimental Commander kept yelling for me to come back. I think I heard him call me a fuckin' little prick."

*

Kohl didn't tell them the rest of the story.

The day after the raid, while Kohl's platoon was in hiding, laughing and telling each and every detail, Kohl got a call on his PRC-10 from the Chief Umpire to report to the Regimental Headquarters. He knew he was going to be reprimanded.

Kohl hiked out of the hills to the nearest road then hitchhiked into base camp. He saw the results of the burned dumpster and as he entered the Regimental Headquarters tent he saw it was in complete disarray. Captain Neal had a bandage on his head and called Kohl a son-of-a-bitch. There were other glares. Kohl didn't know what to expect but he knew the success of the attack did not look good for the Colonel. Kohl entered Colonel Hastings' office. This was Kohl's first encounter with the big intimidating man and before the affair with the Colonel's wife Carol.

"Sit down Lieutenant," said the Colonel.

Kohl sat down on a field chair to the right of the Colonel's desk. He noticed that the Chief Umpire was off to his left, leaning against a field desk.

The Colonel started speaking slowly through clenched teeth. There was a slight quiver in his voice. "Your cowboy act last night caused damage to Marine Corps property and led to the injury of over a dozen troops, plus you stole government property." Gee. Good thing we were just playing. "You broke the rules governing the exercise." No holding. No biting or hitting in clenches. "I am bringing you up on charges of misconduct and you will pay restitution on all personal and property damages."

Kohl glanced over to the umpire. His face gave no sign.

By this time the Colonel's voice had raised in pitch and his words came quicker. His face was beginning to turn red as he continued; "I'm going to see you get court marshaled for this outrageous act of disobedience. You can't go around making up your own rules. You cheated!" he screamed. "Think you're so smart," he yelled as he stood. "I'm pulling you out. As of now, you are through." He mumbled some things that Kohl couldn't hear. Then he added, "You are to go back to Camp Mateo and stand by. Is that clear, Lieutenant!" *You can't talk to Pablo Gilloppo that way. I have my pride.*

Kohl knew he had better keep his mouth shut, "Yes, Sir."

When Kohl walked from the Colonel's office he was met with icy stares and murmured threats.

It was about noon when he got to Camp Mateo, so he decided to go to the mess hall for some chow. When he walked in, he heard whispers and saw people turn in their seats and stare. After he got his tray of food and entered the officer's section, everyone stood, then clapped, and chanted "Viva la Gilloppo. Viva la Gilloppo." He was surprised and embarrassed. He spotted Pete and Mays and headed for their table. They slapped his back.

"That's the way to go there, Senior Gilloppo," said Mays.

They proceeded to tell him what chaos the raid had caused.

Mays said, "The Colonel's so pissed he can't see straight. He got kilt and can't play no more."

Later that day while Kohl was playing pool at the rec. hall, the driver for General Krulak came in and told him the General wanted to see him. Kohl broke out in a sweat as he anticipated the impending doom. *Could I really be in this much trouble? They really didn't say you couldn't use MP vehicles. This is serious shit.* The driver took him to the helo pad where a chopper was to take him to the USS Vancouver, floating five miles off the coast. General Krulac was monitoring the progress of the war games and planning for an amphibious assault.

Kohl's knees were shaking so bad he had difficulty walking as he was escorted to the General's quarters. He was still dressed in his guerrilla uniform that was covered with dirt and grime. The General's aid met him at the hatch.

"Welcome aboard, Colonel Gillopo."

Kohl looked behind to see if he was speaking to the right person. Then he returned his attention to the officer to his front.

"You are to meet with the General, who is going to try and negotiate a peace with your country. However you will not agree to the terms. Play the roll, Lieutenant. OK?"

Saved. By God, I'm saved. Thank you. Thank you. Sweet Jesus.

Kohl walked into the cabin and the General stood and shook his hand. Kohl was noticeably embarrassed. There were pictures taken. And Kohl played the role.

By that evening Kohl was back leading his band of Guerrillas in the hills. Eventually many of his men during the exercise were either killed, wounded or captured, but Pablo Gilloppo was never caught. And the charges that Colonel Hastings had told him he was going to make were never heard about again.

17 God Has a Sense of Humor

It was Sunday. It was like any other day except there were church services up by the helo pad. The services were scheduled for 0800 and Kohl, with about twenty other Marines, were sitting on the ground or on their helmets talking and waiting for Chaplain, Navy Lieutenant Pat O'Riley to finish setting up his alter.

Chaplain O'Riley was six-foot-four and weighed about two hundred and thirty pounds. He had his red hair cut in a short crop, freckles, pock-marked face and a nose that had been broken in Philadelphia street fights. He usually wore camouflage utilities and a thirty-eight-magnum revolver strapped to his hip, but this morning he had on a white silk robe with a gold embroidered white stole.

A field desk was to his front. From a footlocker, he took out and unfolded a white silk cloth. He laid it over the top of the field desk. He smoothed it out. He took a one foot high gold cross from the locker and set it on top of the cloth. The next object was a golden goblet. He wiped the goblet clean with a white cotton cloth and placed the cup down on the desk and covered it with the cloth. He removed a small flask of wine, lifted the cloth cover from the goblet and poured the wine and replaced the cloth. He then took a cardboard box out of the locker and removed just enough wafers for the service and placed them in a silver tray. He covered them also. He adjusted his white stole. He blessed his work and crossed himself. He stepped around the altar to the front and faced the Marines. He closed his eyes and lifted his heavily muscled arms to the clear, bright, blue sky.

"All that's good, God gives us from Heaven."

Kohl heard the "whopp, whopp" of an approaching helicopter. It feathered about fifty yards away to land. Chaplain O'Riley turned to try and hold his altar. Great clouds of billowy dust rose and blew the wine over onto the white silk cloth, but soon parts of his alter were flying over the heads of the ducking Marines. The congregation ran for cover.

Kohl crouched behind his jeep and saw Chaplain O'Riley running through the flying dust towards the helicopter. He saw him climb into the cockpit and grab the pilot by the throat. He could see the pilot's helmet flopping back and forth.

A few minutes later the chopper left and the dust settled. The scattered congregation slowly returned carrying pieces of the altar. Chaplain O'Riley walked back to his tipped over field desk. His lips were moving. His normal red face was several degrees redder. The men gathered his altar and placed the items in a pile at his feet.

"Men?" he said through clenched teeth. "I'm going to call off services for today. Go get some rest. The pilot sends his apologies and has assured me that there will not be any helicopters flying in on Sundays from now on."

*

It was about 2345 when Sergeant Fontain called Kohl on the tac line.

"Lieutenant?" asked Sergeant Fontain.

"Yeah?"

"Could I talk with you a second up here?"

"Sure. Be right up."

Kohl crawled out of his makeshift bunker and climbed up to the road. He could faintly see Sergeant Fontain in the dark.

"Sorry to bother you, Lieutenant, but could you go down and talk to Thorogood? He's pretty bummed about his wife. I'd talk to him but he doesn't know me very well yet. I think it would be better coming from you."

"Why? What's he doin'?"

"Beach told me he's going to find a way to get home. He told Beach he was going to kill the guy his wife left him for. I just don't want him doing anything crazy."

"He got a Dear John today?"

"Yes, Sir."

"Women seem to have the best goddamn timing for this shit."

Kohl used the tactical line to call Thorogood's bunker.

"Post 2? This is Alpha One."

"Post 2."

"Reb, send Handle up. I'm comin' down. Don't shoot my ass."

"Don't worry, Sir."

"I am worried or I wouldn't have said anything."

"Roger that, Alpha One."

Kohl crawled down to Thorogood's bunker.

"Hey, Lieutenant."

"Evenin', Reb."

"What's up?"

"I heard you got a Dear John today. Mind telling me what's the deal?"

"Actually I got a letter from my Mom. She told me my wife moved out of her folk's house and moved in with this guy. I know 'im too. Fuckin' asshole. Messin' around with my wife. I'm going to kill that mutha fucker. Do you think the Corps would let me go home?"

"I don't think the Corps will let anybody go home to kill someone."

"Oh, I'm just pissed. I wouldn't kill him really, just hurt 'im real bad."

"Well that makes all the difference in the world," said Kohl sarcastically.

"I'm serious, Lieutenant. If I could get home I think I could get this whole thing straightened out."

"They usually only let someone go home if there is a death or an impending death. I don't think your wife's' boyfriend's impending death counts here. If we were stateside, you could have emergency leave to take care of things like this."

"Could you check on this for me?"

"When you talked with the Chaplain O'Riley, did you ask him about getting back home early?"

"No."

"Ask him tomorrow morning what he thinks. I'll check with him too, but I just want you to know that I doubt that your request will be granted."

"I just know if I could talk to her. Fuck. I only have two more months, Lieutenant. She waited all this time. She couldn't wait a lousy two fuckin' months. Shit. My life's shit. I have no reason now. You know?"

"You've got lots of reasons, Reb. I just don't want you to do anything stupid. We'll probably be out of here in another month anyway. So hang in there. Don't give up. Shit, you're only twenty. Got a hell of a long life ahead of you. I want you to try and stay focused. You have a squad to think about. Don't let your mind wonder because you have to stay alert. I really am sorry, but like my Mom always said, 'Maybe it's for the best'. She said, 'Things always happen for a reason.' You never know but this might be a good thing. I know. I know. But hear me out. If your wife wouldn't wait for you now, maybe when something else would come up later in the marriage, she'd split on you. You want somebody who'll stick by you through good and the bad. Keep writing her. Don't give up. Maybe she'll come around and when you get back home, you can straighten everything out. OK? I just don't want you to get weird on me. Hang in there. OK, Reb?"

"I'll try, Lieutenant. Thanks."

"Keep your eyes peeled and don't shoot Handle on his way back."

18 Hunting

Kohl's clothes were wet with sweat from the heat of the day. It was getting dark and the reconnaissance platoon was settling into their assigned places on the perimeter after running patrols all day. For a time, after the sun goes down, there is some relief in the heat. But it wouldn't be long before the mosquitoes would come for their evening meal. His clothes never dry out. Kohl looked at his watch. It was 2330. It was going to be another night of catnaps. He arranged the mosquito net over his face trying to keep it from touching his skin and making sure there were no holes for them to get in. He wished he could put something in his ears to keep out the buzzing noise but he couldn't do that. He needed to hear. Any exposed skin was fair game. He could brush away the mosquitoes but couldn't slap, because it made a noise the enemy could hear. He had been in Vietnam long enough now that his sense of smell was more acute and his night vision had improved. He didn't wear deodorant, use cologne, or shave with shaving cream. When he was in the bush he wanted to smell like the earth. To tell the truth, he stunk and so did the rest of the men. Blend in. The Viet Cong are good at it. Very good.

As Kohl rolled over to get more comfortable, he exposed an area to the cool night air. It was like being wrapped in a wet blanket. The night of no sounds, and no light only increased the feeling of loneliness He looked at his watch: 2345.

It was the end of March. Kohl and his men had been dropped off the night before, by the slow and noisy H-34 helicopters, on top of Hill 368. There was an increased concern from headquarters that China might enter the war and come raining down on them like a yellow horde much like they did in Korea. *Sure seems like a lot of ground to cover from China to Danang, Vietnam. Surely someone could spot the thousands of Chinese troops before I could.*

He watched a few lights flicker in the valley, wondering if they were signals to the VC. He looked at the stars and noticed the constellations were different from those at home. He sang songs in his mind. He imagined what kind of job he would have when he got home. He thought of how beautiful Julie was as she had walked down the aisle. He looked at his watch: 0015.

There was an unmistakable pressure for him to return from the four-day patrol with evidence of the VC presence. "Go Git me a VC ear, Lieutenant," the Battalion Commander had said.

The ground was hard and it was difficult to find a comfortable position.

How can it be so stinkin' hot during the day and so friggin' cold at night? If there was a breeze it kept the mosquitoes away, but it only made it colder. What would you rather have, mosquitoes or cold?

Do I have to make a choice here? Couldn't I just settle for a cold beer on a warm beach? What time is it?

He checked his watch, 0237.

What was that? I hope the troops on watch are awake. The VC probably knows we're up here. I wonder what Julie's doing?

Kohl dreamed an uneasy and restless sleep. It was 0312.

He awoke with a start. For an instant he couldn't remember where he was. He looked at his watch: 0448. His clothes were still wet.

It started with a faint glow in the east, and then he saw the first ray of the sunrise from the ocean. Soon he would be able to experience a time of comfort when he would be warm without being cold. Then he would trudge through the jungle in the stifling heat, looking forward to the brief comfort from the heat at dusk, only to be followed by another cold, long, restless, lonely night.

*

Thorogood was point, Hernandez was second, followed by Handle, Schultz, Kohl, Doc, Ford and Beach, as rear guard. Thorogood stopped. He squatted down on the ground. He motioned for Kohl to come up. Kohl crept forward and knelt next to him. He saw what brought Thorogood to a halt. This was the second day of reconning the various small valleys that ran down from the prominent ridge of Hill 368. They had been looking for evidence that the VC were using this area of mountains to hide their travel from one side of the valley to the other. Nothing had been found until now. The ravine they were walking down had been steep and very thick with vegetation. It had a small stream that ran into a larger stream from the northwest. There was a trail at the fork. The grass had been worn and pushed down and in a bare spot in the dirt was a footprint.

*

Grandpa stopped and Dusty stopped too. Just like he had been taught. His Grandpa knelt down. Dusty watched. Grandpa motioned for him to come up to where he was. He walked quietly forward, knelt next to him and looked at the print in the muddy part of the trail. To Dusty it looked like a big hand print. Must have been close to ten inches long but at the end of the fingers were claw marks. *Bear tracks?*

"Bear." Grandpa said. "Perty fresh too, I reckon."

Kohl looked around. *How fresh is too fresh.*

Grandpa grinned his mischievous grin.

They were deer hunting and walking along an unused logging road for about the last forty-five minutes. A damp October mist clung to the Doug Fir and the white bark of the Alder appeared stark, naked and leafless. Dusty never saw a bear during hunting season. He had seen a bear that his uncle had got one year, but he had used dogs. Another time he saw a bear eating berries, down by the river, when they were fishing. He knew his Grandpa used to hunt bear and even trapped a few a long time ago. He had heard stories.

Dusty was excited about the prospect of hunting and shooting a bear. In his mind he could see himself lying on a bear rug or wearing a bear claw necklace.

"Can we track it, Grandpa? I've never shot a bear before. I 'd sure like to git me a bear. Wouldn't you? Huh, Grandpa?" Dusty's eyes were wild with excitement.

"I reckon we could track it a ways, Sonny. But ... "

Oh, nuts.

"Trackin' a bear is more fun than killin' it."

Dusty was surprised. *Why not kill a bear?* He had seen Grandpa kill rabbits, chickens, ducks, geese, calves, sheep, pigs, deer, and even a horse once that got sick. Why he had even seen him kick a cow in the ribs so hard the cow fell over and when he got mad he would throw rocks at his dog.

Maybe he's afraid I'll get hurt. Or maybe it's too dangerous.

"Grandpa, I'm not afraid."

Grandpa straightened up with a groan and walked over and sat on a fallen log. He took the Bull Duram sack out of his left breast pocket, took a leaf of Zig-Zag paper, dipped it in the middle and sprinkled the tobacco into the fold, pulled the draw string with his teeth, licked one edge of the paper and rolled the cigarette into a tight roll, twisted the end, struck a kitchen match on his pant leg and lit his cigarette. As he smoked and talked he lifted the cigarette off his lower lip with his tongue and moved it from one side of his mouth to the other. Dusty sat down beside him, pulled his Snickers bar from his coat pocket and took a big bite.

"Bear ain't really nothing' to be afraid of. Most of the time they're more afraid of us and go runnin' off before you can say scat. Only time they're really dangerous is if they have a cub around or if they're eatin'. Naw, we're the hunter. How old are you now?"

"I'll be fourteen in September," Dusty said proudly.

"Hell, Son. That's eleven months off," Grandpa chuckled.

"Well, yeah. I guess it is," said Dusty.

This was his second year of having a deer license. He knew how to handle a rifle because he had gone hunting before and had carried his Dad's old Marlin 30-30 at first without any shells. Then last year ... almost got one.

He had shot five times so fast he didn't take time to aim. The deer, a big four point, was running and Dusty was running through brush, stumbling and falling over limbs and rocks. Finally the deer stopped. Dusty tried to calm himself. He was out of breath and still shaking. He tried to take careful aim. Squeeze. Click! He was out of shells. He fumbled in his pockets for more, but by the time he found one, the deer was gone. He heard his Dad and Uncle laughing up above on the road.

"If we're going to track that bear, don't you think we'd better get going, Grandpa?"

"No need gittin' in a big tither."

There was a long pause. Too long for Dusty's impatient desire to kill a bear.

He couldn't stand it any longer.

"Aren't we going, Grandpa?"

"Naw. Let's leave 'im be."

"Don't you want to kill a bear, Grandpa? You done it before. You think he's real big? Black bear, right?"

"Black bear. Big too. Probably about four to five hundred pounds."

"We ain't goin', are we?"

"Let me tell ya somethin'. There was this one time, back in '43 it was, I had tracked this bear that I had trapped. He'd been so damned big he lifted up the log I had the trap tied to and carried that sucker off. Holdin' it in his arms like he was carryin' a stick of firewood.

By the time I caught up with him, I had gained a lot of respect for that bear. He stood there lookin' at me, standin' on his hind legs, holdin' this big log. He was plain tuckered out. I sat down and tried to figure out what to do."

"What did you do?"

"Nothin' I could do to save 'im. The trap was on his leg. I couldn't get close enough to take it off. So, I shot him. But my shot didn't kill 'im right off. He didn't roar at me. He didn't try to rush me neither. He dropped the log, sat on his haunches and cried."

"Cried?"

"Yeah, bawled like a baby. Sounded just like a youngun, it did. Cried. Damnedest thing."

Dusty felt uncomfortable. He had never heard Grandpa talk like this before. He thought maybe he was playing one of his jokes, or that maybe this story was one of his tall yarns.

"Then what did you do?"

"I had to kill 'im. So I shot 'im again. That time it did the ol' bear in." Grandpa didn't say anything for awhile just looked off and smoked his cigarette. Then he continued, "I wenched him up a tree and dressed him out and peeled his fur off down around his hind legs... I'd done it times before ... but it seemed like it was the first time I really looked ... I mean took notice ... hangin' there in that tree ... that ... it looked like a ... man's body. The white skin and muscles ... well ya know what I mean, don't ya Sonny boy?" Dusty shook his head yes. "So Sonny, I don't have any hankerin' to shoot me a bear or have you shoot one either. It just ain't right. They're too much like us."

"What about all those other things you killed, Grandpa?"

"As farmers and ranchers, that's how we live. A bear is different and the meat's no-account anyway. Ya don't want to kill somethin' just for the killin'. There should be a reason. Food. Self-protection. Things like that. Just because we can kill somethin' doesn't mean we havta. Animals don't kill their own kind, ya know. Now you take a dog. They'll fight ... but once one of them has the upper hand the other will roll over and give up or run off. And you'll find that with most animals. They don't fight to kill. It seems that only humans kill each other."

"Grandpa? Did you ever kill anyone?"

"Well, I don't think that's a right proper question to ask."

"Well, I heard ... " Dusty started then stopped. Grandpa had given him 'The Look.'

"Do you think Dad did when he was fighting Japs?"

"I don't know. You'll have to ask him."

"He won't tell me."

"Probably has his reasons. Ya see, Sonny, killin' someone ain't all it's cracked up to be in books and movies. Life's a precious thing. As ya git older, ya all begin to realize how short a time we have on this here land. When someone's kilt at the hand of another, well you're ... you're takin' more than his life. You're takin' someone's son, or someone's father or brother. His dreams, hopes and plans. We've been lucky, Sonny. Your Dad and Uncles got through the War safe. That is except for John's boy, Charles, who was shot down and kilt over Europe somewhere."

"What about killin' Japs?"

"War is a little different. The Japs attacked us at Pearl Harbor. When you've got someone shootin' at ya, you shoot back. But even in war, you don't kill women and children. I'm still not all that sure about war either. Kind of a waste, if ya ask me. Never had a hankering for it myself. Never did trust those damn Democrats, Roosevelt, nor Truman for that matter. Damn politicians." Dusty noticed that Grandpa was starting to get all worked up like he would listening to 'Gabriel Heater and the News.' "Yep, we're all going to kick-the-bucket sooner or later. Fertilizer for some daisies. I sure wouldn't want anything to ever happen to ya there, Sonny boy."

"You neither, Grandpa. Grandpa?" Dusty reached over and put his hand on top of his grandpa's wrinkled and knurled hand.

"Yeah, Sonny?"

"When I grow old, I want to be old like you."

Grandpa looked over at Dusty, smiled and ruffled his hair and said self-consciously, "Naw, Sonny. Ain't no need thinkin' about gettin' old nor bein' like me. Neither worth lookin' forward to. Don't have an education. Can't read much nor write worth a tinker damn. Ya don't want to be like me. We came to this here country from Oklahoma so ya kids could do better. Naa. You don't want to be like me."

But I do, Grandpa. I love you. I love your stories. I love the way you laugh. I love the way you treat me. I love being with you, just like this. Sitting on this log and talkin'. You think just because you don't have an education that it's a bad thing. Well it ain't. And Dad told me how hard you had to work on the farm. That the nearest school was a boarding school and besides that, it cost money that your folks didn't have. It doesn't matter, Grandpa. What matters is that you are here. With me. Sittin' on this log and tellin' me about life. Both real and fantasy.

Grandpa, with the eager help of Dusty, built a fire in the hollow of a busted Doug Fir that had a slab of pitch exposed where it had been struck by lightning. As they sat by the fire, Grandpa told Dusty about the first time that he had met Grandma. How he had just come off a trail drive down in the badlands of southeastern Colorado. Dusty sat by the warm fire and listened to his Grandpa's story. From Grandpa's lips, he weaved sounds of bears growling and wolves howling. His laugh and mischievous grin were tucked away in Kohl's young mind, hidden like jewels.

*

The print showed the markings of a tire tread sandal heading up the canyon. It appeared there was just one person. Kohl looked around. His men were squatting along the creek bed, each about ten to fifteen feet apart, facing to the out side, except for Hernandez who took over the point when Thorogood stopped.

They continued down the streambed for another hour and stopped to wait for dusk before continuing to their ambush site. While they were sitting on the side of the stream, Kohl watched a small bird that was flitting among the branches above. A white salvo of bird dung landed on Kohl's forehead to the delight of the troops. In their effort to be quiet, their laughs were muffled by various body parts. At dusk they moved out slowly, inching their way down the thickly vegetated creek bed. Thorogood ducked under a growth of bamboo and when he lifted his head up on the other side he saw a Vietnamese walking up the trail towards him.

"Dung li!" shouted Thorogood.

The Vietnamese turned and ran down the streambed and Thorogood shot a half a clip at the retreating figure.

Kohl dove to his right into the underbrush. He pulled out his forty-five and crawled up a small rise above the streambed. He could see Thorogood walking cautiously forward, followed by Hernandez. Handle was lying on his stomach with his M-14 aimed in cover. The Vietnamese jumped from a bush to the left of the creek about fifty feet in front of Thorogood. Both Thorogood and Hernandez let rip a short burst as he dove into the brush further down the creek. Then all three fired into the brush. Kohl could see where he went and yelled for Thorogood to duck as he threw a grenade. The throw landed at the base of the bushes where the Vietnamese had entered. There was a "Ka Rump" and out ran the Vietnamese followed by another series of shots. He quickly disappeared into the thick jungle.

Kohl's heart felt like it was in his head. He looked at Doc who had crawled next to him. Doc had his forty-five out too. They both looked at the pistols in their hands and muffled a laugh. Kohl and Doc were thinking the same thing. *What the hell am I doing with this piece of shit gun? At five feet they are great. Blow a hole as big as softball. But at fifty feet, I'd be better off throwing rocks.* Kohl remembered when Hoppalong Cassidy, with his pearl handled six-gun, shot bad guys off rooftops at a hundred yards. Kohl knew it only happened in the movies.

*

Kohl had shot "expert" and had been on the Camp Pendleton pistol team.

"There's only nine holes, Lieutenant," said the range NCO.

"That's impossible, Sarge. Maybe two bullets went into the same hole, Ya think?" asked Kohl looking closely at the cluster of holes in the target.

"I don't think so, Lieutenant. You must have flinched."

"You mean I missed the whole fuckin' thing."

"Happens all the time, Sir."

*

"Doc, I've got to get me a serious weapon."

"You and me both, Lieutenant."

Ford crawled up next to Kohl for a better view of the creek bed below. They watched Thorogood and Hernandez leap frog down the creek bed while Handle provided cover. They disappeared around a bend in the small gully.

"Kohl! Front!" said Thorogood. He didn't have to say it loud because the sound carried in the gully even with all the vegetation. Kohl climbed down the rise onto the trail and walked cautiously past his kneeling men toward the front. As he rounded the bend, he saw Thorogood and Hernandez standing over the body of the Vietnamese.

"We got the son-of-bitch, Lieutenant," said Thorogood. His voice was shaking with excitement.

"Hernandez? Go on down the trail a ways and stand by," said Kohl.

"Yes, Sir."

Handle came up, followed by Schultz. Doc and Ford were still on the rise and Beach was at rear guard.

The small man was lying on his back. As Kohl stood over him he saw his eyes open and flutter. Bubbles were coming out of a hole about the size of softball on the right side of his chest.

"Doc, up!" commanded Kohl.

Blood flowed from his back in a ribbon of red, marbling, blending pink into the creek water. His left leg twitched. The Doc came to his side. He felt his neck for a pulse and leaned over and put his cheek next to his face to try and detect any breathing.

"I don't get a pulse, Lieutenant. It looks like he got it through the lung and probably damaged his heart and major arteries, Sir. I don't think there's anything we can do. He's dead."

There was another twitch of his left leg. A bolt action carbine was at his side. He was dressed in camouflage utilities and he had a blue cotton backpack.

"Did I kill 'im?" asked Thorogood. His voice screeched and scratched like a tightly strung instrument. His breathing was in short gasps.

As the others started gathering around, Kohl said, "Keep spread out. This is no cluster fuck. Move it! Thorogood, go up to where Hernandez is and have him move down another fifty feet or so. Keep him in sight though," ordered Kohl.

"Aye, aye, Sir," Thorogood said.

Doc stood up and said, "He's dead, Lieutenant. He's a VC, isn't he?"

"Yeah. He's VC, I think," Kohl answered. But he knew that he really didn't know for sure.

"How can you tell?" asked Doc.

"Well, you can't really. No one else is supposed to be up here. And besides he ran and he had a rifle. Sounds like VC to me," said Kohl.

"Let's cut off the gook's fuckin' ear," said Handle grinning as he bounced from one foot to the other clearly excited.

Kohl ignored the comment as he removed the VC's pack and was going though it, when he noticed Handle remove his 'K' bar. "What do you think you're doing, Handle?" asked Kohl.

"Goin' to cut off his ear," sneered Handle.

"Fuckin' A, Lieutenant. The Aussies do it. Show it to the Colonel. He's the one who told you he wanted a VC ear," said Beach enthusiastically.

That was true. The Colonel said he wanted proof. He said something about a VC ear but Kohl thought he was kidding.

"Ain't nobody cuttin' off any ears," said Kohl.

"But ... " started Beach.

"That's final, Beach. I don't want to hear another word," said Kohl sternly. He took him aside and said, "You're the squad leader, for Christ's sake. Show a little leadership here."

Kohl continued to look through the pack. In the pack was a small pot, hammock, first aid packet, rice, ammo, poncho, a notebook hand written in French, and a letter. He opened the letter and inside was a picture wrapped in plastic. Kohl looked at the man in the picture and at the man lying dead. It was hard to tell if he was the same person but assumed it was. Standing proudly next to him was a pretty young girl who had a small child in her arms.

"Well, we can't carry this fuckin' slope head back. How are we going to prove we kilt us a VC if we don't take his fuckin' ear?" asked Handle.

"They'll just have to believe us, is all. We'll take all this stuff. Ford, you, Doc and Handle dig out a spot so we can bury him," said Kohl.

"You got to be fuckin' kiddin'," sneered Handle.

Ford hit Handle in the pit of his stomach with his trenching shovel. Handle dropped to his knees gasping for breath. When he got his breath back, he rose with clinched fists and glared at Ford. He took a menacing step towards Ford. When Ford raised the trenching shovel, Handle backed off.

Private Handle didn't fit in with the elite recon platoon. He was a hot head, mouthed off, and had a surly attitude. Sergeant Fontain told Kohl that he suspected Handle could be using drugs.

Ford, Doc and Handle dug a shallow grave and slid the slight body into it. They started to cover the body with dirt.

"Wait!" said Kohl. He took the letter from the pack and slipped out the picture wrapped in plastic. "Wait," he repeated softly.

He walked over and knelt next to the grave. He leaned over and pulled the VC's arms up onto his chest and in his hands he placed the picture. Satisfied, he raised up and said, "OK."

Kohl, Schultz, and Ford covered the body with rocks, dirt and brush to cover the small grave.

Ford said, "Can I say a short prayer, Lieutenant?"

"Well, I'm not standin' an' bowin' over this fuckin' gook," snarled Handle, still mad at Ford.

Handle picked up his rifle and pack and headed down the trail where Thorogood was crouched.

"Yeah. Sure, Ford. I mean, it would ... well ... but hurry. We've got to get out of here. It's getting dark," said Kohl haltingly.

"Lord, please forgive us for the taking of another human life. Give us strength to do God's will. Lift this man into your Kingdom, Lord. Protect us, Lord with your battle shield. Give us guidance so we can walk the fields of battle unharmed and be forever ..."

Kohl cleared his throat as an indication for Ford to bring his gravesite ceremony to a close. Ford stopped his prayer and looked up. Tears were rolling

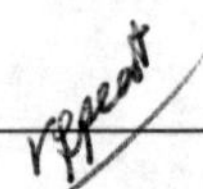

down his brown cheek. Kohl, Schultz, and Ford covered the body with rocks and dirt and placed brush over the top to hide the small grave.

"Let's move out," said Kohl.

19 Body Count

Kohl reported to the S-2 tent. While he showed Mays and Major Wellington what they brought back, he told them of the encounter with the VC.

"What did you do with the body?" asked the Major.

"We buried him, Sir," answered Kohl.

The Major looked at the items in the pack and checked the rifle. "It's a Russian carbine, Kohl."

"No, shit."

"Yep." Then he left to get Colonel McGraw. They returned just as Kohl was finishing up his recon report.

"How come you didn't bring the VC body back?" asked the Colonel.

"Sir, we were way down in a ravine. It would have been a real bitch to carry him out. Plus, we were on our way to an ambush site and it was getting dark. It would have slowed us down and would have increased our noise, Sir"

"Couldn't you have picked him up on the way back?"

"We came back a different way, Sir. I didn't want to change our preplanned patrol route without clearing it through headquarters, Sir."

"Did you call and try to change it?"

"I called, Sir, right after we killed the VC. But we couldn't raise anybody. Like I said we were down in a canyon, Sir. I didn't think it was that important to bring back a dead VC anyway, Sir."

The Colonel paced and worked his jaw muscles. He glared at Mays then at Kohl and said, "Lieutenant, I want you to go back and get that VC body."

Kohl tried not to show his surprise or his frustration at the order. He wanted to ask, why? But he couldn't. An order was an order. He could tell the Colonel was upset and didn't want him to get any angrier than he already was. He also wanted to ask how he was going to bring the body back, but he knew he was going to have to work out that problem himself. He looked at the Major and Mays to see if they had the nerve to ask the obvious question.

"Yes, Sir," said Kohl finally.

"Major, take care of the details," ordered the Colonel.

"Will do, Sir."

After the Colonel left, Kohl turned to the Major and asked, "Why is he making such a big deal about a dead body, Major?"

"General Walt is coming in tomorrow for a look see. All the reports we have been getting about VC killed have been unconfirmed. They have either crawled away in the brush or have been carried off by their comrades. The Colonel wants proof of confirmed kills. So, he wants bodies. We already have two VC's in the FLSU freezer in Danang." *Got 'em in there with the ground round, uh?*

"Before I go back could I get some rest? I've been out four days and I'm beat."

"I'm afraid you're going to have to go back as soon as possible. The longer it lays out there, the more it will start decomposing, plus an animal might dig it up and drag it off. Let's see, here. It's about 1000 now; how about ... can you be ready by 1400? Will that give you enough time before dark?"

"That's pushing it, Major. How 'bout 1230? Get this fuckin' thing over with."

"Okay. Mays, make the chopper arrangements and let regimental headquarters know that we'll have men out there."

Mays also arranged for Kohl to take a stretcher and body bag. The chopper would drop them off at the top of hill 368, where they would hike down the ravine, retrieve the body, then continue down the canyon to be picked up at the bottom. That way they wouldn't have to carry the body back up the hill.

Kohl hated the idea of telling his troops that some of them had to go back to pick up the dead VC, especially Handle and Beach. He could hear them whispering, "I told you so."

"Sergeant? The Colonel said that we have to go back and pick up that dead VC."

Sergeant Fontain gave Kohl a disgusted look but didn't say anything. Kohl knew he wasn't mad at him.

"Pick out four or five men. We're leavin' at 1230."

"I'll go, Lieutenant. You stay here and rest."

"Naw. You don't know where it's at."

"I'll take ... "

Kohl interrupted Sergeant Fontain and said, "No Sarge. I'll go back."

The five-man squad of Ford, Grant, Thompson, Spallenski, and Kohl headed down the ravine where they had been the previous day. The sun was high in the sky. Even though the ravine was shaded, it lacked a breeze. It was like walking in a sauna. Within fifteen minutes their utilities were soaked with sweat. They were tired and irritable. It seemed every vine reached out to grab their legs. Elephant grass cut their arms and faces. Sweat filled their leather boots causing their feet to blister. The boot eyelet hooks caught the vines and constantly tripped the men, causing then to stumble and fall. The M-14 rifles were heavy and cumbersome and the flash suppressers caught on vines. The utilities hadn't changed since the Second World War. Kohl wandered why the ARVN troops and Army got the new lightweight camouflage type? In fact they had all the latest gear.

The tired squad stumbled and fought their way down the ravine. As they were climbing up a series of rock ledges, Spallenski's radio antenna caught a vine while he was stepping from one rock out-cropping to another. As he heaved himself up, the vine acted like a spring and jerked him backward off the rock. He fell silently about eight feet and landed on his back at Kohl's feet. It knocked the breath out of him briefly, which was good because once he got his breath back he let out a stream of New York cuss words Kohl had never heard before.

"You okay, Ski?" asked Kohl.

"Fuck, no. I'm fuckin' through." He wiggled out of the packboard the PRC-10 was on. "I'm tired of carrying this fuckin' piece of shit thing." He kicked it. He wasn't yelling at Kohl. His anger was at everything and everybody.

The men sat down and watched Ski swear, kick and stomp around until he finally got so exhausted that he collapsed in a heap in some grass. As he gasped for air he said, "I'm not ... carrying ... that fuckin' thing ... another foot. I'm not. Someone else. My legs are fuckin' rubber."

"Ski, you're our radioman. Grant and Thompson have to carry that goddamn dead VC," said the exasperated Kohl. "We're all tired. Just a few more hours, man and we're outa here."

"I'll carry it," said Ford as he climbed down the rock. He threw the pack on and the team continued down the canyon.

They found the gravesite and uncovered the body. There were flies and maggots in the open wound, eyes, mouth and ears. And it stunk. Nobody wanted to touch it.

"What should I do with this?" asked Ford as he held up the picture wrapped in plastic.

Kohl glanced at Ford then looked off down the trail. He finally said, "Give it to me." And tucked it into his left breast pocket.

They reluctantly shoved the VC into the body bag and strapped it on the stretcher and continued down the ravine. At the site where they had set up the ambush the night before, they rested next to the falls that came off the rocks. Kohl, along with the men, stuck their heads into the cool water. It felt good and refreshing. Kohl and Ski carried the stretcher the rest of the way down the canyon. The chopper came and took them and the body back to camp.

*

Mays was made the official body gatherer. By the time Kohl had got back, the number of VC bodies in the freezer had risen to four, five counting Kohl's dead body.

"I can't believe I'm doing this shit," said Mays.

"Well, it's nothing to write home about. When's the General coming?" asked the exhausted Kohl as he collapsed onto a folding chair.

"Tomorrow at 1000. I'm supposed to have all the bodies piled up next to the battalion headquarters tent. You know, this is bullshit!"

"I'm so fuckin' tired. To go all the way back there and lug that body back, just to be put on display is..." Kohl was searching for the right word. Weird, gruesome, pitiful, sad, bizarre, morbid, distasteful, grotesque. "... perverted. That's it. It's perverted. Perverted people do perverted things. Too bad we couldn't throw in the other stuff we killed like goats, cows and monkeys," pondered Kohl. He looked at Mays and saw a sparkle in his eye and they both started laughing. Kohl laughed so hard, he rolled off the chair onto the floor.

"Dead goats?" howled Mays.

"You pervert," roared Kohl. They were laughing so hard tears were streaming down their dusty cheeks.

"Okay. Okay. I'll check with Joss, Wheeler and Krout," said Mays.

"And I'll check with Sergeant Higgens. You know Childers thinks the animals are VC and kills a bunch every night with his 81 mortars."

"Man, this is going to be great."

"Since you're responsible for the bodies, aren't you worried about getting the blame?"

"Deny, deny, deny. I can even use my dumb look. How's that?"

"I think you look dumber just lookin' natural," laughed Kohl.

*

It was raining and had been all night, which was a welcome relief from the heat. But the rain had turned the dust into a gooey quagmire. Mays and his driver went down to the FSLU freezer at 0730 to pick up the bodies. There were now six. They stacked the stiff bodies in the trailer. People stared at this pile of bodies as they drove down the road. At one point they hit a ditch and one of the frozen bodies slid out. During its fall one of the frozen arms broke off.They stopped and lifted the mud soaked corpse and threw it and the arm back into the trailer. By 0900 they had all the frozen bodies stacked alongside the headquarters tent. Some of the bodies were mangled and in pieces. They were starting to unthaw and smell. Mays and his driver wore masks and rubber gloves but they still had a hard time to keep from gagging.

Kohl had recruited Wheeler to help collect the dead animals and they arrived with their load at 0930. They drove behind the communications tent and waited for Mays to give them the signal that the General was coming. As they sat in the rain giggling and gagging, they saw Mays' signal. They quickly drove over next to the VC bodies and dumped off two cows and four goats. Since they hadn't been frozen, they were in varying degrees of decomposition. They were bloated, covered with maggots and flies and stunk.

Kohl stopped briefly and looked at the dead VC's. He leaned over and picked up the severed frozen arm and stuck it in the armpit between the body and severed portion of the upper arm. Kohl stood back to admire the disjointed arm that was sticking up. From his left breast pocket he pulled out the picture and stuck it in-between the frozen, knurled fingers. It was raining so hard that no one noticed.

As Kohl climbed back into the jeep Wheeler asked, "What's that all about?" Kohl didn't answer. He pulled his poncho hood over his rain soaked cover, drove off, and parked back behind the communications tent.

Colonel McGraw was walking next to General Walt followed by the General's entourage and the Colonel's staff officers. Talking to Mays was Lieutenant Fitzsimmons, the General's Aide.

As they rounded the tent, the Colonel said, "And this, General is our VC body cou ... What the ... "

While the Colonel's eyes were wide in surprise and puzzlement, the

General's gaze showed an anger building. The collection of frozen VC bodies and dead, bloated stinking animals left the whole contingent in shock.

"What's going on here, Colonel?" asked the General sternly.

"It's a VC body count, Sir. But ... I ... I..."

The press corps recovered quickly and started taking pictures.

The General's Aide moved swiftly and blocked their view. "Please gentlemen. Hold off a second. There's been a mistake." As they tried to get around him, he continued to plead, "Please allow us to..."

"What are those animals doing here? Is this some kind of a morbid joke?" continued the General.

"I ... I ... " stammered the Colonel.

Curious as to what Kohl and Wheeler had done, Mays walked over and pulled the picture from the clutched fingers of the severed arm.

"Lieutenant Mays?" yelled Major Krinshaw who recovered first.

"Yes, Sir."

"What, may I ask is going on here?" continued the Major.

"I brought the VC bodies this morning at 0900, just like I was ordered. I don't know where those came from, Sir," he pointed. He also gave one of his best ever-dumb looks.

"You mean to tell me that someone just ... just ... " stammered the Colonel.

"Does anybody know how these ... What's that you got there?" asked the Major.

"Looks like a picture, Sir," said Mays.

"Let me see," as Fitzsimmonds grabbed it from Mays. He looked at it and then handed it to the General.

General Walt, whose big muscled neck was red and swollen, looked at the picture of a young man standing next to a beautiful girl holding a baby. He turned and walked off a few yards and looked off into the valley below. Everybody was watching the General.

After a few moments he returned, glared at the Colonel, and said through clenched teeth, "Colonel? I don't give a shit about the goddamn animals. I don't know what possessed you to think that I wanted to see dead frozen enemy soldiers displayed like game trophies. It's a disgrace to our uniform and to our country. To desecrate a human being in this manner is abominable. It's beyond human dignity. I want these soldiers shown the respect due our profession. This is disgusting. Turn them over to the Vietnamese for proper burial. Now get them out of here!" he yelled." He glared at the Colonel. "Is that understood?"

"Yes, Sir. Sorry, Sir." Then the Colonel turned and said, "You heard the General, Lieutenant Mays. See that his wishes are carried out."

"Aye, aye, Sir."

The General caught Mays' eyes. Mays told Kohl later that he thought he saw just a trace of a smile, like maybe he knew.

Fitzsimmons came over next to Mays and said, "Isn't that Kohl and Wheeler over there?" He nodded his head in the direction of the communications tent.

"Yeah. I think it is," answered Mays.

"What's he doing here?"

"He's got a recon outfit."

"No. I mean, what's he doing parked over there?"

"To see the General, I'd guess."

"Did he and Wheeler have anything to do with this?"

"You mean ... Naw."

"Yeah, I bet. This has Kohl written all over it. And you too."

"Well, you can think all you want, Fitz. Now you'd had better get your fuckin' brown nose up there with the General. Don't you think?"

Fitzsimmons wheeled and slogged off in the mud after the General.

The General continued his inspection of the facilities and the troops. When he came to Kohl's platoon, he spotted Sergeant Fontain, strolled over and gave the Sergeant a slap on the back.

"Good to see you, Pee Wee," said the General.

The troops looked surprised, first at the familiarity that the General showed to their sergeant and secondly for the name. Pee Wee. There were a few giggles.

"Good to see you, General. Now that you're here maybe we can start kicking some VC ass," grinned Sergeant Fontain.

"Is this your outfit?"

"Yes, Sir. First Platoon, A Company, Third Recon., Sir."

"Fine looking outfit, Pee Wee."

The General spent at least a half-hour talking with the troops. Kohl was very impressed by the General's attention. The questions he asked displayed a genuine concern for the troop's opinions, comments, and welfare.

Later Sergeant Fontain was cornered by his troops who teased him about his nickname, PeeWee. They found out that the General was his platoon commander in Korea

After the General left, the Colonel was in a screaming rage. "I want to get the bottom of this. I was humiliated." He thundered on for another fifteen minutes. His staff had their head's bowed and were shuffling their feet uncomfortably. "Somebody's going to pay for this!" he yelled.

20 Childhood Innocence

Kohl and Schultz were on their way to the Danang Air Base for some supplies, when Schultz pulled the Mighty Mite behind a six-by that had stopped alongside the road. There were five Marines buying bottles of Coca-Cola from a cute Vietnamese girl. Kohl guessed her age at about twelve. Every day she would be at the bottom of the hill selling Cokes to the Marines. Many walked down daily to tease and joke with the girl. She carried the Cokes in a metal box made out of smashed tin pop and beer cans, filled with ice, carried on a flimsy wooden cart.

Kohl and Schultz got out of the jeep and started walking over to get an ice cold Coke. Kohl felt the ground shudder and a blast of hot air hit his face. Then he heard the sound. Ka Boom! Schultz, who had been two paces ahead of Kohl, had been thrown into him. Both found themselves lying on their backs. Kohl couldn't see.

"Jesus. My eyes. Oh shit. They've been blown clean out. Oh, dear God, I'm blind," cried Kohl.

He was trying to build up the courage to touch his face to see if his eyes were lying on his cheeks. He slowly reached a hand to his face. He couldn't tell if the wetness he felt was blood or sweat.

"Lieutenant? You okay?" asked Schultz.

"Are my eyes blowed out, Schultz?"

Kohl heard Schultz scoot closer. "I don't think so. Looks like they're full of dirt."

Schultz grabbed the canteen from his hip and washed out Kohl's eyes.

Kohl could hear the moaning and screaming of others and men running down the road.

Kohl's eyes stung but he could see. Thank God. Schultz's arm was bleeding heavily, so Kohl wrapped a compress on it. Both of them were peppered with glass, dirt and rocks. As he looked around he was shocked at what he saw. There was a crater where the little girl had been standing. The bodies of the five Marines were lying twisted and mangled in the dirt. Kohl could see that two who were moving and moaning while the other three looked like they had been blown into pieces. The first men on the scene were frantically trying to stop the flow of blood until the medics arrived. Kohl and Schultz were sitting in shock, when Sergeant Fontain and Doc Marcellius came running down the hill. The Doc made them both lie down while he administered first aid.

Kohl recalled when he was a kid and had a TNT bomb go off in his hand. The whole front of his body felt like his hand had felt, numb and tingly from shocked nerve endings.

"What happened? Were we hit with a mortar round?" ask the bewildered Kohl.

Sergeant Fontain answered, "It looks like that girl blew herself up. Must have had a bomb of some sort in the Coke case."

"She blew herself up?" asked Kohl.

"Sure looks like it."

"On purpose?"

"Could be."

"How could someone do that? Just ... just ... she was just a little girl. How could a twelve-year old girl blow herself up? It just sounds ... unbelievable to me."

"Well, Lieutenant, several things could have happened here, but who knows. She could have been a VC sympathizer, or her parents could have been held as hostages and would be killed if she didn't do what the VC wanted, or the VC could have placed the bomb into her Coke box without her knowing it. But I doubt that. It's something that is going to happen here, Lieutenant. I saw it in Korea. There's a difference in the way they see life and the way we do. They have been in a war for centuries. Most recently with the Japanese during WW II, then with the French and now with us. They have seen family members die along with their friends and villagers. After awhile they get used to death, I guess. Don't care. Life seems to have lost its meaning. In some cases they would prefer to die of their own hand than face starvation or death by disease. In Korea the Chinese would blow their horns before an attack. The first wave of troops didn't carry rifles, only a few grenades. Their dead bodies were used to hold down the concertina wire and to detonate the land mines to make way for the next wave. In the second wave, one out of every five of the soldiers would be carrying a rifle. When a comrade with a rifle fell, the next soldier who didn't have a weapon would pick it up. I don't mean to preach here, Lieutenant. I'm doing this because I don't like the idea of seeing the man I'm here to protect splattered all over kingdom come.

"Like I was saying. We have a problem with how to treat women and children. We flirt and tease the girls not knowing they can kill us just as dead as any man. And the same with kids. We give them toys, candy and play with them, take them to the Base Doctor when they are sick. The VC knows this. Damn rights they do. And they'll use them as weapons. Beware, Lieutenant. Beware. The girls will hide top secret messages up their private parts because they know we wouldn't dare search. This is a different game here, Lieutenant. The VC has no rules. They have one objective. To kill as many of us as they can. They don't care how. Let's get you both to the medical tent. You're both bleeding from the ears. Got a little carried away. Sorry."

"That's all right, Sarge. Thanks. I just never thought about it much. You know twenty more feet and I'd a been hamburger meat."

21 Dead Drunk

Kohl picked up the supplies they needed and had Schultz drop him off at Pete's, then sent Schultz back to camp.

"What the hell happened to you?" asked Pete.

Kohl looked like he had a bad case of the chicken pox. He had scabs where the rocks and glass had hit his face. He told Pete what had happened then sat down in a captain's chair and Pete handed him a cold beer out of his cooler of ice at the foot of his rack.

"Can't get much better than this, eh Pete?" said Kohl. This was his first beer in a long time.

"You've been out in the sun too long. You know, you could have been blown to hell. Luck," said Pete.

Kohl looked around and said, "For some goddamn reason I don't feel so lucky. There's several kinds of luck. There's very good luck. Then there's just plain luck. Then there's unlucky. And I swear if it wasn't for the fact that I'm unlucky, I'd have no luck at all."

"Sue's going to have a baby," said Pete nonchalantly.

"Jesus Pete, you're really poppin' those babies out. Married two years and two kids. This doesn't look good for Sue at this rate. Haven't you ever heard of birth control?"

"We're Catholic. We use the rhythm method."

"Oh, yeah, sure. I think you're using the wrong kind of rhythm. You've been doing, 'One two, one two, three and a four. One two, one two, three and a four.' Wrong method there ol' buddy. Give me another beer. Man, this is the life. Can't get much better than this. Where's the can?"

Pete pointed.

Kohl returned after almost a half an hour.

"You fall in? Get lost? Played with your wanger?"

"Man, I've got the shits bad. That makes the fifth crap today. I'm usually so plugged up from eating "C" rations that I have to pry the turds out with a crowbar. Give me another beer."

They sat, drank and talked for the next two hours with an occasional trip to the outhouse by Kohl. Kohl heard the jeep before he saw it. It skidded to a halt outside Pete's tent. In rushed Sergeant Fontain.

"Jesus Sarge. What's the gawd all rush," slurred Kohl.

"Excuse me, Lieutenant. We're going out on patrol in about an hour."

"Fuck me. Sarge? I'm shit faced. We were supposed to have three days before we go back out."

"We've got everything all set up for you, Lieutenant. Don't worry. Come on. Chop, chop."

Schultz floored the jeep and headed, in a cloud of dust, back up the hill. When they arrived, the chopper was already there. Sergeant Fontain helped Kohl out of the back of the jeep. The troops noticed Kohl's condition and looked worried. Kohl felt dizzy and the ride up had almost made him sick. His gear was waiting for him. They lifted him into the chopper and left for hill 368.

It was dusk by the time they had arrived. They assembled and moved out to an area near the western point of the ridgeline. They were to set up a LP/OP. Kohl threw up after he got off the chopper. They hadn't gone too far when he had to stop to take another crap. It got dark quickly. Kohl didn't know where he was or where they were going. He shuffled and staggered along the trail. Every once in a while he would miss where they had turned and they would have to catch him and bring him back. He stopped to go to the bathroom again. Everybody behind him had to stop and wait for him to finish. It was very dark now. When he got through, there was nobody in front of him. When he stopped Ski was to his front but he wasn't there now.

Doc asked, "Lieutenant, is there anybody in front of you?"

"I can't see anybody."

Which didn't mean a hell of a lot because he couldn't see but just a few feet anyway.

Doc moved cautiously around Kohl and said, "Don't move."

"OK."

Harris came up and said, "Where's Doc goin', Lieutenant?"

Kohl tried to think. *Boy, I really fucked up this time.* "He went up to see if he could find Ski."

Harris said, "Shhhhh. I think I hear something. Halt! Who goes there?"

"Don't shoot Harris. It's me, Doc. No can find."

"I'll go back and tell Sarge," said Harris. A few moments later Sergeant Fontain appeared next to Kohl.

"How far'd you go, Doc?" asked Sergeant Fontain.

"Not far. I didn't want to get lost nor shot."

"All right. We stay here. Once Ford realizes that we have been separated, he will continue on to the LP. They have the radio, so we'll just sit up here. I don't want us shooting at each other. Stay quiet and alert."

"I'm sorry, Sarge."

"No problem, Lieutenant. We couldn't have done anything tonight anyway. No biggy."

"Hey Doc?"

"Yeah, Lieutenant?"

"I fucked up this time. Hit me."

"Naw... I"

"Hit me. I hit you. Now you hit me. Hit me right here," Kohl said pointing to his cheek.

"I can't hit you, Lieutenant."

"Yes you can. I'm ordering you to hit me."

"Shut up, Lieutenant, before I hit you," growled Sergeant Fontain.

"Yes, Sir."

There were a few chuckles as everyone settled in for the night. It was understood that no one would sleep that night. It was about 0300 when Kohl heard a thump. He quickly rolled to his stomach and covered his head with his hands. It was the same sound you heard when a grenade lands before it explodes. He waited for the explosion. No explosion. He had been told that the VC would throw rocks to make the Marines think they were grenades and listen for them to move or run for cover. Then they would throw the real thing. Please don't move anybody. Kohl heard another thump. Close this time. He felt something roll against his leg. Panic ceased him by the throat. He was frozen in terror. He gritted his teeth and closed his eyes. *Oh my God. There goes my leg. It's all my fault. They know where we are. Man, I don't want to die. Boy, did I fuck up.* He waited. Listening. There was no explosion. Finally he slowly slide his hand down to the object next to his leg. It felt cold and hard ... smooth ... *This in not a rock.* He let out a short gasp. In his hand was a grenade. *A dud. It could go off. What shall I do with it? Should I throw it? They might hear me.* He sat up and threw it. He heard it crash through the brush. *Did they hear me? Do they know where I am?* Kohl thought he was going to pass out from not breathing.

I've got to take a shit. Bad. I wish I were scared shitless.

Why Kohl, you made a little funny there. I'm surprised considering your situation and all.

Kohl heard another thump. Further off this time. He relieved himself in his pants. *How fucking humiliating.* At 0400 he saw a dim light in the eastern sky. *Just a little longer and I've made it through this nightmare.*

They had been coming out here on hill 368 on several occasions now. Kohl had warned Major Krinshaw that they needed to change the patrol routes. "The VC know we are out there now and it won't be long until we get nailed in an ambush," he told him. Tonight was a close call. *We were lucky tonight. Would that be just normal luck or very good luck? I'd say very good luck. Think about it Kohl. That grenade that rolled against your leg was a dud. Lucky. Yesterday you were almost blown to bits by a little girl selling Coke. Lucky. It's only April. You have six more months. You can only be lucky so long and your luck runs out. The odds are not in your favor here, ol' buddy.*

Kohl had to go again. He relieved himself in his pants for the second time. He cried softly.

Oh dear God. I'm sorry. So sorry. I haven't been the best, I know. Haven't called on you except when I want something and that ain't right, I know. But, right now I need help, Lord. I'm scared to death. I crapped my pants. I put my troops in danger. I can't get down, Lord. They depend on me. It seems like I'm having my life sucked out of me. Please give me the strength to get through this one night. Please help me. I feel like I'm falling off the edge. I need you. Are you listening? Give me a sign. Amen.

Kohl listened and looked into the night of stars mounted on a black curtain. A shooting star? No, just a flare. He watched the light slowly creep into the eastern sky. He could smell himself. *This is so disgusting.*

Kohl heard something crawling through the bushes. He raised his forty-five. Then he saw the face of Sergeant Fontain. He lowered his weapon and gave a weary, self-conscious smile.

"You okay, Lieutenant?"

"Yeah."

"It got a little hairy, but every body's fine." The Sergeant sniffed.

"I soiled myself, Sarge. Don't tell anybody, okay?"

Kohl rolled over, grabbed his canteen and crawled into the brush. He took off his pants and shorts, then cleaned himself. He buried his shorts.

When he returned the Sergeant said, "I'm sending Grant's squad out to find

Ford."

Grant came back within minutes and told them that Ford and the rest of the platoon was about fifty yards down the trail.

Kohl suffered through most of the day without water because he used all his water to clean himself. At about two in the afternoon heat Kohl crumpled to the ground. Marseilles was next to the Lieutenant when he fell. He noticed his pail and clammy skin and pulled him into the shade. The platoon used what little water they had left to bring the lieutenant's temperature down. Kohl was so weak they had to carry him to the helo pad for their evacuation late that afternoon.

*

It had been two months since the 3rd Battalion, 9th Marines had arrived in Danang. By now the battalion had erected a mess tent and was serving "K" rations, which are "C" rations in bulk. Kohl was sitting next to Chaplain Pat O'Riley drinking coffee and listening to the Grand Ol' Opry on a little transistor radio. Johnny Cash was singing "Amazing Grace."

Amazing Grace
how sweet the sound
That saved a wretch like me!
I once was lost but now am found
was blind but now I see

'Twas grace
that taught my heart to fear
and grace my fears relieved
How precious did that grace appear
the hour I first believed.

Tho' many
dangers, toils and snares
I have already come
'Tis grace has bro't me safe thus far
and grace will lead me home.

The Lord
has promised good to me
His word my hope secures

He will my shield and portion be
As long as life endures.

At the end of the song Kohl had tears running down his cheek. He put his head down on the table and began to sob. Reverend O'Riley put his muscled arm around Kohl's heaving shoulders. He let him weep. Kohl finally said, "Pat, I need help."

"Talk to me".

Kohl didn't know how or where to start. What had happened to bring him to this point of despair? He said,"I have felt like a lightning rod ever since I came here. The lightning is striking all around me and I have this feeling that eventually I'm going to get hit. I completely blew it two days ago. I could have gotten my whole outfit killed because of my stupidity."

"Don't blame yourself too much, Dusty. You didn't know you were going to go back out so soon."

"But that just goes to show you, Pat. I have to be always ready. I can't let my guard drop. I have to be there for my troops. I have to be able to think clearly. I've only been here two months and I'm exhausted."

Pat said, "You know, I get up in the mornings and see the beauty in this land. Then the first instant I see a Marine it reminds me of the horror of war. Somehow sin entered into this beautiful setting and settled around us like a poison fog. The best that both you and me can hope for is to find some purpose, a reason why we're here. I have a pretty good idea of why I'm here. You will have to find your purpose, Dusty. There was this Jewish psychiatrist named Victor Frankl that I read about. He was in Auschwitz. The Germans exterminated his whole family. Only through luck, good fortune, or divine intervention did he survive. He spent years trying to find a meaning to the chaos. Why was his family all dead and he left to live? He later wrote that he believes that his whole life has meaning. He said, 'We just don't always figure it out.' You may not know now, Dusty, what your purpose is. Why you are here? But you have a purpose, Dusty. God has a plan for you. It's up to you to find it.

"Dusty, right now you're physically very weak. You're also spiritually weak. Currently you are walking through the Valley of the Shadow of Death. I believe you'll get through it. Now what you have to do is believe that you will get through. It's not going to be easy and you won't escape untouched.

"Do you understand what I'm trying to say, Dusty?"

"I think so."

"Join me in prayer, Dusty."

The reverend looked to the night sky filled with white jewels.

Even though I walk through the Valley of the Shadow of Death,
I fear no evil;
For thou art with me;
Thy rod and thy staff,
They comfort me.
Thou preparest a table before me in the presence of my enemies;
Thou anointest my head with oil,
My cup overflows.
Surely goodness and mercy will follow me all the days of my life;
And I shall dwell in the house of the Lord forever and ever.
Amen.

Kohl was silent for several minutes and said, "Thanks Pat. It's hard to believe that there's a purpose to all of this. I find it hard to believe that God has a plan. How could a just God be involved with this? Can we really make a difference here?"

"Dusty, God has already placed his protective hand on you. Think about it?"

"I think you're right, Pat. Thank you."

"It's my purpose, Dusty. Live so you can find yours."

22 God's On Our Side

Kohl: God's on our side.
Charlie: Oh, no he's not. He's on our side.
Kohl: No he's not.
Charlie: Yes he is.
Kohl: Oh, Yeah? He's on our side.
Charlie: What makes you think he's on your side, huh?
Kohl: Because we're Americans. He's always on our side.
Charlie: Just because you're Americans doesn't mean he's on your side. He could be on our side more than yours.
Kohl: How do you figure that?
Charlie: Because we are in the right.
Kohl: You're not in the right. We are.
Charlie: No you're not. We are.
Kohl: Oh, yeah?
Charlie: Yeah.
God: You're both wrong.
Kohl: Who's that?
Charlie: I don't know.
Kohl: Who is that?
God: I'm the Lord.
Kohl: Oh, thank God you're here. Maybe you can settle a little argument.
God: I'll see what I can do.
Charlie: Whose side are you on?

God: I'm not on anybody's side.

Kohl: What? That can't be. You've always been on our side.

God: Who said so?

Kohl: Well everybody has. George Washington, Andrew Jackson, Abraham Lincoln, Franklin D. Roosevelt, Harry Truman, Dwight Eisenhower, Lyndon Johnson. I mean we are a country founded on Christian values."

Charlie: He's our God too, you know.

Kohl: No. He's ours.

God: Hold on here. I'm everybody's God and I don't show favorites. You guys are missing the point. In the beginning, I gave you free will. I did that so I wouldn't have to dilly-dally in everyone's affairs, break up fights, settle arguments, in other words take sides."

Kohl: Well the Bible says that you are on the side of promoting justice and righteousness. That you will protect us from harm and even sometimes you will use your influence to turn nature against our enemies.

God: Oh, I did a few things like that in the beginning. You know, to help jump start civilization. But now, it's all too complicated, even for me. My only hope is that people be good, kind, generous, helpful, things like that. I really don't like war. In fact, I detest it.

Kohl: What are we to do then? The politicians sent us here and we have to follow the orders of our officers. They all say it is the right thing to do.

Charlie: Same with me. I'd rather be home humping my wife and farming rice.

God: I'm sorry. I can't answer your question. I can only say to try and do what is right and honorable. There are times when you will have to stand up for your principles, to protect your life, the lives of others and your property. That's your choice. Just choose wisely. A lot of times there are other ways to solve problems than to fight. You should take the time to try and understand one another. Most of the time you will find that your enemy is no different than you. Different color and lives in a different place, but the soul is the same.

It amazes, even me, how resourceful you people are sometimes. All those gadgets you use to blow each other to smithereens. Seems like your energies can be used in other ways to help mankind instead of destroying it. There's no doubt you're in a pickle here. All I can say is don't worry too much about what the politicians say. They are all liars. They certainly don't have the right speaking for me, saying whose side I'm on. The way they are behaving, they will all find their way to their own private hell."

23 Ghost Riders In the Sky

Kohl was on patrol with Beach's team. Thorogood was point, followed by Beach, Schultz, Kohl, Doc and Woods bringing up the rear. They were patrolling in a steep vine-choked ravine when Kohl heard "Ka Rump".

"Oh, my God!"

Kohl could not see Beach, but he recognized his voice.

"Oh, my God! Oh, Jesus!" continued Beach frantically.

"What's wrong?" Kohl asked. "What happened?"

"Oh, shit! Don't move Schultz. Stay back," cautioned Beach.

Kohl crawled forward, passing the kneeling, wide-eyed Schultz. "What happened, Schultz?" Kohl still could not see around the bend in the ravine and through all the brush. Schultz shrugged his shoulders.

"I think Reb's hurt," Schultz said.

As Kohl continued around the bend, he saw a smoky mist hanging in the still hot air like a gray backdrop. He saw Beach kneeling, looking into the smoke.

"It's Reb, Lieutenant," Beach cried.

"Check it out. Be careful," cautioned Kohl.

Kohl turned and said, "Doc, up."

"He's alive. Oh, thank God. He's alive. Oh, Reb buddy," sobbed Beach.

Kohl moved forward trying to step where Beach had stepped.

"Follow me, Doc," said Kohl.

Kohl smelled the burnt powder and a smell that reminded him of a gutted animal. A sweet, warm scent filled his nostrils. The smell brought the bile from his stomach into his throat. He knelt next to Beach. Reb's stomach was a mangled mess. Some of his insides were lying next to him on the ground. He had been a victim of a 'Bouncing Betty grenade.' Reb's eyes fluttered. Kohl reached for his hand but it was gone. It wasn't at the end of his sleeve.

"Oh, fuck!" said Kohl.

Reb opened his mouth. Doc was tucking his guts and the severed hand back into his stomach cavity. Reb was humming a song. Kohl heard instruments playing. When he turned his head he saw Beach strumming a guitar, Schultz was playing the violin and Woods was playing a stand up bass. He looked back as Doc was placing bandage packs over Reb's seeping stomach wound. Kohl began to sing.

I see the man before me
all crying and wretched in pain
a callin' for me to help him.
He calls me by my name.

(Then Reb sings.)

Come over yonder.
Come over by my side.
I'm dying and I want you to stay here
and pray with me, he cried.

I want to go over home,
to the valleys and green trees,
where my Mother is waiting for me,
a waiting tenderly.

Hold my hand.
Listen will you Kohl.
My heart is growing weaker.
I know that I may go.

Tell mother I'm so sorrow.
Tell of my good-bye.
hold and comfort her,
and tell her not to cry.

I'm so cold, so very cold.
Cover me will you Please.
I know it's not much longer
until my life will cease.

Pray for my soul.
Pray that I will go
where the valleys are so lovely
and the trees are white with snow.

My war will soon be over.
Please won't you try,
to see my Mother, please, Sir,
and tell her of my good-bye.
Tell her of my good-bye.

*

"I will."

"It's time to go, Lieutenant."

"I will. I'll tell her."

"Lieutenant! Wake up. It's rise and shine time. You can tell her later," Sergeant Fontain said laughing.

"What?" said a startled Kohl as he sat up.

"Time to get ready for our little walk in the jungle, Lieutenant."

"Okay. Thanks Sarge."

24 *Playing by the Rules*

It was May 5th. For the first time Kohl's platoon had on their battle gear of helmets and flack jackets. They had always traveled light before. They were preparing to return to hill 368 this time with Mike Company. Things were beginning to change. Just twenty-five miles south of Danang the ARVN's had a major clash with the Vietcong forces.

Captain Reeser was the company commander. The weather was stifling. Mike Company could rotate their troops on patrol, but Kohl's squads went out every day. After the third day they were exhausted. Mays called Kohl on the radio.

"You're going to have company, my boy."

"Yeah? Who?"

"Our beloved XO from Recon. Battalion is comin' out to see you."

About 1600 hours the chopper came and out jumped Lieutenant Commander Horgan. Kohl had never seen him before, nor knew what he looked like. He was impressive. He was a big man with a barrel chest. Kohl swaggered up to the helo pad to greet him. Just to show what a great Marine he was, Kohl had four grenades hanging from his flack jacket pockets and his newly acquired forty-five-caliber submachine gun slung over his shoulder. The Colonel gave Kohl a long studying look. Kohl was watching for some kind of a signal that the Colonel approved of his attire but said nothing.

"Good afternoon, Sir, and welcome to Vietnam," Kohl said with a smile.

"Lieutenant Kohl?" he said sternly.

"Yes, Sir."

"Where are your men?"

"Most of them are out on patrol, Sir, that is except for my radio operator and corpsman, Sir."

He looked around with his big hands on his hips. "What's your mission?"

"Since we have been out here before, we are acting as guides to the combat patrols of Mike Company, Sir."

"Can you explain to me why you're wearing those grenades in your vest, Lieutenant?"

"Well, Sir. They're handy, easy to get to."

The XO gave Kohl an annoyed look. "Uh huh. A good way to get yourself blown up. A bullet hit one of those and there'd be nothin' left of you but burnt flesh. And this?" he said pointing at Kohl's Submachine gun.

"I felt that I needed a little more fire power when I was on patrol, Sir."

"Uh huh. Well, it's against regulations, Lieutenant. And there's a reason why officers do not carry any other weapon besides their forty-five. You are aware of those reasons, aren't you?"

"Yes, Sir, I am."

"Uh huh."

This is not going well.

At this point he turned and walked from Kohl and started heading north off the ridgeline. "Sir?" asked Kohl.

He stopped and turned slightly.

"Sir? May I asked where you're going?"

"Going back," he said as if annoyed.

"Sir? Aren't you going to wait for the chopper? I'll call."

"I'm walking back."

Walking? "Sir, it's over ten miles, more like fifteen. You'll be lucky to get back before dark. We don't know what's down there in the vills, Sir."

"I have my forty-five."

Well, Hi-ho-Silver, Lone Ranger. You just gallop on down there then, you muscle-bound hairball.

"I can send a rifleman back with you."

"No, that won't be necessary." Without another word he turned and disappeared into the brush.

Good bye, fat ass Lieutenant Commander Horgan. I hope you get your fat ass shot to shit.

By this time Captain Reeser came up to greet the Lieutenant Commander.

"Where'd he go?"

"Left."

"What do you mean, left?"

"Gone, Captain. He started walking back."

"Why didn't he take the chopper back?"

"Captain, I really don't know and to tell you the truth, I don't give a shit."

The Captain gave Kohl an annoyed look.

"Well I don't. I offered to send for a chopper and he said no. I offered to send a rifleman with him and he said no. I told him that I didn't know what was down in those villages and he said he had his forty-five."

"Well, call Battalion and tell them what he's doing. They'll probably send a jeep for him."

"Okay, Sir. Will do."

*

The Second Platoon Commander was a Second Lieutenant Flynn. Kohl was sending Sergeant Fontain and Grant's squad of Woods, Flowers and Harris to act as guides. They were to set up an ambush at the northwest base of hill 368 near the village of An Ngai Dong. They were in full combat gear and Kohl could hear them crashing down the canyon. *Here we come everybody.* After it got dark, they went into radio silence. At about 2130, from atop the hill, Kohl saw a red flare. *This was a new American game. Guess who's waiting in ambush? Surprise! Now that we have been here awhile it has given the big mucky mucks time to come ashore and give us "the rules of engagement." Apparently we gung-ho Marines, have shot a few friendly ARVN's and innocent civilians that have been traipsing around in the dark. Rule number one, if you see or hear anything you throw a red flare. If they are friendly, they will throw a red flare back. If they are not friendly, they'll throw something back and it won't be friendly. Now just in case they are friendly and forgot and left their red smoke grenade at home on the kitchen table, the ever-to-be-fair-Marines will throw an illumination flare. That's rule number two. Light up the place. Up on the hill Kohl saw the illumination flare. By the book, Lieutenant Flynn. This is to visually identify, to see if it really is the enemy. Pay no mind to the fact that there is a curfew and anybody found out running around in the dark had been, until now, fair game. But noooo. We have war rules. No, no, mustn't do. That's another foul on you.*

"Fertilizer Fox, this is Fertilizer Fly, Over."

Captain Reeser was with Kohl and took the call, "This is Fertilizer Fox, Over."

"Fertilizer Fox, this is Fertilizer Fly. We have captured a woman and two children. Waiting for instructions. Over."

"Roger that, Fertilizer Fly. Wait one. Out."

Captain Reeser called Battalion Headquarters for instructions. Kohl remembered what Sergeant Fontain had said how the VC use the women and children. Kohl was glad that he was there to help Lieutenant Flynn. That is if the Lieutenant would take his advice. *Remember. After dark, enemy.*

"Captain? They should bring them in as VC suspects," suggested Kohl.

"We'll wait and see what battalion says, Lieutenant."

"Fertilizer Fox, this is Fertilizer Fly, over."

"Fertilizer Fly, this is Fertilizer Fox, Over."

"Fertilizer Fox. We are trying to interrogate the captives but the woman is carrying on something awful, wailing and crying and we can't understand her. Waiting for instructions. Over."

"This is Fertilizer Fox. How old are the children? Over."

"Fertilizer Fox. This is Fertilizer Fly. It's a guess. But I'd say one is eight and the other could be ten or so. Over."

"This is Fertilizer Fox. I copy and I'll call back with instructions. Out.

"See. If we hadn't taken this extra precaution we would have probably killed an innocent mother and her two children."

The Captain then called battalion headquarters again. They told him to wait for instructions from the Battalion Commander.

Fifteen minutes later Fertilizer Fly came back up on the radio. "Fertilizer Fox, this is Fertilizer Fly. Waiting for instructions. Over."

Fertilizer Fly, this is Fertilizer Fox. Will get back to you. Out."

"Captain? We should probably get the men out of there. They're just sitting ducks, Sir," said Kohl.

"We'll wait."

"Okay."

Some time later Battalion Headquarters called back. "Fertilizer Fox, this is State One, Over." Kohl recognized the voice of the Colonel.

"State One, this is Fertilizer Fox, over."

"Fertilizer Fox, have Fertilizer Fly, bring the prisoners in for interrogation. Over."

"State One, Roger that. Out."

Told you so. Told you so. Na, na, na, na, na.

"Fertilizer Fly, this is Fertilizer Fox, Over."

"This is Fertilizer Fly, Over."

"Fertilizer Fly, bring the prisoners in for interrogation, Over.

There was a long pause at the other end.

"Fertilizer Fly, Fertilizer Fly. Did you read, over."

"Fertilizer Fox. Roger that. Wait one. Over."

There was another long pause.

"Fertilizer Fox, this is Fertilizer Fly. We can't bring the prisoners in."

"Fertilizer Fly. Why? Over."

"Fertilizer Fox. Because they ran off. Over."

"Fertilizer Fly. You mean to tell me you just let them run off? Over."

"Fertilizer Fox. While we were waiting for instructions on what to do, they ran away. What should we do now? Over."

It was now a little after midnight.

"Tell Lieutenant Flynn to maintain the ambush site," said Captain Flynn.

Kohl couldn't believe his ears. "Captain, Sir. If I may? Don't you think that the ambush has been compromised?"

"If I did, I wouldn't have had them stay there."

"But what about the flares, Sir. They could be seen for miles. With all the noise the woman was making, I'm sure, Sir, our ambush site is no longer a secret, Sir. To keep them there is..."

"That's enough, Lieutenant, if you don't mind."

"But Sir..."

"I said enough!"

Kohl muttered, "you crazy fucker."

"You say something?"

"No, Sir."

"Well I'm getting sick and tired of you telling me what to do."

"Yes, Sir."

The next morning as the patrol returned, Sergeant Fontain walked right past Kohl without a glance. His little, frail body was wet with sweat. His handle bar mustache was hanging down below his chin. His eyes were like gray glass and as cold as steel. He walked straight towards the Captain. *Oh, fuck. Is he pissed!* Kohl was debating if he should try to restrain him or let him go. He knew he was a professional and wouldn't do anything to jeopardize his career. He hoped.

"Excuse me Captain. May I have a word with you?"

Sergeant Fontain took the Captain's arm and led him off so they couldn't be heard.

"Take your hand off my arm, Sergeant."

Sergeant Fontain removed his hand from the Captain's arm.

"You'd better watch what you're about to say Sergeant and just calm down."

The Sergeant's words slipped between clenched teeth, like a razors edge he hissed, "If I wasn't calm, I would have gutted you with my fuckin' "K" bar by now. You fuckin' moron ... You could have gotten us all killed by your utter stupidity.

I haven't a clue what possessed you in ... You must be fuckin' brain dead."

The Captain interrupted the Sergeant before he could continue. "You are on the verge of a court Marshall, Sergeant."

"Don't interrupt me again, you fuckin' jerk off. Our ambush site was compromised. First by all that flare horseshit that could be seen for a hundred fuckin' miles. Second, by your lack of a quick decision, we stood around with our thumbs up our ass for two fuckin' hours. That woman and two kids were VC and as soon as they took off, you can bet your miserable ass, they told everybody in the village where we were. We were lucky. If anything would've happened to those kids, I would've kicked your ass up between your ears. I hope you're not too fuckin' dumb to take heed to what I say. Then maybe, just maybe, you can get out of this war alive and without fuckin' things up too much. This is not a fuckin' war game here, Captain. It's for real. You had better get your shit together, Captain."

"You can't talk to me like that. I'm the officer in charge here. I don't know who you think you are talking to me that way. I'm going to write you up for insubordination and showing disrespect to an officer. I'm ... "

"You miserable shit. You are one dumb mutha fucker. You so much as report me and I'll have your ass on the next flight out of here. And if you don't think I can do that, just try me. Just try me." He twirled as he concluded his last comment and stormed off.

The Captain walked over to Kohl, visibly shaken, embarrassed and very angry. He said, "Did you see that?"

"Yes, Sir. I did."

"I want you to be my witness."

"Sorry, Captain. I saw it but I didn't hear a thing."

"He can't get away with that. He threatened me. Said he could get me relieved of my command. Isn't that absurd?"

"No it's not, Sir. He can do it."

"No way. He's just a Staff Sergeant. He couldn't do that, could he?"

"You bet. The Sergeant and General Walt are thick, Captain. Real thick. If I were you, I'd forget the whole thing."

Kohl stayed clear of Sergeant Fontain. It took him two days to calm down. He was yelling and hollering at the troops unmercifully. But they understood and respected the small giant. He would protect them and keep them safe. He was their savior.

25 From the Jaws of Death ...

When they got back from patrol they found their battalion had moved off the hill and replaced by another battalion. Kohl also found that he had orders. He was going back to Okinawa. That means off the hill and out of Vietnam. His platoon crawled down the hill April 11. They acted wild. They looked wild. They were wild. Kohl had asked for and received the approval of the new Battalion CO to take the troops to the China Beach. They had beer, soft drinks, and hot dogs. There were Vietnamese children that gave back rubs. They played tackle football and frolicked in the waves. They got drunk and forgot.

The next day Kohl's relief arrived, Second Lieutenant James Fortney. Kohl was scheduled to leave the next day at 0500. About a third of Kohl's troops were scheduled to rotate back stateside within the next month. Sergeant Fontain came to the Officer's tent.

"Lieutenant? The troops want to see you before you go."

"When?"

"Now, if that's all right, Sir."

"Sure. Ford's meritorious promotion just came in and I want to give him his stripes. That is unless you want to, Sarge?

"No. You do it, Sir."

They walked over to where the troops were billeted. Corporal Ford brought St. Joe Alpha Platoon to attention as Kohl approached. Sergeant Fontain disappeared into the shadows near the tent. Ford did a left face and saluted Kohl.

"St. Joe Alpha Platoon present and accounted for Sir," said Ford.

"Thank you ... Sergeant Ford." Kohl returned his salute.

Ford looked surprised and bewildered. There were murmurs among the troops.

"At ease, men. I have here a letter from Colonel Pratt, Commanding Officer of Third Recon Battalion. It says,

> Corporal Ford has been filling a Staff Sergeant billet as Platoon Sergeant of a reconnaissance platoon for the last six months. He has not only filled this job but has excelled in all phases of the leadership that is required.
>
> Corporal Ford has done an exceptional job in training and preparing his platoon for combat. He has displayed under enemy action and on reconnaissance patrols, quick, automatic and well trained decisions. He has excelled in the gathering of pertinent information. And in the final test, he has shown courage and bravery, which has been displayed on his frequent patrols into enemy territory.
>
> It is for a combat situation that he has been trained. It has been in these combat situations that he has performed and has excelled. And it is under these circumstances that I, Colonel Pratt, Commanding Officer of Third Recon Battalion, here by, recommend that Corporal Ford be meritoriously promoted to Sergeant E-5.
>
> Congratulations.

The letter from the Colonel was almost verbatim of the letter of recommendation that Kohl had sent almost two weeks ago. He remembered Ford pounding on the ship's bulkhead to tell him all the troops were present and accounted for. It seemed like eons ago but it had only been four months. Kohl walked forward and gave the sergeant stripes to a beaming Sergeant Ford.

Sergeant Ford said, "Lieutenant, I speak for St. Joe Alpha, when I say we will miss you. You have been the pillar of strength that we needed to succeed. You brought us down the hill all in one piece. You have been an inspiration to us all. God Bless you in your life, what ever you do, Sir."

Kohl walked over and shook Ford's hand and gave him a hug. He whispered in his ear, "Who wrote the speech?"

Ford whispered back, "Marseilles, Sir."

Kohl turned and faced his platoon and said, "Thank you for the words Sergeant Ford. You guys mean a lot to me. I have mixed emotions about going. I'll be glad to get out of here, but I feel like I'm deserting you guys." Kohl walked along the line of Marines.

"Go back to school, Doc. Be a speechwriter for Governor Brown. Ski, you piece of shit New York radioman, your constant complaining always reminded me where we were. Grant you are one fine Marine. I'm proud to have had you in my platoon. Woods, you goddamn hillbilly. You have been a lot of fun. You are one tough son-of-a-bitch. Bubba. You would be a good career Marine and the Marines would be proud to have you. Harris, don't forget your dreams. Without dreams there is no hope. Sale, you're one of the best field Marines I've ever had. You've got that instinct that makes a man a leader. Hernandez, you're one crazy Mexican. If it hadn't been for you keeping us all in stitches we'd have been all loony by now. You're a good person and I respect you for what you have done. Thank you. Thompson, I'll never forget that first time we met. You have grown into one hell of a man. Charlotte, when you get home, keep a place for me so I can come up fishin' or huntin' sometime. OK? Beach, you have a lot of potential to give. Don't cut yourself short. I enjoyed your company. Schultz, from Athol, go back to school Schultz. There's more to life than humping hills and girls." Last in formation was Thorogood. "Reb, you saved our asses more than once. You're the best damn point in the Marines. Be careful." Handle wasn't there. Sergeant Fontain had caught him smoking weed, wrote him up and was in the brig. Kohl turned to leave before he choked up.

"Lieutenant?" said Flowers. "We want you to have this." He handed Kohl a poster that read "Kohl's Raiders 1965". Flowers had drawn the whole platoon in caricatures along its boarders.

"Thanks men. Lock 'n load and be careful."

*

Kohl found Gunnery Sergeant Hellens in the S-4 tent and said, "Gunney? I'm headin' out tomorrow morning so I need to find my foot locker and sea bag."

The Gunnery Sergeant gave Kohl a long steady look, like he had something on his mind.

"Is there a problem, Gunney?" asked Kohl.

The Gunney got up without a word, nodded to Kohl and motioned him to follow. Kohl stepped in behind the Gunney who briskly walked to a jeep then climbed behind the wheel. Kohl climbed into the passenger seat. They drove off towards the airfield. Still without a word. Kohl didn't ask any questions. He assumed he was taking him to get his gear. He just must be a man of few words. They drove through a security gate and Kohl recognized the area as the place where they bivouacked back in March. The Gunney stopped in front of a Quonset hut, got out and motioned Kohl to follow him. He took out some keys; found the one he was looking for and opened the padlock on the metal doors. He swung them open and he and Kohl stepped inside. Kohl couldn't see anything at first until his eyes became adjusted to the darkness. And then his eyes began revealing slowly what was in front of him.

"Holy shit!"

"That's what I say every time I walk in here, Lieutenant," said the Gunney in a slow drawl.

In front of Kohl was a stack of sea bags and footlockers that reached from wall to wall and went almost to the ceiling. This went on for the whole 100-foot length of the Quonset hut.

"How am I going to find my gear in that?" asked Kohl.

"Well, Lieutenant. There's no way we can find it by tomorrow. What I've been trying to do ever since I got here, is to get a crew down here and go through and sort this goddamn fuckin' mess into units and alphabetical order. But I can't get friggin' bodies. Low priority, they say."

"Gunney, I don't have anything but my utilities. Shit. I can't believe this shit."

"Amen, to that, Lieutenant. When we get it sorted, all I can do right now is to tell you that I'll send it to you."

"I would appreciate whatever you can do for me, Gunney, but I know that my chances of seeing my gear again is next to zero."

The Gunney glared at Kohl as a result of his last comment and said slowly, "Lieutenant, I want to assure you that it is my duty to see that each and every piece of gear here is accounted for and documented. I can assure you that there will be no pilferage."

"Sorry, Gunney. I apologize. My God-All-Mighty. I can't believe they just piled it in here like this. What the hell were they thinking? I can't believe this shit. Thanks for showing me this. I never would have believed it. It'll probably stay this way until some Colonel wants to get his gear."

"I doubt there's any officers gear here that's above captain, Sir. But you're right. It'll probably stay this way until somebody with some clout raises hell. Seen enough?"

"Yeah. Let's go."

*

That evening Kohl tried to get in touch with Mays and Pete to say goodbye. He was able to reach Mays but Pete was busy supervising offloading gear down at the docks in Danang. Kohl met Mays at the Air Force Officer's Club, at the Danang Air Base.

Mays said, "You're one lucky son'bitch."

"Yeah. I guess I am."

"Guess?"

"Well, I have mixed feelings. I feel like I'm deserting the troops, and..."

"But, it's not your choice. You got orders."

"I wonder if it had anything to do with the dead animal thing."

"Naw. If Colonel McGraw had found out it was either of us, he would have sent us out on patrol with nothing but sticks. He sure as hell wouldn't have sent you back to Oki."

"True. Do you think it was because I was drunk on patrol?"

"Don't think so. I'll tell you what I think."

"Okay."

"You're not Pratt trained. They probably sent out Lieutenant Commander Horgan to check you out. But I think the decision was already made. You were history. You see, here's the deal. In you came in January, just in time for a ninety-day cruise with a platoon that was due to rotate back stateside in four months. They were just taking care of some loose ends. By putting you on board ship with troops that were going back stateside was a no sweat, no strain kinda deal. They want recon brown bars to raise for the next three years, not you with less than a year. They did the same with me. Stuck me in Recon S-2 and loaded me on board ship. Just like you. But they didn't plan on this little war. Now they have to do some serious switcho-chango. You are the first recon combat officer, but you're not one of them. They've got gung-ho officers just itchin' for glory. You're history, man."

"How do you know all this shit?"

"I'm S-2, intelligence, remember?"

"Oh. I keep forgetting. Will you excuse me? I've got to take another crap."

PART III
OKINAWA

Pass the Booze
By
Gene Northington & Ray Butts

I've been with friends all day
It's no good I'm still lonely
Seems like I just can't forget my one and only.

So there's just one thing left to do
If I intend to sleep tonight
Put the bottle on the bar and let me do it up right.

Please put the bottle on the bar
Where I can pet it
Take my address down before I forget it
I've got a feeling someone's gonna have to take me home this time
'Cause I'm gonna set here
Till I get her off my mind.

My baby's gone, gone, gone
And I'm alone, oh so alone
And I've got nothing else to lose
So bartender, pass the booze.

26 *Make Like a Bird and Get the Flock Outa Here*

Schultz came by to pick up Kohl at 0430 to take him to the Danang Air Base. On the way down to the airport, Schultz told Kohl that Ski and Beach got hit the night before. He said the Sergeant and the new Lieutenant got into a shouting match because of it.

"Sarge was pissed because the Lieutenant sent them out to an LP/OP in an area they hadn't checked out and in broad daylight. The Lieutenant hadn't consulted Sarge about it, I guess. Really pissed him off. Ski was hit with grenade shrapnel. He's not hurt bad but might loose some of the sight in his right eye. Beach is okay. Sarge got us together and went out and brought them back. Boy was he pissed." Schultz let out a deep sigh. "Ski wouldn't have got hurt if you had been there, Lieutenant. No, Sir."

"Oh, I doubt that, Schultz. We were bound to get hit sooner or later."

But Kohl knew that if he had been there, maybe he could have made a difference. First he would have consulted Sergeant Fontain. If Major Newcomb was persistent about when and where to set up the LP/OP and Kohl didn't agree he would have argued his case.

I may not be Pratt trained, but I do have the experience and the training. In Vietnam you learn fast.

Kohl said goodbye to Schultz and checked into airfreight. They said they wouldn't start loading until about 0900. He had almost four hours to kill. He went over to the Air Force Officer's Mess and had breakfast. After breakfast he went back to the terminal and climbed into a chopper and went to sleep.

A Marine guard woke Kohl and helped carry his gear to the GV. They had left the back hatch open and he was able to watch Vietnam disappear. I'll never have to see that sweat box again. But Kohl's emotions were mixed.

What is it, Kohl?

It just don't seem right. Part of me can't wait to get out-a-here and the other part doesn't want to leave. I was replaced yesterday and last night they got hit. Could I have made a difference if I was still there?

You would have listened to Sergeant Fontain and probably argued with Major Wellington. Maybe you would have made a difference. And maybe Ski wouldn't have shrapnel in his right eye.

Damn.

As Kohl settled back with the steady drone of the engines he wrote Julie a letter.

*

April 17, 1965

Hi Sweetheart,

I'm on my way back to Oki. I can't believe I'm actually leaving this sweat hole. I don't know what I'll be there doing there but it's for sure I'll never see this place again.

Last night one of our recon outposts got hit. One of my men was wounded. Lucky I'm outa here.

This place was starting to get to me. The picture I'm sending you was taken outside our recon supply tent. I'm sure a good lookin' warrior, aren't I tho'? I love you darling. I just keep plunging into one day after another. It's going to be so good when I get back home. I think of you so much. I should be able to write more often now that I'm out of the jungle. How I love you. My situation in this world would be impossible, it seems, with out you.

I got a letter on Thursday. So that was a pretty good timing. I tried to get a hold of Pete last night to say good bye but he was down at the docks unloading ships.

Man, I can't believe I'm outa here. Came close to losing my mind but I'll never lose the part that remembers you. I love you with all my heart. Be careful and study hard.

See ya, sooner than you know,
Dusty

*

His friend, First Lieutenant John Ralston, met Kohl at Kadena Air Base. They greeted each other and made small talk until they got in the jeep and headed toward Camp Schwab and Third Reconnaissance Battalion Headquarters.

"Well, what the hell happened, Kohl?"

"What do you mean, what happened? I'm fuckin' out of there, man."

"I heard that you got 'relieved of duty'."

"Relieved? That's horseshit. Where did you hear that?"

"It's been going around for about the last two weeks now."

"That's bullshit, John. I wasn't relieved. What exactly did you hear?"

"The scuttlebutt is that the Colonel has been getting messages from Dole."

"Spade?"

"He was there with ya, right?"

"Yeah. He had the other recon platoon. What did he say?"

"Well, it wasn't good. I don't know any of the specifics. I think Spade was cutting you to make himself look good. Word was that if it hadn't been for him you would have been up shit creek. Rumors really started flying after Lieutenant Colonel Horgan got back. Shit. There are about five of us that have known you from Basic School. We know you're a fuck-up."

"Shut up."

"Just kidding," laughed Ralston. "We knew something wasn't right. It just didn't fit."

Kohl told Rolston about the XO's ten-minute visit.

"He said that you hadn't made arrangements for transportation and he had to walk all the way back to camp in enemy territory."

"That's bullshit."

"And he said you were dressed up like something out of a John Wayne movie."

"He was right there, I guess." Kohl paused and said, "This pisses me off. I know this sounds weird and I'm glad to be out of that fuckin' place and I don't ever want to go back, but I don't like this one bit. I'm going to try and get to the bottom of this. I can't believe Spade would do that to me. He didn't show any animosity towards me. We got along fine. I even got to like that muscle bound gung-ho prick."

"Listen. It was no secret. Spade was sent for a reason. Everybody knew he had his nose so far up the Colonel's ass, he had a brown ring around his neck."

When Kohl arrived back at Camp Schwab, he reported into the duty NCO and checked into his BOQ room. Immediately he was bombarded with questions about what had happened and what it was like in Vietnam. He told them that he was tired and wanted to get some chow and go to bed. He took a long warm shower and slept a restless sleep. The next day was Sunday and Kohl and Rolston went to Kossa for shopping and drinking. It was raining hard just like the first time he was in Okinawa back in January.

Monday morning at breakfast, Ralston and Lieutenant George Briggs, another buddy from Camp Pendleton, joined Kohl at the table.

"Got some scoop for you, Kohl," said Briggs.

"Yeah. Me too," said Rolston. "I've been checkin' with Sergeant Hilton, communications. And I got to see some of the copies of transmissions that came in. The deal appears to be that," he leaned closer so others couldn't hear, "if it hadn't of been for Spade tellin' you what to do and how to do it, you and your platoon would have really been in trouble."

"I can't believe this," said Kohl shaking his head. "I mean. Mays knows. Major Wellington knows. Sergeant Fontain had confidence in me. Were any of these allegations confirmed?"

"Not that I'm aware of. Except for that visit by the XO. But listen. It makes sense, if you see it through Colonel Pratt's eyes. Here's what I think the deal is. You're not Pratt trained. And because you're not Pratt trained, you are a fuck up. Plus they don't want to admit they made a mistake by sending you afloat and into Vietnam without recon training. That's what I think."

"Mays said the same thing," informed Kohl.

"I heard you've got orders," said Briggs.

"Where?" asked Kohl.

"Don't know. But it's some place other than here."

Kohl was upset. He spent the rest of the morning trying to anticipate what he would say at the meeting with the Colonel. He formulated the questions in his mind. *Was I relieved? If so, Why?* He wondered if he would get an unsatisfactory fitness report and if he should ask for and file a Request for Mast?

Kohl received word that Captain Heart wanted to see him. He walked into the Quonset hut, said hello to the Top, then proceeded into the captain's office. The Captain asked Kohl to write a report entitled "Lessons Learned in Vietnam." This surprised Kohl considering the information he had been given. At least the Captain wanted to know what kind of information he had to offer.

Kohl spent the afternoon writing the report. He praised the men in Saint Joe Alpha, especially Sergeant Ford. He complemented Third Recon. Battalion for the caliber of men and the training they received.

He expressed his concern that his platoon had not been utilized properly especially when they had been assigned to scout for rifle companies. He also criticized the lack of proper equipment and supplies. He complained the ARVN troops had Hewys, while the Marines still used the H-34's.

They had the lightweight jungle fatigues and the Marines still were wearing the utilities from WW II.

They had jungle boots while his troops' leather boots got wet and rotted, plus the eyelets would get caught on vines. The Army had new light M-16's and the Marines were carrying M-14's. Most of the gear was from the Korean War and some even from WW II. But Kohl's harshest criticism was in regard to the "Rules of Engagement." Kohl wrote,

> "Rules of engagement were imposed just before I left. When we were out on patrol we were to throw a red flare if we came upon persons unknown. If they were friendly, they would respond by throwing a green flare. If they didn't respond with a green flare, we were supposed to throw an illumination grenade, in order to identify them as friendly or enemy. It was a joke. For one thing you couldn't tell who was the enemy. The Viet Cong wore ARVN uniforms. The rule when we first got there was if anybody was out after curfew, they were enemy, fair game. But because we killed some "civilians," they imposed these identifying rules. Needless to say ambushes were a waste plus placed the troops in perilous situations."

There were other problems that Kohl didn't mention in his report. He knew the Marine Corps brass didn't like to be criticized. He felt he had probably stepped outside the bounds already. The problem was with the Marine 782 gear. This was equipment like packs, blankets, web belts, ammo pockets, canteens, helmets, etc. The problem was when Marines are issued their 782 gear from supply they got whatever was available. Most of it was in terrible condition. When it came to inspections, the troops were criticized and given unsatisfactory reports for poor gear. In turn the troops would go to the Army/Navy surplus stores and buy new gear with their own money in order to pass inspections, a common practice in the Marine Corps. So what happened when the Marines packed for their 90 day cruise, not knowing that they were going to be landing in Vietnam, they had the old worn out 782 gear and left their good stuff back in Oki. Their old stuff was falling apart.

*

Kohl was called into the Battalion Commander's office the next day at 1500 hours.

Here goes.

"Come in, Lieutenant. Have a seat," said a smiling Colonel Pratt.

"Thank you, Sir."

To the left of the Colonel sat Lieutenant Colonel Horgan. He smiled and nodded to Kohl.

Hi, fat ass Horgan.

All smiles.

"We want to congratulate you on a job well done, Lieutenant," said Colonel Pratt smiling.

"Thank you, Sir. I did my best, Sir. But a job well done was not what I heard when I got back, Sir. I heard I had been relieved. Now why would I hear one thing from my friends and another thing from you, Sir? I don't like the idea of being shit-canned and if I have anything recorded in my fitness report that is detrimental to my performance of duty, I'm writing a statement in rebuttal."

"Now, wait a minute, here, Lieutenant. You're on the verge of being disrespectful," the XO said.

Colonel Pratt gave the XO a confident wave of the hand as an indication that he had control of the situation.

"Lieutenant Kohl, let me assure you that what you have heard has been just rumor. No truth to it. You were not relieved. Your orders came form Division Headquarters. Our hands have been tied," he said with a shrug. "We would like to keep you here to help us train the troops who will soon be heading for Vietnam. But ... You are apparently needed elsewhere. I wish you the best and ... Do you have anything to add Colonel?" He asked the XO.

"No. Nothing, Sir."

"Thank you again, Lieutenant. That will be all."

Short and sweet. Now get the fuck out of here. Kohl stood up, came to attention and said, "Aye, aye, Sir." He did an about face and marched smartly from the office. *They are pacifying me. I could stay and fight this.*

Fight what? And if you stay, they could send your ass back to Vietnam.

I don't want to be here anyway. I just didn't like the way it was done.

They didn't ask me one question about Vietnam. It was like I'd never existed. Like I was never there. I was there, Goddamn it. I was there

With Kohl it was a matter of honor, duty, obligation and pride. True he complained about being in Vietnam. There's no doubt he'd rather be someplace else. And he was less than pleased about the Marine Corps. But he felt a responsibility to his troops. It was his duty. He felt his duty and honor was being questioned. That he didn't measure up to their standards. Duty, honor, and pride were not only the creed that the Marines stood by; it was Kohl's creed too.

He heard the XO call his name. He turned and the XO handed him an envelope.

"Oh, by the way, here's your request for an early release. We never got to it."

Fucker!

*

Kohl was still having problems with diarrhea so the first chance he got he went to the camp infirmary. He told the male nurse what his problem was. The nurse had him go immediately in to see the doctor.

"Hello, Lieutenant. How can I help you?"

"I've got diarrhea real bad, Doc. I just got back from Vietnam last week."

"Yeah, well, you probably picked up amebic dysentery."

"What's that?"

"You probably drank some bad water or ate some contaminated food."

Kohl was trying to recall what he had eaten. All the food had been "C" or "K" rations. The water had all been treated with Halizon tablets. That is except the time he was bringing the dead VC body back and he stuck his head under the water fall and inadvertently drank some. Even though the water ran clear and cool it must have been infested with bacteria.

The doctor asked Kohl to remove his clothes down to his socks and briefs.

"Here. Step up here," the doctor said pointing to the scale. Kohl stepped up and stood still while the doctor adjusted the ballast. Kohl watched it move down and down. It finally balanced. "A hundred and fifty-five," the doctor said.

Holy shit!

"Have you lost a little weight or are you just naturally emancipated?" said the doctor.

Kohl was thinking. When he got to Okinawa, he weighed between one hundred and eighty-five to one hundred and ninety pounds. He lost about ten pounds on board ship and then he must have lost the rest in Vietnam. He looked at his body in the mirror. He was nothing but skin and bone. "I've lost about thirty pounds, Sir."

The doctor whistled. "I'll give you some pills for your dysentery and some vitamins to take, plus some Milk-o-Magnesia." He scribbled some instructions and said, "Here, give this to the nurse."

"Thank you, Sir."

I might have left Vietnam but it didn't leave me.

*

Two days later, when Kohl went to the bathroom he happened to glance into the bowl. This was not an everyday occurrence to check out the condition of his bowl movement. It wasn't that exciting to see diarrhea in various shades of brown. Within the confines of the bowl he thought he saw movement. He bent over for a closer look and saw two reddish worms about eight inches long. He panicked, hyperventilated and passed out, bumped his head on the sink and rolled to the bathroom floor. It was only a few seconds when his breathing returned to normal and he regained consciousness. *I've got fuckin' worms. Holly shit.* He got up off the floor and walked shakily over to his rack and sat down. He waited until he had calmed down, then went back to see the worms again. He was wondering if he should take the worms to the Doc ... but dismissed the idea. *I'll just give him a good description.*

"Is the Doc in?" Kohl asked the nurse.

"Yeah. What's the problem? You look a little pale."

"Man, I shit some worms."

"I'll tell the Doc you're in."

Kohl was shown into the Doctor's office. The Doc said, "Passed some worms, uh?"

"Yeah. Two brown fuckers about eight inches long."

"Did you bring them in?"

"Are you serious? That's fuckin' disgusting, man."

"Did you flush the toilet?"

"No," said Kohl softly. He didn't flush; thinking there might be a chance the doctor wanted to see the worms. He hoped not. But now it was obvious that he was going to go back and fish those worms out of the bowl. The Doc gave him some rubber gloves and container. "Are you sure you need to see those things?"

"Yes."

27 Headquarters

Kohl's luck was making a big turn for the better. He was taking the place of an action, starved 0302 as the Assistant S-4 of Force Service Regiment. Kohl knew he was going to like Major Newcomb soon after they met. He had a quick friendly smile. His manner was courteous and he spoke to Kohl in the confident way of a teacher not that of a superior officer.

"You are my assistant, not my lackey. I will ask you to share my workload and if we both do our part, we will have time to have a little fun on the island. Make our stay here as pleasant as possible. Life's too precious to waste. Don't you think?"

He gave Kohl the list of his duties. Kohl's eyes focused on the long list. *This doesn't look like sharing to me.* He was officer-in-charge (OIC) of the Officer's and NCO Mess, BOQ, the Officer's and NCO clubs, Fire Marshall, Regimental Safety, Labor Relations, Athletic and Recreational Activities, Utilities Control, Embarkation and Movies.

"Just looks impressive," the Major said. "Nothing to it, really. You have outstanding NCO's, Lieutenant. Trust them and let them do their job and you'll do fine. All you have to do is peek in on them every now and then."

"Don't worry, Major. I'm not one to play the high and mighty. It's not my style," said Kohl.

And the Major was right. Kohl had a Warrant Officer in charge of the Officer's Club, a Master Sergeant in charge of the Officer's Mess, a Fist Sergeant in charge of the BOQ and he was also in charge of the labor relations that included the locals that worked on the base. It was the same with all of the other duties he had, all were E-7's and above. They had seen their share of snot-nosed ninety-day wonders. These men knew their jobs. They sure didn't need nor want Kohl telling them what and how to do something. The problem was that it didn't stop a lot of young officers from trying to tell NCO's what and how to do something that they knew absolutely nothing about. But it didn't take the NCO's long to see that Lieutenant Kohl showed them the respect they deserved and in turn the respect was reciprocated.

Kohl told the Major that the khakis he was wearing were borrowed and that his gear was still in Vietnam and didn't have any idea of when or if he would ever get his gear. The Major made arrangements for a clothing allotment.

Finally a 7:30 to 4:30 job, soft rack, and a nasain to wash my cloths and clean my room, a hot shower, a bar and good food. Now this is livin'.

As BOQ Officer he got one of the best rooms, but he had to be careful. It couldn't be nicer than a major's or colonels. He could have chose to live alone if he wanted, but Marines were coming in fast for the build up in Vietnam. He thought it would work out okay if he had a roommate.

He was an east coaster.

What's your problem with east coasters? Are you prejudiced?

No. They just seem so uptight.

He had black hair, milky white skin, and a long, thin nose above a thin mustache and full lower lip. He reminded Kohl of the movie star Earl Flynn.

"Your name Kohl?"

"Yeah. What's yours?" as they shook hands.

"I guess I'm your roomy. Name's Charley Stern," he said as he threw his sea bag on his rack and began unpacking. "I'm in Engineering Battalion. How is it over here?"

"I've only been here a little over two weeks myself, so I don't know a hell of a lot. It's been raining mostly."

"Man, let me tell ya. If my trip over was any indication of how things are going to be, I'm going to have a ball. We sailed out of San Diego on a ship full of military dependents. It was like a two-week cruise. Fucking beautiful. Horny chicks everywhere. I met this broad that was on her way to Japan to be with her flyboy husband. And I could see why he wanted her near. She was one horny woman. We screwed all the way over to Japan, in all positions and in all places."

He proceeded to provide Kohl with all the sorted details. "Man, what a lay. Apparently her hubby had heard about her running around and got the Air Force Chaplain to get permission for him to bring his wife over in order to save his marriage. The way she was banging, it was going to take more than what he had to keep her. She was one sex-starved lady. Man-o-man. I'm planning on having one hell of a good time. Glad the Marines don't let their wives come over."

"You married?"

"Yeah, and have a kid too. They're back in Providence. I've been married five years. I need a fuckin' breather. Five years is like forever, man.

"There was this girl I met in Diego while I was waiting for the ship. She was going to San Diego State. Man, I fucked her beautiful brains out for two days. I ..."

He kept talking about his sexual escapades while he unpacked but Kohl had already tuned him out. He returned to the book he was reading called "The Devil's Advocate." To Kohl he seemed like a nice enough guy, but he didn't have any respect for officers that fooled around on their wives.

Goddamn east coaster.

28 Ed Ames Sings Indian Songs

Kohl went to see some of his old 3/1 buddies who just got in from Camp Pendleton. He found them in the officer's club drinking beer and they were bitching already. Kohl called Rolston and Briggs, who were at Camp Schwab, to come down and join them. It was 2100 by the time they arrived. After a few more beers, Kohl, Rolston, Briggs, and two of the 3/1 buddies, Thorton and Shelbee, got a cab and went to the Kadena Air Force Officer's Club. They were on their second round of Singapore Slings when in walked Joe Wheeler. They saw him and waved him over.

"Man, I've been following you guys from bar to bar," said Wheeler.

"What are you doing here?" asked Kohl.

"Got orders out of the sweat box. They're sending me to some prisoner of war interrogation school or something like that. Some shit, huh?"

"How are things going back in Nam?" asked Kohl.

"Same ol' shit. We are getting more contact now. Say, your old outfit got hit a couple of days ago."

"Anybody hurt?"

"Yeah. Got the shit kicked out of 'em. I recall hearing that the lieutenant got zapped."

Kohl wanted to ask Wheeler more questions but before he could Wheeler called the waitress. She came over to the table to take his order. "Bring me six bottles of champagne," ordered Wheeler.

"Champagne?" questioned Briggs.

"What's the occasion?" asked Shelbee.

"Well for starters, I'm out ah Viet-fuckin'-nam, and secondly I got an inheritance in the mail yesterday."

"Somebody die?" asked Rolston.

"I had a rich uncle. Swear to God. He died over a year ago and the estate had been in probate. It finally got settled and I got a nice chunk of change."

"How nice a chunk?" asked Rolston.

"Big chunk," answered Wheeler.

"You miserable rich turd, are you going to tell us or not?" sneered Rolston.

Wheeler was enjoying teasing them. He looked at his fingernails and bit off a hangnail. "It was for over $600,000."

"Holy shit!"

"So, if you fuckers are through with your questions, let's celebrate."

They each worked the corks and popped them over the heads of the unsuspecting patrons of the club.

"Cheers," Wheeler said as they raised their bottles and took drinks. The bottles foamed and fizzed, running from mouths and noses, coughing and choking, Champagne frothing from the opening onto the table and down the arms of the Marines.

"Let's go take in the show. Ed Ames is singing," suggested Kohl.

"Who in the hell is Ed Ames?" asked Shelbee.

"He was the Indian on the TV show ... shit, aah." Thorton was cut off by Briggs.

"Davy Crocket with Fess Parker, wasn't it?" said Briggs.

"Yeah. That's it," said Thorton.

"Singing Indian songs?" asked Shelbee.

"No. You dumb fuck. He just played an Indian. He's not a real Indian. He sang with the Ames Brothers," said Kohl.

"What are some of their songs? The name doesn't ring a bell to me," asked Briggs.

"Well, no wonder, with that country shit you listen to," sneered Thorton.

"Come on you clowns. Let's go listen to the Indian without his brothers sing 'Kilt him a bar when he was only three," sang Rolston.

They all joined in the chorus, "Davy, Davy Crocket. King of the wild frontier."

They got up singing and entered the showroom where Ed Ames was in the middle of 'You, You, You.' Their noisy arrival caused a disturbance, each carrying a bottle of Champagne and pulling out chairs. After the song Kohl raised his hand and asked him if he would sing 'Harbor Lights.'

"How'd you know he sang that?" asked Rolston.

"I like their music. Shhh. Listen," whispered Kohl.

Even though Kohl was trying to listen to the music, his buddies were becoming more rowdy as the night wore on. Then the second round of Champagne bottles arrived. Ed Ames was showing extreme patience and had just finished "The Naughty Lady of Shady Lane" that brought hoots and hollers from the Marines. But some of the other patrons were becoming increasingly annoyed at their behavior. Rolston broke out with the Marine Corps Hymn and was joined by his drunken comrades. The officer's club management had had enough and kicked them out. It was raining outside. They wandered around the street with their Champagne bottles trying to find cabs back to their respective camps. By the time they got cabs they were soaked. Kohl made it back to his BOQ. He staggered over to a downspout and stood under it, letting the water flow over his spinning head. He slogged down the hall leaving a trail of water in his wake. He passed out on his bed.

29 Here's To Ya

Kohl awoke sometime around 1100, still in his wet cloths. *This is the grand daddy of all grand- daddies'. Man, am I hurtin'. Really bad. Champagne hangover. Bad. Bad. Bad. I'll never do this again. I promise.*

He got up and took a long shower. He called the base hospital in Okinawa. He gave the nurse a list of names from his recon platoon to see if any of them were there. PFC Julian Hernandez was there.

Hernandez was in room 317. When Kohl peeked into the room, Hernandez was sitting up in bed eating lunch. His face lit up in wide grin when he saw his platoon commander.

"Hey, Lieutenant. I made it out. I gots me a fuckin' ticket home."

Kohl walked into the room. He tried to control any expression on his face. Hernandez' head was wrapped up. "You look like a fuckin' A'rab," Kohl said as he shook Hernandez' hand. He pulled out a chair and sat next to the bed. "I saw Lieutenant Wheeler last night and he told me you guys got hit. I called here to see if any of you guys were here. How you doin'? What happened anyway?"

"I'm doin' fine, Lieutenant. Got my fuckin' top of my head blowed off. Look."

Before Kohl could say, "Don't do that," he lifted off the turban.

"No big deal. Comes right off. See?"

Kohl couldn't control his surprise. The left side of Hernandez head was bald, covered with scabs and an L shaped ten by eight-inch jagged scar and stitches that looked like barbed wire.

"Jesus, Hernandez."

"Got me a metal plate right there," he pointed.

"Well, tell me what happened."

"The whole platoon was on patrol walking along that road at the bottom of hill 368 out of Hung Fuck (Huong Phuoc). Fuckin' turd brain Woods saw a rifle layin' next to the road and left the column to go and pick it up. But before he did Sergeant Fontain hit Woods in the back with a rock, then yelled at him to leave it the fuck alone. Sure 'nuff it was booby-trapped. Sergeant saved his ass.

"You want this tapioca pudding shit, Lieutenant?"

"No."

"It was about 1800 when we got hit. Machine guns, mortars and small arms fire. They must have been tipped off, Lieutenant. They knew we were coming. I bet it was the fuckin' ARVN's. It was the first time we had been out there. I was point and was hit right off. Harris was killed."

"Oh, no."

"Lieutenant Forney was killed too, draggin' fat ass Thompson behind a dike. Thompson got it in the leg. Charlotte got hit. And so did Bubba. I heard they're both okay.

"Where're they at?"

"Phu Bi, I think. At least that's what I heard. Anyway, we were pinned down for about forty minutes before the A-4's came in and covered our ass while we shagged ass out-a-there. Doc saved my ass, Lieutenant. I understand he might get the Silver Star. He was out-fuckin-standing. Sergeant Fontain took over after the Lieutenant went down. Since we had all automatics, we were able to lay down covering fire to get out of the kill zone and behind a dike. Some shit, uh, Lieutenant?"

Lieutenant Fortney dead. And I'm sittin' here in Okinawa. Somebody has reached out and touched me.

Kohl ate Hernandez' tapioca pudding and talked until he started dozing off. Kohl quietly got up and left. He walked out of the hospital and into a bar across the street. He sat down at an empty table in a dark corner.

"Bring me a fifth of scotch and a big glass of ice, please."

When the barmaid came back with his request, he asked her to tell the bargirls to leave him alone and he handed her a ten dollar tip

He remembered when Harris had got in trouble with Major Blue in the Philippines and how he had tried to help him. *A man so big and strong, it's hard to imagine him dying. Damn. Here's to you, Harris. Hernandez got the top of his head blowed off, but thank God he's alive. Here's to you, Hernandez. And here's to you, Charlotte. Damn it, Bubba Flowers. The*

Corps was supposed to be the break for you. Here's to you, Bubba. Here's to you, gung-ho-fuckin'-Fortney. You with your fantasies of war and now ... What the hell. It could have been me, Fortney. It could have been me. I don't know what to say. I don't know how I should feel. Sorry that I'm alive? Here's to ya, Fortney. Here's to my fortunate departure. Here's to my new job in the safety of Okinawa. Here's to my wife. Here's to you, Sergeant Fontain.

Kohl silently drank. He remembered how he climbed up on that rock, oblivious to the dangers. He drank to the safety of his buddies who were still there. He toasted to the ghosts. He drank remembering and trying to forget. And when he passed out, the owner of the bar called the MP's. They took him back to his BOQ, carried him to his room and laid him on his rack.

30 Conduct Unbecoming

Kohl was appointed to serve on a panel of officers for a court marshal. The Marine Corps was prosecuting Corporal Thomas Penny for Conduct Unbecoming a Marine. The prosecution stated that Corporal Penny was caught having a homosexual encounter in a bar rest room in Naja. The prosecution was asking the court to give Corporal Penny a dishonorable discharge.

The arresting MP, under examination by the prosecuting attorney, said the bar was a known hang out for local Okinawan homosexuals and had the establishment under surveillance. It was also listed by the Armed Services as out-of-bounds. He said that Corporal Penny was caught with his penis in the mouth of another man.

The defense provided testimony from Corporal Penny's platoon sergeant as to his character. The Sergeant said what a fine Marine he was and, to his knowledge, he was not a homosexual. The defense attorney also had some of his buddies, who were with him that night, testify on his behalf. They said they were all drunk and did not know that the bar was a 'queer' bar or knew that it was out-of-bounds.

Then Corporal Penny was called to the stand. He looked like a Marine Corps poster boy. He had a square jaw, blue eyes, tall and well built. He was noticeably nervous. His voice was barely audible when he took the oath and his head hung in desperation and shame.

The defense attorney asked, "Why did you go to the 'San Francisco Bar,' Corporal Penny?"

"Sir, I was drunk, Sir..."

"Just answer the question, Corporal. Why did you go to the bar?"

"There was no reason, Sir. It was just there, Sir."

"Did you know it was a homosexual bar?"

Kohl recalled how he and Mays accidentally walked into a homosexual bar in Hong Kong. Then Mays started a fight. It could have been an embarrassing situation if the cops would have caught them. No telling what would have happened. The Marines were paranoid about homosexuals within their ranks.

"No, Sir."

"What did you do once you were inside?"

"We sat down at a table, Sir."

"Then what?"

"We ordered drinks, Sir."

"When did you notice that this bar was different?"

"Like I said, Sir. I was drunk. I didn't notice anything different."

"How did you come to have oral sex with another male, Corporal Penny?"

Corporal Penny had tears rolling down his cheek. He said, "When I went to the bathroom, Sir."

"Tell us in your own words, what happened in the bathroom."

"I went into a stall to take a leak, Sir." He paused and took a deep breath. The panel could barely hear him and the President asked him to speak up. "I heard a female voice in the next stall."

The defense lawyer interrupted him and asked, "How did you know it was a female?"

"Because it sounded like a female, Sir."

"You didn't know it was a man?"

"No, Sir."

"Didn't you think it was unusual that a woman would be in a men's rest room?"

"I didn't think about it, Sir. I was kinda drunk."

"Couldn't you tell by looking?"

"No, Sir."

"Why not?"

"Because she was on the other side of the partition, Sir."

"Go on. What happened then?"

"Well ... she ... aah ... he ... asked me if I wanted to be ... aah ..."

"Go on."

"Aah, sucked off, Sir," he said as his voice trailed off into a murmur.

"Speak up, Corporal," said the President of the panel.

"Sucked off. He, she ... asked if I wanted to be sucked off. But I didn't know. Sir. I was ..."

"When you had this sexual encounter, Corporal, couldn't you tell it was a man?"

"No, Sir. There was a hole in the partition and I stuck my ... aah ... I used that and it was very dark, Sir. I couldn't see very well, Sir."

"Corporal Penny? Have you ever had a homosexual encounter before?"

"Oh, no Sir. Never."

"Do you have sexual feelings or ever had sexual feelings for men?"

"Oh, heavens no, Sir. I wouldn't ... Well, you know, Sir."

"That'll be all Corporal Penney. That concludes testimony for the defense Mr. President."

"So be it. Corporal Penny you my step down."

After the council's summation, the panel retired to chambers. The panel consisted of a major, who was President, two captains and two lieutenants. Kohl wished he could do something for Corporal Penny. He knew that he wasn't a homosexual. He was in the wrong place at the wrong time. But Kohl knew the Marine Corps and how it felt about homosexuals within the ranks. It would and could not be tolerated.

The two-man pup tent would be a thing of the past. "Yohoo! Who wants to sleep with PFC Smithers tonight? We're pulling straws. Who has the longest wins."

Or the squad bay shower scene could change forever. "Here comes Smithers. What ever you do don't drop your soap. That's why we all have soap on a rope."

But with Corporal Penny it wasn't a matter of whether he was or wasn't. It was what he did and he got caught. The President asked for a vote. The vote was unanimous; Corporal Penny was guilty of homosexual activity and given a dishonorable discharge for Conduct Unbecoming of a Marine.

31 Hello, World, Over?

Kohl had heard that people were calling home on short wave radio. Sergeant Green operated the radio on weekends as a service to men who wanted to try and call home. He explained that he could radio a place on the Oregon coast and they in turn would call by telephone to the person you wanted. So Kohl called Julie.

"Hello?" said Julie.

Kohl couldn't believe his ears. It was her voice. He also heard the voice of the operator from Oregon asking if she would accept the collect call from North Bend, Oregon. North Bend meant nothing to Julie but she haltingly said she would accept the charges.

"Hi, Julie. It's me, Dusty. Over."

With radio communications you have to say over so the radio operator can switch from transmit to receive.

"Oh my God! Oh my God! It's you. Is it really you? Oh my God. I can't believe it." There was a pause.

The voice Kohl heard next was the operator in North Bend telling her that when she finished talking to say 'over.'

"What?" asked Julie.

"Say, 'over' when you finish talking."

"But I'm not through yet. Can I say more?"

"Yes. But before he can talk you have to say 'over.' Then I switch from transmit to receive then he can talk. Got it?"

"Okay. ... Over?" She said in a puzzled voice.

"What are you doing, Julie? Over," asked Kohl from a list of questions to ask and things he wanted to tell her about.

"Nothing much." She paused then remembered to say over.

"How's school? Over."

"It's boring. I don't like my major. I think I'm going to change. What are you doing? Over."

"This is a pretty neat deal. The ham radio operator here calls this guy in North Bend, Oregon and he calls you. So we only have to pay for the call from Oregon to Huntington Beach. What time is there? Over."

"It's about ten o'clock ... at night ... Saturday. You sound different. I guess it's because it is a long ways, huh? What's it like in Okinawa, Dusty? Over."

"It's been raining a lot but today it is about 72 degrees with big white puffy clouds and a few showers. I sure miss you, my darling. I can't wait to see you again. I think of you all the time. Over."

Kohl didn't hear anything.

"What happened, Sarge?"

"Lost it."

"How much of my call did she get?"

"Don't know. I'll keep trying."

It was no use. Kohl wished he could have had more time. He felt disappointed that he didn't get to tell her how much he loved her. Maybe next time. *Damn, that was bitchin'.*

32 People-to-People

Okinawa was hit a glancing blow from a typhoon. The wind knocked out the electricity late in the afternoon, so Major Wellington told everyone in the office that they could leave for the day. Kohl sat in his dark room for a while. It was too early to go to bed so he went to the officer's club. It took him awhile for his eyes to adjust to the candlelit room. Sitting at the bar was Lieutenant Olson a friend of his from Pendleton. It wasn't hard for Kohl to see him. He was over six foot six and weighed close to two hundred and forty pounds. Kohl sat down next to him.

"Olson? When did you get here?"

"Yo, Kohl. Been here for two months already."

"Where're you stationed?"

"I'm Procurement Officer. I go out to the ville and buy stuff from the locals. It's our new 'people-to-people program'."

"I heard it was called 'peehole-to-peehole program'."

"Very funny, Kohl," said Olson but he wasn't laughing. "How's Julie? And how'd the wedding go?"

"She's still in school and the wedding was great. Sorry you couldn't make it."

"Well, you know. Christmas with the folks in New Hampshire."

In the candlelight, Kohl showed him some of the wedding pictures he carried in his wallet. In turn Olson pulled out a picture and showed it to Kohl. Kohl had a hard time making it out in the candlelight.

Olson asked, "What do you think?"

"Who's this?"

"Her name's Lori. She lives in Naja."

"What? You have a ranch?"

*

Kohl noticed soon after he had arrived at Camp Henderson that many of the BOQ rooms assigned to some officers were seldom used. They stored some gear and used it sometimes during the day but by the evening, they were gone. He asked his BOQ NCO, First Sergeant Myers where they went.

"They probably have a ranch, Lieutenant."

The thought of a ranch in Okinawa didn't make sense. "I'm afraid I don't follow you, Sarge."

"A Ranch is what we call a rented flat in the ville. It comes fully equipped with furniture and living accessories. That includes a nasain who cooks, washes clothes, keeps the flat clean and provides all the comfort and needs of her man. If you know what I mean".

He also told Kohl that after a standard thirteen month tour many of the nasians fell in love and so did many of the Marines. Some of them had children, got married, and brought them back stateside. Some of the nasains thought it would be an easy ticket to the United States, but most of the time they were left behind. The nasains would wait for the next Marine. With some of the higher-ranking officers one would leave and his replacement would inherit his house and nasain. A Ranch.

*

"No," Olson said irritated that Kohl asked the question. "I don't have a goddamn ranch. I met her during one of my people-to-people buying trips. Her folks have a furniture store. I met her there and we started going out."

"Are you living together?"

"No. She lives at home with her folks and goes to college. In fact she has to sneak out to be with me. Her folks do not allow her to date Americans, especially servicemen." And then Olson added, "I'm in love with her."

"No, shit?'

"We've talked about marriage and her going back with me."

"Are you sure this is the right thing to do? You just got here, man. Don't you think that's awfully fast."

"She treats me like a king."

"Is that why you're in love with her because of the way she treats you?"

"No," said Olson showing his irritation at Kohl's questioning. "She's beautiful and intelligent. She has a great body."

"Don't give me that. These girls over her have no tits and flat asses."

Olson glared at Kohl.

"It's true," continued Kohl. "Olson? You know the game the girls play over here. Get a hold of an American serviceman, marry him and then leave his ass once she's state-side."

"Well, Lori's not like that."

"I think you're in love with the fact that she's putting up with all your bullshit. Don't give me that look. It's true. When we were roommates in San Clemente, how many times have I fixed you up..." Kohl paused. "A lot, right?"

Olson nodded.

"First of all, you try and impress them how strong you are by throwing 'em around like dolls. It scares them. They realize that if you wanted too, you could do anything you wanted to and they couldn't do anything. And secondly, you treat women like shit."

"Do not."

"How many girls will go out with you again? Huh?"

"Well, if they don't like the way I am, to hell with 'em. I can do anything and Lori doesn't mind."

I bet once she gets stateside and this 'I can do anything shit' will come to a screeching halt. Have you thought of that?"

"I don't believe that. She really loves me. She's not one of those bargirls. She's got class. We're going to get married."

And that was that. Kohl knew that Olson had made up his mind and any further discussion would find Kohl on the floor. He knew he could only push Olson so far. He remembered the time at Officer's Candidate School when Olson got pissed at him and threw him across the concrete floor.

They talked for hours in the candlelight. Kohl needed help to get back to his BOQ room. Olson threw Kohl over his shoulder and carried him to his room, dropped him on his bed and left.

33 A Dollar Drunk

Kohl worked through the hangover on Friday. Wheeler, Rolston, Briggs, Shelbee and Thorton came looking for Kohl after work. They found him in his room. They all left for Friday happy hour. There was a complimentary spread of dip, chips, Buffalo wings, sushi, sashimi, fresh vegetables, and an assortment of breads and crackers. A glass of draft beer was ten cents, a bottle of Hinnegan's was fifteen cents, and mixed drinks were twenty-five cents. They played liars dice. Kohl had a lucky streak and had only bought two rounds all night. They ended up drinking through dinner and Kohl ended up snockered for the second night in a row.

Kohl stayed behind while his buddies left for a bar down town. He picked up the five Hinnegan beers he had accumulated from the table and moved to the bar next to Lieutenant Joe Peters, a mild mannered, soft-spoken H & S officer.

"You wana onea my beers?" asked Kohl.

"No, thank you. I'm drinking a vodka gimlet," he answered in a refined clipped Massachusetts accent.

"Wall, whoop-dee-doo."

"What do you mean by that?"

"That you're a candy-ass. That's what."

"I'd say that you have had too much to drink, Kohl."

"You can bet your sweet bippy. I have an' I got fo ta go. Fo mo, Joe," chuckled Kohl.

"Don't you think you've had enough?"

"Fuck no. An' who ass ya ta be my Mutha ... fucker." This brought another chuckle from Kohl. "I got to go pee pee." Kohl turned from the bar and fell off the barstool. Peters picked him up.

"I can do it myself," as Kohl twirled around. "Where is it? Oh, there." He ran into the wall and while he was there he used the wall to hold himself up as he navigated down the hall. When he returned Peters was gone. He leaned over to a man he didn't know and asked, " Where'd the man go who was sittin' here?" he pointed.

The man shrugged.

"Ass hole," said Kohl.

"Who are you calling an ass hole, buddy?" snarled the man.

"I am," said Kohl confidently.

"What?"

"Here, you can have these beers ... buddyyyy ... on me ... " and then Kohl leaned over and whispered in his ear,"Ass hole," and left weaving in the direction of his room. It was still pouring rain from the typhoon. Kohl stood in the rain. He tilted his face up and opened his mouth and stuck out his tongue. Then he fell over backwards. He rolled over and got on his hands and knees and crawled over and sat under a downspout and let the rainwater fall over his spinning head. "He was an ass hole," he mumbled. "I could just tell."

Two Marines came out of the club and noticed Kohl sitting under the downspout. "Hey, man. You planning on spending the night there?"

Kohl made an effort to answer. He tried to wipe the water from his face so he could see. They went over and picked him up under his arms and drug him to his room.

*

The alarm went off at 0630.

"What the...? " Kohl tried to open his eyes. They were glued shut. He pried one eye open. He looked at the clock. "What the hell's goin' on?" He reached for the clock and knocked it to the floor, still ringing. "Oh, please stop." He rolled over and groped around, trying to find the clock. "Fuckin' thing." He bumped it and it slid under the bed. He rolled back over and covered his head with his pillow. He could still hear it. *Why is it goin' off at 6:30 in the fuckin' morning? It's a goddamn Saturday, for Christ's sake. Ooooh, I don't feel so good.* The fog was lifting. I remember. The truck was to leave at 0715 from the parking lot. He was Officer-in-Charge of an M-60 machine gun exercise at the firing range. He put his feet on the cold floor trying not to move his head too rapidly. He lowered himself slowly to the floor and found the ringing clock and stabbed the alarm button off.

Oh, man. Maybe they wouldn't miss me.

Not a good idea, Kohl. Not showing up for duty is a punishable offense. It doesn't matter how you feel. You gota go. Over did it, did you? That's two nights in a row. Now get your ass up and in gear.

All right, all right. I could die of a brain hemorrhage ya know. This could be a terrible shock to my system. I can't imagine all day with a 50-caliber machine gun firing. My head will explode.

34 Drunk and Disorderly

All day at the range Kohl felt his head explode every time an M-60 machine gun thundered. He yearned for the quiet comfort of his bed ... and sleep. He couldn't wait. The bouncing ride back was an additional insult to his pain. His temples were pulsating. His ears were ringing from the constant firing of the M-60's. His eyes hurt from the glare of the sun. His head was a ball of agony. Bed.

He crawled from the cab of the six-by and shuffled to his room.

He opened the door in anticipation... but someone was there. Sitting in a darkened corner. It was Mays. Empty beer cans were strewn around the trashcan in the corner. At his feet was a cooler full of ice and more beer.

"What the..."

"Surprise!" Mays threw Kohl a beer. Kohl caught it, looked at it and then back at Mays.

"What are you doing here?"

"Well, that's a fine how-de-fuckin'-do."

Kohl walked over and shook his buddy's hand. He was glad to see him.

Mays said, "I was replaced by one of Pratt's men, just like you. Now, I'm right here at H and fuckin' S. Just like old times, eh buddy?"

"Yep. Just like old times."

"Well, don't cream your jeans with excitement. What the fuck's wrong with you? You look worse than you act."

"Aww, Mays. My head is about to explode. I've got a shittin' hangover, bad. I've been on the range all day listening to M-60's and my head's about to explode."

"You fuckin' candy ass. Come on. Shower, shit and shave and let's go party."

"Oooh man. Mays, I'm beat. Besides, I've been drunk the last two nights. If I don't watch it I'm going to turn into an alcy. I'm fuckin' goin' to bed."

"Don't give that cry baby horse shit. Don't drink then. I don't give a rat's ass. What about me, asshole? Huh? What about me? I'm a deprived man. I've been waitin' for your skinny white ass for two fuckin' hours. That's drinkin' and whorin' time a waistin'. Now, come on. Cut the whining shit and get your butt in gear. We're meetin' everybody over at the Cortney Club. Come on. Chop, chop."

Kohl reluctantly gave in to Mays, like always and took a shower, shaved, gulped down a hand full of aspirin and got dressed.

At the Cortney Club they met Rolston, Briggs, Shelbee, Wheeler and Thorton. It didn't take long for Mays to hit his stride. They had only been at the club for about an hour when Mays took over as MC. He told a bewildered Air Force Lieutenant to go fuck himself and took the mike away from him. The band was from Australia and was playing songs from a new group from England called the Beatles. Mays was trying to get everybody drunk by chug-a-lugging their drinks. But as always it was Mays who was getting plastered.

"All right everybody let's give a round of applause for the Aussie band. What's your name?" he asked as he leaned over. They told him. "The Wallabies."

Everybody cheered.

"Now let's all toast to the Wallabies. Now, now. Not everybody's toasting," he scolded. "Here you sissies, like this," as Mays chugged down a glass of beer. Then burped. "Now let's try it again. Wait. Hold it. My glass is empty." Someone with a pitcher filled it up. "Now down the hatch," as Mays emptied another glass. He stepped down from the stage and the band began playing, 'I Wanna Hold Your Hand.'

Couples were dancing and Kohl watched Mays armwrestle a big Air Force Officer and beat him. He stood up beating his chest and gave a Tarzan yell. As Mays continued his self-appointed MC duties, he was progressively showing the effects of his drinking.

"You ass holes aren't drunk yet," he yelled into the mike. "I just got back from Viet-fuckin'-Nam and I want every body to drink to my return. Ready? Bottoms up."

To Kohl's amazement Mays did something really weird. He put the beer next to his right ear, tilted his head and poured the beer into his ear. Some of the people howled and laughed but others gave him a disgusted look.

"What did you do that for?" asked Kohl when Mays returned to his barstool. The whole side of his shirt was wet with beer.

"What's it to you, you fuckin' queer," sneered Mays.

Kohl could see the ice in his eyes.

Mays slid off his stool and started crawling onto the dance floor. Kohl gave an "uh ooo." He saw Mays do the same thing at the Sandpiper in Laguna. The dance floor was crowded and Kohl started to go and retrieve the crawling Mays. Then he heard the scream.

"He bit my butt. The pervert bit my butt," screamed a pretty short blonde.

The crowd parted and there was Mays on his hands and knees with a big grin on his face. The big Air Force guy that Mays beat arm wrestling walked over and kicked Mays in the side. Mays let out a grunt. There was a slight wince on his face. Kohl let out a groan. Mays growled and grabbed the big man's leg and started chewing on it. The guy was cussing and stomping up and down trying to shake the gnawing Mays off his leg. Then Rolston tackled the big guy and started punching him in the face. Another Air Force guy was trying to pull Rolston off when Briggs hit the guy on the side of the head. Kohl saw Thorton thrown into a table and Shelbee get hit from the blind side and knocked off his barstool. Wheeler was bouncing around and jabbing like Cassius Clay when the Air Force guy he was showing the finer points of boxing kicked him in the balls. Kohl didn't want any part of this. It wasn't his fight and he started inching his way to the door.

"Where do you think you're going, Jarhead?"

*

"Where do you think your going, Dusty?" said the kid that lived down road.

"I'm going home."

"Well, you have to go by me."

Dusty tried to stay clear of his next door neighbor. He was always trying to pick a fight. They were in the same grade, but he was older and bigger. Dusty was afraid of him and the kid knew it. They stood facing each other and Dusty started to walk past and the kid moved in front of him. Dusty tried to go around. The kid blocked him.

"Hit me," said the kid.

"No. I don't want to fight."

"Chicken. Come on hit me. Come on."

Dusty poked him on the shoulder. Nothing more than a tap. Then Dusty felt a crunch on the side of his face. He started crying and the kid left laughing. When he got home, he tried to get into the bathroom without his Dad seeing him.

"What's wrong with your face, Sonny?"

"Nothin'"

"Nothin', my foot. Come 'er."

Dusty walked over with his head down and he started crying, "He was bigger than me and he hit me for no reason." He told his Dad about what the kid down the road said, "He wanted me to hit him first."

"Well. Did you?"

"Kinda. But not really. It was ... just a..."

"Come 'er, Sonny. Sit down. You ain't hurt."

"Am too," cried Dusty.

"Now listen. Listen. Are you listening?"

"Yeah," he sniffed.

"You've been boxing ever since you were old enough to hold up the gloves. You're good. Look at me. You can hold your own with anybody especially that kid down the road. Most fights only last one or two licks and that's all. So if you are in a situation that you can't get out of, knock the crap out of the guy. Hit him first and hit him as hard as you can. Nine times out of ten that will be it."

"What about if he hits me back?"

"Then box him. Here let me look at that eye."

*

Kohl hit the man as hard as he could with a straight right to the chin. He knew the man wasn't looking for an answer and he sure wasn't expecting the punch that sent him crumpling to the floor. The band started playing a slow song but with the yelling and screaming it was hard to hear. Kohl saw that the door had become blocked. Wondering how he was going to get out of this mess, he dropped to the floor and crawled behind the bar. *Goddamn Mays. All for one and one for all just goes so far.* He sat down with his back against a cooler. He looked to his left and sitting about five feet away was the bartender. Kohl gave him a sheepish grin and put his finger to his lips. Then around the corner of the bar, crawling on all fours, with her blonde hair hanging down, and her tight mini skirt hiked up around her butt crack came the girl Mays bit on the butt. She stopped crawling when she ran into Kohl's leg. She looked up and pulled her long blonde hair from her face. Large brown eyes looked at Kohl.

At first she looked surprised, then she smiled and asked, "How come you aren't out there fighting with your friends?" She turned and leaned up against the booze rack and pulled her knees up under her chin. She was small, maybe a little over five foot tall. Her lips were full and she settled those big brown eyes on Kohl. "Well?" she asked.

"Not my fight, Ma'am."

"That was my husband you hit."

"I'm sorry. I ... "

But before Kohl could finish he heard the MP's come in. Everything was starting to quiet down as they removed the people involved in the fight. There was some protesting and cussing but soon all was quiet. The bartender rose to his feet and looked around. He looked at Kohl and the girl. The bartender told the remaining people that the bar was closed and they shuffled out. The band packed up their instruments and gear and left. The bartender picked up broken glass, overturned tables and chairs while Kohl and the girl remained seated behind the bar looking at each other. All was quiet.

"Do you want to take me home, Mister-Marine-man?" she purred.

"What about your husband?"

"He's probably being taken to the guard house. Don't you think?"

"Probably. But it's after he comes home that I'm worried about."

"Take me to your place, then."

I'd love to take you back to my room and fuck your beautiful brains out. Kohl could feel the heat in his crotch. He still had a bad headache but he was thinking about the offer. Making love could take all the hurt away. *All the blood would move from my throbbing head to my throbbing pecker.*

"Well?" she asked with impatience.

"You can come out now," said the bartender.

Kohl and the girl stood up and looked around. Every body was gone. Kohl felt guilty for not joining the fight. Choosing instead to hide behind the bar.

You're a Goddamn chicken shit. You know that?

Yes, I know.

"Well, I guess I had better be on my way," he said to the girl.

She stood with her hands on her hips and a pout on her full red lips and asked, "Are you just going to leave me here?"

"Sweet thing, I'd love to lick you all over but I can't. I hope you'll except my apology. I'm flattered," he said. Then turned to the bartender and asked, "Where do you think they took them?"

"Probably down to the base brig."

"Where's that?"

"Take the road out front, here, go east about five or six blocks and it's around the back of hanger 37."

"Hanger 37?"

"Yeah."

"Thanks. Good night." Then Kohl turned to face the little girl. "Good night to you, sweet thing. I know I'll regret this."

"Good night, Mister Marine man."

Kohl gave the bartender a nod and left.

Man, you are one dumb mutha fucker. You see that? Tits and ass and those big brown eyes? Shit for brains. And you walkin' down the street with your cock pokin' out like a magic wand, just because you feel guilty about cowering behind the bar.

No, that's not it. I'm married. Remember? And I didn't cower either. Mays started it. It wasn't like I didn't do anything to help. After all I nailed that one guy.

Yeah. And you could have nailed big brown eyes too.

Kohl walked into the brig mumbling to himself. He knew he was probably going to take a ration of shit from everybody since he was the only one who didn't get picked up. He entered the guard office and walked up to the MP sitting behind the desk.

"Yes, Sir. Can I help you?"

"Do you have any Marine Officers in the brig back there?"

"We have one."

"What's his name?"

"His name..." he looked at a list of names on a roster. "...Mays. First Lieutenant Paul Mays."

"Is he the only one that has been detained?"

"There was an Air Force Lieutenant also."

Must be the big fucker.

"Where did the others go?"

"They were all released on their own recognizance."

"Is it possible that I could take Lieutenant Mays home?"

"I don't know about that, Sir. I'll have to ask the Lieutenant, Sir. Just a second." The MP left his desk and entered a room to the rear. It was 2:30 in the morning, Kohl's headache was killing him and had been all evening. He was exhausted and wanted to go to bed. He saw the MP bring the officer-in-charge.

"I'm Lieutenant Porter. How can I help you?"

"My name is Lieutenant Kohl, Lieutenant. A friend of mine is here by the name of Paul Mays. I'd like to take him home, if I could please."

"I'm afraid that's out of the question. He's been brought up on charges of being drunk and disorderly, civil disobedience, destruction of property, assault and resisting arrest.

"I understand, Lieutenant, but he doesn't have to stay here does he? It's not like he's going to flee from prosecution. We're on a fuckin' island here. He just got back from Vietnam, man. Give him a break. I'll vouch for him. Okay?"

"Where are you stationed?"

"Henderson."

"Okay. Yeah. I'll approve it."

"Thanks, man. Really appreciate it."

An MP brought out Mays. Mays smiled when he saw Kohl but only one side of his face responded. His left upper lip was swollen to the size of a golf ball. And his left eye was bruised blue and swollen shut. His right ear had dried blood on it and he had a scratch that ran down his forehead to the bridge of his flat nose.

"Hi there perty boy," Mays said. "I see you didn't get that beautiful California beach boy face messed up. We sure kicked some fly boy ass, didn't we?"

"Yeah. It sure looks like it. You don't look so good, Paul. Has the doctor looked at you?" Kohl asked as they walked out into the night air to wait for their cab.

"No. The only thing that really hurts are my fuckin' ribs. Right here," he pointed.

"Probably where that big fucker kicked you."

"Yeah. He was a big fucker wasn't he?"

"Yep. Big fucker."

Once they got into the cab, they both fell asleep.

35 How Do You Spell Cherries?

It was a beautiful Saturday morning. There were a few showers with some sun breaks. Kohl worked at the office that morning but now he was through for the day. He felt good. He liked his job. The Major would tell him what to do and leave him alone to complete the task. After noon chow he returned to his room to write some letters or maybe do some reading. He didn't know. Just relax. He propped his pillow up and lay down, let out a big sigh and closed his eyes for a short nap.

"Kohl! Phone!" came the call from down the hall.

"Shit!" Kohl said as he got up and walked down the hall to the phone.

"Lieutenant Kohl."

"Lieutenant? This is Colonel Knoach. We've got a serious problem here and I want something done immediately."

"Yes, Sir. How can I help?"

"You're BOQ Officer, right?

"Yes, Sir."

"Well, you've got a problem with one of your naisons. She had the gall to refuse to launder and press my dress whites. This behavior in unacceptable. I have just got off the phone with your Commanding Officer, Colonel Pachelli, and he said for me to inform you that he wanted you to make a full report of the action taken to resolve this matter. He confirmed my concern that this act of disobedience can not and will not be tolerated. I can see no recourse but to have her fired immediately. Colonel Pachelli thinks so too, I'm sure. You understand of course why it was so important to have my dress whites by tonight, don't you?"

"No, Sir. I'm sorry I don't."

"You don't?"

"No, Sir."

"You should know, Lieutenant. You're the Officer's Club Officer, right?"

"Yes, Sir."

"You mean to say that you are not aware of what is going on at the Officer's Club tonight?"

"I don't know, Sir. I just can't remember what's happening tonight."

"Don't you read the schedule?"

"I told you before, Sir. I don't remember." *Are you going to let me in on your little secret, Colonel? Or are we going to continue this little guessing game?*

"Not being aware of the club schedule for an event such as this gives me the impression that you are negligent in your responsibilities. Isn't that a reasonable assumption, Lieutenant?

"If you say so, Sir." Kohl was getting a little tired and irritated at the Colonel's charade.

"Well, for your information and information that you should have known, tonight is Colonel Skinner's farewell party."

"Oh, yes. I recall now."

"Don't patronize me, Lieutenant. You can't even keep your naisons under control. Now what are you going to do about this matter? She should be fired and Colonel Pachelli thinks so too. Don't you agree, Lieutenant?"

"I'll see what I can do, Sir."

"You didn't answer my question, Lieutenant."

"I thought I did, Sir."

"I want her fired. Is that clear?'

"I'll get back to you on that, Colonel," said Kohl and he hung up.

Jesus fuckin' Christ. What a fuckin' asshole. Sure made a point that he talked to Colonel Pachelli.

Kohl walked over to see if First Sergeant Myers was in his office on a Saturday afternoon and he was.

"Thank God, you're here, Sarge."

The Sergeant looked up from a book he was reading and smiled at Kohl and motioned him to sit down. "Coffee, Lieutenant?"

"Sure. Thanks."

"What's up?"

Kohl poured himself a cup, sat down in one of Sergeant's lounge chairs and told the him about Lieutenant Colonel Knoach's call. The Sergeant had girls in charge of each BOQ building and each floor had about ten girls that cleaned the rooms and took care of the officer's laundry. He knew their names and could understand and speak some Japanese. He accompanied Kohl to the BOQ area where they worked. When they arrived the naison in charge and the naison who Kohl came to see were in the bathroom showers where they washed the officer's clothes. The naison who had the confrontation with the Colonel was crying. Neither of the girls could speak English but with Sergeant Myers help they found that Colonel Knoach had waited to the last minute to turn in his dress whites to his naison. She had too many dress whites to do for the going away party and didn't have time to do his. The naisons worked regular hours from eight to five six days a week. Kohl asked Sergeant Myers to ask her if she would stay longer today and do the Colonel's dress whites, if he paid her extra. She talked and argued with her floor boss and finally turned back to the Sergeant and said that she would. She cried that she didn't want to get fired.

While Kohl and the Sergeant were walking down the hall, Sergeant Myers said, "You know, Lieutenant, there's a problem here. We do not want to set a precedent for the naisons to work longer than their contract time. Nor do we want to start a process where the officers can pay them extra for extra duties. Could lead to problems. Know what I mean?"

"I get ya, Sarge. Has this happened before?"

"It happens all the fuckin' time. I know it's hard Lieutenant, but don't let the senior officers run over your ass. You're the boss."

"I sure don't feel like it. See ya later."

"Later, Lieutenant."

Kohl walked on down to Lieutenant Colonel Knoach's room and knocked. A man standing in his Marine Corps issue boxer shorts and v-necked tee shirt opened the door. He had short cropped blond hair, blue eyes, thin lips and freckles sprinkled across his small nose. He reminded Kohl of the Pillsbury doughboy because his body looked round, smooth and soft. His voice was high and thin which he tried to make up for in volume.

Little twerp.

"Lieutenant Kohl?"

"Yes, Sir."

"Come in," he said as he walked over to his desk with his flip-flops making a slapping noise. He picked up his unfinished cigar, poked it in his mouth and said around the edges, "Did you fire her?"

"No, Sir. I did not," Kohl said as he closed the door behind him.

The Colonel's face turned red and he said, "Now, why is that, may I ask?"

"Because, Sir, it's not her fault. She already has too many whites to do, Sir. However, I have talked to her and she has agreed to stay late this afternoon in order to do yours, Sir."

"If it's not her fault, are you insinuating it's mine?"

"Well, not exactly, Sir. I ... She..."

"It's too late," he interrupted.

"Too late?"

"Yes, too late," he glared at Kohl. "I had to make arrangements to have them done off base at an additional expense because of her insubordination and because of your dereliction of duties."

"Sir, you have to understand..." Kohl started.

"I don't have to understand anything, Lieutenant. It's you who needs to understand. She refused an order and she should be fired."

Kohl had a hard time taking the yelling Colonel seriously. Red faced, with a cigar sticking out of his mouth, standing in boxer shorts and thongs, he looked like Elmer Fudd.

Kohl took a deep breath and said, "Sir, she's a civilian, not a soldier. She works for a contract service. She's not your personal maid."

"I've had about all I can stand from you," he yelled. "It's apparent that you have a problem with authority. I am going to report your disobedience to your Commanding Officer, Colonel Pachelli. I'm sure he'll have a thing or two to say about how you mishandled this situation."

"Yeah. Whatever," said Kohl in an exasperated tone. Then turned, opened the door.

"I haven't dismissed you yet, Lieutenant."

Kohl turned at the door, looked at him, walked out of the room and down the hall.

"Get back here! I'm talking to you, Lieutenant! I'm going to call your Commander!"

Kohl kept walking as the Colonel continued to yell at him. Fuckin' little prick. He walked back to his room, went to the sink, turned on the cold water and let it run into his palms, then splashed water onto his face. He leaned on the sink with his arms extended and looked into the mirror. *What the hell is happening here? All this over a naison and a pair of dress whites. For what? Is this really important? What does this have to do with world peace? To kow-tow to that little piece of shit control freak is horse-shit. Send the little fucker to Vietnam. Maybe he'd find out what the VC will do with his dress whites. Shove 'em so far up his ass the sleeve will come out his mouth. Fuckin' ass hole.*

*

"Kohl, phone," came the call down the hall.

Shit, now what. What earth-shaking piece of shit do I have to do now?

"Coming, Kohl?"

"Yeah. On my way."

"Lieutenant Kohl."

"Lieutenant? This is Colonel Stevenson. I would like to see you ASAP. That's room A22.

"Is there a problem. Sir?"

"I want to bring a matter of concern to your attention."

"I'll be right up, Sir." *Now what the fuck's wrong. What's all this ASAP shit?*

Kohl walked over to building A and up to room 22 and knocked on the door.

Lieutenant Colonel Stevenson opened the door and immediately asked, "Did you fire that Jap girl yet?"

What the hell's going on? Doesn't anybody above major have anything to do today? Is this 'Let's fuck with Kohl's head day'?

"No, Sir. I did not."

"Are you going to?"

"No, Sir. I am not."

He stood in front of Kohl and glared. "I hope you have a good reason."

"I don't have to have a reason for you, Sir."

The Colonel's face turned crimson and with his teeth clinched he said, "I want her fired. That's an order."

"It's not your order to give, Sir."

"Are you disobeying my order, Lieutenant?" The emphasis was on the Lieutenant.

"No, Sir."

"Well, what about this," as the Colonel shoved a menu into Kohl's hand.

Kohl looked with surprise at the menu of the Officer's Mess for the coming week, wondering what does this have to do with anything.

"Have you read this menu, Lieutenant?"

Am I having a bad dream here? I want out! Show me the door, the secret door. Help!

"Yes, Sir. I have," he lied. He had read some of it but usually only glanced at it and signed his okay.

"So, how do you spell cherries?"

"What?" Kohl looked puzzled. This was a big jump from firing naisons to spelling cherries.

"You heard me, Lieutenant. How do you spell cherries?"

I hate spelling bees. I was always the first one to sit down. Never could spell worth a damn, but I do know how to spell cherries for whatever god-damn reason this dip-shit wants to know. I just have to keep my cool.

The Colonel continued, "Is this how? C-H-E-R-R-Y-I-E-S?"

"No. What's this about Colonel?"

"Look at the menu. There." He pointed out to Kohl. "Inattention to detail, Lieutenant. You can't expect to be a proficient officer if you do not pay attention to details. You can't gloss over a problem and expect it to go away. But what can I expect from a Reserve Officer."

Follow the bouncing ball, Kohl.

He was a Reserve Officer and not a Regular Officer. That was true. The difference between the two is the Reserve has three years reserve duty after active duty while the Regular Officers are in for a career. But he didn't see the connection.

"What makes you think I'm a Reserve Officer, Colonel?"

"Oh, I can tell by your lackadaisical attitude and how you have allowed the Officer's Mess to go down hill. And besides the toast hasn't been done."

"Toast?"

"Yes, toast. It's not done."

Kohl couldn't contain himself any longer. "Toast? Fucking toast! You're bitchin' about untoasted toast." He started laughing and shaking his head in disbelief.

"You find that amusing!" yelled the colonel.

"You're a fuckin' idiot!" yelled Kohl as he turned and walked down the hall.

"You can't call me that! I'll have your ass, Lieutenant! Get back here! I'm not through with you! Get back here!"

Fucking untoasted toast. I can't believe this shit. Even though it's day-light, I swear there must be a full moon. Kohl muttered down the hall. And for the second time in two hours he had colonels yelling at him.

*

Kohl dreaded walking into the office Monday morning. He spent most of Sunday trying to write an 'Action Taken Report' for Colonel Pachelli. He thought he justified everything except for his encounter with Colonel

Stevenson. Even though Kohl's patience had been pressed to the limit, he couldn't justify calling a superior officer an idiot. That comment could lead to Office Hours for showing disrespect for a superior officer. He knew he was in trouble again.

As Kohl walked into his office, Major Newcomb looked up and grinned. "Well, Kohl. Did you have an exciting weekend?" said Major Newcomb.

At least he's smiling. That's a good sign.

"Here's my 'Action Taken Report,' Major."

"Yep. Got my ear chewed off at Colonel Skinner's going away party. Both ears, in fact."

"Colonel Pachelli, too?" grimaced Kohl.

"No doubt," said the Major as he began to read Kohl's report. He smiled and said, "Nothing's in here about your conversation with Lieutenant Colonel Stevenson?"

"No, Sir. The conversation was hard to explain, Sir."

"Did you call him an idiot?"

"Yes, Sir. I did. I know there's no excuse, Sir. I just lost it after the untoasted toast thing."

"Untoasted toast?"

"Yeah. That and not spelling cherries correctly."

"What the hell are you talking about?"

"And being a Reserve Officer..."

"Hold the fuckin' phone."

"I'm tellin' ya, Major. It was weird."

"I didn't hear about any of that."

"Well, it happened."

"He complained because the toast was not toasted?"

"Yes, Sir."

"You've got to be kidding?"

Kohl shrugged and said, "Nope."

The Major shook his head and laughed, "Colonel Stevenson ... I'll handle the Colonel Knoach thing. You did the right thing by not firing the naison. He was out of line," he said as he ripped up the report. "I'll handle everything with Colonel Pachelli. However you will have to apologize to Colonel Stevenson. He won't let it go until he has you grovel before him."

*

Later that day when Kohl was walking to noon chow, he saw Colonel Pachelli in the passageway. Kohl tried to duck around the corner before the Colonel saw him, but was too late. He motioned for Kohl.

Oh, shit. He saw me. I'm fucked. Man, am I going to get yelled at. Maybe worse.

As Kohl walked toward the big man, his legs felt like they were going to fold. He was shaking with dread. *Damn. Why can't I just keep my mouth shut?*

"Well, well, well. If it isn't Mister BOQ man, himself," said Colonel Pachelli smiling.

"Yes, Sir. That's me," Kohl said as he waited for the boom to fall.

"So you called Colonel Stevenson an idiot, did you?"

Right to the point. No need prolonging the agony. I'm dog meat.

"Colonel Pachelli, Sir. I am so sorry. I was way out of line, Sir. I can't explain it, Sir. It just came out. Sir. It won't happen again, Sir. I promise. I'm going to apologize to him right after chow, Sir."

The Colonel laughed and said, "You don't have to say shit, Lieutenant. I got briefed by Major Newcomb and just had a little chat with Lieutenant Colonel Stevenson. He's a God damn geek-necked turd." Then he paused and looked at Kohl and said, "Just don't make a habit of calling colonel's idiots." He wheeled and laughed, as he continued down the hall.

"Oh. No, Sir. It won't happen again. Thank you, Sir."

Thank you, sweet Jesus. Thank you. I'm saved from the ravages of hell one more time.

No more. No more. I promise to keep my nose clean and mouth shut.

Humm. You've said that before, Kohl.

I know. But, I mean it this time. Really.

36 The Dirty Duty

For the first time in Kohl's brilliant military career, he was glad he had weekend duty. Being drunk three weekends in a row had weighed heavily on his physical well being. He needed a weekend to recover. Plus last weekend's fiasco. Kohl's chance of getting into trouble, while on duty, was remote. Duty started at 1700 hours on Friday and concluded at 0800 on Monday. He was called the Officer of the Guard. Sergeant Myers was the Sergeant of the Guard and he assumed most of the responsibilities for the supervision of the guards and sentries that stood watch or patrolled the base. Kohl's duties included 'The Inspection of the Guard' Friday evening, Saturday and Sunday mornings, and inspections of the mess halls and received and forwarded all incoming secret communications. Every hour he would have to write into the duty logbook, "all posts were secure." The sergeant handled the troop guards. So on a quiet weekend there wouldn't be much to do. He read books, wrote letters, played cards with the sergeant, and took catnaps. Boring. But that was okay.

Friday night went by without incident. So far, Saturday had been quiet. It was a little after ten o-clock on Saturday evening. Kohl had just finished making his rounds, settled down at his desk and began reading accident reports from the previous Friday night.

"Injury: Broken nose. Reason: While playing basketball, I went up to catch the ball but I caught an elbow instead. Injury: Broken toe. Reason: I was playing handball and got mad because I missed the ball. So I kicked the wall and broke my toe. Injury: Broken front teeth. Reason: A guy called me over and he hit me twice in the mouth for no reason. Injury: Broken wrist. Reason: I ran into a truck with my horse. Injury: Broken hand. Reason: As I was reaching for a cigarette, PFC Andrews hit my hand with a hammer. Injury: Broken nose. Reason: While I was riding in the back of a six-by, I smarted off to some Corporal and he hit me in the nose. Injury: Lacerated hand. Reason: I was pinning on my good-conduct medal when PFC Higgens snapped me with a towel and when I hit him in the mouth I cut my hand on his teeth. Injury: Broken forearm, strained wrist, muscle spasms in my back, numerous bruises and abrasions, twisted knee, and broken little finger. Reason: I was hit all through the football game."

37 *The Fickle Finger of Fate*

Kohl finally got his gear from Vietnam. Surprisingly everything was intact. He had also signed up with the University of California to take a correspondence course in California History and had been busy working on his first assignment. He had been selected by the Special Services to give scuba diving lessons starting next Saturday. He found a place to have his suits made and was scheduled for measurements as soon as he got the money. With the Doctor's help his bowel movements started to take some shape other than the diarrhea he had since his return from Vietnam. Rather than spending his free time drinking and feeling sorry for himself, he had finally decided to try and use what time he had left on Okinawa to be put to some useful purpose.

It was 0800, Monday, June 28th when Kohl walked into his office. Major Newcomb looked up and told him that Colonel Pachelli wanted to see him. As usual, Kohl pondered what kind of trouble he was in. He asked himself if it could be the fight at the Cortney Club. Sometimes it takes a while for the word to get around. Mays had received office hours for his role in the melee. He didn't want trouble now that he had a job he liked and commanding officers who were good.

Kohl reported to the adjadent and he led him into the Colonel's office.

"Lieutenant Kohl reporting as ordered, Sir."

"At ease. Have a seat Lieutenant."

Kohl sat down as his mind raced through all his misadventures. He was looking at the Colonel's face for any sign. He had practiced his excuses for the fight at the Cortney Club.

"Lieutenant, I'm going to send you back to Vietnam."

The comment caught Kohl off guard. Because his mind was practicing excuses, he didn't hear and what he heard didn't make sense. He thought he heard Vietnam. And the room began to spin and black dots appeared before his eyes. Sweat broke out on his forehead and under his arms. His breathing matched the increased beating of his heart. He thought he might pass out. Kohl leaned over and put his head between his legs.

"What are you doing, Lieutenant?"

"Excuse me, Sir. I don't feel so good."

What's happening here? Are you a chicken shit? Buck up! You've been there before and you can do it again. No big deal. Now breathe deep.

The black dots disappeared and Kohl raised his head. He stared at the Colonel. He didn't know what to say. The Colonel looked confused.

"Are you all right?"

"Yes, Sir. I'm fine."

Kohl sat looking at his hands, long fingers and the nails that he bites, short, no white showing.

These hands should be holding breasts not guns.

The Colonel broke the silence and said, "You will be assigned to the 3rd FSR Unit in Chu Lai."

"Sir." It came out in a squeak. Kohl cleared his constricted throat. "Excuse me, Sir. Was it anything I did or didn't do?"

"No, not at all. In fact both Major Newcomb and I have been pleased with your performance. It's my job to organize this new unit for Chu Lai. An air strip is being built for the support of the 9th Marines who will be stationed there."

Kohl said softly, "But Sir, I've already been to Vietnam. There's a whole bunch of officers just itchin' to go. Send them."

"The reason I'm sending you is because you've been there. You know what's happening and what to expect. I need your experience. Especially for the job I have for you."

"And what's that, Sir?"

"You are going to be one of the officers responsible for the security of the air field and the perimeter security for the 3rd FSR Unit."

Damn! Buggered again.

As Kohl sat slumped over looking at his hands, the Colonel said softly, "I need you there, Lieutenant."

"Who's going to be the Commanding Officer, Colonel?"

"Lieutenant Colonel Knoach."

Oh, no! Not Elmer Fudd. And that rain cloud just keeps following me around.

"When do we leave, Colonel?"

"The Unit will start loading up Wednesday morning the 30th on board the USS Tulare."

"Is Mays going?"

"Yes."

Good. Misery loves company.

"Do you have any more questions?"

"No, Sir."

"Well, you can take the next two days and get your gear and affairs squared away. On your way out get your orders from the First Sergeant. That'll be all, Lieutenant. Good luck."

"Thank you, Sir," Kohl said as he rose to leave. He turned at the hatch and said, "And, Sir? If I may? I would like to say that you and Major Newcomb have been two of the best senior officers I've ever had the fortune to serve under, Sir. Thank you again."

"Thank you for the compliment, Lieutenant. Be careful."

"I will, Sir."

Kohl returned to his office, cleaned out his desk, and said goodbye to the Major. When he got back to his room and before he could sit down to reflect on his situation, the door flew open. Bursting through the door, with his face red with excitement, was Second Lieutenant Blaylock, Colonel Knoachs' Adjutant. He was grinning ear to ear.

Lieutenant Blaylock strutted and posed to compensate for his lack of physical stature. He was of average weight and height but his body was white soft. He had been a supply officer ever since he got out of Basic School. He talked constantly about wanting to be a grunt.

"Have you heard? Have you heard? This is great. Vietnam. Finally. Man, this is outstanding."

Kohl sat on the bed and looked at him. "You miserable little fuck. Get out of here and leave me alone."

"You haven't heard, have you?" Blaylock continued.

"I've heard."

"Bitchin', Huh?"

"Yeah. It's out-fuckin'-standin'."

"I can tell by your tone that you are less than thrilled."

"Thrilled? Blaylock baby, you've got it all wrong. I can hardly contain excitement."

Blaylock let out a humph and sat down on the New York Jew's bed, who was never there since he got 'a Ranch', and said, "Colonel Knoach wants you to get him a bed."

"I can't do that."

"Yes you can. You're BOQ Officer. You have beds around."

"They are all on inventory, asshole. I can't just go down and load up a bed. Why can't he sleep on a cot like the rest of us?"

"He's our CO, Kohl. He can't sleep on cots like the rest of us. Besides he has a bad back."

"I don't give a rats ass. Fuck 'im."

"I guess you could say it's an order from the Colonel, Kohl."

"Fuck you."

"You sure are testy this morning."

Kohl had just about all he was going to take from Second Lieutenant Jefferson T. Blaylock from Connecticut, a product of some wealthy family, eastern prep schools and a graduate in journalism.

Damn east coasters.

"I'll see what I can do. What do I get out of this?" asked Kohl.

"What do you want?"

Kohl thought for a while before answering. *What do they have that I could use for trade and something that I would like? K-Bar.*

"I want five K-Bars."

"That's impossible."

"You want the bed? Five K-Bars."

Blaylock licked his lips and said, "Three. I'll give you three."

"Fuck you, you little shit. I'm not in a fuckin' mood to bargain. Git outa here. Fuckin' ass hole."

"All right. All right. Jeez. Five K-Bars. The Colonel will be pleased, I'm sure. Thanks Kohl."

"The Colonel can eat my shorts." Kohl glared at Blaylock and he left.

*

Kohl and Mays sat at the Henderson Officer's Club bar and drank beer with whiskey chasers. Mays was drunk. It was one of the only times that Kohl could remember that Mays wasn't loud and obnoxious and wanting to fight. They talked about their wives and what they were going to do when they got back, back to the world.

*

Kohl got up at 10 the next morning, showered, dressed and went to lunch.

After lunch he went to see Sergeant Myers about the bed for Colonel Knoach.

"Good afternoon, Lieutenant. You don't look so good. Heard the news. Sorry to see you go. I enjoyed working for you."

"Yeah. Me too, Sarge."

Kohl walked over and poured himself a cup of black coffee and sat down in a large recliner. Being a supply sergeant had its advantages. Sergeant Myers office was adorned in fine furniture. It looked more like a family living room with a desk. They sat in silence for a few minutes and then Kohl said, "I need a favor, Sarge. I hate to ask but I'm kind of over a limb here."

"I'll do whatever I can, Lieutenant. You name it."

"I need a bed for Colonel Knoach."

Sergeant Myers looked at Kohl, leaned back in his chair and grinned.

"Some shit, huh?" said Kohl.

"No biggy, Lieutenant. These things happen more than you think. These goddamn officers, no offense, Sir, think they can just snap their finger and get anything they want and then when our inventory comes up short they scream bloody fuckin' murder that we are pilfering. So who's left hanging by the short hairs? You and me, Lieutenant. You and me. But ... I haven't been in the fuckin' Corps for 17 years without covering my ass. No sirree. I know these cock suckers."

"Do you have any ideas? Can it be done? I have signed for all this shit. Thousands of items and thousands of dollars."

"Let's go talk to Sergeant Wilson."

They left and walked in the afternoon sun over to one of the headquarters' warehouses. Their eyes had to get acclimated to the dark warehouse.

"Wilson?" yelled Sergeant Myers. "Where's your black ass."

"Myers. Don't chew come in 'er hollerin' like dat. I can't sleep wit' you bellowin' like a beached white whale." And out saunters a short, heavily muscled Marine. His white tee shirt was stretched across his broad chest. "Now what's all this yellin' about?"

"The Lieutenant here wants a bed," said Sergeant Myers.

"Not for me, Wilson. It's for Colonel Knoach," explained Kohl.

"Lieutenant?" said Sergeant Myers. "Wilson's my man. When I have little tasks like this," Myers points, "he's my man. That right Wilson?"

"Oh, the trials and tribulations of being a Buck Sergeant."

"Well?" asked Kohl.

"Why, I declare," Wilson said as he looked at his inventory sheet. "If my inventory don't show 735 officer beds but I jus happen to know I got more." He winked at Myers and smiled at Kohl. "You want one too, Lieutenant, to take to Nam?"

"No. One's all I want. Can you do it?"

"It's done."

"Just like that?" asked Kohl.

"Just like that," answered Wilson.

"Here, Sarge." And Kohl handed Wilson a K-Bar. "You too, Sergeant Myers."

"I would have done it for nothin', Lieutenant," said Myers.

"Will let me have yours then, Chester. Your Momma told me you shouldn't play with knives. Poke your eye out," said Wilson.

"My Mama don't talk to colored people, Wilson."

"Oh, that right? She didn't talk but while I was bangin' her, she was moanin' somethin' awful."

"Well, that's more than your Mama does. She just lays there."

"Yeah? And you know why?

"No, Why?"

"She said she couldn't feel your little-bitty-white dick. That's why."

Wilson was laughing and Sergeant Myers was telling something else about Wilson's Momma while Kohl walked outside.

He decided to go see if Sergeant Green was at the ham radio shack. He wanted to try and reach Julie one last time before he left. He had tried several times before but the weather conditions had always been bad except for that time in May. Sergeant Green tried all afternoon to reach North Bend, Oregon but there was a big storm off Hawaii and he couldn't get through. Dejected, Kohl left, bought a bottle of Jack Daniel's at the PX and spent the rest of his waking hours alone in his room reflecting on his sad state of affairs.

PART IV
CHU LAI

Detroit City
By
Danny Hill & Mel Tillis

I wanna go home.
I wanna go home.
Oh, how I wanna go home.
Last night I went to sleep in Detroit City
and I dreamed about the cotton fields and home.
I dreamed about my mother,
dear ol' papa, sister and brother.
And I dreamed about the girl who's been waiting for so long.
I wanna go home.
I wanna go home.
Oh, how I wanna go home.
The home folks think I'm big in Detroit City.
The letters that I write they think I'm fine.
But by day I make the cars.
And by night I make the bars.
If only they could read between the lines.
Cause you know I rode a freight train headin' north to Detroit City.
And after all these years I find I've just been wasting my time.
So I think I'll take my foolish pride.
And put it on the south-bound train and ride.
And I'll go back to the love ones.
The ones that I left waiting so far behind.
I wanna go home.
I wanna go home.
Oh, how I wanna go home.

38 Recurring Dream

Kohl woke with a start. He sat up. He was drenched in sweat and it wasn't from the heat of the confining quarters on board the USS Tulare. It was the dream. The recurring dream. The same dream he had in Vietnam when his throat had been cut by a VC who had crawled through the gun turret hole. He gasped for air. His windpipe was severed. He was drowning in his own blood. He waited until his breathing normalized. Even though his legs were still weak he left the cabin and climbed the stairway topside to get some fresh air. He stood at the railing and let the warm tropical breeze brush his skin. It felt good. It cleared his mind of the dream. The ship cut florescent curls, pealing the fear into the blackness.

*

July 4th, 1965

Hi Sweetheart,
Yesterday I got your post cards from Mexico. It sure looks beautiful down there and by the messages on the cards; it appears that you are having a wonderful time.
Well, I was waiting until I knew for sure before I told you. I didn't want to upset you. But I'm on board the USS Tulare heading back to Vietnam. It's not like before, Hon. I'll be in a place called Chu Lai with the Force Service Regiment. Rear echelon stuff. I probably

won't even get out of the compound. Believe me, I'll be safer than you driving on the LA freeways. Mays is with me too.

It finally warmed up and quit raining. Now it's hot. While I was at Oki it rained almost ever day. The day before we left Mays and I went to the beach for the first time. Now I'm on this goddamn boat heading back to Vietnam. All the officers are bitchin' up a storm about how hot it is. The room I'm in is about 15 feet by 15 feet. We have nine men and all our gear in this room, one electrical outlet, and seven fans. I told them if they're bitchin' now about the heat and accommodations, they haven't seen anything yet.

And it's nothing compared to the troop quarters in the hold.

We had fire works off the fantail tonight. I must say it was impressive.

I miss you so much. Say hi to everyone for me. I'm keeping the faith and maintaining my sanity. I keep saying things could be worse, not much though.

I send you all my love. We are on the down slope now. Only five more months to go.

Love always,
Dusty

*

On the morning of July 7th the engine room became silent. Kohl stood on the port bow of the ship as Danang came into view. The blue ocean and white beaches glimmered in the morning sun. Monkey Island's dense foliage was variegated in all shades of green. The highlands to the west gradually rose to meet the clear blue sky. Kohl let out a big sigh.

This fuckin' place is beautiful.

Mays came up along side and said, "Dejavu, Mutha fucker."

"Dejavu," answered Kohl.

Other marine officers began to cluster around Kohl and Mays and peppered them with questions.

"Is that the air field?"

"Where's Danang?"

"Where are we going?"

Kohl felt like an old salt. But there was another feeling that began to crawl into his throat while he looked toward shore. He was beginning to feel the fear of night patrols, the buzz of mosquitoes, the stifling heat, dust, sweat, fatigue. Was fear another word for being afraid?

I'm not afraid. A little apprehensive maybe but not afraid.

What about scared? Are you scared?

I think I'm worried more than anything.

Worried about getting killed?

No. I just wish I knew what the hell's going on.

Kohl and about twenty troops climbed over the side and down the cargo net into the Mike boat and headed for shore. He wasn't paying attention but something wasn't right. He got up out of his crouch and saw that they were heading toward White Beach. The same beach they landed on in March. At the briefing he understood that they were to land at the Danang pier. He walked back to the coxswain.

Kohl asked, "Excuse me, sailor?"

"Yeah?"

"Aren't you supposed to take us to the Danang pier?"

"Where's the Danang pier?"

"It's over there," Kohl pointed.

"Oh."

Jesus. I swear I'm surrounded by idiots.

They docked and climbed out of the Mike boat. Kohl told the troops to stand-by while he tried to find transportation to the Danang FLSG. He found a first lieutenant from shore party and asked if he could get them a truck. He said he could and made the necessary arrangements.

Another Mike boat came in and unloaded more troops and a Major. The Major walked up to Kohl and said "Morning, Lieutenant."

"Howdy, Major."

Howdy? What the fuck are you thinking?

Kohl's mind was a thousand miles away with Julie. He was aware that a Major was standing to his side and he acknowledged his salutation but other than that he stood in silence and stared off toward the sea, to the east.

"Excuse me, Lieutenant," the Major said with his eyes narrowed in annoyance.

Kohl jerked his head back to the voice. The Major stood with his hands on his hips and said, "Well?"

Kohl looked around. He was confused. "I beg your pardon, Sir. I ... I'm sorry, Sir. Did you say something?"

"Are you on dope or something? I'm a superior officer and you didn't salute. What kind of an example are you? Well? Are you going to salute or just stand there with your stupid mouth open?"

"Sorry, Sir."

"Well, do it."

"Yes, Sir." and Kohl saluted.

"Jesus fuckin' Christ. Insubordinate prick," the Major muttered as he walked off, down the dock.

The trucks came and Kohl and his troops climbed aboard. As they drove through Dog Patch the Vietnamese kids yelled "Ello. Ello. Marine."

Kohl got off the truck, saw Mays, and waved. They both walked to the tent where they had last seen Pete two months ago. He was still there. Same place. There was a swirl of activity around him. More troops, tents, and supplies but Pete seemed oblivious.

"You miserable sack of shit," yelled Mays.

Pete looked up, smiled, jumped from his desk and waving his arms, ran towards Kohl and Mays. They grabbed each other, slapped backs, and grinned.

"Did you come to save me?" Pete asked.

"I'm afraid not, Pete," said Kohl as they walked back to his office.

"Man, I thought you guys were long gone. What happened?"

Mays said, "We couldn't leave you, man. So California boy and I volunteered to come back and keep you company. It's no fun having wet dreams without you, Pete."

There was a continuing banter between Mays and Pete but Kohl lagged behind. There was a matter pressing on his mind, in the recesses, around the corners where anger had built. He wasn't conscious of the fact until ... he had thought about it ... but it welled up bursting to the conscious.

"Where's my old outfit, Pete?"

"Oh, they are all gone by now."

"Do you know Lieutenant Spade?" asked Kohl.

Mays gave Kohl a side-glance and said, "Leave it be."

"I just want to talk to him, that's all. Can I use your Jeep?"

"Sure," said Pete.

Kohl walked off toward the Jeep and Pete said, "When will you be back? We've got some serious partying to do."

Kohl didn't answer. His mind was on how he was going to confront Spade. Ever since he had returned from Vietnam and found out that it was Spade who had betrayed him, he had envisioned how he would confront him. In his mind he would daydream of how he would get back at Spade. In his fantasy he would send a struggling Spade to the ground in a flurry of punches. In his vision he would see a bloody face and a cowering Spade. He could safely dream his dream because he would never see him again. But coming back to Vietnam had not been part of the plan. He climbed into the Jeep and drove to where the old 3/9 CP used to be. 1/9 was there now and as he drove into the compound he heard a familiar voice call his name.

"Lieutenant Kohl, Sir!"

Kohl stopped the Jeep and turned to see Sergeant Ford jogging toward him. "Sergeant Ford," Kohl said as he got out and shook his hand. "Good to see you, Ford."

"And you, Lieutenant. You're back, uh?"

"Yep. I guess they can't fight the gooks without me."

"Are you sure, Lieutenant?" Ford said with a wink.

"Oh, shut up."

"What are you doing here, Sir?"

"I'm going down to Chu Lai."

"Yeah, I heard they were setting up an air field down there."

"They have me in charge of airport security."

Ford turned slightly and looked into the valley below and asked, "Say, Lieutenant. Is there a chance I could be your Sergeant ... again?"

Kohl felt a feeling of pride that Ford wanted to be with him again. He also relished the thought of having a gung ho sergeant like Ford and what a help it would be to him.

"Aren't you 'bout due to go back state-side, Ford?"

"Re-upped, Lieutenant. Re-upped."

"Re-upped. No shit. Well, I sure could use you, Ford. I'll ask my CO and see what we can work out, okay?

"Outstanding, Lieutenant. Did you hear about the airfield attack last week?"

"No. What happened?"

"Mortars. They set up in the ARVN sector, Lieutenant. The ARVN's are a joke. The attack knocked out six planes, killed an airman and wounded three others."

"Maybe things will get better. I can see there has been quite a build up since I left. Where's Sergeant Fontain?"

"He got sent up to Khe Sanh. Special Forces are pulling out and the Marines are going in."

"Is Spade still around?"

Ford looked questioningly at Kohl before he answered, "Yeah, he's still platoon commander of L Company."

"Where're they at?"

Ford pointed, "Over there."

"I'll see you later, okay?"

"Sure, Lieutenant. Later." Ford watched Kohl walk towards L Company Third Recon.

Kohl saw Spade sitting on a pile of sandbags drinking a Coke.

Damn, he looks bigger than I remember.

He is big, you dumb fuck.

Yeah, I know. But I forgot how his fuckin' shoulders, neck and head all blend into one big fuckin' muscle.

Are you sure you want to pursue this?

No.

Well, you had better turn around before it's too late.

Spade stood up when he saw Kohl walking toward him and he smiled with all those big bright white teeth. Kohl hit Spade as hard as he could with a right hand to the side of Spade's head, neck, shoulder. It didn't matter they were all connected. They were the same. Big muscled mass. Kohl felt the shock run from his hand, to his wrist and up his arm.

Damn that hurt.

Spade's head turned and the blow knocked him back a few steps but he didn't crumple to the ground.

Uhoh. Kohl. You are now in deep dog shit. This is not good. Dreams do not come true. You'd better turn and run like hell, because you are about to get the livin' shit kicked out of you.

Spade brought his heavily muscled left arm up. Kohl flinched. But Spade put his hand to the side of his face and rubbed it and said, "Jesus, Kohl. What the hell did you do that for?"

Kohl was breathing hard as adrenaline rushed to all the parts of his body, which didn't leave much for his brain. "Because ... Because, you ... you." *Spit it out Kohl before he rips your tongue out.* "Because you betrayed me."

"What?"

"You told the Colonel that I wasn't doing my job."

"I did not."

"You did too. They told me all about it when I got back. It was you."

Spade sat back down on the sand bags and said softly, but there was a chill in his voice, "You know I could break you like a fuckin' twig."

"Yeah. I know," answered Kohl. He let out a self-conscious giggle.

"Then why did you do that?"

"I had too. I couldn't let you just ... just say things that were not true."

"Hey. You didn't want to be here anyway. So I thought I was doing you a favor."

"If I want a favor, I'll ask for it."

"Sorry."

"Fuck you."

"No, I'm sorry man." Spade held out his hand. "I mean it. I didn't know it meant that much to you. You were always bitchin', you know."

"Yeah, but I thought it was between us, man."

"I'm sorry."

Kohl looked at the outstretched hand. He had seen Mays do that to a guy once and when the guy shook his hand Mays pulled him into a smashing left fist.

Could Spade be doing the same thing?

Kohl looked at the smiling Spade and back at the out stretched hand. Kohl took it. Spades grip was like iron. Kohl watched his every move, wary of his sincerity, but Spade didn't hit him.

Kohl let out a big sigh of relief. "I'm sorry too," said Kohl finally.

They hugged each other self-consciously and talked about things ... things that didn't matter. They talked around the edges of dark holes. They talked, joked, and laughed. Spade talked about his girl back home and Kohl talked about Julie. They talked about food, cars, and the fireworks on 4th of July. They drank Cokes and watched the sun go down over the highlands. Soon it was dark. They sat silently. Spade looked gaunt and Kohl noticed a slight twitch under his left eye. He remembered the first time he met the gung-ho Spade at the Kadena Airport when he arrived at Okinawa. And then again in April when he came charging up the hill, excited about being in Vietnam. He didn't look excited now.

"Be careful, Spade."

"I will, and you too. God be with you, Kohl," he added as an after thought.

Kohl thought he saw a glint of a tear in the dimness of the early evening. He said goodbye and drove back down the hill. He didn't feel like partying, but he didn't want to go to sleep either. Maybe if I got drunk, I wouldn't dream that fuckin' dream. All those times he went out on patrol, he wasn't afraid ... but that dream, with his throat cut, unable to breath, it turned his skin to ice. He could taste the fear.

I know what fear tastes like. It's metallic and sticks to my pallet. It's bitter and like alum, it takes the moisture out of my mouth that leaves a tongue lowing, feeling foreign and unneeded.

*

Pete's alarm went off at 0500 and kept ringing until Pete reached out from under the mosquito net and slapped the innocent alarm into submission. The sleeping occupants of the tent began to stir.

Kohl sat up in his cot and looked through the mosquito net at the enclosed shadows. He couldn't remember where he was. The shadows began to filter into recognizable forms. He remembered coming into an empty tent last night. He had pulled a pint of Johnny Walker out of his sea bag and ...Kohl said, "What time did you guys come in? Did you party without me?"

"There wasn't any party," snapped Pete.

"Well good. Then I didn't miss anything?"

"You missed the meeting," said Blaylock.

"What meeting?" asked Kohl.

"Boy, is the Colonel pissed at you," continued Blaylock.

"Will you guys shut up! I've got to finish fuckin' my rubber lady," mumbled Mays as he pulled his blanket over his head.

"What meeting?" said Kohl again.

"Where'd you go anyway?" asked Blaylock.

"What's it to you, Blaylock. Now, Pete. What meeting?" asked Kohl again.

"The Colonel called a meeting of all the officers that are going to Chu Lai," answered Pete.

"Fuckin' ruined our party time, man," moaned Mays.

"Why did you have to go, Pete?" asked Kohl.

"Man. He's one of us. Some shit, huh? We are going to be one happy-fuckin'-family," said Mays as he got out of his canvas cot and stretched. "Got me a rock hard-on and no place to put it. Bend over Blaylock."

Blaylock got red as Kohl and Pete laughed.

*

After morning chow Blaylock found Kohl back at the tent reading. He said, "The Colonel wants to see you ASAP. Boy, you're in trouble."

"Jesus, Blaylock. You go on like a broken-fuckin-record."

"Well, he is."

"Okay! Okay!" yelled Kohl. "You really piss me off. Where's he at?"

"I'll take you."

"Damn you, Blaylock. If you don't get out of my fuckin' face I'm goin' to spread your nose all over yours. Got it?"

Blaylock grumbled to himself and pointed, then said, "He's at the Regimental CP. Know where it's at?"

"Yes, I know. Been here, remember? You dumb fuckin' moron."

Kohl walked to the regimental CP and found Colonel Knoach sitting behind a field desk piled with papers. Even though it was a little past 0800, the Colonel had sweat running down his round, white, flushed face.

"Morning, Colonel. Heard you wanted to see me."

The Colonel looked up annoyed at the disruption and at Kohl. "I knew you were a mistake. I knew it. I could tell, from the way you ran the Officer's Mess. I could tell by your attitude, when I ordered you to fire that naison back at Henderson. You were disobedient then, you're disobedient now, and by all indications you will be continue to be disobedient. I just knew it. So if I knew it, why are you here? Well, it sure wasn't my choice. I wouldn't have you within a hundred miles of me, if I had anything to say about it. It was because of Colonel Pachelli. He told me I had to take you. He probably didn't want you around either.

"So. Where were you last night? You missed a meeting, you know. You didn't get my permission to go anywhere. Who do you think you are? You just think you are on your own here and can do whatever you want? Well, Lieutenant you can't. I'm your commanding officer and you answer to me. Even though it's not my choice. I'd prefer, in fact, I require that all my officers be the best. I hate incompetence, and you, Lieutenant Kohl, are incompetent. I'll try and do my best to make you a better Marine but I doubt I can do you any good. I don't see how you made it though OCS. If I had been in charge, I would have sent you to Camp LeJeune. You are a sorry excuse of an officer. I've read your fitness reports. Marginal! And you still haven't told me where you were."

After the first couple of sentences, when Kohl perceived the direction of the monologue, his mind began to wander. He had been watching an individual droplet of sweat roll down the Colonel's forehead, down the bridge of his small nose, over his red upper lip into the flapping mouth. Some of the sweat dripped off his chin onto the pile of papers, leaving little gray round circles.

"Tell me! Lieutenant?"

Focus Kohl. Focus. I think he's asking you a question.

"I beg your pardon, Sir, did you ask me a question? I didn't sleep well last night with all the planes, mosquitoes, generators, artillery rounds, and all. I seemed to have ..."

"Lieutenant!" he shouted. "I don't want to hear your feeble excuses. You went into Danang, didn't you? Probably was with a whore, while we were having our meeting. Weren't you? I know your kind."

"No, Sir. I went to see a buddy of mine up on the hill."

"That's no excuse. You were supposed to be at the meeting."

"Sir. I didn't know there was a meeting 'till this morning."

"Everybody else was there, Lieutenant. Our FLS Unit is like a finely oiled machine. All the parts have to work together. And that includes you, Lieutenant. You are not to go any place without asking me. Understood?"

"Yes, Sir. Can I go now?"

Kohl thought the Colonel's head was going to explode. It was red and spittle was starting to run from the corners of his mouth. "Get out! Get out!" Colonel Knoach lifted his arms to wave Kohl out, but the sweat had glued some papers to his arms and he began flapping his arms trying to rid himself of the clinging papers.

Kohl turned and left.

"Don't you leave this compound. You hear?" yelled the Colonel.

"Loud and clear, Colonel. Loud and clear."

When Kohl walked out of the Colonel's office he sighed. He looked over and saw Sergeant Major Jurgens grinning.

Kohl smiled and said, "Hi, Sergeant Major."

"Morning, Lieutenant. I see you got your AM ass chewing."

"I needed to get my day on track," said Kohl sarcastically, then added, "Say, Sergeant Major. I need a favor."

"No. You can't have a transfer," the Sergeant Major said laughing.

Kohl laughed too and asked, "There's a Sergeant stationed here with 1/9 by the name of Ford. He's an E-5. I would like to have him as my Airport Security NCO. He's good. He was my platoon sergeant when I was recon platoon commander back in March. What do you think? Could you swing it for me? Huh?"

"Why don't you ask the Colonel?" he asked grinning.

"I don't think he likes me very much," said Kohl smiling.

"I'll see what I can do, Lieutenant."

"Thanks, Sarge."

39 Chu Lai

(Stars and Strips)
Chu Lai, Republic of Vietnam.

How would you like to build your own city? Begin with a desolate strip of sand, baked in 100 degree plus temperatures, and try to make it livable.

The infantry marines kept going inland when they landed, finally stopping atop a ring of hills that circle the base to the west. But the Group Utilities Section began building a city for the thousands of marines that would come ashore to man the future airfield.

The first thing you do is to plot your street system. But when the streets are going to lie on shifting sand you have problems. So they brought in clay.

Next they would erect row upon row of tents.

Then electricity provided by diesel generators.

They filled rubber tanks atop 14-foot platforms for running water.

They dug trenches for toilets and covered them with plywood that had holes cut on the top.

They constructed the mess halls, showers, and factories for the repair and maintenance of equipment.

Chu Lai. Sand in your food. Sand in your sack. Sandy beaches and blue water and not a girl in sight.

*

The GV (Hercules C-130) banked hard to the west. Kohl could see a little of the turquoise ocean out of the back end. The large GV had four turbo-prop engines and carried both troops and cargo, the seats were made of web strapping, and the passengers faced to the rear. This was to protect the passengers in case of a crash or ditch. At least that's what Kohl was told. Because he was facing backwards he couldn't see where they were going but he could see where they had been. Mays was sitting next to Kohl and had the luxury of a small window he could see out of. On the other side of Kohl was a noisily sleeping Pete. Also in the plane was Colonel Knoach and sitting next to him was Lieutenant Blaylock. Sergeant Major Jurgens was talking to Sergeant Ford. The Sergeant Major had known what strings to pull in order to get Sergeant Ford transferred.

Mays was looking out the small window.

"What's down there, Mays?" asked Kohl because all he could see was a big crate covered with a straining cargo net and a small sliver of blue sky.

"Sand."

"Come on. What else?" continued Kohl?

They were dropping fast. The engines were being pulled back and feathered.

"What now? Do you see the air field?"

"Jesus!" groaned Mays.

"What? What?" asked Kohl again more startled. "Jesus, what?"

"We're going to land on that?" exclaimed Mays.

Kohl couldn't stand the frustration any longer but he couldn't move because of his seat belt and shoulder straps that held him firmly in his seat.

"Fuck me. Hold on," commanded Mays.

The plane dropped at least thirty feet straight down and Kohl's stomach stayed at the altitude they had just left. They hit the landing strip with a thump and a jolt. There was the sound of tires running over ridges or grooves, Kohl couldn't tell. The engines whined in shrill complaint as the pilots sent them into reverse thrust. His body was thrust backward, which was actually forward but if you're setting backward, backwards is forwards. Kohl was watching the straining cargo nets that held shipping crates of supplies. *If one of those go, it'll squash me like a pancake.* The engines roared in a final ear splitting protest and the plane shuddered, shook and jolted to a stop, then turned port, slowly rolled and jostled it's way back down the way it came. After a few minutes the plane came to rest. The engines wheezed to a gasping halt.

There was nervous laughter and exclamations about the landing from the twenty Marines on board. Kohl had to wake up Pete. He had slept through the whole ordeal.

Pete wiped the back of his hand across his mouth and said, "What?"

"We're here, Pete." Then turned to Mays and said, "That was the shortest damn landing I've ever seen."

As the Marines filed down the ramp of the GV, Kohl glanced quickly from horizon to horizon wondering where this place called Chu Lai was. To the east he saw a row of tents. And beyond that were the hills of sand with a sprinkling of small shore pines and brush. To the west rose the tangled-forested mountains. Now that the GV had landed, dozers and earthmoving machines came back onto the strip and began where they had left off. He was standing on metal matting. He saw working crews carrying pieces of matting down by the dozers and hooking them together. This was the airstrip, about the size of two football fields.

The FLSU contingent was taken by six-by to their compound, located north about two miles of the airstrip. Kohl could hear the surf along the bluff where the tents were located. Captain John McKillip, Commanding Officer of the advance party, was there to meet them upon their arrival. The Captain, with a friendly smile and sharp salute introduced himself to Colonel Knoach. His freckled face was sunburned and red.

There was a collection of tents that comprised the mess hall, supply, maintenance, communications, S3-S2 offices, the Colonel's office and troop quarters. The living quarters for the officers consisted of four four-man tents.

With their sea-bags over their shoulders, Kohl, Mays, and Pete were taken to the last tent in the row. Blaylock was also in their tent but he was still with the Colonel. Next to their tent were two large diesel engine generators. They were so loud the ground shook.

"Jesus. We're going to be next to that?" Mays pointed. "How're we going to sleep with those things going all night? With all this space, why do they have to have them next to our tent?"

"I don't know. I'm going to see if I can catch DeBoise before he takes off. See if he has any words of wisdom about the airport," said Kohl

Kohl walked into the S-2/S3 tent. Second Lieutenant Bill DeBoise was cleaning out his field desk.

Kohl asked, "DeBoise, isn't it?"

"Yeah," answered the small young man without looking up.

"Hurry Up, Lieutenant," said the corporal who Kohl assumed was driving the Lieutenant to the airbase.

"I'm hurrying. Got my stuff from the tent Jennings?"

"Yes Sir. Plane leaves in fifteen minutes, Sir."

"Shit. Shit. Shit," declared DeBoise as he rustled through papers of a bottom drawer.

"Come on, Lieutenant. What are you looking for?"

"Go on out to the Jeep. I'll be right out."

DeBoise reached behind a drawer he had pulled out and extracted a brown paper bag that was rolled and taped. *Is that what I think it is?* He stuffed it into a small gym bag, got up and was startled by the sight of Kohl standing there looking at him. He turned without saying anything, ran to the jeep, and roared off toward the airstrip.

Kohl had hoped DeBoise would be able to give him some information about the airport security. He heard that the air base was getting hit almost every night. Sniper fire mostly. With DeBoise gone Kohl left the tent and walked toward the beach. He came to a small bluff, climbed down the trail, and stood next to the waves that lapped lazily at his feet. About fifty yards out was a reef of rocks and corral that enclosed the small bay on two sides. The water was a clear opal blue/green. Kohl sat down in the warm sand, leaned against the bluff, and fell asleep. The next thing he knew he felt a thump on his foot then heard Pete say, "Hey! Hey! Kohl! Wake up! I knew I'd find you down here. The Colonel's having a meeting. Come on."

"Pretty, isn't it?"

"Yeah. Come on. We'll be late. Come on."

"What do you think?"

"About what?"

"The beach. Pretty neat, huh?"

"Yeah. Not bad, I guess. Not bad."

When Kohl and Pete walked into the Colonel's office everybody was sitting in a semicircle in front of the Colonel's desk. The Colonel glared at Kohl. *Will, glare at Pete too.* They took their seats along with Captain McKillip, Navy Lieutenant Dr. Austin, Lieutenant Hockett, Captain Van Loon, Warrant Officer Shaffer, Lieutenant Mays, Navy Lieutenant Peterson, and Lieutenant Blaylock. To Kohl's surprise Lieutenant DeBoise was there too. Kohl gave him a shrug with upright palms. DeBoise, visibly upset, looked away. *Missed his plane searching for his stash.*

"Where's Major Ponds?" asked the Colonel.

"Probably down by the pier, Colonel," said Captain McKillip. He reminded Kohl of Ikabod Crain. He had kinky curly red hair, a prominent Adam's apple and freckles. When he talked the words came out southern smooth. His mouth opened from one side as though only that side of his face had the muscles to work his mouth. He had been the CO until now.

"Did you tell him there was a meeting, Captain?"

"Yes, Sir."

"Then why isn't he here?"

"He's off loading an LST, Sir."

"When I have a meeting, I want everybody here. Where's ... aah ... "the Colonel looked at a roster of names, "Captain Hawes?" he asked looking up.

There was silence. The Colonel glared at Captain McKillip.

"Sir, we didn't have meetings like this, Sir," explained McKillip.

"Well we do now. It's very important that the FLSU operates proficiently. I must be kept appraised of, and the progress of our duties to provide the support necessary for the successful operation of 1/9. It's up to us..." The field phone rang and the Colonel turned in his chair to answer. "Colonel Knoach. Yes. Yes. I'll find out, Major and get back to you.

"Captain McKillip?"

"Yes, Sir."

"How come the trucks haven't arrived at the Ammo Dump?"

"I told Lieutenant Shaw this morning, Sir."

"By the way where is Lieutenant Shaw?" the Colonel asked. The field phone rang again. "Colonel Knoach. No, he's not here. Try the Shore Party Pier. You did?" The Colonel glared at McKillip. "I see. I'll take care of it."

"It appears that our Mr. Ponds is not at the pier, Captain," the Colonel said through clinched teeth. The Pillsbury DoughBoy look couldn't generate fear. Neither could his high pitched voice. He used his rank to instill the fear. He continued to glare at McKillip.

The Captain shrugged and said, "He could be away from the phone, Sir."

"Then he should have someone by the phone at all times. And that goes for all of you. When it comes to crunch time, I want to be able to get a hold of each of you instantly. Minutes could mean lives."

Oh, brother.

"By the way, where is Lieutenant Shaw?"

"He's gone, Sir," said McKillip.

"I know that!" shouted the Colonel. "I want to know where."

Warrant Officer Shaffer was the Maintenance Company CO. He was the only officer there in a tee shirt. Around the mid section, grease had a tendency to collect on the prominent protruding gut. He spit a brown stream of tobacco juice into a can. He wiped off a brown string of drool with the back of his hand and drawled, "Sheeeit, Colonel. He's in Danang by now. Left on the plane that DeBoise was supposed to be on. Ye jist couldn't leave us, huh DeBoise?" laughed Warrant Officer Shaffer.

"Warrant Officer? There will be no profanity in this office and further more; you will not chew tobacco in my presence. Spit it out."

"Sir?" asked the eldest officer.

"Now."

Warrant Officer Shaffer looked from side to side. None of the officers would meet his eyes. Instead they looked down at their hands and feet or out the sides of the tent. Kohl was the only one that caught the eye of the embarrassed officer.

A Warrant Officer, rank wise, was lower than a Second Lieutenant but rank was seldom enforced. They were Mustangs. Enlisted NCO's that were extremely proficient in their field. Kohl had never seen any officer ever chew out a Warrant Officer. Never.

"Yes, Sir," he said and he spit the wad into the can.

"And, another thing, Mr. Shaffer." The Colonel was heavy on the Mister. "You look like a slob. Dress in the proper attire. Understood?"

The air could have been cut with a K-bar. The Warrant Officer's neck was red. His eyes closed into slits. Kohl watched his muscled, grease streaked arms twitch. Each muscle fiber exploding. Knurled fingers and skinned knuckles clawed and clenched to the under side of his chair.

"Now. Since Lieutenant Shaw is supposedly not here any longer, Captain McKillip, don't you think it would be an appropriate decision on your part to inform the current Motor Transport Officer, Lieutenant Mays here, about getting the ammo picked up and delivered to the ammo dump? Think so?"

"Yes, Sir. I'll get right on it, Sir."

"We will have a meeting tomorrow evening here at 2000. That's every officer. Do I make myself clear?"

"Yes, Sir," they answered.

Kohl and Pete walked slowly and silently back to their tent. Kohl was thinking how miserable this was going to be. He would rather be out in the field than to spend five long months playing mind games with the Colonel.

Really? You'd rather be out in the boonies?

Yes.

You're safer here.

I know.

When the three arrived at the tent Kohl complained, "How in the fuck are we going to be able to sleep next to those generators?"

Pete said, "I'm so fuckin' tired. I don't care."

Kohl brushed his teeth, wiped a damp cloth over his face, arms and torso and climbed under his sheet. They didn't need mosquito netting because the breeze from the ocean kept them away. He lay on his back and looked at the dark interior of the tent and listened to the constant drone of the diesels. He found some toilet paper, tore off a piece, wadded it up and put it in his mouth to add moisture, then put it in his ear. He did the same thing for his other ear. It helped. *Maybe I can get some rifle range earplugs tomorrow. The artillery people will have some.* He rolled over and pulled the pillow around his head. He heard Blaylock come in. Later, he heard Mays come in. He looked at his watch. It was 0200. He heard Pete get up to take a leak. Mostly, he heard the diesels.

*

Dust hung over the oval track. White light turned orange by the dust illuminating the cars roaring down the straight-a-way and sliding into the turn and roaring down the straight-a-way again and again and again. Why would anyone ever watch a jalopy derby? The noise was deafening. Besides it was boring.

A drop of water hit Kohl on the forehead. Maybe it'll settle the dust. Then another one. This one hit his closed right eye. He opened his left eye and recognized the inside of the tent. The roar of the diesel hurt his teeth. Another plop hit his cheek. *What the hell's going on?* It had started to rain. Gentle soothing sounds of rain were hitting the top of the tent. He sat up and lifted his right arm and touched the canvas above his head. There was a hole about three inches long. He got up and dug around in his travel bag and pulled out a bar of soap and stuck it in the hole.

40 Airport Security

It was two days later that the Marine Airbase Commander sent for Kohl. Kohl took Second Lieutenant Cobain and Sergeant Ford and reported to the air base headquarters. They were met by Major Phillips, who was the coordinator for setting up the airport security. Kohl was to be the officer-in-charge. Sergeant Ford would be the security NCO. Kohl and Cobain each would have two weeks on and two weeks off. On their off week they would be responsible for FLSU security and any other S-2 duties that Colonel Knoach deemed necessary. Sergeant Ford would be permanently on airbase duty until Kohl could find another sergeant to share the load. The troops used for security would change every two weeks and would be pulled from the ranks of the rear echelon. Kohl was to determine how many troops were needed and to set up a quota system for each of the FLS Units to fill.

The Major took the three to a map of the area and pointed out where everything was located. Kohl's area of responsibility would be primarily to the west and northwest, MP's monitored the roads into the area, Shore Party covered the eastern shoreline, FLSU the northern shoreline and Regimental Headquarters covered the south.

The three toured the perimeter of their AOR and started making notes of fields of fire, mapping gullies, trees and areas to clear brush. They would have to dig bunkers. They needed sand bags, concertina wire, landmines, clamors, illumination, and hand grenades.

The activity around the airfield was deafening. Engineer Battalion, with the help of an American civilian construction company, was clearing, leveling and laying down runway metal interlocking matting.

Sand was everywhere.

*

It was 0900 the 13th of July. The troops were assembled to Kohl's front. Lt. Cobain and Sergeant Ford brought the dirty, unshaven motley crew to some semblance of rank and formation. Most of the puzzled young faces were recent arrivals, leaving behind sweethearts, high school football, wives, children, and parents. They had left their warm beds, home cooking, hot showers, TV shows and back yard bar-b-ques. They locked their hotrods in the garage they used to 'tool' around town in, park at the drive-in eating burgers and fries and drinking cherry cokes. Their Jerry curl and ducktails were replaced with the high and tight Marine haircut. Turned up collars and pegged Levis were exchanged for green utilities. In their hands, with the butt resting in the sand, was the M-14 rifle. They were mechanics, drivers, electricians, clerks and cooks. Some hadn't been in the field in months and for some of the older Marine NCO's it could have been years. Now they had been chosen and called upon to sit night after night for the next two weeks listening and watching. Mostly there was nothing to hear, and with the night so dark, nothing to see. But the night plays its tricks with the human ears and eyes. The wind stirs the branches; animals rustle the leaves and grass; and the VC watch the watchers. Will it be tonight, tomorrow night, next week, next month? Kohl didn't know the answers, but he did know that it would happen. Would they be ready?

To the rear about 50 yards were the big black rubber balloon fuel tanks. If blown, the explosion and flames would fry anything within 200 yards and suck the air out of the lungs of those who survived. Another 200 yards were the A-4 Skyhawk bombers all in a neat row.

Kohl told the motley crew that the VC herded goats and cows to trip the flares. They also tried to get the Marines to fire their weapons, especially the automatics so they could plot the positions. He told them that they used children with satchel charges strapped to their backs to infiltrate the lines and lie under a plane and blow themselves and the plane to smithereens. The troops gave him a skeptical look. For emphasis, he told them about the girl selling cokes at Danang. He described how she had blown herself up in a shower of glass, rocks and dirt. The bodies of the men standing next to her were torn to pieces. Instead of firing at noises and shadows, he wanted the men to throw illumination grenades. Then when a target was identified as enemy, throw a grenade.

"However, I don't want any John Waynes,'" he told them. "I want all the grenades kept in the containers." He told them about a Marine had a grenade hanging from the pin on his belt. As he climbed into the back end of a loaded six-by the grenade got hung up on something and the pin pulled out. The grenade rolled to the front of the truck bed and blew up. Ten Marines were killed and the rest were critically wounded. Kohl nonchalantly pulled a grenade from his field belt and without looking at the troops he pulled the pin. There was a gasp from the troops. Some ran and others fell to the sand. While others remained standing, looking puzzled. Sergeant Ford had a smile on his face. Earlier that day Lieutenant Cobain, who was the OIC of the Underwater Demolition Team, had defused the grenade. Kohl continued to talk as the troops cautiously came back to formation, "I don't know why it is that when someone pulls the pin on a grenade fear and panic sets in. As long as you hold the spoon down, this grenade is as safe as it was before I pulled the pin. So if you use a grenade and you pull the pin, take a deep breath and try to relax. Then throw it. We have the most effective grenades in the world. Just make sure their effectiveness is used on our enemy and not us. Be careful.

"After dark," he told them, "nobody leaves their positions. Not even to take a shit or piss. Nothin'. Got it? Anybody after dark walking or crawling is enemy. So if you don't want to get your ass shot, stay in your foxhole. Right after I first came to Danang, back in March, a Marine shot two of his buddies who had crawled out of their foxhole to check out something they thought they heard.

"Keep a cool mind. Being in a critical area like we are I want you to be alert but not to the extent where you become jumpy and scared. On the other hand, I don't want you to be so relaxed and laid back that you don't take your job seriously and fall asleep on post. Remember that your fox hole buddy depends on you and you on him. If a VC finds you asleep a lot more can happen then a few planes being blown up, you could have your throats cut.

The VC has a tactic of traveling in pairs or maybe threes. One will approach what they think might be an outpost or foxhole, just walking along like some dumb ass Marine. The Marine sentry will call out "halt." And the VC will disappear while the other one will move to the side and throw a grenade at the unsuspecting occupant of the foxhole. That's why we will have four men to a position. Two people will be awake at all times. One reason is the one situation I just mentioned and the other is to keep one another awake. Remember men, when you stand that watch and your buddies are grabbing a few winks before it's their time, you have their lives at stake. In fact you have all our lives at stake. If you're lucky, Luke the Gook will try to come through your area and you'll be ready and waiting for this scrawny, little, piece of shit.

"Here," Kohl said as he pitched the hand grenade at an unsuspecting Marine. The Marine instinctively caught it. The troops scattered like a covey of quail, while the unfortunate Marine dropped the grenade at his feet and ran and dove into the sand. It was a dirty trick and Kohl knew it. He hadn't planned on doing what he did. He was upset because these young men didn't realize what was at stake.

When nothing happened, they slowly got up and walked cautiously back where Kohl was now standing holding the dud grenade.

"Are there any questions?"

"Sir? I want to submit a P.A. form for the grunts. I didn't join the Marines to work in the mess hall ... Sir."

"So, providing beans, bullets and Band-Aids is not your idea of being a Marine? Is that right?"

"Sir. Begging your pardon Sir. I didn't join the Corps to sit in some mess hall making bread, Sir."

"When'd you get here, Marine?"

"Three days ago, Sir."

"You have a long way to go, Marine. The Marine Corps gave you the MOS you have and they sent you here because we need you. We need you and every one of you to do your jobs. You all will be working long hours. I know you won't pay any attention to what I've got to say on the matter but believe me it ain't all it's cracked up to be. But here's what I'll do Marine. Just to make you happy I'll put you in an L and OP. If you can handle that I'll see what I can do. After two weeks out there you might have a change of heart about being a grunt."

"Thank you, Sir."

"Don't thank me yet, Marine. You might be dead in two weeks."

*

July 13, 1965
Hi Baby Doll,
Well, here I am in Chu Lai. It's seems to be cooler here than in Danang. I think it's because we have a breeze off the ocean. It is remote. Man, there's nothing around.
I am the Intelligence Officer, (don't laugh). I actually am the airbase security officer. No big deal, really. The chow is pretty bad and living conditions

are poor but not as bad as it was in Danang. It's funny. We have to walk a mile and a half to shower and by the time we walk back we are all smelly and sweaty again.

Pete has lost a lot of weight. He came down with Mays and me. He is the Force Logistic Support Officer for the 10,000 Marines that are here now. Sue is due sometime this month. He's feeling pretty bad about not being there.

I haven't received any mail in 13 days. I know it's having a rough time catching up with me.

Say Babe, I would appreciate any kind of food, cookies, Kool-Aid. You know the presweetened type. Even though we are a supply outfit, we have limited supplies. I miss a hell of a lot more than cookies but that's about all I can receive in a box.

There's a big full moon out tonight. I don't want you to worry but I'm at the airfield now. It's no biggy. We have been spending most of our time building our bunkers and filling a lot of sandbags. That's one thing in our favor we have lots of sand. I've been out here for a week and have a week to go then two weeks off. That moon up there sure is pretty tonight.

I remember the first time I saw you. Remember? I was home from college for Christmas and me and some of my buddies from high school went to the Rendezvous Ballroom in Balboa. I remember that Jan and Dean was playing. I saw you standing with a group of girls. And it was kind of weird. It was like I was in a 3-D movie. You stood out from everything. You had on that pink dress that had a poodle on it and a white cashmere sweater that stretched in all the right places. You had your long blonde hair in a ponytail. When I got the nerve to walk up to your group, I saw you glance at me but you quickly turned away. All your girl friends smiled at me but you acted like I wasn't even there. Remember what you told me? You told me that you thought I was coming to ask one of your girl friends to dance. But you were wrong. It was you. And when we kissed good night down on the beach, I swear I've never been kissed with such tenderness.

I told the guys that night that I had found the girl I was going to marry. They said "Oh, yeah. That's what you always say." I said, "No. I mean it. This is it. She is the one."

Good night, my darling. You will be in my dreams tonight.

Love, Dusty

*

It was 0700 when Kohl came riding into the FLSU compound in his jeep.

He got out and headed for the chow hall. All he had eaten for the last two weeks were C-rations, so he was looking forward to the K-rations. For breakfast he had scrambled eggs. They were made from powdered eggs and powdered milk. He had toast from a can that had the consistency of pound cake. The grape jelly he tried to spread on it rolled like purple ball bearings. He drank warm milk made from powdered milk and water laced with Halazone tablets, a lot like drinking swimming pool water with chalk in it. It was hot and better than C-rations but not much. Pete came in and slid in next to Kohl.

"Jesus. You stink," said Pete with his nose wrinkled. He moved over.

"Fuck you. You'd stink too if you spent two weeks where I've been. Fuckin' ass hole," replied Kohl.

"We didn't have the luxury of showers out there."

"Colonel wants to see you. Told me to tell you as soon as you got in."

"Pretend you never saw me. I'm fuckin' beat, man. I'm goin' to shower and catch some needed sleep."

Pete shrugged and said, "I'm leavin' for the pier anyway. See ya later."

Kohl finished breakfast and walked the half-mile to the showers. He was so sleepy his eyes hurt. He had been looking forward to sleep since about 0300. That's when it's the hardest. Every body function starts shutting down. It was difficult to rest, let alone sleep on airport security. At night he and Sergeant Ford split the eight-hour watch. But the four-hour rest was constantly interrupted by gunfire, artillery fire, illumination flares, and frantic calls on the field phones from frightened young Marines. At daybreak they had to work on their bunkers. Then when they had time to get some sleep the noise was deafening. With the short runway the A-4D's used Jayto bottles necessary for the speed that they needed for lift off. Then there was the heat, flies and sand.

Even with the roar of the two diesel generators next to his tent, Kohl fell into a dreamless black tomb.

Kohl felt something touch his shoulder. Lying on the ground in a half-finished bunker for two weeks changed the way Kohl slept. He might sleep but his sense of hearing and feelings were still acute. When Kohl felt something on his shoulder he immediately responded in a manner to protect his safety. Reaction was quick. Reflexes responding in an instant. He didn't see but he felt his left fist connect with something hard. It was Blaylock's head.

Kohl bounded to his feet. With his heart racing, he saw Blaylock sitting on the dirt floor of the tent. "What the heck did you do that for, Blaylock?" said Kohl angrily.

"What are you yellin' at me about? I'm the one who got hit. What did you do that for?" whined Blaylock.

Kohl was still shaking and apologetically said, "Sorry Blaylock. I'm a little jumpy. What were you doing anyway?"

"The Colonel wants to see you and I'm getting sick and tired of this bull shit. Every time I inform you that the Colonel wants to see you, I either get a ration of shit or you physically assault me."

"Gee, Blaylock, maybe I'm trying to tell you something, like maybe now is not a good time."

"The message that I get is, there's never a good time."

"Okay. Okay. What does the Pillsbury Dough Boy want now?"

Blaylock took the derogatory comment as a personal affront. "I don't know. I'm not like you. I do my job without playing ninety-one questions." Blaylock stomped out of the tent.

Kohl slowly got dressed and made his way to the Colonel's tent, walked in and greeted the Colonel, "Morning, Colonel."

"Good morning, Lieutenant Kohl. I wanted to see you the first thing when you got back. Didn't Lieutenant Peterson tell you?"

"No, Sir. I saw him leave just as I came in, Sir."

"I've been waiting two weeks for you. We've got a lot of work to do. I want you to make sure the compound is secured and provide the necessary safety for our troops in case of an attack by the VC."

"What is it you have in mind, Sir."

"Come on. I'll show you."

The Colonel indicated to Kohl where he wanted a trench dug in the middle of the rows of tents at both the officer's and enlisted quarters. Plus he wanted anti-aircraft guns placed on both ends of the compound.

"Anti-aircraft guns?" asked Kohl.

"Yes."

"The VC don't have any planes."

"They don't but the North Vietnamese do, so do the Chinese and the Russians."

"They're not in the war, Sir."

"But they could be. We have to be prepared."

"Those old guns won't bring down a MIG."

"What is it with you? Can't I ever tell you what to do without you arguing with me? Why don't you just do what I tell you? ... Huh? ... Why?"

"Sorry, Sir. I'm just tired."

"I also want you to set up a night time perimeter security system, with LP's and OP's, plus post sentries on the road. We can never be too careful. Better safe than sorry."

"That's true, Colonel. I'll get right on it, Sir."

"Don't forget about the meeting tonight."

"Do I have to be there?"

"There you go again, asking questions. Yes, you have to be there," answered the annoyed Colonel.

41 Meetings

At 1900 hours the officers filed singly into the Colonel's office. There wasn't the usual banter. Most nodded or said a restrained greeting.

Captain McKillip was fifteen minutes into his report when he said, "Sir, the water point coordinates are 530084, 517043 and 553055."

"The last coordinate ... 553055, where was that?" asked the Colonel.

"That would be 1/9 Artillery, Sir."

"They got water?"

"Yes, Sir."

"Then why, may I ask, did I get a call from Major Latham that as of 1600 this afternoon, they had not received water?"

The Captain was at a loss for words. He looked at Lieutenant Mays for assistance.

"I sent the truck, Captain," said Mays without waiting for Captain McKillip to ask.

"Well, it's apparent that the truck didn't arrive and I want to know why," said the Colonel as he glared at Mays.

"I'll have an answer for you in five minutes," said Mays as he got up and jogged out the tent heading for the communications center.

"I need to know those things before the meeting not during or after, Captain."

"Aye, Aye, Sir."

"Captain Hawes," the Colonel said.

Captain Charles Hawes looked up from his notebook. He was the CMT-33

CO (Engineering). He had the bulldozers, earth moving equipment and road graders. He himself was big. The small field chair looked as though it was going to buckle from the 250 pound bulk. Thick black eyebrows ran helter-skelter along a prominent ridge above his dark eyes.

"Yes, Sir," he said in a voice that was used to being heard above the rumble of a tractor.

"I have a report from Regimental S-2, Captain, that your men have been shooting at the Vietnamese villagers down by the dump. And that three have been killed. Is that true?"

"No, Sir. That's not true. My men have been shooting but only above their heads to scare them off. They won't move and there's a chance that the Cats will run over them, Sir," explained Haws.

"Then how do you explain the three indigenous personnel that were shot three days ago?" continued the Colonel.

"Colonel, I heard that those people were found in the village, Sir. Who knows how they got shot? They could be VC for all we know."

"Can't you keep them out of the dump without shooting them?"

"Sir, I told you we didn't shoot anybody."

"I don't want your men shooting any more villagers. Okay?"

"But, Sir..."

"What did I say, Captain?"

"They're thick as fleas down there. Some of them are going to get killed. Women and children, Sir," Captain Hawes persisted.

"No more shooting. Got that?" yelled the Colonel.

"Yes, Sir."

"Captain McKillip?"

"Sir?"

The field phone rang and the Colonel talked to Major Defleffs who had been patched through from Danang. The call took over forty-five minutes. Kohl doodled in his notebook and squirmed in his chair to get comfortable. He dozed off briefly, falling from his chair, landing in a heap on the floor. The Colonel didn't notice as Kohl sheepishly and cautiously returned to his chair. There were a few muffled snickers.

"Okay. Where was I? Oh yeah. Captain McKillip, you will need to make arrangements to get aviation gas delivered from bulk fuel by Thursday. Got that."

"Yes, Sir.

"Bye the way McKillip, I got a call from Regimental S-4 this afternoon. He said the last shipment of fuel was bad. Know anything about that?"

"No, Sir. Bad in what way?"

"Water," the Colonel said, then waited for a response from Captain McKillip. When none came he asked, "What ship, goddam it? What ship?" The swear word took the officers by surprise.

The Captain leafed hurriedly through his notes.

"Well? You don't seem to be very well organized, Captain."

"Sir, it's here. I'll ..." and the Captain's search became more frantic.

"You're wastin' my time and everybody else's. Find it and let Mar-Div know. Now," and the Colonel looked around to see who his next victim was going to be. His eyes set upon Lieutenant Kohl, who figured if he didn't look up he wouldn't be called. Just like he did in school. Then the Colonel asked, "What happened to Lieutenant Mays? Longest danged five minutes I've ever seen. Oh, yeah. Lieutenant Kohl?"

"Ye..."Then the field phone rang. Saved by the bell.

"Colonel Knoach. Yeah. Got that. Yeah. Uh, huh. Sure. When's he going to be here? Yeah. Dang. That doesn't give us much time." And the Colonel continued talking. It was almost 2300 when the Colonel covered the mouth piece, turned to his officers and motioned with his hand that they could leave, that is except for Captain McKillip and Lieutenant Blaylock.

Once out of the Colonel's office, they all walked silently to their tents.

Kohl broke the silence by asking, "Wonder why the Colonel asked McKillip to stay?"

"Who gives a rat's ass," snarled the usually easy-going Pete. "I am beat. I've got to be at the pier in less than three hours."

*

Kohl spent the next day organizing the Unit's security as per the Colonel's instructions. He was having trouble finding the manpower to man the posts. The officers and NCO's were complaining bitterly about the lack of manpower. By 1900 hours a disgruntled group of officers were sitting in front of the Colonel.

"By the way, Lieutenant Mays?" asked the Colonel who was perched upon his office chair like a king on a throne.

"Yes, Sir."

"What happened to the trucks that were supposed to show up at the ammo dump yesterday? You left here last night and said you'd be back in five minutes. That was over 24 hours ago. I was trying to get a hold of you all day. Why wasn't I informed? Care to elaborate?"

"The trucks were diverted and sent to the pier, Sir."

"By who's authority?"

"Lieutenant Shaw, Sir."

"He's gone."

"He must have done that before he left, Sir."

"How come I wasn't informed?"

"About him leaving?"

"No, for cripes sake. I know he's gone. I want to know why you didn't tell me."" Sir, by the time I found out what happened last night, Sir, the trucks were already there and everything had been taken care of."

"You were to notify me."

"I told Blaylock."

"You did not, Mays."

"Why you little..."

"Hold it right there, Lieutenant Mays," the Colonel warned.

"Lieutenant Kohl?" The field phone rang again. "Oh, that darn phone. Colonel Knoach. Yeah. Okay. It'll be tomorrow sometime..." And the conversation continued for over thirty minutes. Kohl was timing the length of the calls now. They had placed bets to see how many minutes he would be on the phone tonight. Blaylock didn't want to play.

He finally returned the phone to its cradle and asked Kohl, "How are you coming on the FLSU security?"

"I've got the outpost set up, Sir. And field phones out to each position."

"What about the anti-aircraft guns?" asked the Colonel, followed by somebody's chuckle. The Colonel's head swiveled to the sound to find its source. When his searching eyes failed to find the culprit, he returned his gaze to Kohl. "I haven't seen any trenches being dug."

"No, Sir. Not yet."

"We could get hit with a motor attack at any time, Lieutenant and because of you a loss of life could result."

Captain McKillip jumped to Kohl's rescue and answered, "Sir, we have a shortage of personnel, Sir. We keep pulling them off their duties for airport security and various other work parties, Sir. We aren't getting our jobs done, Sir."

The Colonel's face turned red when he answered, "You stay out of it Captain. I gave an order, Lieutenant. You carry it out. I don't care how it's done. I want it done. Not the next day or next week. Got that?"

"Yes, Sir," answered Kohl.

"We've got to get some lightning rods, Lieutenant Hockett."

"Oh. Yes, Sir. Lightning Rods. Right away, Sir. Lightning Rods. Right." Kohl could see the little squirrel running the wheel in Hockett's head.

"Excuse me, Sir. I know this may sound stupid, Sir, but am I supposed to have lightning rods?"

"No. I want you to get me some."

"How many, Sir?"

"I don't know ... hundred, maybe ... two hundred."

"Sir?"

The Colonel's jaw muscles worked and his face flushed. He didn't like questions. He wanted answers and results. "What?" he barked.

"Where do I get lightning rods and if I may ask, Sir, what for?"

"Mister Hockett. You and your whiny questions are beginning to annoy me. You're the Supply Officer, you find them and as to the what for? It's really none of your danged business but I'll tell you anyway. Two days ago three Marines from 1/9 where killed when lightning struck them as they sat on top of their bunker. Regimental needs lightning rods to put on the top of bunkers." Then the Colonel asked sarcastically, "Do you have any more questions?"

"No, Sir."

"Well, I guess it's getting late. That'll be all for tonight. I'm sure you've got a lot of work to do this evening. We have to get more accomplished than what we have been doing. So let's get rollin'. Good night."

*

"Let's get rollin'," Kohl said sarcastically.

As Mays, Pete, Kohl and Blaylock were walking back to their tent Mays said, "Blaylock, you fuckin' slime ball, I'm going to tear your fuckin' gizzard out."

"You didn't tell me."

"I did too, you fuckin' turd brain. Last night when I got back to the tent about oh-two-fuckin'-thirty, I went to your rack and told you. Shook you awake and told you. You fuckin' maggot fart."

"Oh, yeah."

"Oh, yeah, my ass," and Mays lunged at Blaylock. Kohl and Pete knew where the conversation was going and were prepared for the charging Mays. They caught him before he could grab Blaylock's throat, squeeze it and pop his head like a pimple. "I'm not through with you, you fuckin' brown nosed faggot."

"I'm sorry, Mays. I forgot, really." Blaylock expressed a genuine concern for his safety and future well being. He added, "I'll tell the Colonel tomorrow. Honest."

Grumbling and exhausted they fell asleep to the drone of the twin diesels.

*

The week before when Kohl was at airport security, he had an opportunity to meet a civilian construction engineer named Bill Spears from Terre Haute, Indiana. His company was hired by the Department of Navy to help build the airstrip. They were the main company that had developed the matting system that was being tested at Chu Lai. He invited Kohl to his air-conditioned trailer and over a cold beer, the first beer Kohl had had for over a month, they talked about home. Bill said he could make two years pay in six months. The thing he missed most was not being able to see his boy play high school football this fall. But he'd be home for Christmas and probably come back next February for another six months.

*

Kohl drove down to the airbase to see if he could find him and did. Bill Spears was talking with a survey crew. He waved at Kohl as he drove up. They exchanged greetings and shook hands.

"Didn't think you were due back for another two weeks," said Bill.

"I'm not. I came to ask a favor," answered Kohl.

"No you can't have my trailer." He laughed at his joke. "Ask away. I'll see what I can do."

"I'd like to borrow a backhoe for a day and an operator if you've got one to spare." asked Kohl.

Bill took his Indiana Hoosier hat off and rubbed his bald head. "When do you want it?"

"Sooner the better. I've got to dig some trenches at our compound in case of mortar attack."

"I could break one loose tomorrow."

"Great. I'll have a lowboy here first thing in the morning. I really appreciate this Bill."

"No sweat. Anything for a fellow Marine."

"No shit. You were a Marine?"

"Yep. Korea. Fifty-two."

As they sat on a sandbag bunker, he told Kohl how he had lost two toes to frostbite at Inchon.

When Kohl returned to FLSU it had turned into a hot and sticky afternoon much like the day before and probably the next day. Kohl met with Sergeant Major Jurgens.

"What's on your mind, Lieutenant?"

"I've been thinkin', Sergeant Major. Could you get me three CP tents?"

"What for?"

"Well, I was thinkin' that it's about time we set up some tents for an enlisted club, NCO and Officer's club. I know we don't have any beer for the enlisted club or soft drinks but it could be a place for them to gather and relax and play cards and listen to music. We can get the hard stuff for us. So what do you think?"

"I'll see what I can do Lieutenant. I think it's a good idea. The troops have been working 14 to 16 hour days seven days a week. They need a place to hide and wind down. We'll get some beer in here one of these days."

"I hope so. I'm a deprived man."

"I thought all you officers drank martinis," laughed the Sergeant Major.

"Oh, Sarge. You've got us mixed up with the Navy Officers. See what you can do, okay?"

"I'll do what I can, Lieutenant."

*

When Kohl returned to the tent from chow, Pete, Mays and Blaylock were setting on some flimsy folding chairs made from aluminum tubing and plastic strips. Mays picked the chairs up in the ville. They were smoking cigars.

"Where in the hell did you get cigars?" asked Kohl. Pete handed Kohl one and lit it for him. "Well, what's the deal?"

"Pete's a proud Papa," said Mays.

"No shit."

Pete said, "Got the word from COM about fifteen minutes ago. Michael James, born July 10th. He weighed in at 8 pounds 10 ounces."

"Well, no shit, Pete. Congratulations, man. That's great. Any word from Sue?"

"The Red Cross guy said that Sue and baby are doing fine. Sure wish I could've been there."

Tears were welling up in Pete's eyes. Kohl said, "It won't be long now, Pete. Less than five months to go. Be over sooner than you know."

"We need a goddamn drink," announced Mays.

"Let's go to the fly-boy club," suggested Kohl.

"Can't do that. We have a meeting in an hour," reminded Blaylock.

"Fuck! Fuck! Fuck! Fuck!" grumbled Mays.

"This calls for a celebration. We can't let a little ol' meeting deter us," said Kohl. He looked at the droning diesel generators, then smiled.

"What?" asked Blaylock.

"Quiet!" yelled Mays. "He's thinking."

"If he's thinking, it could take a while," said Pete laughing.

Kohl said almost to himself, "What would happen if we lost electricity?"

"It would be dark. That's a dumb question," said Blaylock.

Kohl continued to muse, "If it's dark, you can't see."

"I get the picture. What do you have in mind, Kohl?" asked Mays.

Kohl, Pete and Mays hurriedly collected five-gallon cans and began siphoning diesel from the generators.

"What good's that going to do?" questioned Blaylock. "They'll just see that they ran out of gas and fill them back up."

"Not as easy as it sounds, Bubble Ass," said Mays.

"Why?"

"When a diesel runs out of gas the only way you can restart it is to take off the line to the fuel pump and prime it. Takes a while. And by that time we could be long gone and partying," said Mays.

Blaylock left the tent in a huff.

*

Kohl, Mays and Pete arrived at the meeting smelling of diesel. Blaylock was sitting next to the Colonel and glared at them. The other officers trickled in and were all seated by 1900 hours.

The Colonel cleared his throat and the officers became silent. "Okay, gentlemen. Let's begin the reports. Let's start with you Lieutenant Hockett."

"Sir. I'd like to begin, if I may, Sir, by asking the Colonel a question?"

Jesus, Hockett. Where are your balls?

"Go on," said the Colonel.

"I've got a shipment of cold weather gear, Sir."

That comment brought on a few muffled chuckles.

"Like what?" asked the Colonel.

Second Lieutenant Hockett looked uneasy and continued cautiously, "Uh, we got down mummy sleeping bags, parkas, cold weather boots and soft covers with ear flaps, wool socks and Mickey Mouse boots, Sir."

Everybody was laughing now. Even the Colonel had a smile on his face, then the lights went out.

Everyone quit laughing and sat quietly. The whole camp was in complete silent black.

"Could be a VC attack," whispered the Colonel.

Kohl answered, "Yeah. We'd better hold tight, Colonel. I don't want any of my security people shooting anyone."

"Yeah. Good idea, Lieutenant. We'll just stay here awhile. Is it just us that's lost electricity, I wonder?" asked the Colonel.

"It's probably the generators," said Blaylock.

It was a good thing it was dark, because if Blaylock could have seen the look on either Kohl, Mays and Pete's face, he would have realized that he was in deep trouble.

"Go check that out, Blaylock," ordered the Colonel.

"Yes Sir." And Blaylock felt his way out of the tent, commandeered a flashlight and retrieved two men from maintenance, then disappeared.

They all sat quietly for about five minutes, when Mays said, "Well, Colonel. Looks like it's going to be awhile. Shall we call it a night?"

"Naw. Let's give it a little while longer. Blaylock will be back if he can't find the trouble."

It was then that Kohl saw Blaylock walking back to the tent with the flashlight bobbing up and down as he walked. "All taken care of, Colonel. The lights will be back on in a few minutes, Sir."

"What was the problem?" asked the Colonel.

"The generators ran out of gas."

"Both of them?"

"Yes, Sir."

"That's funny," the Colonel said. Then the lights came back on. "Well, let's get back to work. Where were we?"

The three lieutenants glared at Blaylock and he quickly lowered his gaze to the floor.

"Hockett's got cold weather gear in South Vietnam and it's 100 degrees out, now that's out-fucking-standing," said Captain Shaffer.

"I told you men before that there will be no swearing in this tent. Got that Mr. Shaffer?" said the Colonel sternly.

"Yes, Sir," said Shaffer.

Then the Colonel returned his attention to Hockett, "Send it back, Hockett. It's for dang sure we don't need it here."

"Aye, aye, Sir."

"Sir?"

"Yes, Captain McKillip."

"Sir, I had Lieutenant Mays send down his trucks to off-load the ammo from the LST this morning at 0345. I asked for five trucks and I only got three."

Mays said, "Captain, I only had three. All the others are broke down or out."

"Well, anyway. I want to know why the ammo went to the ammo dump, Mays, instead of going to 1/9 howitzer?"

Mays responded, "Because the Colonel told me to, Captain."

"Colonel, 1/9 is conducting a sweep at dawn. The Howitzer Company's conducting fire support and they do not have enough artillery shells. I had it all worked out with Major Riddle, Colonel, to take the shipment directly over to artillery," asked McKillip.

"That's not the way it's supposed to be done, Captain."

"I know, Sir. But I had it all worked out. Both the major and I thought it would be a critical waste of time. Excuse me, Sir, but I can't have you circumventing my authority."

Kohl said nonchalantly, "Pete's wife had a baby."

"What?" asked the Colonel.

"Pete's wife had a baby, Sir," Kohl repeated.

The Colonel looked confused. "Baby?"

"Yes, Colonel a baby. Michael James Peterson."

"Well that's nice but what does that have to do with anything?"

"Well, nothing really, Sir. I just thought you'd like to know. That's all."

The Colonel still had a puzzled look on his face as he continued to look at Kohl's smiling face. He returned his gaze to Captain McKillip and tried to retrieve his thoughts. He continued, "In regard to me circumventing you, Captain, I will, if you're not doing the job you're supposed to do."

"I'm in charge of logistics, Colonel. I can't have you second guessing me at every turn, Sir."

"That's enough, Captain. You have it all wrong. I'm in charge of everything. You're on the verge of being out of line."

"How can I work under these kind of conditions, Colonel? It appears to me..."

Then the colonel cut McKillip off, "That's enough, Captain. It appears to me, that if you can't work under these conditions then maybe I should send you some place where you feel more comfortable. Lieutenant Hockett?"

"Yes, Sir."

"As of now you are my new S-4."

That comment was followed by the group of officers mumbling nervously.

McKillip said, "You can't do that."

Hockett said, "I'm only a Second Lieutenant, Sir."

Kohl said, "Gung ho."

"What was that, Lieutenant?" asked the Colonel.

"I'm only a Second Lieutenant," whined Hockett.

"No. Not you. What did you say, Lieutenant Kohl?"

"I said, 'Gung ho, Sir. You know. Everyone pulling together. All for one and one for all."

"Are you patronizing me, Lieutenant?"

"No, Sir. I'm just making a point."

"The point is, Lieutenant, that things will be done my way, the right way. Well, I've had about all the insubordination I can handle for one evening. Captain McKillip? You'll report to the 1/9 Regimental CO tomorrow morning. I want you out of here by 0800. You are hereby relieved of your duties.

"With pleasure," said the angry McKillip as he threw his notebook on the ground and stomped out. He was followed by the rest of the officers all in amazement at what just transpired. The men were mumbling and grumbling. They were gathering around Captain McKillip.

"What are you going to do, John?" asked Shaffer.

"Get the fuck outa here," said McKillip angrily.

"Is this going to mess you up career wise?" asked Charley Hawes.

"Well, let me put it to you this way. It isn't going to do me any good."

"I'm sorry, Captain," said Hockett self-consciously.

"Ahh, it ain't your fault. I saw this comin'," said McKillip with a sigh. "And by the way, Kohl, thanks for trying to derail the situation."

Kohl said, "If everyone around here wasn't such a candy ass..."

"Now just hold on a goddamn minute here, Lieutenant," said Major Ponds angrily. "I don't have to put up with any of your shit or anybody else's. You leave me the fuck alone and I'll leave you alone. Got that?"

Mays walked up to the Major with a sneer on his face and wild eyes and he said, "Major, you're not seeing the big picture." Mays grin was held in a tight line. "Kohl was right in what he said in there. We have to work together, cooperate with one another. You can sit down there with your Cape Cod bungalow if you want, Major, but you will need us as much as we need you. Are you reading me, Major?"

Everyone was looking at the Major. There was electricity in May's voice.

Major Ponds said, "Are you threatening me?" but his voice was without strength.

Mays said, "I don't threaten, Major."

Pete said, "Come on guys. We can work this out. Let's call it a night. Sorry to see you go Captain. I'll talk to you before you leave in the morning. Good night everyone."

42 A Blanket Party for Blaylock.

That night as Blaylock lay sleeping, his breath deep and steady, Mays, Kohl and Pete stood over him. Pete held one end of the blanket while Kohl held the other. Then they threw the blanket over Blaylock. Pete held the blanket over his face, to muffle the sounds while Kohl held the blanket around his feet. Blaylock jerked awake and struggled against the strong grips of Pete and Kohl. Then May's smashing right fist sunk into the soft belly of Blaylock. Other blows immediately followed, pummeling Blaylock's wreathing body in massive sledgehammer like blows. Mays sought the soft parts of Blaylock's stomach and ribs with his hard fists. Grunts, groans and muffled whimpers disappeared into the blanket. Mays was breathing hard as he repeatedly pounded the now unresponding body. Pete reached over and held back another powerful fist that Mays was to deliver into Blaylock's motionless body.

"That's enough," Pete said softly.

Pete and Kohl released their grip.

Mays said, "That ought to teach that brown nosed mutha-fucker."

And they climbed into their racks. Kohl heard Blaylock whimper, groan, and cry softly during the night.

*

The next morning they watched Blaylock try to get out of bed. His eyes were downcast. He tried to sit up but couldn't. Instead he rolled over, pulled his feet off the cot and placed them on the floor, then used his arms to push his body into an upright sitting position. Tears ran down his cheeks from the pain. He tried to reach for his pants and groaned. Kohl walked over picked up his pants and handed them to him. Blaylock mumbled a thank you. In turn each of them silently helped him get dressed. Mays tied his boots. Nobody said a word.

*

The roar of the backhoe brought the Colonel out of his tent to see what was going on. Kohl had left a lime mark in the sand where the operator was to dig the trench. Kohl was standing to the side when the Colonel walked briskly up behind him.

He yelled, "What the heck's going on?"

"I'm digging the trench you wanted," Kohl said nonchalantly.

"You're not supposed to dig trenches like that," he yelled to be heard above the roar of the backhoe.

Kohl gave the Colonel a quizzical look and asked, "How are you supposed to dig a trench?"

"With men, not machines."

"I tried, Colonel. We don't have any men to spare. So I got this. Pretty cool, huh?"

The Colonel let out a humph sound and said, "I want you to shut this thing down and get men out here to dig the trenches, the way it's supposed to be."

"Colonel, if I may, Sir, and with all due respect, Sir, may I ask, why?" *Hello, Kohl. Seems we've been through this before. It's not for you to ask, why, but to do or die. Does that ring a bell?*

"You are arguing with me again, Lieutenant Kohl."

"I know, Sir and I mean no disrespect but the backhoe and operator are here. I can do all this in just a matter of hours. If I used men, Sir, that is if I could get them, it would take days, Sir."

The Colonel walked in tight circles with his hands behind his back and finally said, "Okay. But next time you let me know what you're doing. You just can't go off and do your own thing, which by the way seems to be a problem you have. From now on you clear it with me. Is that clear, Lieutenant?"

"Yes, Sir." *Dejavu. I've heard that before.*

I know. I know. But finally reason prevails.

*

That night in the meeting, Blaylock began to respond to a comment another officer had made. He stopped himself and looked at Mays, Kohl and Pete.

The Colonel looked at Blaylock and asked, "You were saying, Blaylock?"

Blaylock shook his head negatively, and said quietly, "Never mind, Sir. It wasn't important."

*

Kohl knew from his first encounter with Colonel Knoach in his BOQ room in Okinawa that he was going to be difficult to get along with. Now the Colonel was playing one officer against the other, keeping them separate so he had control and became the stronger one. Officers, trying to protect themselves, would sacrifice anybody in order to deflect the blame. They would fight and argue among themselves. At the meetings it was a poor display of cooperation and coordination of efforts. The Colonel seemed to like it that way. He seemed to encourage the behavior and relish in its turmoil. Kohl imagined him grinning as he surveyed the men hanging, squirming, twisting and turning from the ropes they clung to. When the officers' feuded among themselves, he was their savior because he would know what to do. He had all the answers. He was the stabilizing force. The pillar of strength. And for a Colonel who was barely five foot eight and one hundred and forty pounds and talked as though he was a castrated choirboy, it was a stretch.

Kohl, Pete and Mays talked about the situation. They knew something had to be done. The other officers were good men. But the senior officers were career officers; they had to get along with the Colonel. And the younger second lieutenants, according to Kohl, didn't know any better. It was important they receive good fitness reports in order to be promoted. However the senior first lieutenant's were getting out in less than six months. To them the reprisals were insignificant. Captain McKillip was the logical choice to be called upon to organize the officers but he had just been relieved of duty

They needed a coordinator that had nothing to loose, someone who had the knowledge and respect of his fellow officers and the NCO's. Kohl knew Pete was the man for the job. Pete, as S-3, was good at his job. He got along well with everybody; the Colonel even liked him. Even the DI's at Basic School couldn't get mad at him. It was up to Pete to get things organized.

It was just a matter of convincing Pete.

Kohl, Mays, and Pete were sitting outside the tent drinking cognac out of tin cups. They had just finished evening chow of sauerkraut and wieners and were relaxing before the next marathon meeting. Pete and Mays were both exhausted. For over the last couple of weeks both of them hadn't averaged more than four hours sleep a night. Both Mays and Pete could have and would have relied on their NCO's for more assistance but the Colonel would have none of that. He wanted his officers to carry the complete burden.

Kohl said, "This is bullshit. We're going to miss the fuckin' movie, man."

"We never get to see the movies," moaned Mays.

"Do you know what they have playin' tonight? Elvis, in 'Blue Hawaii'," complained Kohl.

"No, shit. Man I love Elvis. And those chicks in the movies ... Hawaii, fuckin'-A-man," continued Mays.

"All that round-eyed pussy in skin-tight bikinis, tits a floppin', Man, shit, fuck," said Kohl.

"Sun, sand, blue water ... "

"Sounds like this place," said Pete laughing.

"Oh, yeah. Except for one small detail. No fuckin' broads," answered Mays.

"No movies for us. Fuckin' Colonel," complained Kohl. "I mean, we could have a meeting and cover everything in twenty fuckin' minutes; but not Pillsbury Dough Boy. No. He has to quiz us on every goddamn detail that he knows the answer to. And then talk on the phone line for another fuckin' goddamn hour, shit. I'm not shittin' ya. We could start at 1930 and be outa there by 2100 easy. Each of us gives our reports, the Colonel could ask his stupid fuckin' questions, and we could be outa there. But does that happen? No. He's talkin' on the fuckin' phone or waitin' for someone to talk to him. We're sittin' there with our thumb up our ass. He's got us all fighting, bitchin' and complaining to each other. That's bullshit, man. We've got to do something about it."

Kohl looked at Pete.

Mays said, "Yeah." And he looked at Pete.

"What?" asked Pete.

"It's you, Pete. It's you. You're our fuckin' savior, man," said Kohl as enthusiastically as he could.

"What are you talkin' bout. You're crazy."

"Kohl's right, Pete. You're the man. You're what the Marine Corps stands for. All for one and one for all. Gung Ho, mutha fucker."

"You're crazy."

"Think about it, Pete," persuaded Kohl, "You have the ability to organize. You have the confidence of the NCO's."

"I do?"

"Yeah, ya do. You can do it," encouraged Kohl.

"Why not you or Mays?"

"I'm at the airport two weeks at a time and plus the Colonel hates my fuckin guts and Mays here, is a fuckin' asshole," said Kohl.

"I'm not an asshole," Mays said, but the retort was without enthusiasm.

They finally convinced Pete. Then they began planning their strategy.

*

Second Lieutenant Hockett, feeling very important about his new job as S-4, started to cause some problems at the meetings, but after Kohl put sugar in his rack for two nights straight, those little red ants began to bring Hockett around to Kohl's way of thinking. Pete would come to the meetings prepared with notes and information. The well-oiled machine the Colonel had always talked about and wanted was working, but not the way he had envisioned it. The phone magically stopped ringing during the meetings. The Com Chief stopped transferring the calls and began taking messages. And much to the delight of the Chief he saw a fifth of Southern Comfort on his rack every Friday night. As each meeting progressed the Colonel saw his power eroding and Pete began gaining more and more control. Pete knew the information and more of the officers began seeing the advantages of cooperating. He was the coordinator. He was good. He was smooth. And the Colonel yelled and threatened to no avail.

*

July 25th, 1965

Hi Sweetie,

Be damned if it ain't your lover-boy.

I got three letters from you yesterday. Plus I got one from the folks and believe it or not I got one from my cousin Lenard.

It's raining today.

Something's wrong with me. When I go to bed after about two or three hours I get sick at my stomach. This has happened for the last week and I have had a bad headache too. The Doc doesn't know

what's wrong either.
I figured out the other day how much I get a month. My base pay is $461.00, separation pay is $30.00, and $120.00 living expenses that goes to you and $55.00 combat pay.

Sorry. I got called to the Colonel's office late last night for a meeting. He wanted me to check up on where BA279 Batteries were. So I had to go find them. Then by the time I got back I had to write a Logistical Status report for Pete. By the time my day is done it's about 10 or so at night. So I didn't finish the letter.
It's almost August. I have about 92 days left in Vietnam. Three months. I'm into the home stretch. Won't be long and I'll be in my babies arms. What a wonderful day that will be. I don't think the Marine Corps will extend me but there has been talk. I'll be home for Christmas.
I know you have been scared to death but to tell you the truth, it's no big deal where I'm at. I hate being over here. This is not my idea of fun. I just want to get home to you and out of this place.
I want to offer you an explanation. I got five letters today and I'll give you the dates. Then maybe you'll see how fouled up the mail is. The post marks on those five letters were July 18th, 20th, 20th, 22nd, and 23rd. The three letters I got the day before were postmarked July 17th, 19th, 21st. So you see honey, a lot of times when you refer to something in one letter I might not have seen it yet.
We have been having beautiful sunrises and sunsets lately. And it's been raining almost every afternoon. It kinda cools things off a bit and settles the dust.
There's no place to call from over here.

Got interrupted again.
Well, I'm not the only one that gets balled out for not writing. A lot of the men here are getting similar complaints from their wives and girl friends. You'll have to try and understand that the situation here is not conducive to writing, nor do we have a lot of time to write, plus the mail service is not the best in the world. There was a period of time that I didn't get anything for three weeks.
Well I think that's about covers everything for now. I'd better get this in the mail. It's 8:30 in the morning and it's already hot. It's

Friday, only three more working days till Monday. Every day is the same. Thank God for your letters.
Sure do miss you. The days are slowly passing bye.

Love ya loads,
Dusty

43 Watts Riot

It was Saturday August the 14th. Kohl was sitting at the Marine Air Officer's club tent on the beach drinking a beer and listening to the radio playing music from Radio Hanoi. They could listen instead to the Armed Forces Radio out of Saigon but he and the others at the bar liked Radio Hanoi because it had better and more up to date music. The girl they called Hanoi Hanna was talking about the courageous Negro people who were rising in revolution against the oppression of the fascist United States. The radio program was peppered with propaganda messages but for the most part the Marines laughed at its absurdity.

"... The white suppression of the Negroes is taking its toll and the burdened Negroes have retaliated in open rebellion in the streets of Watts. Watts is a segregated ghetto near Los Angeles, California. Millions of Negroes are raging through the streets burning white establishments, killing the white suppressors. The United States government has sent in troops and tanks to smash the rebellion but all is in vain as the people of all color gather in strength. Negroes from cities all over the United States are uprising. Soon the United States will be in chaos from the Negroes who embrace the communistic views. In our country we are all free and do not discriminate of those of another color. We are all-equal and love one another as comrades.

"How can the American capitalists talk of freedom when they discriminate against people of color? They try to dictate to us, the Peoples Republic of Vietnam, on how we should rule our country when we know what we want. They continue to bring more soldiers to kill our women and children, destroy our fields of rice, rape our women all in the name of freedom. But it's only for their own selfish reasons, to line the pockets of the industrialist.

"So, join us Negro soldiers. Throw down your weapons and come to us where you will be treated with respect and dignity. Join your comrades back home in the revolution against the white imperialists. You are fighting a war you can't win here. You are losing more men every day. For what? What have we done to you? Nothing. If we came to your land, wouldn't you fight for what you believed in? That's what we, the people of Vietnam, are doing. You have been sent here to make war because the American imperialists need war. You are killing innocent women and children in order to make Wall Street capitalists more money.

"Now, let's listen to Julie London sing "Cry Me A River." And while she sings think of your loved ones back home.

Kohl listened to the whispery, velvet voice of Julie London.

Now you say you're sorry
You cry the whole night through.
Well, you can cry me a river, cry me a river
I'll cry a river over you,

Kohl finished his beer and walked out the side of the tent into the early evening dusk toward his bunker in the sand. The song followed him out and played in his mind as he hummed the tune.

Now you say you're sorry
For being...

The A-4D that came screaming down the short runway erased Julie London from his soothed brain. About 200 yards before the end of the runway, the pilot kicked in the Jato bottles. The added blast of rocket fuel shot the small bomber into the red sky.

"Halt! Who goes there?"

Kohl was surprised by the challenge. But he stopped. It was still light enough to see. However, he could understand the caution. He replied, "Lieutenant Kohl."

"Advance to be recognized, Sir."

The sir comment brought a smile to Kohl's lips as he advanced.

"Halt! ... Recognized."

"Hello, Corporal. How goes it?"

"Good, as can be expected, Sir."

Kohl stood by the foxhole and looked off toward the mountains in the west. It always seemed strange to him to see mountains in the west. In California, the San Bernadino mountains and Sierras were to the east and watching the sunset in the Vietnam mountains opened a window unfamiliar to him. He was in a place he did not know.

"What's your name, Corporal?"

"Jones, Sir. Jimmy Jones."

"Where're you from, Jones?"

"Compton, Sir."

"When I was in high school, we used to go up there for the Compton Relays."

"I ran track, Sir. Did you, too?"

Kohl looked at the tall lanky black man and could see him as a runner. "Yes. I ran the quarter. Wasn't very good, though. I got creamed. What did you run?"

"I ran the hurdles. I wasn't very good either. If I'd been better, I'd be in college now instead of here. Know what I mean, Sir?"

"Know what you mean. When did you go to school there?"

"Uh. ' 61 to '63. Dropped out my senior year and joined the Corps."

"Did you know Charlie Dumas?"

"No, Sir. I know of him. He went to Centennial not Compton, didn't he Sir?"

"Oh. That's right. He was a hell of a high jumper, wasn't he?"

Kohl had seen the two sleeping figures in the sand and asked, "Who are they?"

That's Sergeant Heller, there," he said pointing. "And that's Sergeant Powers."

"Two sergeants and a corporal in one hole. How come?"

"Just the way it worked out, Sir."

"I just heard about the trouble in Watts on Hanoi Radio. Have you heard any thing about what's happening?"

"Yes, Sir. I heard."

Kohl waited for him to finish or add to his comment but he didn't. He asked again, "What happened?"

"Well, Sir. I don't know. Just what some of my friends have told me."

"What did they say?"

"Happened a couple of days ago. Could have been a week for all we know, Sir. The cops stopped some black dude and it got out of hand, I guess. Don't know much, Sir."

"That's hard to believe that something like that would happen in California. Maybe Alabama or Mississippi but not California. I've never seen any prejudice in California."

"Really? Where you from, Lieutenant?"

"Huntington Beach."

"How many blacks you got in Huntington Beach, Sir."

"We didn't have any that I know of but we had some Mexicans and some Japanese. We didn't have any problems."

"You ever been to Watts, Sir?"

"Yes."

"Drove through it on Imperial, Sir?"

"Yes."

"Probably fast, with your doors locked and the windows rolled up. Is that right, Sir?"

Kohl suddenly felt guilty and ashamed because that was exactly what he did.

"Sir? I felt the same way when I would drive in downtown Tarzana."

"Really?"

"Really."

"Sorry."

"Not your fault, Lieutenant. There are problems ... even in the Marine Corps."

That comment didn't surprise Kohl because he knew it was true. "I think it's getting better. It's not like it used to be. Well, listen. It's getting dark. I'd better get going. I don't want to get my ass shot. See ya, Corporal Jones. Keep a clear eye."

"Aye, Aye, Sir."

*

Kohl had just got his breakfast from the chow truck and had settled on a bank of sandbags near his bunker and started to eat his breakfast before it got cold. The early morning brought a chill off the ocean. He found it hard to believe that he could be concerned about his breakfast getting cold when in a matter of a few hours he would be sweating and looking for shade. He relished the warm breakfast because the air port security only got warm meals two days a week and since this was Sunday, it was one of the days.

Sergeant Ford walked up and said in a reluctant tone,"Lieutenant? I think we have a little problem."

He looked at Ford and said,"Well?"

Ford nervously looked around. He gently tugged at Kohl's arm and said, "Let's go over there."

"Damn it, Ford. Can't you see I'm eating?" Right after he said it, he regretted it. *You sound like a dog growling and hovering over your food bowl. The Sergeant probably hasn't even eaten yet.*

Kohl sat his plate down and followed Ford toward the strip where he stopped on the backside of an eight-foot high mound of sand. Sitting on the other side was a black Marine with his head resting on the top of his arms that were crossed over his knees. When the man heard Ford and Kohl, he looked up.

"What the fuck?" muttered Kohl. The upturned face was swollen and bruised. His left upper lip was swollen and split, his right eyes was closed shut and his cheek under it was discolored. Then he recognized the tall thin man. It was Corporal Jimmy Jones.

"It was my idea, Sir," said Ford. "I noticed Corporal Jones in the chow line. He didn't want to bring it to your attention, Sir. But I convinced him to tell you what happened."

Kohl continued to stare at the swollen face of Jones in disbelief. After about ten seconds, Kohl asked, "Well, what the hell happened? I can't believe this shit."

Corporal Jones wiped some spittle mixed with blood from the corner of his mouth. He tilted his head to one side so he could see the Lieutenant with his good eye. He licked his lips and had trouble forming his words because of their swollen condition. He said,"It's nothin', Sir. Forget it."

"Forget it, hell."

"You don't understand, Sir. If I talk to you, it'll only get worse. I could be in trouble already."

Ford said in a reassuring tone,"The Lieutenant's okay, Jones. Tell him what happened."

Jones looked suspiciously at Kohl and said,"Lieutenant, there's nothin' you can do. I have to return to my unit tomorrow and one of the Sergeants that did this to me is my unit chief. It could only get worse, Lieutenant."

"So, it was the Sergeants in your hole that did this?" asked Kohl angrily.

Jones didn't answer and lowered his head back on his arms.

Kohl turned to Ford and asked,"What do you know about it, Ford?"

Ford looked at Jones. Jones didn't look up. Then Ford said,"If he won't tell you, then I guess I will." Ford paused before continuing, trying to formulate his thoughts. "It appears that Jones, here, had watch last night from 2000 to 0200 and Sergeant Heller and Sergeant Powers split the watch between 0200 and 0600. Jones complained about it and they did this to him."

Kohl knew Corporal Jones was right. After tonight's watch they would all be going back to their units. He didn't have any authority over the two Sergeants. If he made a report and had Jones bring charges no telling how long it would take. And considering how shorthanded they were, he doubted that transfers or disciplinary action would be made. Kohl asked Ford, "What units are the Sergeants in?"

"Heller is in maintenance, Sir. What's Sergeant Powers' unit, Jones?"

"Transportation."

Bingo. Sergeant Powers' ass is grass. Kohl knew he could count on Mays to make things very difficult for Mr. Powers. As far as Heller was concerned, he could inform Captain Shaffer of what happened but he couldn't guarantee that any action would be taken.

"Jones?" said Kohl. "If any reprisals are made against you for talking to us about this, I want you to inform Sergeant Ford, here. He in turn will let me know. Unfortunately I cannot guarantee your safety back in camp but I can here. Ford?"

"Yes, Sir."

"I want you to split up Heller and Powers. Don't tell them why. And move Jones to southeast perimeter."

"Aye, aye, Sir."

With that, Kohl returned to his cold breakfast and found that the ants were in the process of carrying off what was left of his unfinished scrambled eggs, sausage links and toast. He buried the food and the ants under the sand. He tried to do it fast before the ants realized what they were in for. But it wasn't fast enough because some pissed off ants got under his sleeves and started biting. For breakfast he heated some hot chocolate over a can of sterno.

Charlie? Admire us. We are Americans. Land of the free and home of the brave. We want you to be like us. Where all men are created equal ... but it's apparent that some men are more equal than others.

*

Kohl walked into the regimental headquarters for a meeting with Major Phillips the regimental S-2. Accompanying Kohl was Lieutenant Cobain and Sergeant Ford. Much to Kohl's suprise Lieutenant Joss was there to meet him.

"Major," said Kohl in salutation, then took Joss in his arms in a bear hug.

"Good to see you, Joss."

"Good to see you, Kohl," answered Joss.

"What are you doing down here?" asked Kohl.

"I came down here to play in the sand for a little R and R," smiled Joss, "but the Major had other ideas."

"Oh, I'm sorry," Kohl said as he realized that he hadn't introduced his men. "Major, You remember Lieutenant Cobain and Sergeant Ford?" The major nodded in the affirmative. "And men this is one of my buddies from OCS, Lieutenant Joss."

Joss said, "I remember you, Sarge, from the hill."

"That's me, Lieutenant."

"What are you doing here, Joss?" asked Kohl.

The Major cleared his throat and said, "He's my mew Assistant S-2. Now, If you don't mind. You can do your catching up later. I've asked you men here to brief you on rumors and information we have received about possible suicide missions by the VC. We have word that they will try to infiltrate and destroy planes, runways, fuel storage areas and so on."

The Major wanted to know the state of readiness of the troops and what were the preparations for enemy infiltration. He wanted Kohl and Cobain to increase the number of troops, improve fields of fire, and install more concertina wire. Now that Kohl had finnished his two-weeks of security it was Cobain's turn for his two weeks.

During the briefing it had started to drizzle. By 1700 the drizzle had turned into a steady rain.

"So much for your R and R, Joss," said Kohl as they left the regimental S-2 tent.

Cobain and Ford said their good-byes then left for the airfield.

Kohl continued, "Let's go down to the Marine Air Club."

"You have an officer's club here?" asked Joss.

"Don't get your hopes up. It nothing but a tent, ammo crates, gook aluminum chairs and booze. Beer is in short supply. They might have it and then again maybe not. And the same goes for mix for the hard stuff. Mostly we have to drink the hard stuff straight or with Halizon water."

"Quit bitchin', Kohl. I havn't had a drink since we were back in the Phillippines."

The quarter mile walk soaked them both. Like always, the rain was warm and the humidity was high. It took a long time to dry off. It seemed that Kohl's crotch, arm pits, and feet were always damp. When they arrived they saw Mays sitting in a bent aluminum chair. He had just brought truck loads of troop replacements for the next two weeks of airport security.

"Hey, Mays. Look who I brought? Your favorite sheep herder." Kohl regretted what he had said as soon as it left his lips. Heads turned. Mays smiled brightly. Joss's face got red from embarrassment. Kohl could tell that Mays was not one of Joss's favorite people. Mays teased him constantly. Mays got up and shook Joss's hand and gave him a slap on the back as they sat down.

They talked under the pounding rain on the tent. Kohl inquired about Joss's aunt and uncle in the Philippines. Joss said that they write him often and had asked about Kohl. He said he also got a letter from Wendy. This brought a note of interest to Mays' face.

"She asked about you, Kohl. Wanted to know how she could write to you."

"Got a little nukie in Manila, huh, Kohl?"

"No, I didn't, fuckhead," growled Kohl. He turned, ignoring Mays and asked, "What did you tell her?"

"I told her that you were happily married and to leave you alone."

"Yeah. That's probably best." Kohl's memory drifted back to that night when he fell asleep on the grass and woke to see her silhouetted in the light in that white cotton dress. At this moment he was so horny, just the thought of that evening gave his sweaty crotch a stirring of motion.

The water was pouring off the sides of the tent in a solid sheet. The rain pounding on the tent was so loud it was hard to carry on a conversation. The bar didn't have beer so Mays was drinking Jim Beam and water, Kohl was drinking Cuttysark, and Joss was sipping on the same Martini he had ordered when they arrived. Mays was drunk. Kohl on the other hand assured himself that he was in complete control of his senses. Joss excused himself, said good bye and walked out into the pouring rain to his quarters. Kohl was proud of Mays. They had talked all that time and Mays didn't make fun of Joss once. He must be getting soft.

Mays yelled so he could be heard above the wind and swirling rain, "Let's git the fuck outa here."

"Okay," yelled Kohl.

They both stood up for the first time that evening. Both grabbed the cable spool table for support, then lurched out of the side of the tent.

They both stood on wobbly legs sprawled for balance. Mays turned his head to the night sky of water, opened his mouth, and rubbed his face with his hands.

Kohl asked, "Where's your jeep?"

"I don't have one no more."

By the way he sounded, Kohl thought he was going to cry.

"He took it from me," Mays continued.

"Who?"

"The Colonel did. He took it from me. Now I don't have a jeep. Where'sures? Colonel take yours too?"

"No. Ford took it back to the airstrip."

"Let's go get it."

"If we do we'll get shot by security."

"Let's call," said Mays confidently.

"Who?"

"Pete. Let's call Pete."

"What time is it?' Kohl asked.

"I got a watch that glows in the dark. I do."

"What time does your fuckin' glow in the dark watch say? I'm getting wet."

"A little water never hurt no one." Mays grinned at Kohl. Water was streaming down his smashed face. "Where did you say your jeep was?"

"Ford has it."

"I'm fuckin transportation officer. I can get us a ve-hickal. Come on."

They started walking towards regimental headquarters.

"You're drunk, Mays," Kohl said it with sudden revelation.

"Am not."

"Are too. I can tell."

Mays stopped and looked back, "How?"

"I can tell by the way you walk. You walk all bent over."

"I don't either. You're full of shit. Here's a truck." Mays walked over to the driver's side of a six-bye, opened the door and climbed in.

"Keys in it," yelled Kohl.

"SSShhhh!"

"What?"

"Shut the fuck up, you moron," yelled Mays.

"Oh."

Mays found the keys in the glove box and Kohl climbed in. The truck starter shattered the night with it's grinding sound and what seemed like a long time the truck burst into pounding pistons and choking exhaust. Mays ground the gearshift into second and lurched out of the parking area on to the main road heading towards camp.

"Turn on the windshield wipers," hollered Kohl.

Mays fumbled around, drove off the road, swerved back, but found the wipers.

"That as fast as they go?"

"Yeah. Now leave me alone. I'm drivin," Mays said angrily.

"Can you see? I can't see shit. Do you have the high beams on?

"Yeah."

"Maybe you should have the low beams on. With the high beams all I can see is rain. Turn on the low beams maybe we can see the fuckin' road."

"Jesus, fuckin' Christ. You're worse than some goddamn woman. Shut the fuck up."

Kohl sat in silence for a while and then asks, "Do you know where you're going?"

"Fuck yes, I know where I'm going. Goddamn moron. Drive this road bunches."

"I don't think we're going in the right direction."

Mays whirled around in the seat, let go of the wheel, and started slapping Kohl on top of the head. Kohl pulled his arms over his head to ward off the blows. "I thought I told you to shut the fuck up."

"Jesus. You didn't have to do that. I just thought I saw us go by the turn off, was all. Looked like it," whined Kohl.

"Think so?"

"Think so. How fast are you driving? Maybe if you slowed down, we could see better."

"I'm barely goin' twenty miles an hour."

Then the truck hit a big hole or ditch. Both Mays and Kohl hit their heads on the roof. The truck rose, then the back end hit the hole. Mays stopped the truck and they both looked at each other in the dim glow of the panel lights. Their bewildered look was apparent.

"What was that?" asked Kohl.

"I don't know. Go check."

"Fuck you. You go check."

"I'm the driver."

"So? What's that got to do with anything?"

They sat without talking and looked out into the darkness and listened to the rain pound on the tin roof and the slap of the windshield wipers moving in non-syncopation.

Mays broke the silence and said, "You fuckin' dick." And climbed out into the swirling wind and rain. Kohl couldn't see him until he walked in to beams of the front lights. Mays unzipped his pants and took a leak. He stood for what seemed like a long time watching his stream. When he finally finished he turned his back to Kohl and in the beams of the truck he dropped his pants around his knees bent over and mooned Kohl.

Kohl was laughing when he rolled down the window and yelled, "What did we hit?"

Mays disappeared from the glow of the headlights as he walked to the rear of the truck. He swung the driver's side door open and climbed in and said, "We hit a ditch."

During a rain the roads turn to a red muck. Because of the sand of Chu Lai, the engineers brought in truckloads of red clay for the road base. There were no signs, guard rails, mileposts, roadside reflectors, or lights, just the red mucky clay.

"There aren't any ditches on the road back to camp."

"I know that."

"Then where are we?"

"We're not on a regular road. In fact I don't even know if we are on a road at all. How far back was that turn off?"

"About fifteen minutes. I don't know how far."

Mays ground the transmission into reverse, backed up, made a U-turn and headed back the way they had come. Kohl wiped the fog off the inside of the window so they could see but visibility was still nonexistent.

"How far back was it?" Mays asked.

"Fifteen minutes at least. I don't know how far."

"How far back was it?" Mays asked.

"I said, fifteen minutes. Jesus."

Mays continued driving slowly forward. He asked, "Has it been fifteen minutes yet?"

"Hell, I don't know. You've got the fuckin' glow-in-the-dark-watch."

"Think that's it?"

"It hasn't been fifteen minutes yet."

"I just asked you that, shit for brains. I ought to stop right the fuck here and kick your ass."

Mays brought the truck to a stop.

Oh, shit. He's going to kick my ass.

"Does that look like the turn off?" asked Mays.

"Shit, man. I can't tell."

"Fuck it." Then Mays swung the truck into the turn.

"Man, this doesn't look familiar at all."

"How can you tell? You can't see shit."

"Well, neither can you."

"That was a hooch."

"A hooch? You're crazy," yelled Mays. "There's no hooches on the way back to camp."

The truck lurched forward, dropped front end first into something soft. The lights seemed to shimmer and glow. They heard a gurgling sound.

"What the fuck..."

"I think we're in some water."

"Water?"

"We're in the fuckin' river, Mays."

The front of the truck appeared to be moving to Kohl's right, which would be probably down stream.

"Bail out," screamed Kohl as he pushed the door open. Below him was a swirling black murky cauldron. He could see the bank reflected from the truck taillights. The back end of the truck was sliding off the bank into the current. Kohl jumped. *Boy that sobered me up.* He came up with a mouth full of water and gasping for air. He tried to get his bearings. He saw some grass clumps sticking out of the rushing current. He grabbed one and tried to find some solid ground under him. He pulled himself up and waded about ten yards to shore. He was wet and cold and then he saw the truck float past him. But in the dim glow he saw something else. It was ... Mays. He was standing on top of truck cab like Captain Ahab. *He's going down with the truck. What a brave man.* Then he saw Mays jump. Kohl ran down stream and retrieved the thrashing Mays from the river. They sat on the bank breathing hard.

"Well, that's a fine mess you got us into," Kohl said angrily.

"It's the Colonel's fault. He took my jeep."

"Why did he take your jeep?" asked Kohl.

"His broke down and took mine until we can fix it, which will take fuckin' forever."

"What time does your glow in the dark watch say?"

"It two-fuckin'-thirty."

"Now what?"

Mays glared at Kohl and growled, "Why don't you call a fuckin' cab?"

"Oh. It's too late. You'd never get a cab at this hour." They both howled in laughter so hard that they rolled on the rain soaked ground. Finally Kohl stopped laughing long enough to ask, "What about the truck?"

Then Mays got up and started walking. He stopped, looked around, and finally said, "What truck?"

They laughed and sang their way back along the red muck road to camp.

44 The General's Coming

The Colonel asked Pete to write a report. The report was to expound on how well the Colonel had been doing since his arrival. The problem with the assignment was that weekly and monthly reports pointed out how ill equipped the Marines were. Trucks and equipment were breaking down at an alarming rate with little or no repair parts. Ordered parts were either slow in coming or when they came they were the wrong parts. Supplies would come they didn't need, such as the cold weather gear. For the most part though, parts never came at all. The sand at Chu Lai was destroying bearings, plugging filters, and choking carburetors. The sand was getting into every crack and crevice, basically grinding and scratching surfaces of rods, shafts and gears until the machine would come to a screeching halt. There was a standing order that the Marines could not pilfer from other broken down equipment to repair others. In some areas Marines could steal Army, Navy or Air Force parts and equipment but in Chu Lai they couldn't do that. There were only Marines in Chu Lai. So in order to keep trucks and equipment running they pilfered from broken down equipment or jury-rigged it so it would work at least until the parts were available. A lot of improvising was being done. The report was to be available for the upcoming inspection by General Walt.

Mays, Pete, Kohl, and Blaylock were sitting on their racks in the tent talking. Kohl couldn't believe how much Blaylock had changed. He seemed happier, even laughing and making jokes. Pete had turned in a preliminary report to the Colonel but it didn't portray the Colonel in the gleam of heralding light he wanted. The truth did not look good. The Colonel wanted Pete to redo it so the results would be more favorable.

"How am I going to change ten operating six-byes into forty-four?" asked Pete.

"You think you've got problems. I'll be lucky to have ten running by the time the General gets here," said an exasperated Mays.

They all sat silently until Kohl hesitantly suggested, "What if you forgot about the number of trucks running and used miles run instead."

"Yeah. I could do that," said Pete. "Can you get me the info, Mays?"

"I guess so. It could work. And make us look good. I run those ten trucks twenty-four hours a day. I know they are all going to take a big dump any day now."

"I've got problems with ice too," continued Pete.

"What do you mean?" asked Kohl.

"Well, for starters, remember when for two weeks we didn't have any ice at all because the generator went down."

"Yeah, so?" said Kohl.

"So, the Colonel wants me to change that too."

Mays said, "Average. Do an average. Like amount of ice per day or week. You know like 40,000 pounds per week. Something like that. But I still don't know what to do about my trucks, man. If the General comes to inspect the Company, he'll see ten trucks that run and look like shit because they are run almost constantly. Then he'll see the bone yard and have a fuckin' cow. And my ass will be grass."

"You know the Colonel will want all forty-four out," piped in Blaylock.

All that progress Blaylock and you blow it all in one statement. Once a kiss ass, always a kiss ass.

"That's fuckin' impossible, you fuckin' idiot," yelled Mays.

They all sat with their heads resting in their hands as gloom settled on the tent.

*

But Pete did it. He had the pounds of ice. He had the miles of transportation. Pete wrote a dialogue about a water truck made out of scraps that maintenance built for the health and safety of the Marines that would make a grown man cry.

Every thing is beautiful, Colonel. You horses ass. Nothing is wrong. Everything is AOK. Everything is peachy keen.

*

Kohl noticed the General's advance party when he went to morning chow. After chow he returned to his tent and started cleaning his 45 pistol. He was scheduled to return to the airbase for perimeter detail late that afternoon. He heard someone walking toward the tent. He could see the legs of freshly ironed khakis and shinny black boots.

"Knock, knock," said a voice that Kohl recognized.

"Well, no shit, Fitz. You take the wrong turn in the South China Sea? This is Viet-fuckin-nam not the Philippines."

First Lieutenant Fitzsimmons gave a nervous laugh, entered the tent, and shook Kohl's outstretched hand. He said,"I came looking for you, you know."

"Well, that's awfully sweet of you, Fitz. I didn't know you cared," Kohl said sarcastically.

"I don't. I just came to have a little chat with you."

All right. Cut the crap. Say what's on your mind.

"It seems that every time you're in the vicinity of the General something always happens."

"Like what?"

"In the Philippines you got drunk and started a fight with a Major, remember?"

"Yeah. That wasn't anything. It wasn't really a fight just a difference of opinion. That's all."

"You might think that was all there was to it but the Major you insulted went straight to the General. And I got chewed out for letting you up there. And then, what about the dead animals and the frozen bodies in Danang? What about that, huh?"

"I don't know what you're talking about."

"Don't give me that. I saw you, Kohl, sitting in a Mighty Mite the morning all that stuff happened. You and Mays both were involved some way."

"I think your imagination is running away with you, Fitz."

"Cut the Bullshit, Kohl. The General is coming and I don't want any of your..."

"What?"

"I don't want you to do anything that will embarrass me or the General."

"You've got me all wrong, Fitz ol' buddy. Nothin's going to happen, I promise."

"Promise?"

"Scout's honor. But ... sit down, Fitz. I need to ask you a favor."

"Oh, brother. I knew it. Just knew it."

"I'm not going to do anything. Just listen. Please."

"Why should I do you a favor? You pull all this shit, then ask for a favor?"

"Mays and Pete are in a spot. I really don't have anything to do with this fucked up inspection. But the shit's goin' to fly. I want to warn you abo..."

"I knew it. I knew it. You're in on something."

"Now, wait. Goddamn it, Fitz. Hear me out. Things are fucked up here. We don't have supplies to fix trucks and equipment. Things are fallin' apart left and right. Colonel Dough Boy wants us to white wash everything. You have the ear of the General."

"I don't have the ear of the General. I'm not an aide."

"But you could steer him. Because what he's going to see isn't the way it is, Fitz."

"I don't understand?"

"Mays is supposed to have over thirty six-byes running and he's got ten. And that's just the tip of the iceberg. Maintenance is machining most of their parts. This sand eats up gears, carburetors and bearings as fast as they can replace them."

"Okay. What do you want me to do?"

"Mays will have all his trucks out for inspection, like he's supposed to. But only the front line trucks will have all their working parts. The trucks in the back rows will be on hidden blocks and some won't have motors, transmissions, and rear ends. Get the picture?"

"The General will definitely want to see this."

"I know. But if the General finds out at the inspection, it will be Mays who gets the shaft not the Colonel. So what I'm asking, Fitz, is getting the General through the inspection, then tell him afterwards. He can even talk to us in private if he wants. Can you do that for me?"

"I'll do it if I can. I'm not promising nothin'. The General is damn independent and does as he damn well pleases."

"That's all that I ask, Fitz. Thanks."

"Don't thank me yet. See ya, Kohl."

"See ya, Fitz."

"You had something to do with those frozen animals, didn't you?"

"Not me, Fitz. You got me mixed up with someone else."

"Yeah, yeah. See ya."

"See ya."

45 Care Packages

Kohl was at sick bay talking to Doc Austin, while he was in getting a quart jar of Kay-O-Pectate.

"How many times have I told you guys not to drink the water," the Doc said.

"I didn't drink no water without that Halizon shit," said Kohl.

"Well, you got the shits from something."

Then Kohl remembered about his dunk in the river the night he and Mays got lost in the truck. He recalled getting a mouth full of water several times during the ordeal. He hoped he didn't get those worms he had before.

"I got worms before, Doc. I don't want those shittin' things again."

"I'll give you something for the worms."

The Doc laughed at something he thought of.

"What?" Kohl asked.

"I just got a letter from my wife. She had asked me what it was like over here and I sent her a letter with sand in it."

"That's perty funny, Doc."

"Yea. But that's not the funny part. She writes back all pissed at me for sending the letter with sand because she opened it while she was eating dinner and spilled sand all over her food. I wrote back, 'Now you really know what its like'."

Kohl laughed and said,"Ain't that the truth. We goin' to the vill Thursday?"

"Sure. Comin'?"

"If you want me too"

Every Thursday Kohl and the Doc would go into the small village called Ap Tan-Rinn. Kohl helped the Doc get the women and children lined up for shots, treated infections and sicknesses of various kinds. But mostly Kohl handed out candy and discarded C-Rations to the children.

*

Kohl was going to the bathroom for the third time in two hours. He was sitting in the bright morning sun reading when Corporal Krumgold walked up with his bucket of lime, and rolls of toilet paper.

"Morning, Lieutenant."

"Morning, Corporal."

"You've been sittin' a lot on the crapper, lately, Lieutenant."

"Got the friggin' trots. Say the edges of the holes you cut in the plywood are like sitting on nails. It's rougher than hell. Can't you smooth 'em out some?"

"I'd need sandpaper. And the sandpaper we have is so damp from the humidity it just falls apart. Besides the crapper's used for taking a dump and not for leisure reading."

"Don't get smart with me, Krumgold. I'll write and tell your folks about what you did while you were in Vietnam. Corporal 'Honey Dipper'. Sound impressive?"

Corporal Krumgold's other duty was to help Doctor Austin at the morgue. Doctor Austin was also base coroner. Krumgold helped prepare the bodies for shipment home. This was going to be Krumgold's occupation once he got out of the Corps, where he would join his brother and father in the family mortuary business in Oxnard, California.

"Say, Lieutenant. If you're tired of Marine chow you can come over to my tent. Tonight we are having lobster."

"You're shittin' me."

"I ain't shittin' ya, Lieutenant. I have a snorkel, fins, face mask and spear gun and out in that lagoon, I got five lobsters this morning early."

"No, shit?"

"Out-fuckin-standin', Lieutenant. Big fuckers, too."

"How'd you get the skin diving gear?"

"Folks sent it. Lieutenant, it's beautiful out there. Tropical fish and pink and purple corral. Absolutely beautiful. Hard to believe, huh?"

"Yeah, it's hard to believe. Say Corporal. You know that I'd like to talk to you, swap stories and all, but if you don't mind, take care of what you're supposed to be doing and get the fuck outa here. I'm trying to pass the lima beans and ham we had for chow last night."

*

August 21, 1965

Hi Babe,
My day would have been a complete nothing if it hadn't have been for the care package I got from you. Every thing was just perfect. The chocolate chip cookies were great. Everyone in the tent is envious of me for having such a fine cook. They said to send my regards to the chef.

(Actually the box the cookies came in was a mangled mess. And when Kohl excitedly opened the box there wasn't a piece of cookie bigger than a nickel. Besides that, ants had already found their way inside.)

The pictures you sent were ... how can I explain ... I'm at a loss for words. I apologize though. I couldn't help myself. I know you didn't want me to show them to anybody but I was so proud.

(The pictures showed Julie in a white bikini with blue Pokka-dots. She had said she had had a few drinks in order to get up the courage to take the cheese cake pictures.)

I hope these pictures don't ruin. I wrapped each picture in onion skin paper and put them in a plastic bag. It gets so damp here, plus hot and dusty.
I'm still working like mad. I think I'd feel better if I felt like I was accomplishing something. I do a job and there's two more to take its place. This friggen dirty, hot, screwed up place. We don't have any gear to do our job and we have to scrape, beg, borrow, steal to get a vehicle off deadline, no parts and short handed. Force Logistics Supply Unit, that's what we are called but we aren't supplying hardly anything. It's like get what you can, when you can, anyway you can. Great War.
Pete and I sneaked away Friday morning and went to the beach. Had my icebox, aluminum chair, scrounged up a couple of beers, swam, and relaxed. That was the first time that happened since I've been here. I've heard that R &R trips are being planned for either

Hong Kong or Bankock. That would be cool.
Can you imagine getting a cold when it's over 100 degrees? Well, I've got a cold. I'm trying for pneumonia. Think they would send me home?
Well love, thank you for the goodies. I wish I could get you in a box. I look at those pictures you sent me and I look and look and then I do pushups. Sure do love you Julie. Take care and study hard, be careful, stay happy. I'll be home sooner than you know.
Love always and ever,
Dusty

*

It wasn't the thought of good food. It wasn't the feeling of having a good night's sleep without the roar of the diesel generators. It wasn't the relief from the insufferable heat. And it wasn't sex, although sex was way up there on the deprivation chart. What Kohl wanted more than anything was a letter from home. It was the slim thread that kept Kohl and his fellow Marines connected to the real world. Mail call was the most important time of every day. There wasn't a moment that went by that Kohl didn't think of mail call and considering how much he thought about sex, mail call was on his mind a lot. It could also be a source of problems from Dear Johns, to an ill parent, or death of a loved one, and to some it could mean other hardships. Whatever the circumstances it was a letter from home. It was a source of endless conversations with tent mates all sharing in the news from home. Letters were read over and over again. Some were folded and placed in a breast pocket or hurriedly crumpled into a pant pocket to be retrieved and read when time would allow or when a moment of despair would rise to the surface.

Blaylock got mail, but as time progressed Kohl and the others noticed that when every one was sharing what was happening at home, Blaylock didn't have anything to offer. It was then that Kohl began to notice what Blaylock received. They were magazines, catalogues, letters of inquiry, but no letters from home.

Kohl was not one to pry into another's personal affairs but the four men in the tent shared everything. That is except for Blaylock.

*

It was late in the afternoon when the supply clerk, PFC Fields announced himself outside the Kohl's tent.

"Anybody here?" asked PFC Fields.

"Yeah, Fields. I'm here," said Kohl. "Come in. What's up?" Kohl added.

"Came to pick up Lieutenant Blaylock's gear."

"What for?" asked Kohl. He thought that Blaylock had been transferred.

"Got word he's dead."

Kohl almost fell over as his knees buckled. He had just finished washing some clothes and was preparing them to be hung outside on the clothesline.

"What? You're crazy," Kohl said, not believing what he had heard.

"Sorry, Sir. I've got the COM sheet right here."

"Let me see that," said Kohl as he grabbed the sheet from PFC Field's outstretched hand.

As he read it, he couldn't believe it. He saw Blaylock this morning. They had gotten up, got dressed, went to chow and as far as Kohl was concerned, Blaylock had gone to the Colonel's tent and did his Colonel duties like he did every day. He never went anyplace. How in the hell could he be dead?

"Have you checked the CP?" asked Kohl.

"If he's dead, Lieutenant, why would he be there?"

"Because I don't think he's dead. I think there has been some kind of a mistake."

"Gee, Lieutenant. I don't know. I was told the Red Cross has already notified his parents."

"Don't they have to verify this shit before the parents are notified?"

"I don't know, Lieutenant. I'm just the Supply Clerk. I was told to come and pick up his gear to be sent home."

"Stay here, Fields. I'll be right back." Kohl left the tent in a trot. The CP tent was only about 100 yards away.

Kohl reached the tent and went in. Looked where Blaylock usually could be seen working on some useless piece of shit the Colonel wanted him to do and there he was.

Surprised at Kohl's look of concern, he said, "What's wrong?"

With the Colonel sitting there at his desk, Kohl didn't want to go into what was going on, so he said, "Nothing." and left.

When he got back to the tent he told Fields that there had been a mistake, and that Lieutenant Blaylock was alive and well in the Colonel's tent.

"But Lieutenant, I have the COM sheet."

"If you don't believe me, go take a look."

"Roger that, Lieutenant. I don't understand though."

"Neither do I, but he's alive, I assure you."

*

Kohl didn't say anything until after chow when he, Mays, Pete, and Blaylock were sitting in their aluminum chairs outside the tent drinking Cointreau Liqueur after eating canned hot dogs and sauerkraut at evening chow.

Kohl said, "I had a little visit this afternoon from PFC Fields from supply, Blaylock. You need to thank me for the clothes on your back or they would have been in Oki by now."

Blaylock squinted his eyes in confusion. So did Mays and Pete as well.

"Pete. Mays. We are looking at a ghost," Kohl continued enjoying his little guessing game. Besides what else was there to do?

Mays lost patience and said, "What the fuck you talkin' about?"

"It appears that our friend Blaylock here, is dead."

Blaylock looked down but Kohl could see a small grin cross his lips.

"PFC Fields came to pick up his gear to ship home. Appears he had a COM sheet stating Blaylock had been killed in action. And we all know that he has no action, never had no action, and never will have action. He's a no action kind of a guy. But I'm confused Blaylock? Where did that COM sheet come from? Huh?"

Blaylock looked up. All three of them were staring at him. He shrugged and said, "I envy you guys. You get letters from your mothers and wives. Kohl even gets letters from his cousins, and his aunts. You Pete, get letters from friends from high school and college. Mays gets letters from a school of junior high kids, for Christ's sake. And me? Nothing. Nothing. Oh, sure I get catalogues and magazines but I don't get any mail from anybody. Not my parents. Not from a girl friend. Not from anyone. I just thought it would serve my Dad right. I mean, after all, I might as well be dead. No one cares. No one."

With that last comment tears began to roll down Blaylock's red chubby cheeks. "To them I'm not even alive. They sent me to boarding school and then I would spend summers at some camp or other. Prep school, then science camp, or as a parent-imposed volunteer in the Sierra Club. Then college. I don't even know my dad. My mom I never knew. Dad just said she left. I don't have anyone."

Mays said, "If you weren't such an ass hole..."

"Shut up, Mays," said Pete.

"I was just kidding," whined Mays.

"We're your family, Blaylock," said Kohl. "We may not be all of what you expect but we are here."

"Ditto, to that," said Pete. "There's not many families that are as close as we are."

"I have to admit that Blaylock is not the ass hole he once was. And to tell the truth I've got more of those junior high kids to write to than I have time. I can't answer all their goddamn letters if I was here for another fuckin' year. So maybe you could help me out. Huh, Blaylock?" asked Mays.

*

The care packages were the best. Better than letters. Better than sex. It had taken months to get the process started so Kohl and his buddies could receive care packages. First Kohl had to communicate that he wanted Kool-Aid. The kind that had sugar already added. He wanted Rooten-Tooten Raspberry, Jolly-Olly Orange, Goofy Grape, LoudMouth Lime, and the big hot item Chinese Cherry. Halizon in the drinking water was like drinking Listerine mouthwash. When Kohl added the Kool-Aid it made it palatable, barely. The cookies and cake packages continued to be a problem. If the box wasn't pulverized by the time it got to Chu Lai, then came the problem of trying to keep the ants out. Kohl put the left over cookies in a plastic bag, sealed the bag, and put the bag in the icebox. The next day when he went to get a cookie the ants were there. They had eaten a hole in the plastic bag. He didn't know how they got in the cooler. Keeping the ants out proved to be almost impossible. The best solution was to eat everything when it first came.

*

The FLSU Officer's Club, called the Pangi Pit, was nothing but a tent with wire spools for tables and ammo boxes for chairs. Kohl and the others usually brought down their rickety aluminum chairs. The bar was a board laid across more ammo boxes. Behind the bar was more ammo boxes for shelves and inside were every conceivable kind of liquor. And it was the good stuff. However there were a few items missing. There wasn't any beer, soft drinks, or ice. The officers either drank it straight or with Halazone water.

"What the shit is that?" asked Mays as he walked up to the make shift bar.

Kohl said with a slight air of dignity, "Why, it's Goofy-Grape and Vodka."

"Uughhaa," Mays shivered. "Can you believe this shit, Sarge?" Mays asked Sergeant Brisco who was the bar tender.

"I must admit, Lieutenant. That purple shit looks perty bad."

"Here, Mays, taste it."

"No way, man. I'll do my shit straight."

On this night, there was quite a contingent at the club. Besides Kohl, Mays, Pete and Blaylock, there was Warrant Officer Shaffer, Second Lieutenant Hockett, Lieutenant Cobain and Captain Hawes. The officers had a rare night without a meeting. The Colonel had been called to a meeting at 9/1 Headquarters. With everyone drinking straight liquor, except for Kohl, it didn't take long before inebriation set in.

They had a record player and only two LP's. One was called "Candyland" by Pete Fountain and the other was "Detroit City" by Roy Drusky. And when the song 'Detroit City' came on everyone joined in the chorus.

I wanna go home,
I wanna go home,
Oh, How I wanna go home.

Everyone was making fun of Kohl's blue mouth. Then the dark, quiet night exploded into automatic rifle fire and screaming red tracer bullets. In a 50-caliber machine gun one out of every seven bullets is a tracer round and when fired at night they put on quite a show. When the sound of the first rounds filtered through the drunken minds of the officers, some just stood while others hit the deck. Kohl was one of the first. It was his first instinct, drunk or not. Then the lights went out. There was a lot of conversation as to what was going on and considerable discussion on what to do. What persisted most was the forgone conclusion that they were being invaded by the Viet Cong from the sea, just like what the Colonel had feared. Slowly the Officers left the tent for the trench.

Kohl got to his hands and knees and crawled behind the bar.

Dejavue, Kohl. Seems like this is a favorite ploy of yours. Trouble and you crawl behind the bar. You some big chicken shit or something?

You seem to be forgetting, the last time this happened there was this sweet young thing sitting across from me.

I remember. And I also recall she invited you home and you refused.

Rest assured if she was sitting across from me right now, I'd nail her right there on the ammo box.

Are you going out to fight the gooks?

You won't see me out running around in the dark. A good way to get yourself killed. No sirreee, Bob. You ain't seein' me out runnin' round.

Kohl heard movement over to his left.

"I sure hope that's you Sergeant Brisco."

"It's me, Lieutenant Kohl. You ain't seein' me out runnin' around."

"Same here, Sarge."

"What do you think is happenin', Lieutenant?"

"I'll bet you a jelly donut that one of the OP's got scared, heard something and let rip. And that of course does the thing that dominoes do. One causes the other to do the same thing. Betcha?"

"Probably right, Sir. Just sit tight then, I guess."

The field phone rang and Kohl nearly jumped out of his boots,"If that's the Colonel, he's probably lookin' for me. Probably wants me to go and check the OP's for Christ's sake. Tell him I'm not here."

"Yes, Sir. Sergeant Brisco. Yes. Not now. Yes. No, he's not here. No, I don't know where. Yes, Sir. Yes, Sir. Yes, Sir." Then the sergeant put the phone back in the cradle after several attempts.

"Was that our grand leader?"

"Yes, Sir. That was the Man, himself."

"Was he looking for me?"

"That he was, Lieutenant."

"This surely calls for another Goofy Grape drink."

"Can't see, Lieutenant."

"I'll do it by feel. Say, Sarge, since I'm BOQ Officer, I hereby absolve your duties as Club bartender. Be free."

"Is that so, Sir."

"Sure. I can do that. Now you can have a drink with me. I hate drinking alone."

"I can't do that, Lieutenant."

"Why not?"

The Sergeant shrugged but Kohl could see it. "First of all you're an officer. And second your white."

"How do you know. You can't see me."

"Quit your foolin', Sir. I know your white."

"Pretend you're drinking alone."

"I don't like drinking alone either, Lieutenant."

There was a long pause while Kohl searched for a bottle. Found one and drank from it. Then poked Sergeant Brisco's shoulder and handed it to him. Kohl could hear Brisco swallow.

"What shall we talk about?" asked Kohl.

"I don't know."

"You know what?"

"What?"

Kohl chuckled silently to himself, then said,"I just thought of something."

"What's that?"

"Couple of nights ago I got to sneak down to the movies without the

Colonel knowin' and I saw this western called 'Quick Draw' and I got to thinkin' about my old trusty forty-five here. So here is my version of the Marine Officer quick draw. One, he unbuckles the flap that holds his forty-five in. Two, he draws his forty-five. Three, he takes off the plastic cover, you know Sarge to keep the dust off. Four, he unbuckles the ammo pocket. Five, he takes out the ammo clip. Six, he puts the ammo clip into the forty-five. Seven, he slides a round into the chamber. Eight, he fingers the safety off. Nine, he finally aims, then fires"

During the dissertation the Sergeant was rolling on the floor laughing.

The war raged on.

*

Kohl licked his lips and got a mouth full of dirt. Still too groggy to think clearly, it didn't register in his drink-induced slumber why dirt was in his mouth. He had to pee. He also felt sick to his stomach. His right arm had no feeling. As his discomfort began to swim slowly from point A, B, C, and D to brain headquarters, the fog began to clear. He spit and slowly cracked one eye open.

In the gray early morning light he could see something brown and solid in front of his face.

What's that? Where am I? Looks like dirt.

He spit again and rolled his dry tongue around the inside of his mouth, trying to gather enough saliva to spit more of the dirt from his mouth.

As Kohl's one eye began to focus and comprehend what he was looking at he realized he was lying in the dirt and it looked like some kind of a hole, then panic seized him.

I'm buried alive.

"Help! Help!" he croaked.

Save your breath. If you're buried alive, you have to save your strength.

Yeah. Right. But... I can see. There's light from above.

Then you're not buried.

Kohl sat up slowly. Dirt and blue slobber was hanging from the corner of his mouth. His body ached. His head felt like a bowling ball and his right arm was hanging limply from his shoulder. He could see that he was in the trench that they had dug with the backhoe. It was for protection.

He saw a shadow cast on the side of the trench wall and a figure looming overhead. Kohl careened his head around and squinted in the direction of the figure.

It was Warrant Officer Shaffer and in his Texas drawl he asked, "What the fuck you doin' in there? You afraid of the iddybiddies gettin' you?"

"Musta fell in here last night. Don't remember. I thought I was buried alive."

"Here, let me help you out," said Shaffer as he stuck out his hand. With his help Kohl climbed out of his tomb and brushed the dirt and sand off his body.

"Were we overrun with VC last night?"

"No. One of the OP's got spooked was all."

46 Who Wants to Sleep With Cobain?

Kohl came grumbling into the tent.

"You've got to quit talking to yourself, Kohl. People are beginning to notice," kidded Mays.

"The fuckin' Colonel really pisses me off."

"What else is new, shit for brains. You're always pissed off at the Colonel."

"I just went over to give the Colonel the latest shipping report he asked for this morning. So I go over there and he tells me he already knows, and then when I ask why I had to go through all this today, he just looks at me like I'm a dumb ass."

"You are a dumb ass," said Mays.

"Fuck you. He has to be the most egotistical, neurotic, self-indulgent individual I've ever met. He absolutely drives me crazy. Just trying to out guess him is impossible because nothing he does makes fuckin' sense. I'm tired of his little games. To hell with him. I'll just do my job and if he doesn't like it he can go to hell. I almost blew it. I came close to hittin' the son-of-a-bitch in the mouth. Thank God I caught myself. I really don't know what the hell goes on in that pea brain of his. He thinks he has to treat people like dogs in order to get the best results. He needs to take a human relations course."

The last comment brought howls of laughter to Mays and Blaylock.

"What's so fuckin' funny? I'm going to take a shower and try to cool off."

Kohl took off his clothes, put back on his socks and boots, wrapped a towel around his waist, strapped on his forty-five, and walked toward the shower. Kohl's experience in Danang had taught him to always take his boots and side arm wherever he went.

It was about a quarter of a mile now to the showers. They had moved them all to a central location north of camp. As Kohl was walking leisurely along the bluff above the shoreline in the late afternoon sun, he noticed a line of about twenty to thirty men standing out side the morgue. Curious, Kohl turned and walked toward the men. Some saw him coming and left.

Kohl walked up to a tall skinny Marine and asked,"What's happening?"

Marines could tell that Kohl was an officer even if they hadn't seen him around camp because of the forty-five he wore. Only NCO's and officers wore forty-fives. And Kohl was too young looking to be an NCO.

The Marine answered,"Nothin', Sir."

Yeah. Right. Marines don't stand in line for nothin'.

Kohl peeked around the corner of the morgue tent flap and saw Corporal Krumgold take money from a Marine in front of the line and lead him behind a screen. When Krumgold turned around, he saw Kohl. Kohl saw Krumgold's face turn white. It was then Kohl knew Krumgold was up to something that wasn't right.

Krumgold walked over to where Kohl was standing and on his way he waved the men in the line off. He told some who lingered around to leave.

Krumgold gave the Lieutenant his best grin and said, "What's up, Lieutenant?"

"Krumgold? Why do I have this funny feeling that not all is what it seems? All these men were lined up. Why?"

Krumgold didn't answer. He moved sand around with his boot. Kohl knew he was trying to think of an answer to the Lieutenant's question but was having a hard time figuring out what lie would be best.

He finally said,"I'm sorry, Sir. I can't answer your question."

Everyone was out of the tent now. Kohl gave Krumgold a stern look and said,"That's not good enough, Corporal. I'm going to ask you one more time, what's going on here? And if you don't give me a legitimate answer, I'm writin' your ass up for insubordination and failure to follow an order. I'll have your ass stripped down to Private. Do I make myself clear?"

"Yes, Sir," he said weakly.

"Then let's have it."

"Uhmm. Well, Sir." He paused. "If I tell you will I get in trouble?"

"Jesus, Krumgold. We're not negotiating here and I'm not promising nothin'. Now out with it. I'm tired. I want to take a shower. Now quit fuckin' around."

Even though there wasn't anyone in the tent, Krumgold talked in a whisper, "This morning, Sir. Well, this morning this journalist lady got..."

"Yes?"

"...Killed."

"So?"

" Well, she's a looker, Lieutenant and fresh..."

"Oh, shit, Krumgold. Shit! Shit! Shit!" Kohl kept saying it over and over as he stomped in circles in the sand. "What's this place doing to you, Krumgold? You're better than this? Jesus-fuckin'-A- Christ-all-mighty. Selling a peek at a dead women's breast and her... Jesus, man. She's dead, for God's sake," Kohl yelled. "Where's your dignity?"

"I'm sorry, Lieutenant. I don't know. I wasn't thinking. I..."

"I know what you were thinkin'. Money. And the shit-for-brains standing in line were thinkin' with their dicks."

Krumgold begged, "Oh, Lieutenant. I fucked up, Sir. I..."

"Shut up! Just shut the fuck up!" yelled Kohl. "It's so disgusting that I can't even see how I can report it. How many saw her?"

"Ten or fifteen."

"Shit! Shit! If this gets out... Oh, shit. What am I saying? Sure it's going to get out. Fix it, Corporal. Make it go away."

Kohl walked out of the tent. His feelings were a jumbled mix. He felt disgust at what Krumgold had done and was disappointed he would do something like that. He felt sorry for the horny Marines. He felt sorry for himself. It had been eight months since he had sex. All the Marines were in various stages of depravation of the female gender. Some men frequented the brothels of Okinawa and Philippines. In Vietnam, where the Marines were, most towns and cities were off limits. Venereal decease was rampant. The doctors didn't have a name for the VD they had in Vietnam. So they called it NSU (Non-specific urethraitis). He climbed down the bluff to the beach in his towel, boots, and side-arm, then he sat in the sand, and looked east out across glimmering sea. Home.

*

"Hey, guess what?" said Cobain gleefully as he entered Kohl's tent. "I got Malaria."

Mays said, "That doesn't sound too exciting to me. Especially after watching you shiver and sweat the last two days."

"They're going to send me home."

"No, shit?" asked Pete.

"Yeah. I have to go down to La Trang first thing in the morning. Then the good ol' US of A."

"Jesus, Cobain," said Kohl. "I'll miss your ass. But hell that's better than shootin' yourself in the foot."

Cobain went back to his tent to rest. Kohl and his tent mates went to chow and then to the meeting. After the meeting there wasn't much to do but read or write by candle light or go to bed. Pete was gathering his rubber lady and blanket and was heading out the tent.

Kohl asked, "Where're you goin'?"

Pete showed a sheepish grin and said, "I'm going to sleep with Cobain."

Mays piped up with his usual reply, "Golly, Pete, if I'd known you were that way I would have asked you to sleep with me a long time ago. In fact you can come right over here you big hunk."

"Man, you guys don't have a clue," continued Pete.

"What? I don't get it? Wait, Pete," said Kohl.

Pete stopped, turned, and said, "If Cobain has Malaria and I sleep near him tonight maybe I can get it too and they'll send me home."

Mays said, "No, shit. That's a great idea."

They all grabbed their rubber ladies and blankets and followed Pete.

Blaylock asked, "Kohl? What about our story for tonight? Can you bring your book?"

"Yeah, sure," said Kohl and he went back into the tent to get the book he had been reading to his tent mates the last few nights.

Cobain rose up on one elbow as the lieutenants entered one by one into the tent with their rubber ladies, blankets, and pillows.

Cobain asked, "What are you guys doing?"

Mays said, "We came to sleep with you, you handsome devil."

Cobain, still confused, watched silently as the men picked out their spots on the sandy floor. They all started to settle down.

"What we need is a night cap. Got anything, Cobain?" asked Mays.

"Got a bottle of Old Turkey under my rack," said Cobain.

Mays reached under Cobain's cot and retrieved the fifth of bourbon whiskey. He uncorked it took a pull and passed it to Pete. Pete did the same and passed it to Kohl who followed suit. Then Kohl passed it to Blaylock.

"I can't drink that stuff," said Blaylock.

Mays said, "Blaylock, you big puss, take a pull."

"If I do, I'll need a chaser. If I don't I might throw up."

Kohl said, "Come on, Blaylock. You can't be a candy ass all your life."

Blaylock took a sip, swallowed, then coughed. He looked at his fellow

Marines. Mays glared at him. He took another sip. Longer this time. His body shook, but he didn't cough. He passed it to Cobain.

"I'm sick. I can't drink," reasoned Cobain.

"Drink enough and you can make the mosquitoes drunk," said Pete.

Cobain drank and the bottle made the loop again.

Mays said,"All right, Cobain, show some skin."

"What do you mean?"

"Throw some covers off."

"I've got chills."

"Fuck your chills. You've got to think of others instead of yourself. Sacrifice for the sake of others. You've got to give those mosquitoes something to chew on. They take some of what you got and deposit it in us. Then we can all go home."

"So that's why you're here?"

Mays said,"Fuckin' A. Do you think we were here for a sleep over? Fuckin' moron."

Kohl said, "You know, you guys? We've got a problem here. I've been thinking about it for a while now."

"What?" Pete asked.

"It's our language."

Mays said,"What the fuck's wrong with our language?"

Every one laughed as they passed around the bottle. Not being deterred Kohl continued,"I mean we're getting short, that is except for dipshit here," He pointed to Cobain,"Who's going home and Blaylock who'll be here forever. But I'm talkin' about us, Pete, Mays. In a few short months we are going to find ourselves home with family and friends trying to find jobs and we talk like... like..."

"Assholes," said Mays.

"Mays, I'm serious. I think we need to do something about it."

"You're right," said Pete.

"Hell, I could stop any time. No sweat," said Mays. "But I don't see the need."

"I can see it now," said Kohl. He stood up in his underwear for affect and dignity. "This is Mays in a court room.'I object your Honor.' 'Objection overruled.' 'What?' 'I said, objection overruled.' 'Well fuck you Judge, you fuckin' fagot?'

Everyone laughed.

"You guys think I can't quit, well I can. Cold turkey. Speaking of which. Pass me the fu ... Pass me the bottle, as... Give me that. I can do it." Then he took a long pull from the bottle and passed it to Kohl. "Let's start tomorrow."

Kohl said, "Okay with me."

Everyone nodded. Cobain was falling to sleep but woke up when Mays tried to remove more of the sheet.

"But there's something else," said Kohl. "I think there should be a consequence for cussing." They nodded. "How 'bout a fine jar. Every time we cuss we feed the jar. And we'll only do it when we are in the tent or at the bar. Okay? Now how much do we pay?"

"Quarter?" asked Pete. Everybody nodded yes. Then Pete added, "What will we do with the money?"

Blaylock suggested, "The fine bottle should be bequeathed to the last remaining man."

"Well that's a finc howdy do, since you'll be the last one going home," retorted Mays.

"That's fine with me," said Kohl.

They all agreed. Cobain was asleep and mumbling. He was sweating and shaking. Blaylock was starting to have second thoughts about trying to get malaria.

"How long does Malaria last?" he asked.

"The rest of your life," said Mays.

"Uh, uh. Your lyin," said Blaylock.

"He's tellin' the truth, Blaylock," said Pete.

Blaylock took another swig from the bottle. Blaylock said, "I'm not too sure about this."

Mays growled at Blaylock, "Well, git the fuck outa here then."

Kohl said, "Did you guys here that the fuckin' R&R plane blew up?" They nodded in the negative. "Yep. It did. Cancelled all the R&R's."

After a moment of silence Kohl continued, "Went down somewhere in Cambodia."

"No shit?" said Pete.

"No shit," answered Kohl.

"Can you imagine being taken prisoner of war?" asked Pete.

"What makes you think they were taken prisoner of war?" asked Blaylock. "They could have all died or somethin'."

"That's a good either or," said Pete.

"Better Red than Dead," said Kohl.

"They wouldn't get shit out of me," said Mays.

"What do you have to hide, Mays? What big military secret would you try to keep from them? Huh?" asked Kohl.

"Nothin' really. It's the principle. You know to honor the 'Code of Conduct," said Mays.

"I am an American fighting man. I serve in the forces, which guards my country and our way of life. I am prepared to give my life in their defense." recited Blaylock.

"Jesus, Blaylock. I'm impressed. I thought you were drunk," said Pete.

"Number two," Blaylock continued. "I will never surrender of my own free will. If in command, I will never surrender my men while they have the means to resist."

"I can see that, resisting I mean. As long as I thought that I had a way out, you know," said Kohl.

"When I was up at Bridgeport, they strapped my ass to a teeter-totter-like thing and dipped me in this pond. I knew they wouldn't let me drown. But when I started pulling water in my lungs there wasn't anything I wouldn't have told them to get me off that board. I'm sorry. Call me a chicken shit. I knew I wasn't going to die. What would it be like if we were held in North Vietnam or China?" asked Kohl.

"I think I could trick them. Pretend I was crazy. Shit my pants and stuff," said Mays.

"Number three..."

"Shut the fuck up, Blaylock," said Mays.

"But, even if you said and did what they wanted you to do, in your own mind you would know what was right and what was wrong. As long as you believed. Don't you think, Pete?" asked Kohl.

"The rules are there for a reason, Kohl. You're probably right. But who knows how you would act," answered Pete.

"They aren't gettin' shit out of me," said Mays.

"If I am captured I will...."

"Shut the fuck up, Blaylock and give me that fuckin' bottle," growled Mays as he grabbed the bottle from Blaylock and took a pull. "Fuckin' geek. How'd you remember all that shit?"

"Because I'm smart. I have an IQ of 157."

"Oh, brother," said Kohl.

"I have a pornographic memory," said Blaylock.

Everyone laughed.

"What?" said Blaylock. "I do."

They sat in silence and listened to a mosquito flying. In the candle lit glow they saw it land on Cobain's leg.

Kohl said, "I got a telegram from Fitz today. He said our problem will disappear."

Blaylock asked, "What problem?"

Mays asked, "Do you mean that little talk you had with him paid off?"

Kohl said, "Guess so. We'll see."

"What problem?" persisted Blaylock.

"It's nothing we want to confuse your big-assed pornographic brain about, Blaylock," said Mays.

"I do not," pouted Blaylock.

Then Pete asked Mays, "Are you going to law school when you get back?"

"I think so. My dad's law firm will foot the bill and I've got a spot with the them when I finish law school."

Kohl asked Pete, "What about you?"

"I don't know. My wife's father wants me to go to work for the company he's working for. He's a petroleum engineer and lives most of the time in the Middle East. I don't know if I want to do that. I'll probably get a job with some business in the Bay Area. I don't know. I'll see what comes. What about you Kohl?"

"Shit. None of us will get back much before December. That's too late for me to teach. Might substitute teach but I'll need to make some cash cause Julie's still got a year left of school. So I don't know either. What about you, Blaylock? You've still got two years to do but do you have any idea what you're going to do?"

Blaylock took another swig of bourbon. He held the bottle now like it was his. He was drunk and had a hard time focusing on the discussion. "What?" he asked.

"When you get out, what are you going to do?" Kohl asked again.

"Who's gettin' out?"

"You."

"I'm not gettin' out. I've got two, yes two, two more years. I do."

"We know. Doesn't your father have some kind of a plant or something in Connecticut?"

"Yeah. Blaylock Industries. They make measuring things for construction. Lasers." He pointed his finger and made a buzzing sound.

"You going to work for them?" asked Pete.

"Fuck no. My father's a poop head."

"Poop head?" laughed Mays. "Poop head? Jesus Blaylock if you're going to try and swear, cuss like a goddamn Marine not some candy ass."

"Okay. I'll try to do better," Blaylock said apologetically.

"The company's probably worth millions, Blaylock and it'll be yours when your ass hole father gives it to you. True?"

"I don't want it. I think I'll stay in the Corps. That'll really piss him off. Are you going to read tonight, Kohl?" asked Blaylock.

"Guess so." And Kohl pulled out his book.

Kohl received the book in the mail from one of his fraternity brothers. He already had offers as high as fifty dollars for the book. The book was called 'Candy'.

Kohl lit a candle and sat it on a stand so he could see. He pulled the bottle from Blaylock' grip, took a big gulp, and passed it back to Blaylock, who had disregarded his initial concern for drinking bourbon straight.

"Where was I?"

"You were where she was humping the hump back," said Blaylock.

Kohl began...

> With a wild impulsive cry, she shrieked: "Give me your hump!"
> The hunchback was startled for a moment, not comprehending.
> "Your hump, your hump!" cried the girl. "Give me your hump!"
> The hunchback hesitated, and then lunged headlong toward her, burying his hump between Candy's legs as she hunched wildly, pulling open her little labias in an absurd effort to get it in her.
> "Fuck! Shit! Piss! she screamed......

47 *Beer By the Shipload*

Kohl was on the beach reading when Pete walked up behind him. Kohl turned around when he heard him coming. "Hi, Pete."

"Hey," answered Pete. "Came to tell ya..."

"What the shit? Where's your teeth?" asked Kohl. He immediately saw the gap where his four front teeth were supposed to be.

"Lothed 'em."

Kohl remembered the last time Pete lost his teeth, it happened while they were on the beach in San Clemente. Kohl was trying to teach Pete how to surf and finally Pete was getting the hang of it. He had caught a wave and had risen to his feet and yelled "Hey" at Kohl. And his teeth flew out.

"Where?"

Pete didn't say anything for a while and sat down next to Kohl. "In the crapper."

"What? You're shittin' me?" They both laughed.

"I was takin' a leak and thneethed and they flew out. Right down the hole."

"Did you try to get them?"

"Fuck no."

"You'll never get teeth over here."

"Do you have Malaria yet?"

"Not that I know of. How long does it take?"

"I don't know. Thay, that guy they call Corporal Crapper?"

"Krumgold?"

"Yeah. He came by and gave you thith." Pete gave Kohl a sack and in the sack were fins, a facemask, and snorkel. "He thaid he was being thent back."

"Home?"

"No. He didn't thay that. I heard he got in trouble for thomethin'."

"Oh."

"Anyway, he athked me to give you thith bag."

Pete and Kohl sat in silence and looked at the ocean waves as they swept over the coral reef.

Pete said, "The Colonel'th peeved at you."

"Big friggin' deal. Won't be long now and that little sucker will be history."

"He want to thee us in about twenty minuteth."

"What about?"

"Didn't thay."

They sat and watched the surf without talking for a while, each captured in his own thoughts, then Pete said, "You know what your problem ith?"

"No. But I've got a sneaky feelin' you're about to tell me."

"You have a problem with authority."

"Don't either. I can't help it if my commanding officers are ass holes."

"Think about it, Kohl. You had problemth at O-thee-eeth, Bathic Thcool and in Camp Pendelton you had a run in with Captain Blue. Then there wath the problem with the Regimental Commander. It just goeth on, Kohl. All thith time in the Corp and you thtill haven't learned."

Kohl sat silently and thought of what Pete had said. His immediate reaction was to argue and deny but the more he thought about it the more he realized that Pete was probably right. He had a hard time taking orders. He didn't like people telling him what to do and when to do it and how to do it. He remembered his Dad told him that being an officer was a lot easier than being an enlisted man. He guessed that his Dad knew he would have even a harder time at being an enlisted man.

"You're probably right, Pete. I can't seem to keep my mouth shut. But it's hard to take you serious when you talk like Sylvester the cat."

They got up and walked back up the bank toward the CP tent. They entered the tent and the Colonel motioned them to sit down. He was on the field phone as usual.

"There's an LSU coming in from Danang. It'll be here in about an hour. It's loaded with beer."

Big smiles erupted over the previously solemn faces of Kohl and Pete. Kohl couldn't help but emit an, "Awright!"

"Don't get too excited Mr. Kohl. This beer, all 64,000 cases, is for the troops of the regiment."

Kohl whistled, then said,"64,000 cases. Wahoo!"

The Colonel continued,"But there's a small problem."

I knew it. It was too good to be true.

"On the way down it rained and in the heavy seas that followed the cardboard got wet and fell apart. So what we have gentlemen, is a boat load of beer that will have to be off loaded with scoop shovels."

Kohl and Pete laughed at the idea.

The Colonel continued,"What I want you two to do is get some trucks and jeeps with trailers and meet the LCU as it arrives. It will be coming in at the pier on the river north of here. And the reason I'm having it done this way is to make sure that there is absolutely no pilfering and you two are responsible."

Isn't that like leaving the fox in charge of the chicken house?

"Lieutenant Peterson?"

"Yes, Thir?"

"What happened to your teeth?"

"Lost them."

"Humph. I want you to personally over-see this operation and make sure these trucks reach their final destination. I want you to ride in the lead truck and personally deliver its contents to Third Battalion. Lieutenant Kohl. I want you to make sure the remainder of the beer gets delivered to regimental headquarters. I have made out delivery slips that will have to be signed. I want every can of beer accounted for. Is that Clear?"

64,000 cases. That's aaah. Kohl was doing the arithmetic on his pad. A case is 24 beers times 64,000 cases is 1,536,000 beers. God, I'm in heaven.

"Lieutenant Kohl! Lieutenant Kohl!" shouted the Colonel.

Kohl came out of his reverie,"Yes, Sir."

"I'm counting on you two."

"Yes, Thir," said Pete.

"Sir, I don't understand what the big deal is if a few beers out of two million are missing?"

Pete rolled his eyes and the Colonel glared at Kohl. He said sternly, "I'll have your butt if one darn can is missing. Got that?"

"Yes, Sir," they said in unison.

When they got outside Pete punched Kohl in the arm. "You don't pay any attention to what I thay, do you?"

Kohl laughed,"Damn if you don't sound like a queer."

"Fuck you."

"I can't see what the big deal is. What's a few cans here and there?"

"A few canth here and there and we don't get there with any."

They spent the next thirty minutes rustling up trucks, trailers, and volunteers. The latter was the easiest. They drove the convoy of three six-byes and two jeeps with trailers to the landing. It was a happy occasion. When the LCU pulled slowly and cautiously up to the riverbank and dropped the ramp, the mouths of those waiting dropped too. Beer cans cascaded down the ramp. Some started floating down the river. The volunteers jumped in to save the beer. Piles of beer. Or to be more exact, a big pile of beer. The volunteers began shoveling the beer into the trucks and trailers.

Ssssss. Oh darn. One's popped. Don't waste the precious brew. Just remember to save the can.

Kohl yelled to the troops,"Just suck it from the hole. And save the can."

Funny thing. The beer cans seemed so fragile. They popped at the slightest touch of the shovel.

Kohl reminded, "Save the cans, everyone. The Colonel wants us to account for every can."

"Aye, aye, Sir," said the eager troops.

With the trucks, drivers and shovelers filled with beer, they departed the empty LCU in a flurry of yells and whoops and headed to their destinations. Trucks full of joy.

*

Kohl had to take over Pete's place at the meeting because he wasn't back yet. Kohl was having trouble staying focused because he still had a buzz on. Present were Warrant Officer Shaffer, Major Ponds, First Lieutenant Mays, Second Lieutenant Blaylock, Second Lieutenant Hockett, Captain Van Loon, Captain Hawes, and Second Lieutenant Yates, who took Lieutenant Cobain's place. Cobain was still at La Trang.

Just as the meeting was starting Doc Austin was called out on an emergency.

It was about 2200 hours when Colonel Knoach got a call. Ever since Kohl had made the arrangement with the communications chief, they very seldom had been interrupted by phone calls during the meetings This call was different.

"When?" asked the Colonel. "Uh huh. Yeah," the Colonel's tone was serious.

The officers who sat in wait knew something was wrong. The Colonel cleared his throat and said good bye and hung up the field phone. He looked at Kohl.

Oh shit. He found out about us drinking the beer.

The Colonel said, "Pete's truck hit a mine."

Kohl clutched the side of his chair for fear of falling off. He looked at Mays.

"Oh, no," moaned Mays.

"About an hour and a half ago. He had delivered the beer to battalion and was heading back."

"Is he..." stammered Kohl.

"He's alive but hurt," said the Colonel. "His driver..."

"Corporal Wiggins, Sir," said Mays. "It was Corporal Wiggins."

"Yes. Well. Corporal Wiggins is ... well he's dead."

"How bad is Pete hurt?" asked Kohl.

"His legs got it pretty bad," answered the Colonel.

Images flashed through Kohl's mind like a slide show on fast foreword. All the pictures were of Pete running, jumping and climbing. He was playing tennis, basketball, and football. The great natural beauty of his stride. The strength of his knotted and muscled legs. Pictures. Flashes of the past. Kohl got up to leave. "I've got to go," he mumbled.

"He's been medivaced to La Trang."

"I've got to go," continued Kohl.

"There's nothing you can do. Sit down." Kohl turned and glared at him. The Colonel added, "Please."

Mays reached up and grabbed Kohl's arm and guided him to his chair. Tears began to collect in the corners of his eyes.

The Colonel said, "It's too bad. Things like this happen. It's inevitable. Lieutenant Kohl you'll have to take his place as S-3 officer. The truck is a loss of course. How many does that leave us now, Lieutenant Mays?"

Kohl was dizzy. The room swirled and the Colonel's voice lost all meaning. "Trucks?" he said softly. "Trucks?" Louder. "Trucks?" Louder. "Fucking, trucks. You fucking ass hole," he screamed. "We've got one marine killed and one mutilated and you're talking about a fucking truck?" Spittle sprayed from his mouth as he rose screaming out of his chair. Mays restrained him as he headed for the Colonel, turned him, and led him outside towards the tent.

"It's not his fault, Kohl."

"Is too. He made him go because he didn't want his precious beer to get stolen. He got him killed."

"You're not making sense, Kohl. If you want to get mad at someone, get mad at the fuckin' VC."

They went to the COM tent and made frantic calls to find out about Pete's condition. Nothing. They finally got in touch with Cobain and told him that Pete was there and to find out how he was doing. Kohl and Mays went to the Officer's Club tent and drank themselves into an oblivious coma. Crying and laughing. Crying and laughing.

*

Kohl awoke at first light. Just because he had a hangover didn't keep him from his task of finding out what happened to Pete. He roused the Doc from his sleep.

"Doc. Doc." Kohl shook him gently. "Doc?" The Doc's eyes peered out from half-close eyelids.

"What?" he groaned.

"What happened to Pete, Doc? How bad is he hurt?"

"Bad."

"How bad?"

"Both legs blowed off somewhere between the knee and the hip."

"Oh, sweet Jesus. How 'bout his balls."

"Balls?"

"Yeah. His balls. You can lose your legs but if you lose your balls. Shit, man. It's over. So?"

"I don't know. I think his balls were okay."

*

I'm having a hard time following your train of thought.

It's important to have your wanger.

Pete doesn't have any legs for Christ's sake.

I know and that's bad. But not as bad as being dead.

Maybe for you but it's pretty damn important to some.

I was just thinking what it would be like living without legs. Then I was just thinking how hard it would be to live without a pecker.

I see your point. On a priority list that would be important to have your wanger. Except for one thing, Pete didn't have a choice.

Losing your legs takin' beer to the troops seems so... unimportant.. I don't get it. Do you?

*

As Kohl walked back to his tent, the sun rose in the east. The reflection on the water looked like a smooth orange peel. He picked up the bag of skin-diving gear that Krumgold left and walked down to the beach. The low tide exposed the coral reef. The shallow surf played and lapped at the edges. Kohl put on the gear and backed into the gentle waves. It felt cold but was warm compared to the ocean at Laguna. He spit on his mask and sank beneath the surface. Enclosed, surrounded, enveloped in the surreal comfort of a new world. Quiet except for his breathing through the snorkel. If there was a heaven Kohl wanted it to be like this. Coral purple and pink. Fish of all sizes and colors some flitting and darting, some floating lazily in the surging tide and moving leisurely with slight moves of the tail or fin. Colors. Sand hiding shells. Sunlight sending tentacles of beams to the glowing depths. Kohl always was surprised at the beauty. This morning wasn't any different.

Life is beautiful Pete. I'm sorry, ol buddy. It could have been me. I should have been there for you. I don't know why things happen. You are a great guy, Pete. I love you. I know you. You'll come out of this with that cocky smile of yours. I'm so sorry.

Fish florescent sides of blue strips, yellow bellies, glimmering, shimmering colors collecting, swirling, and swaying with the surge of the waves overhead. Collecting and gathering, eating, feeding together. The varieties of colorful fish were so close. The source cast a shadow on the sandy bottom. It was difficult to look up with the facemask. His snorkel hit the shadow. Kohl came to the surface. He raised his mask to his forehead. It was a body. Dead, bloated, white, purple. Fish food.

*

Kohl spent the night on top of the refrigeration truck. It was parked next to the Colonel's tent. The Colonel's tent was divided into two sections. One section was the office where he did his work and held his nightly meetings. The back section was his living quarters. Behind that was an open area that was enclosed with a six foot high tarp for privacy. It had a couple of lounge chairs and his shower. The shower was a fifty-gallon drum laid sideways on a seven-foot platform. A hose with a showerhead and a handle, when pulled would open the valve for the water. The drum was painted black so the water would be somewhat warm.

The next morning Kohl awoke as the Colonel came out to take a shower. He showered and shaved, got out and went back inside to dress. Kohl climbed carefully down so no one would see him. He went back to his tent before the others woke. The next night he did the same thing. The following morning he saw what he was looking for. As the Colonel showered he began stroking his penis with soap. With the camera Kohl bought in Hong Kong he focused his telephoto lens on the Colonel. First on his face then on his erect member. It was perfect. He adjusted the angle so he had the Colonel's face clear and his erect penis. The click of the camera was lost in the running motor of the reefer truck.

"Got you. You mutha-fucker."

Kohl took the film to Joss who was Regimental S-2. They had a dark room for film development. Underneath the soft glow of the red light the image came into view.

"The detail is beautiful. You can see his face. Look how he's biting his lip," said Joss.

Kohl got Joss to print an eight by ten black and white glossy. Late that evening after the meeting, Kohl pinned it on the bulletin board in the chow hall.

At around 1000 the next morning, Kohl saw Lieutenant Colonel Knoach climb into a Mighty Mite with his duffel bag and leave camp. Without saying a word to anyone, he was gone.

48 Fourth Down and Ten Yards to Go

It was October 24. In six days it would be Kohl's 26th birthday. He only had about 30 days left in Vietnam and this would be his last duty as airport security officer. After four months at the job he didn't have a difficult time recruiting volunteers. Even though they had to stay up most of the nights, they still could sleep and rest all day. It was better than their regular duty of 12 to 15 hour work days, six to seven days a week. They knew that Lieutenant Kohl would have football, soccer, baseball, volleyball games, and special treats when the two-week duty was over. They knew as long as they did their job at night things would go easy for them the next day. If someone was found sleeping on post or opening fire at unwarranted shadows, the next day would be spent on lectures and classes.

Kohl would spend most afternoons at the Marine Air Officer's club listening to music and reading.

Kohl became a friend with a Marine Air Supply Officer Captain Phelps. He flew C-130's from Chu Lai to Australia and back every week picking up fresh vegetables and fruit. Kohl told him this was going to be his last gig as airport security officer, he was planning on throwing a party and asked him if he could bring back some beer? Phelps said he'd see what he could do. Kohl asked Major Ponds, of Shore Party, if they could use a stretch of the beach south of the pier for their party. Shore Party had built a beach cabana out of scrap lumber and palm fronds. Mays and two drivers brought the replacement troops Sunday afternoon of November 7th. Afterwards Kohl picked up the food and ice, then stopped by airfreight, and picked up the precious cargo of beer. Swan Malt Liquor Beer. There were two jeeps and two six-by trucks loaded with supplies and happy troops. It was high tide and they drove down the beach in the soft sand. It would be low tide when they returned. They got to the Shore Party beach area by 1330. The sun was high in the sky and it was hot. It was time for Marine football.

*

"Well Billy Bob, looks like a good day for football."

"You said a mouth full there, Crotch ol' buddy."

"Looks like they've split the two teams into South Security headed by the illustrious leader Lieutenant Mays and North Security led by our fearless leader Lieutenant Kohl. One-team shirts, one team skins. A little argument over the rules, it seems. Two hand touch anywhere, four downs, everyone's eligible, the sea on the left and the beer bottles, boots and clothes on the right."

"Depends on which way your facin'."

"Yeah, Billy Bob. Well, you know what I mean. The flip of the coin and ... it's lost in the sand. Found it. Mays' team kicks and it's a boomer. Off to the right."

"Left."

"Whatever, BB. Anyway it goes into the water and it's scooped up by Corporal Heather. Ooooh."

"Got to let him up or he'll drown."

"He's up and spittin'. Well done Heather! Kohl's team's in a huddle. Sergeant Baker is drawing pictures in the sand. Break. Kohl to the right and Fallery split to the left. Short punt formation and the snap. Baker's back, Kohl's undercut and Baker's smeared. Oooo."

"I thought it was two hand touch, Crotch."

"It is. But it looks like he was touched by many hands. Huddle. More lines drawn in the sand. Second down. The snap and ... Oooo. Our fearless leader just got a forearm in the face."

"Where's Baker?"

"He's under the pile. See his foot sticking out?"

"There seems to be some concern from Mister Baker about the lack of blocking. It appears that everyone is going out for the pass and no one is blocking."

"Huddle. Third down. Baker's back and his pass is away as Kohl and Fallery run a cross pattern across the middle and ... Oooo. Damn, that must of hurt."

"Looks like Kohl and Fallery ran into each other. Baker's bullet pass hit Fallery in the ear."

"In that series they lost twenty yards. Fourth down and the punt's away. Nice high kick and Peg is signaling for a fair catch."

"There's no fair catch rule. Oooo."

"That wasn't fair either. Both Kohl and Fallery hit Peg before he got the ball. Looks like the ball bounced off Kohl's back. They appear to be arguing about the penalty. Mays is marking it off. Okay. Now it's North's turn. They huddle and break quickly. No lines drawn in the sand by quarterback Mays. They line up in a Tee formation. PFC Prichard, a big black dude, is lined up at full back. The ball is hiked to Mays. He hands off to Prichard who is running up the middle. And he falls after tripping over Lance Corporal Bebe."

"It was hard to tell who touched him first and where."

"Second down now. Another quick huddle. It's hiked to Mays who hands off to Prichard up the middle again. He's tackled by Corporal Reed.

"You see that, Crotch? That big assed Samoan nailed his black ass."

"Ten more yards. Mays is arguing with Kohl about tackling. Third down. And it looks like the same formation. Kohl's team is stacking up the middle. There goes Prichard again."

"Holy shit. Big pile of sweaty bodies."

"A lot of cussing and hollering going on. Longer huddle this time."

"It's a beer break."

"Fourth down and fifteen yards for a touchdown. Mays brings his men to the line. The snap and a pitch to Prichard around left end."

"Shooter just creamed the Lieutenant."

"Prichard stumbles and falls five yards short of the end zone. First Down for the South team. Baker's drawing more lines in the sand. Break. And the snap. Baker is back, looking, and throws."

"Who was he throwing to. Nobody there."

"Reed's got a bloody nose. He says that PFC Sloan hit him with an elbow."

"Man if I was Sloan I wouldn't want to piss Reed off."

"You said a mouth full, barley breath. Second down. The snap. Baker roles to his right and passes to Fallery. It's a diving catch. Oooo, shit."

"He hit the jeep. Is he okay? Damn, that must of hurt."

"Reed's got blood all over his face and is yelling at Sloan for hitting him in the nose again with his elbow."

"Fallery is up. Got the breath knocked out of him, looks like."

"Third down, folks. Here's the snap and Baker falls back and throws over the middle. Kohl jumps for it, catches it. Oooo."

"Did he do a flip?"

"Ten! I gave him a ten! Lieutenant Mays hit him low."

"When you do a flip, you're not supposed to land on your back. I give him a seven."

"He's not moving."

"He needs a beer!"

"He's up. Sergeant Ford is leading him back to the huddle. Last down. The snap and ... it goes way over Baker's head."

"Reed's running after Sloan."

"Look at Sloan run. The ball is just lying in the sand. Run, Sloan, run you little shit!"

"Might as well get some more beer. Reed'll never catch Sloan. If he catches him, he'll drowned the little fucker in the ocean."

"What are they doing now?"

"Looks like Sloan has stopped. They're talking. Oh, this is interesting. Sloan is letting Reed take a shot at him."

"He's crazy."

"Damn. You see that?"

"Yeah. Reed nailed him. Jesus. Sloan's getting up. And they're coming back. They're laughing. Arm and arm."

The game continued until Mays faked a hand off to Prichard and bootlegged it around right end. Reed tackled Mays and was quickly followed by five other bodies. The ball popped out of Mays sweaty hands and Kohl caught it in mid air and began running for the only touchdown of the game. Kohl zigzagged down to the waters edge for better footing. PFC Pieffer cut Kohl off and as Kohl turned to his right back up into the soft sand Private Peg and Corporal Shooter tackled him followed by a pile of sweaty bodies. There was a poof of exploding air from the football. That was the end of the game. There were bloody noses, fat lips, one dislocated finger, a hyper-extended knee, a sprained ankle, one arm bite, scratches, and abrasions. The fraternity of Marines laughed and backslapped their way to the cabana and the cold Swan Malt Liquor beer.

*

At dusk they started a fire. One of the troops, a Corporal named Lorren Cummings, played his guitar, and led singing around the fire

"Lieutenant?" said Cummings. "I wrote a song called "Marine" that I'd like to sing if it's okay."

"Sure. Go ahead," said Kohl. The others nodded in agreement.

Cummings, was a dark haired, good looking young man from Missouri. He strummed his guitar and his tenor voice rose above the lapping waves.

*

Now I'm going to tell a story
so sad as it may seem.
It's a story about the life of a Marine.
Everything I tell you is original and true.
So listen up real close and I'll tell it to you.

You can have your Army khaki.
You can have your Navy blue.
But here's another uniform I'll introduce to you.

This uniform is different.
The finest ever seen.
The Germans call them Devil Dogs.
The name is just
Marine, Marine.

They train them in Diego.
The land that God forgot.
Where mountains are high and rivers dry,
and the sun is blazing hot.

He's peeled a million onions,
and twice as many spuds.
And when he gets a little time,
he washes out his duds.
Marine, Marine.

Now girls I've got a little tip
That I'll pass along to you.
Just get yourself a good Marine
There's nothing he can't do.

And when he gets to heaven
Saint Peter he will tell.
Another Marine reporting, Sir,
I've served my time in hell.
Marine, Marine.

Now the moral of my story is
Very plain to see.
That to be in our Corps
A real man you must be.

So before you leave your home
And everyone you love.
You'd better think it over
Pray for guidance from above.
Marine, Marine.

*

As night drew on, the drunken men staggered back to the trucks for the ride back to camp.

Kohl, Mays, and Ford stayed behind while the two six-bys weaved there way north up the beach. They had stayed behind to pick up the cans and trash, but much to their wandering eyes did appear an unopened case of Swan Malt Liquor Beer. They sat around the fire and drank much of the remaining beer. Ford, not being much of a drinker, stopped after just a couple. The talk was mellow and melancholy. They talked about Pete. The night was calm. They could hear the gentle lapping of the waves on the shore. The night sky was filled with stars but was moonless and very dark.

"You may be short, Mays but you ride high in the saddle," said the drunken Kohl.

"What the hell does that mean?" slurred Mays.

"It means you're one hell of a guy. That's what. Even if you tried to kill me in Basic school with a pugile stick and even if you tried to break my neck in the Philippines playing basketball and today you submarined my ass and almost broke my back. Even after all that you're my bud."

"Jesus Kohl, you're not going to try and butt fuck me, are you?"

Kohl and Mays laughed and leaned on each other for support and climbed into the Mighty Mite Jeep. Ford was sober enough to drive. He said that the sea breeze blowing in his face would sober him up. The blowing breeze he was referring to was because the front window of the jeep was lying flat on the hood so as not to reflect light. Also, they would be driving without lights, which was SOP for night driving. The drive back wouldn't be difficult. The beach was flat and straight. It was low tide so the sand was hard. They would drive north until they reached the floating pier and then take the road back to camp.

Kohl climbed into the back and Mays took the front seat. It wasn't long after they left the Shore Party beach cabana that Kohl passed out in the back seat.

*

He heard the sound of waves rolling into a curl and falling onto themselves. The sea gulls were calling to each other as they circled over head. Warmth from the early morning sun began to creep up his body. His legs were cramped, so he tried to stretch out, but his foot hit something hard. From the sounds he heard he thought he was lying on a sandy beach. Encroaching on the consciousness of his drunken mind, he heard sounds that didn't fit. It was a droning hum. Something was tickling his face. Flies. He brought up a cramped arm to brush the fly away and his hand hit something ... wet. He rubbed his face. The smell. It was familiar. Again he tried to stretch his cramped legs and couldn't. They kept hitting something that wouldn't move. The hum. The flies. The smell.

Kohl's discomfort brought a groan through his dry, cracked lips. He thought he heard voices but they appeared to be somewhere in the distance. He cracked one crusty eye open. Just enough to let in too much light and he quickly closed it. The voices were getting closer. He recognized the hum of a running motor. As his mind began its awakening from a dreamy drunken fog, he realized he was probably still in the Jeep. He felt the sun's warmth on his left shoulder. The voices were becoming more distinct and getting louder and closer.

"Oh, shit," Kohl said softly. His voice cracked. *I'm going to have to open my eyes. Then sit up.*

The sun's brilliance blinded Kohl's second attempt at opening his eyes. His vision was blurred and unfocused but focusing. Objects began to take form. Voices began to have meaning. The droning sound was from the jeep motor and he could tell that the back wheels were spinning helplessly in the sand. Images began to swirl and blur. Red, black and crimson stalactites hung in front of his face. Flies buzzing, landing on his face, flittering in front of his eyes. A familiar smell was causing his stomach to convulse. He began to focus on the image just inches in front of his face. The face, upside down, hanging by white cords of sinew and black torn muscle, eyes bulging, tongue blue gray and swollen hanging stiffly, flies filled the cavities and roamed the exposed surfaces. Mays.

Kohl's scream cracked the early morning air like jagged edged glass, braking the silence of early morning waves lapping at the pristine shoreline. The scream ended and with a ragged gasp of inhaling air, he exploded into another scream again and again. He felt hands holding him, lifting, carrying. Sounds, ear piercing like A-4's on take offs, screams filled the mind, spilling from dry swollen lips, choking, gagging, disappearing into moans and groans that ache in whimpers of despair.

It's a dream Kohl. Wake up. Wake up.

It's not a dream. I saw Mays' severed head lying upside down staring at me. It was real.

Kohl heard the frantic voices but he couldn't understand what they were saying because of the screaming.

"Jesus, fuckin' Christ!"

"This is horrible."

"They must have hit the pier cables, Major."

"Yeah. At low tide those cables are suspended out of the water about six feet. They must have ran into it last night."

"Both the driver and that other guy were decapitated.

"Where's the driver's head?"

"Isn't that it rolling at the edge of the surf?"

"Lucky for that guy who was asleep in the back."

"Yeah. Lucky."

*

It is a dream. A beautiful dream. Flowers are every where. Children are laughing and women are singing, their songs fill the air. It is a dream. Yes, a dream. Beautiful lights fill the night. The guns are flashing and rockets drop red flares, casting blood shadows on the fight. It is a dream. A beautiful dream. The rice paddies are green and the skies are blue. Bodies are everywhere. Some are standing, some are sitting, some are lying on the ground with eyes widened in a casting stare. It is a dream. A beautiful dream. Of thoughts of home. Lights are flashing and waves are lapping on the shore as heads stick from the foam. It is a dream. This dream, like most dreams is not real. But the dreamer doesn't know.

*

"Hello. Hello. Hellllooooo."

"How much of that sedative did you give him."

"A lot."

*

Black. Everything was black. Kohl's clouded thought was that he was like the soldier in the book "Johnny Get Your Gun." He couldn't see. He thought that maybe he was blind. He had tried to move his right arm to his face to scratch an itch but it wouldn't move. Then he tried to move his fingers. He thought they moved but he couldn't tell. His heart was pounding so fast he thought his chest would explode. *Thank God I can feel the sheet with my fingers. I have feeling.* He tried to move his legs and found he couldn't. *I'm paralyzed.* He started crying.

"Take that thing off his face," said an angry voice.

Light! I can see.

Kohl could make out the forms as their busy hands removed a strap that was holding his head down. Kohl lifted his head and as his eyes became adjusted to the light he could see the straps that were holding his chest, arms and legs to the bed.

"Where am I?" he croaked.

*

Dear Julie,

First of all, I want to apologize for not writing. I have an excuse. I've been gone for the last week. I've been in a hospital in La Trang. I'm all right. There's nothing physically wrong with me. There was an accident. It happened about five days ago. Paul Mays was killed along with Sergeant Ford and I was with them, but I'm okay. It was just one of those crazy things that happen. It didn't have anything to do with the War. But I did spend some time in the hospital. Again it wasn't anything physical. It was just that I had a hard time. I kind of lost it for a while. The shock of losing Paul and Ford kind of did a number in my head. I just wanted to let you know that I'm back with my Unit and that everything is okay.

Love,

Dusty

*

Yeah, everything is okay.

49 *The Last Detail*

Kohl was sitting in the chair while Colonel Wellington was leaning against his desk drinking coffee. The Colonel said, "This is really hard for me."

"Have I been extended, Colonel?" Kohl interrupted.

"No, that's not it. Regiment has asked for you to take Joss's place to supervise the POW camp and interrogation of the prisoners."

"What happened to Joss?"

"A VC POW stabbed him with a pencil. The little son-bitch shoved that pencil through his eye into his brain. He'll lose his eye but they don't think he has any brain damage. They don't know for sure yet."

"What was the VC doing with a sharp pencil?"

"He was showing Joss where the VC locations were on the map and when Joss leaned over he stabbed him."

"When did this happen?"

"Last night."

"Colonel, I've only got six days left. Why me?"

"You're the only one here that has gone to POW interrogation school, plus with your experience in the field... well?"

"Isn't there any way I can get outa this?"

"I'm aware of your situation, Kohl and I brought this matter up to Major Phillips. You're it. He did convey to me that this was going to be rear eschlon stuff. Two days at the most."

Tell that to Joss. Fuck.

Kohl rode the jeep out to the staging area where three Hueys were waiting to take him and another rifle platoon out to where a Marine company was conducting a sweep south of Chu Lai.

*

The three Hueys were circling high over an area where the rifle company was conducting a sweep. Kohl could see puffs of smoke rising from the thick vegetation of the hills. He leaned over and grabbed the gunner's arm to get his attention.

"What's happening?"

"They want us to hold. May need us to fly a mission." The gunner turned his head away from the wind so he could catch what was being said over his head set. "Strap in, Lieutenant. We are going down for a look-see."

The Huey dropped. Kohl didn't know that choppers could fall like that. His stomach was in his throat. On the roller coaster at Long Beach the drop was nothing like this. As the ground rushed toward the falling chopper, the pilot flared and the Huey zoomed over treetops. Kohl had heard how frightening the Hueys were to the VC. They couldn't hear them until the Hueys were right on top of them with their M-60's blazing and rockets firing.

Kohl was sitting on his flack jacket when a bullet ripped through the floor. He lifted up his feet.

Boy is that stupid. What good is it to lift your feet?

Kohl heard the bullet ping around the inside of the chopper. It fell into Kohl's helmet that he had sitting on his lap. The chunk of lead rolled to a stop. Kohl looked at it, and then he looked at the other men in the chopper.

"Looks like the VC left you a little present, there, Lieutenant," said the Sergeant sitting across from him.

Kohl heard a thunk. The chopper rocked back and forth twice. There was a crunch of mettle grinding. The gunner yelled from his perch in the window, "We're going down! Brace yourselves!"

Six days. The Marine Corps is going to get me killed yet.

The gunner was spraying the tree line to the west with his 60 caliber. Copper casing clattered to the floor. "Here comes!" the gunner yelled.

The chopper seemed to be flying all right. As they got closer to the ground, Kohl could see the rice paddy below. He heard bullets hitting the chopper. Kohl saw the front window blow apart then the chopper fell about twenty feet, it dropped like a rock into the rice paddy.

The jolt clattered his teeth. He put on his helmet and unbuckled his seat belt and bailed. He scrambled to his feet and sprinted about twenty-five yards in a crouch and dove to the ground.

Kohl lay flat on his stomach in the rice field. His face was turned to his left with his arms over his helmet. His eyes were closed. He was breathing hard and his heart felt like it was about to explode out of his chest.

Afraid?

Hell, yes. I'm fuckin petrified.

He heard the zing and zip of bullets whizzing through the grass and an occasional ping, a tink as rounds hit the chopper. The chopper blades had stopped. He heard the chatter of automatic rifle and machine gun fire from the tree-line. He opened his left eye first then his right. His saw what looked like a squirrel about four feet away. It's big brown eyes showed fear too. Must be a mongoose. Its body was flat along the ground much in the same way that Kohl was. It sniffed the air.

Hey, there ol' buddy. What's happenin'? Looks like we're in a bit of a pickle here. Zip. Zip. *I guess I kinda stumbled into your abode. Sorry about that. I guess you live around here someplace. If I were you I'd find that hole and climb in till this is over.* The mongoose looked to his left then back at Kohl. *Hear something?* Ping, ping, ping. *Do you know what's going on? Hell if I do.* Zip. *Damn that was close. Shit! Did you see that? Do you want to be a Communist? You don't care do you? As long as you have snakes to eat, you don't give a shit, do you? I'm here to save your ass, you know.* The mongoose inched a foot closer to Kohl, lifted its head, and sniffed again. *I'm your friend. You can trust me.* Whiz. Thunk. Kohl heard a grunt. *That one might have got someone.* The mongoose inched closer and stretched its neck out and sniffed again. Kohl unfurled his left arm slowly and lay his hand palm up in front of the mongoose. *Are we going to win this war?* Zip. Zip. Zip. I*'ve got my trusty ol' forty-five. Could kill bunches if they get close enough. Do you have a little family of Mongooses or is it Mongoosie? Ever think of dying?* The Mongoose turned his head and sniffed, then inched closer and touched Kohl's finger with his cold nose. Kohl smiled. Zip. Zing. *Friends?* The Mongoose rose to its haunches, rotated its head to the left and right, then a splat and a shower of bone, fur, and blood. The Mongoose was gone.

Kohl felt something hit his foot. He looked down and saw the Sergeant lying at his feet.

"Hey, Lieutenant. I got ahold of ... What's that stuff all over you?"

"A Mongoose. I think. Or what's left of it. Just got blowed to shit."

Zing. Zip. Zip.

The Sarge ducked.

"You know what they say Sarge? You don't hear the shot that killed you."

"Yeah," he said distracted. "I got a hold of air support and A-4's are on the way. Once you hear them come and drop the napalm, get up and run for that tree line over there. Got it?"

"Got it." *Two hundred yards is a hell of a long ways to run in a hail of bullets.*

The Sergeant crawled off.

Above the clatter of the automatic weapons he heard the faint song of the approaching Marine Skyhawks. *Damn those guys are good. When they say close air support the Marine pilots can kiss your ass they are so close.* They were becoming louder and soon became an earth-shaking scream as they flew over head and dropped napalm on the tree line. The fire from the napalm sucked the air from his lungs. It pulled the surrounding air into the fiery ball.

Kohl got up and started to run then stopped. He noticed something move out of the corner of his eye. The gunner was hanging out of the chopper hatch.

Don't leave your dead. Don't leave your wounded.

React don't act. Seconds of indecision costs lives.

Kohl glanced back at the retreating Marines as they ran for cover across the rice paddy to the line of trees. Kohl heard a whoosh, and then a splash of dirt and a Marine doing a cartwheel flip to one side. Something tugged at his pant leg. He looked down and a crimson spot began to spread on his lower pant leg. He didn't feel anything.

Run you crazy son-of-bitch! Run!

I saw something move.

The only thing that should be moving is you. Now get the fuck outa here.

Kohl ran back to the chopper. *The wrong way, you dumb fucker.* He couldn't understand how the VC could be alive and firing after being hit by that big fireball. He lifted the head and shoulders of the gunner. The gunner let out a soft, "Oh."

God, he's big. Remember the time you killed that deer. You pulled him up on a stump and rolled him off onto your shoulders? Remember what happened? Pinned your scrawny ass to the ground, it did.

Kohl put him into a fireman's carry and began the long walk to the tree line. Running was out of the question. The gunner was close to two hundred pounds of dead weight. The Marines in the tree line must have seen what he was doing because they laid down a massive field of fire. Kohl could still hear the splats of bullets hitting the dirt around him. Kohl's legs wobbled and his breath became labored. Pain was spreading though out his body. He stumbled but regained his balance.

Remember the big bear that jumps on your back in the quarter mile.

Yeah.

You got the bear, baby. You got the bear.

The two hundred yards to the tree line was too far. He wasn't going to be able to make it. He heard a splat; a whimper came from the gunner. The impact spun Kohl in a half circle but he didn't lose his grip or his balance. His muscles screamed. He was fifty yards from the tree line when four Marines exploded from the dense cover and ran to Kohl. They took the gunner from Kohl's shoulders then he collapsed in a heap. Two carried the gunner and the other two help Kohl to his feet and drug him to cover. The Sergeant came and kneeled down beside the gasping Kohl.

"The pilot's still there, Sarg," rasped Kohl.

"I know. We're not going anywhere. We've got Second Platoon of Charlie Company coming in and some gun ships for support. Then we'll kick some gook ass."

"How's the gunner?" Asked Kohl.

"Doc's with him. Saved his ass, Lieutenant." The Sergeant pulled out his canteen and Kohl gulped down the liquid. "Your pant leg is covered with blood. Yours?"

"I think so," said Kohl.

The Sergeant pulled up Kohl's pant leg carefully, revealing a bloody calf muscle. In the middle of the muscle was a dark red round entrance hole and on the other side was the exit hole. "Looks like it went clean through, Lieutenant. I'll get the Doc over here to dress it up."

Kohl could never recall all of what happened next. He didn't know exactly what he did. He only recalled glimpses, like fleeting shadows images appeared and then were gone. He heard a voice that kept saying, "Don't leave your dead. Don't leave your wounded." It was like watching a movie as he ran back to the downed chopper. The Sergeant and his men followed the lieutenant, retrieved the dead pilot and wounded copilot and returned to the tree line. Then they returned under an onslaught of enemy fire to retrieve the two downed Marines in the rice field. Kohl could only recall flashes. It was as though he was outside himself. He recalled the sound of the M-60 as he fired it into the tree line where the VC were located. The mental lapses were lost, short circuited, sent to a black vault in the recesses of his mind to bubble stagnantly to the surface when he was asleep, when his mind was left unguarded and exposed.

*

Second Platoon arrived and under the firepower of the Hueys they were able to clear the VC from the hills to the west. The choppers came in to take the dead and wounded back to Regiment. The last chopper took Kohl on to Base Camp where Major Phillips met him.

Kohl's calf muscle was sore now and he walked with a limp. "Sorry about your trouble, Kohl."

"Me too."

"Hurt?"

"Got shot in the leg. It stiffened up on me. It'll be okay. Where's the prisoner compound?"

The Major pointed to an area that was surrounded by triple concertina wire. Inside were approximately twenty VC suspects squatting on their haunches. "We have to watch the ARVNS, Kohl. The rules of the Geneva Convention don't mean shit to them. We're warriors, Kohl not animals."

Kohl had learned in POW and Interrogation School that the Americans got far better results from treating prisoners with dignity and respect than through threats and torture.

"What do you want me to do, Major?" asked Kohl.

"See that hooch over there?" Kohl nodded. "That's where the ARVN Captain Vu Tri is interrogating the prisoners. Just keep an eye on him."

"Aye, Aye, Sir."

Kohl watched the Captain all afternoon without incident. The next morning the Major told Kohl that a Second Lieutenant was coming in to replace him and that he could leave on the same chopper.

Kohl greeted the Lieutenant as he came in.

"Hello and Goodbye, Lieutenant. I'm going the fuck home."

To Kohl's surprise on the chopper with him were the ARVN Captain and two VC prisoners with hoods over their heads. He suspected the Captain was going to take them to the Regimental POW compound. The Chopper lifted off the pad, banked a hard left, and climbed in a circle above the sniper fire. As the chopper leveled out and headed northeast the ARVN Captain took the hood off one of the prisoners and started yelling at him. Kohl couldn't understand what he was saying but he could see that the VC was crying and scared. Kohl had seen them act that way before and he thought it was mostly for show. They weren't usually scared and didn't seem to care if they died. Then to Kohl's horror the Captain shoved the shackled and handcuffed prisoner out the hatch. Kohl heard him scream. The ARVN glared at Kohl. Kohl knew his mouth was still open in surprise. Then the Captain took the hood off the remaining prisoner and started yelling at him.

"No!" yelled Kohl above the roar of engine and wind.

"He will talk," answered the Captain.

The captive was crying and begging as the Captain began dragging the prisoner to the hatch.

"No!" yelled Kohl. "You can't do that."

The Captain looked up at Kohl and moved the prisoner closer to the hatch. The noise was deafening. The screams of the prisoner mingled with the screaming engine and whistling wind through the hatch. In a sudden explosion, Kohl threw himself at the smaller Vietnamese Captain. The Captain saw the charge and brought his knee up into Kohl's groin. Kohl groaned in pain as the Captain rolled to his hands and knees. Kohl leaped on top of him, grabbed him in a cross face with his right arm, and broke him down flat on his stomach. When the Captain tried to push himself up with his arms, Kohl caught his left arm in a chicken wing and brought it high on his back. The Captain screamed in pain. The prisoner scurried on his hands and knees to the back corner of the hold and cowered in the corner with wild eyes. Kohl held the Captain down until they had reached the ground. Then he let him up. The glare that the ARVN Captain gave Kohl was seething with hate.

"You Americans can't help us. You have nothing to lose."

The Captain turned and led the prisoner off to the POW Compound. Kohl turned and started walking back to the terminal.

"Hey, Lieutenant!" shouted the Captain. "Look!"

The Captain grabbed the sleeve of the prisoner and spun him around, pulled his pistol from his holster and shot the man in the face. Kohl saw the back of the prisoner's head explode. He folded onto the tarmac. The Captain smiled, turned, and walked off.

*

Kohl went to the base hospital tent and got his wound dressed and cleaned. His leg had stiffened considerably. It was sore and swollen.

When he got back to his unit he was met by Sergeant Major Jurgens. He took Kohl's hand and shook it.

"Well, Lieutenant. It's official. You'll be leaving God's country the 26th. *Two days and a sleepover.* You'll fly from here to Danang, then from Danang to Okinawa and then you should be home some time around the 30th." *Home.*

Colonel Wellington came out of the headquarters tent when he saw that Kohl was talking with the Sergeant Major. "I heard about what happened. I'm sorry. If something would have happened to you I never would have forgiven myself."

"It almost did. While I was out there all hell broke lose. Got shot in the friggen leg." Kohl told him about what happened.

Kohl went back to his tent and packed his gear. There were two new Lieutenants there. He didn't know their names. He gave all but one pair of his salty utilities to Blaylock. A storm was coming. Clouds were being pushed by blustery winds off the highlands. He went to the club. The rain beat heavily on the canvas tent roof then rolled off in a solid sheet of water. One by one they all said their and good-byes and then Sergeant Brisco gave Kohl his bar bill. He had had over ninety drinks on the tab for a total of $14.90. Then the Sergeant wrote, "Last night in Chu Lai, Vietnam and the Officer's Club 'the Panji Pit'. Bill paid in full."

Kohl walked alone back to his tent. His three tent mates were asleep. He took off his wet cloths and lay down. He felt a thump on his head followed by a stream of water. The bar of soap that he had put in the hole above his head when he first got to Chu Lai had fallen out. He moved his cot and tried to sleep but he was too excited about leaving tomorrow.

*

The next morning Kohl said goodbye to Corporal McTagert, and Demos, Sergeants Olson, White, Hedrick, and Flynn who had helped him stay out of trouble. On his way to the airbase he had Lance Corporal Pieffer take him down by the pier. He knelt in the sand and looked out to the black clouds covering the sea and said his good-bye to Mays and Ford.

*

The GV from Danang was supposed to arrive around noon, it didn't arrive until 1900. As it got darker Kohl was becoming very concerned that he would miss his plane out of Danang. He boarded two hours later and he lifted off the sands of Chu Lai, the first leg of his trip home. Danang seemed far to the north but the ride only took fifteen minutes. By the time Kohl checked into Danang Transit it was almost midnight. The Staff Sergeant informed Kohl that because of Typhoon Cock all flights from Danang and Okinawa had been cancelled, plus the sergeant handed Kohl a list of 22 Marines that he was in charge of for the trip to Okinawa. Kohl looked up one of his buddies from Pendleton and slept in his tent for the night.

*

The next day after breakfast, Kohl spent the day reading and drinking beer. At about 1300 hours Captain Smith jogged up to Kohl and told him his plane was leaving in 30 minutes and to rustle up his 22 Marines for the flight to Okinawa. His buddy from Pendleton found a jeep in salvage that ran and took him to Danang Transit. It was another GV and with engines still running from its earlier landing. They loaded up. Kohl was short 4 men but they left without them.

When Kohl got to Okinawa the first thing he did was go to Sukran to take a long hot shower, the first one since July. He tried to call Julie but he couldn't get through. He went over to Camp Hanson and tried the Ham Radio but the storm interference was disrupting reception. Kohl ended up sending a telegram that told her he would be flying into Travis Air Force Base in Fairfield. He didn't know the day or the time yet.

*

It was 1600 hours on the 29th of November when Kohl was informed his plane was going to leave Kadena Air Force Base in thirty minutes. Kohl hailed a cab and rushed to the airport. The turbo propped C-130 left two hours later for Travis Air Force Base with a short stop in Japan. Kohl thought he could call Julie in Japan and tell her of the change of destination.

When they landed in Japan the pilot told the twenty or so passengers they would have a three-hour layover. Kohl went to the Officer's Club, and had dinner plus a few drinks to calm his nerves. While he was there he heard some Air Force officers talking about flying to Vietnam, Okinawa and Japan from the states. They were reservists doing their weekend duty. Kohl eventually recognized one of the officers as his pilot. He was drinking, and they aren't supposed to drink within twenty-four hours of flying. It was then he realized his plane wasn't going to leave in three hours; they were in the process of making plans to check out the local bordellos.

Kohl went back to the terminal and asked about his plane. One of the dispatchers told him that his plane had developed some mechanical problems and wouldn't have it fixed until sometime tomorrow. Then he gave Kohl a wink.

"Look, man. I don't give a fuckin' rat's ass if I have to fly the fuckin' plane myself. I'm fuckin' goin' home... now!"

"I'm sorry, Lieutenant. That's the only one going... unless?"

"Unless, what?"

"Unless you want to go to Toro."

"Man, that's where I wanted to go in the first place."

"Well, it's loading up now. We have some guys on emergency leave going too. Where are your things?"

"Still on the other plane."

"All that stuff is tied down and we can't get to it."

"I don't care. Just get me the fuck outa here."

He called Julie and was able to get through and told her that he would be at Toro about nine in the morning.

The plane was another C-130. To Kohl it seemed like a snail was making it's way across the Pacific.

The approach into Toro was much like the early morning gray fog of San Francisco. The plane was making its final approach into Toro. Kohl's heart was pounding with anticipation. The wheels skidded onto the runway, the prop's reversed and slowed the C-130 into a turn and then the approach to the terminal. He peered from the window to see. *Where is she? Did I tell her the right time?* The plane came to a stop and Kohl and the passengers began to deplane. He walked down the steps. He looked at his watch. It was 7:15. *No wonder she's not here. We're almost two hours early.* He picked up the two bags he had. He could pick up the rest of his stuff in Travis anytime, he thought. He didn't care. He was home.

Kohl hobbled into the Transport Office and got his orders stamped and new orders were given. His leg had stiffened up from the long plane ride.

"War wound, Lieutenant?" said the Lance Corporal clerk.

"Yeah."

"Sliding into second, eh, Lieutenant?" he said with a grin.

"Fuck you, asshole." The angry comment surprised Kohl as much as it did the Lance Corporal. In all his years in the Marine Corps he had never talked to an enlisted man in that manner. He was going to apologize but...

"Gee, Sorry," the Lance Corporal said but his voice dripped in sarcasm.

People came by two and threes, shadows from the walls appearing, clutching the young men who came home on emergency leave for those sick, dying or dead. There was no joy, no streaming banners, no crowds waving.

Kohl limped down the long empty corridor. Klump, klump, klump. Toward the bank of telephones. He lifted the receiver off the hook, listened for the dial tone, took some change out of his pocket and placed it on the small counter. When he tried to put a dime into the slot his hand was trembling so bad he dropped the coin. When he bent over to retrieve it he noticed that along the wall to his right was a row of benches. On one of the benches he saw a girl lying down. He could only see the top of the girl's blond hair. It was familiar. Kohl's already anxious heart was pounding even faster. He walked silently to the sleeping girl and looked. He swallowed the choking constriction in his throat. It was Julie. She was asleep, lying on her side facing him. *Oh, Julie. My baby. How beautiful you are.*

Kohl sat slowly down on the floor and crossed his arms on the bench seat in the curve left by his sleeping wife. He laid his weary head in his arms and looked. He traced every feature with his eyes as if it were the first time. The way her hair hung loosely over her forehead and how her long eyelashes embraced themselves. He saw her closed eyes dart in a dream: the slight upturned curve of her nose. The lips were full. Even without lipstick they were flush and revealed a slight smile. Her chin was tucked next to her clasped hands as if in prayer. Her breath came long and easy as he watched her breast rise and fall under the white Cashmere sweater.

I'm home. I'm finally home.

Kohl sighed. The air escaped as if confined from a compressed chamber. A year of controlled emotion seeped from his body. Deflated and weeping, it vacated and flowed free like rivulets of blood, taking with it the stamina, the will to survive, the anger, the fear, the excitement, the uncertainty. There was a gaping hole; a cavity remaining in his heart for what was left behind. It had been four days since he was extracted from the jungle, pulled like a pin from a grenade. It came pouring out. He could smell it. It was in his pours and broke free with the sweat. He could still hear the gunfire. He could hear the cries for help. His eyes grew wild as he gasp for air in panic. *Show no fear for fear is contagious.* He took another deep breath. He had realized that he had been holding his breath. His frightened eyes stared at the peaceful beauty. He felt if he looked away she might disappear.

What if?

Don't do that.

If I had been thirty seconds earlier down the hill. If I hadn't returned for my poncho that little girl would have blown me to bits. Thirty seconds. If my replacements would have been a week later, it might have been me they stuffed into a body bag instead of Lieutenant Fortney. And when that dud granade rolled against my leg, I thought my legs would be shredded meat. What kind of shit is that? It could have been me on that truck instead of Pete. I could be coming home with my legs still in some Vietnam rice paddy. I could have been sitting in the front seat instead of Mays. In that case it would have been over. It could have been the end. If just one of those bullets that was whizzing around me four days ago, if... son-of-a-bitch. Son-of-a-bitch, man, fuck.

Was it luck?

All this time Kohl had felt unlucky. He recalled how a year ago he complained about his plight on the plane to Okinawa. Now he felt how insignificant, how unimportant, how self centered those complaints were. He was alive and home. Now he had to live up to something more than the fulfillment of his own destiny, he had to live the lost dreams of Mays and Pete. *What was it that Pastor O'Riely told me? That I had to find my purpose. Could that be my purpose? That it was up to me to live, to come back alive, to live for all those who wouldn't be coming back? It's my purpose.*

He shouldered the pride of being a Marine. He would always be a Marine. He was proud to serve his country, to do his duty, to fulfill the honor for those who paid the ultimate price. Kohl regretted he couldn't have done more, to have made a difference.

I'm here. I'm back.

On the outside nothing had changed. Kohl had been swept from the jungle as though by magic in a flying machine and into Tustin, California in just a matter of hours.

Click your heels, Kohl.

The radio said, "A little fog on the first day of December but will burn off by early afternoon."

People will walk around shopping for Christmas. They will drive to work and take the kids to school.

Hello, everybody. I'm home. Did you know there was a war going on?

They don't seem to care? They don't understand. It was over there. It doesn't matter.

It has to. If it doesn't matter then, why? We are Americans. It has to matter.

Kohl raised his head and looked at his hands. They looked thin as he held them out. They trembled slightly.

I'm the same, aren't I?

Not a chance, Kohl. You are not the same person you were when you left. And that doesn't mean the change is bad. You realize now how precious life is. You realize how important your friends and family are. You know how lucky you are to be alive. You know how lucky you are to be an American. But the bad thing is at night the dreams will come. In moments of solitude when your curtain comes down, you will feel the fear creep out of dark corners of your mind and with its tentacles pull you into the abyss. You are doomed to carry the shadows of this past year for the rest of your life.

But I lived. I survived.

Yes, Kohl. You did live. You're home now. But nobody survived... not even you.

Kohl felt the tension expel from his soul. He saw the same vile demons running along side snarling and growling, "Fresh meat, fresh meat." He was tired. Not relaxed or sleepy, but totally exhausted and spent. Kohl's mind whirled in confusion. *This wasn't supposed to be. Where are the banners and waving flags? 'Where are the cheering crowds?* Images flickered across the kaleidoscope of his vision. He saw flashes in the dark and became consumed by fear. He looked away from Julie but quickly looked back for fear that raged through him was like a firestorm leaping up canyon walls. It could not be contained.

You can show it now. Let down your guard.

The fear? I can? My men won't know?

You're safe now. You can let it go and be free of its gripping talons. You can let it out now. You don't have to be afraid any more. You have a life to live.

What if this is a dream, a trick?

It's not a dream, Kohl. Close the door. It's best that you don't look back. You'll be safe now. You're home. You don't need me any more.

"I'm sorry," Kohl said softly. "I'm so sorry." Heavy coarse sobs of sorrow, relief, despair, and guilt escaped his trembling lips and cries tumbled from his heaving shoulders... then he felt a gentle hand caress his fallen head.

GLOSSARY

Aboard- On Base or on ship. To be welcomed aboard.
Adjedent- S-1. Personnell officer
Afloat- Deployment of Marines onboard ships
Ammo- Ammunition
Ammo Dump- A place where ammunition is kept.
Amtrak- Amphibious tracker, a landing craft with tracks, called the iron coffin.
AOR- Area of responsibility
Article 15- Summary discipline judgement of a Marine by his CO may result in fine and confinement.
ARVN- Army of the Republic of Vietnam (South Vietnam)
Banana Clip- Sub machine gun ammunition clip.
Base Camp- A resupply base for field units and a location for headquarters.
Basic School- A Military School in Quantico, Virginia for Officers.
Berm- A raised mound.
Billet- Assignment or job. Place of residence.
Binjo Ditch- Open sewer.
Bird- Aircraft
Blues- Dress blues
Body Bag- Plastic black bag used for dead bodies.
Body Count- The number of enemy killed, wounded, or captured during an operation. A means used to measure the progress/success of the War.
Booby Trap- An explosive charge hidden so a soldier will hit, step on or trip it.
Boonies- Also called boondocks, the woods or jungle.
Boot- Recruit or a trooper that has just got out of boots camp.
BOQ- Bachelor Officer's Quarters
Bouncing Betty- An explosive that propels upward about 3 to 4 feet then explodes.
Bow- Front of ship.
Brass- Officers
Brig- Jail
Bronze Star- US military decoration awarded for heroic or meritorious service.
Brown Bar- Second Lieutenant.

Buck Sergeant- E-5 Sergeant
Bulkhead- Wall
Bush- The Jungle
C-123- Caribou. Small cargo plane with an open hatch in the rear.
C-130- Hercules. Turbo prop cargo and troop transport plane with an open hatch in the rear.
CP- Command Post
Camp Pendleton- Marine Corps Base in California. Home of the 1st Marine Division.
Carbine- Short-barreled, lightweight rifle used by the Viet Cong and North Vietnamese Regulars.
Caribou- C-123. Small cargo plane.
Charlie- Viet Cong
Chopper- Helicopter
Chow- Meal or mess
Chow Hall- A place where meals are served.
Click- One notch of adjustment on a rifle.
Cluster Fuck- Any attempted operation that went bad. Disorganized.
CO- Commanding Officer
Code of Conduct- Military rules for US soldiers are to live by when taken prisoner. Rules were written as a result of prisoner behavior during the Korean War.
COM- Communications
Compound- A fortified military installation.
Concertina Wire- Coiled barbed wire used as an obstacle.
Contact- Making an engagement with the enemy.
Corps- Short for Marine Corps
Corpsman- Navy Medic serves with Marine rifle platoons.
Cover- Hat
Coxswain- What the driver of a boat is called.
CP- Command Post
C-rats- Short for C-rations. An individual meal containing, can of fruit, dessert, powdered coca, cigarettes, toilet paper, coffee, crackers and gum.
Crotch, the- The Corps
Cruise- Period of enlistment or tour of duty.
Deck- Floor
DMZ- Demilitarized Zone
Doc- Navy Medical Officer usually a Navy Lieutenant. The same as a Marine Corps Captain, or Navy Medic.

Dung Lai- Vietnamese for Halt.
Early Out- Being released from active duty because of an emergency.
Ensign- Navy Officer. Same as Marine Second Lieutenant.
Entrenching Tool- Small shovel used for digging foxholes.
Extended- When a tour or enlistment is moved to a later date.
Fantail- Rear end of ship.
Fatigues- Standard combat uniform (green).
Field of Fire- An area a weapon(s) can cover.
Flack Jacket- A heavy fiberglass filled vest worn for protection from shrapnel.
Flare- Illumination grenade or projectile.
FLSU- Fleet Logistics Support Unit
FMF- Fleet Marine Force
Fox Hole- A fighting hole dug for protection.
Fragging- The assassination of an officer by his own troops, usually by a grenade.
Friendly Fire- Accidental attack on your own troops.
Galley- Kitchen
Gear- Equipment
Gooks- Derogatory name for Asian.
Grease Gun- 45 Caliber sub-machine gun.
Grunt- Marine infantryman
Guerilla- Viet Cong
Gun Ship- Huey Helicopter
Gung Ho- Working together. All for one, one for all. Usually referred to Marines that are highly motivated to be the best.
Gunny- Short for Gunnery Sergeant.
H&S- Headquarters and Supply
Hard Charger- Another name for a Marine that is Highly motivated.
Hatch- Door
Head- Toilet
Hercules- C-130
High and Tight- Marine Corps hair cut
Honcho- Boss/man in charge.
Honey Dipper- A trooper who is responsible for burning human excrement or a person who takes care of the head.
Hooch- Any kind of shelter/home.
Honey Dipper- The name given for a person who takes care of outdoor latrines.
Horn- Telephone.
Hueys- HU-1 Helicopter. Also called a gunship.

Hump- To walk in the hills of jungle.
Jarhead- Derogatory name for Marine.
Jungle Boots- Footwear that looks like a combination of combat boot and canvas.
Junk on the Bunk- Complete clothing and equipment inspection lay out on the rack.
K-Bar- Marine issue fighting knife.
KIA- Killed In Action
K-rations- C-rations in bulk & heated up by the field mess.
Leave- Vacation time.
Liberty- Free time after work or on week ends.
Lifer- A Marine that makes it his career.
Lock and Load- Arm and ready your weapon.
LP- Listening Post
LST- Troop landing boat.
LZ- Landing Zone. A place to land Helicopters or airplanes.
M-14- A wood stock rifle used in the early portion of the Vietnam conflict.
M-16- Plastic stock, lightweight rifle that took the place of the M-14.
M-60- The standard machine-gun.
Maggie's Drawers- A white flag waved from the butts of a rifle range signifying that the round missed the target.
Medivac- Medical evacuation by helicopter.
Mess- Chow hall
Mighty Mite- Jeep used by Marine Corps.
MOS- Assigned job specialty.
MP- Military Police
Mustang- An enlisted man who becomes an officer.
Nam- Short for Vietnam
Napalm- A Jellied petroleum substance that burns fiercely.
NCO- Non-commissioned Officer (enlisted).
OCS- Officer's Candidate School at Quantico, Virginia.
OIC- Officer-in-charge
Office Hours- Summary court Marshall usually held in the Commanding officer's office.
Outstanding- Exceptional. Well done.
Passageway- Corridor or hallway.
Perimeter- Outer limits of a military position.
PFC- Private First Class
Piss Cutter- Enveloped shaped overseas cap. Garrison cover.
Pogey Bait- Candy or snack food.

Point- Marine who is in front.
Port- The left side of a ship.
POW- Prisoner of War.
Prick-10- PRC-10. A portable back packed FM receiver-transmitter radio used for short distances.
PT- Physical Training
Quantico- Place in Virginia where the Marines have Officer's school.
Quarters- Living area/place.
Quonset Hut- A half-round corrugated metal building.
R&R- Rest and relaxation.
Rack- Bed
Recon- Abbreviation for Reconnaissance.
Re-Up- To extend a tour or enlistment.
Request for Mast- To request to be heard by the Commanding Officer.
Rifle Team- The backbone of the Marine Corps consisting of 4 men.
Rotate- One unit goes home while another unit takes its place.
Round- A bullet. Ammunition
Round Eye- All non-Asian girls.
Rubber Lady- Inflatable air mattress.
Rules of Engagement- Specific regulations for the conduct of battles by the US.
S-1- Personnel
S-2- Intelligence
S-3- Operations
S-4- Supply
Saddle Up- To put on your pack and get ready to move out.
Salt- A Marine with experience. An old timer.
Sarge- Short for Sergeant.
Scuttlebutt- Rumors
Sea bag- Duffel bag.
Search and Destroy- To conduct a sweep or run a patrol to look for and kill any enemy contacted.
Secure- Tied down. Everything is in order.
Seven-eighty-two Gear- Field gear.
Short timer- A Marine nearing the end of a tour of duty or enlistment.
Sick Bay- Doctor's office.
Simper Fi- Always Faithful.
Six-by-six- Standard three axle truck.
Sixty Day Wonder- Second Lieutenant out of Basic School.
Skipper- Captain
Skivvies- Underwear

Slopehead- Derogatory word used for Asian.
Smoking Lamp- To be able to smoke. Smoking lamp is lit.
Snoopin' and Poopin'- Reconnaissance of an area.
SOP- Standard operating procedure
Special Services- A branch of the service that offers recreational & educational programs for the troops.
Squad Bay- Barracks
Squared Away- Neat, orderly and organized.
Squid- Derogatory word for sailors.
Stand By- Prepare yourself.
Starboard- The right side of the ship.
Swabbie- Derogatory word for sailors.
TAC line- Tactical phone line
Top- The First Sergeant
Topside- Upstairs. On deck.
Tracer- A round of ammunition chemically treated to glow so its flight can be followed.
Trip Flare- A ground flare triggered by a trip wire used to signal and illuminate the approach of an enemy at night.
Utilities- Olive drab field uniform.
VC- Viet Cong
Viet Cong- Guerrilla fighting force in Vietnam.
Ville- Village
White Phosphorus- Used for illumination.
Willie Peter- White phosphorus
World- The USA
XO- Assistant to the Commanding Officer
0302- Infantry Officer

Chain of Command
Marine Enlisted
E-1 Private
E-2 Private First Class
E-3 Lance Corporal
E-4 Corporal
E-5 Staff Sergeant
First Sergeant
Gunnery Sergeant
Master Sergeant
Master Gunnery Sergeant
Marine Officers

Warrant Officer
Second Lieutenant
First Lieutenant
Captain
Major
Lieutenant Colonel
Colonel
General (No. of Stars)

Marine Corps Structure
Rifle Team (5)
Squad
Platoon
Company
Battalion
Regiment
Division

Three Rivers Publications

You can order by:

- Mail PO Box 283, Hebo, OR 97122
- Email jkesey@wcn.net
- Website jimkesey.com
- For credit card orders **amazon.com**

- -

I would like to order "What Am I Doing Here?"

Qty.	Unit Cost	Shipping	Total
	$19.95	*$2.00*	

Name ______________________________

Address ____________________________

Phone ____________________

Email ____________________

Please dedicate this book to _______________

Method of payment can be either check or money order.

Send to:

Three Rivers Publications

PO Box 283

Hebo, OR 97122